Homeland

Homeland

a novel

by

Cris Mazza

RED HEN PRESS   LOS ANGELES

HOMELAND
Copyright © 2004 Cris Mazza

Cover art *Sugarloaf* (c. 1938) by Sam Colburn.
Courtesy of the estate of Sam Colburn.

Book design by Mike Vukadinovich
Cover design by Mark E. Cull

ISBN 1-888996-71-4
Library of Congress Catalog Card Number: 20031145833

The City of Los Angeles Cultural Affairs Department, California Arts Council and the Los Angeles County Arts Commission partially support Red Hen Press.

Printed in Canada

Red Hen Press
www.redhen.org

First Edition

Acknowledgements

Acknowledgements made to the following publications in which portions of this book first appeared: *Indigenous / Growing Up Californian* by Cris Mazza, City Lights Press, for "Homeland" (portions of chapter one, two and four); *The Milk of Almonds*, Feminist Press, for "Our Father" (portions of chapter one, two and four); *San Diego Reader* for "Homeland" (portions of chapter one, two and four); *TriQuarterly* for "Familiar Noise" (chapter three); *Denver Quarterly* for "A Mistake, an Accident"; *Crab Orchard Review* for chapter one; *Fiction International* for portions of chapter twelve.

for my parents

Chapter One

The shotgun hangs over her father's bed, above one aluminum safety rail that is jammed to no purpose against the same wall. Decorations from home are recommended to cheer displaced geriatric patients. Ronnie had mounted the gun within easy reach, but her father has never once stretched his unimpaired hand to touch the stained wooden stock.

In the late seventies, a lot was sold adjacent to their three-acre farmstead on one of the hills outlining Dictionary Valley. Within a year, a two-story Spanish-style suburban house was assembled. Then a family moved in and added a swing set, sandbox, a tree house built on stilts without a tree, a basketball hoop over the garage, and bikes, which were always left in the driveway. But not too long before her father's first stroke, the unfamiliar, and disheartening, sounds of boys playing capture-the-flag and touch football mutated into something far more disruptive: a stereo that detonated rapid-fire booms like machine-gun cannons.

The little boy next door, Shane Murphy, had turned fifteen and was a *wigger*—a phenomenon explained once on *Phil Donahue*, although after that, Ronnie never again heard the subject on radio nor television. Like the rest of the wiggers, Shane wore blond hair pleated into thin braids all over his head, colored beads swinging at the tips; his jeans mustard yellow or royal purple, big enough to fit a butt three times his father's size; shoulders hunched and spine bowed, head bobbing as he sauntered off to the high school bus stop with no books nor lunch sack. Then Shane was home again by one in the afternoon to begin the daily large-weapon assault with his stereo.

One day a crack appeared in the plaster above the kitchen sink while Ronnie was washing dark green Swiss chard leaves in cold water. Her father glowered at the buzzing pane of his bedroom window. But didn't fetch the shotgun from the closet until another day when he and Ronnie climbed the steps from one of the lower terraces—where they'd been setting up home-grown bamboo poles in rows for climbing green beans—and saw Shane and two friends, one riotously freckled wearing an orange Mohawk, the other black with an unremarkable hairstyle, holding baseball bats and surrounding two workmen who'd been hired to repair eroding asphalt by the residents on the private dead-end lane.

Something had happened, the foreman explained, when he'd finally found other workers to come finish the job after the first two had refused to return. At first the workers had tried to claim it was the color of their sweatshirts and ball caps that had inspired the boys to threaten them; but apparently, they'd finally admitted, there'd also been some words exchanged between the workers and Shane as he swaggered down the lane, so Shane had proceeded to round up his homies—the *wigger* on Phil Donahue had used that word—and they came back to stand their turf.

What the foreman didn't know was that Ronnie's father had clumped into the house straight to the bedroom, without even removing his dust-crusted work boots, to retrieve his shotgun from the closet where it had stood upright in its zipped leather case since his last hunting trip to Mexico many years earlier. The boys had dispersed—one holding his pants up as he ran—while the workers had vaulted into their truck and squealed down the lane. Ronnie's father had peppered the leaves of the lane's biggest eucalyptus tree, right over their heads, with a blast of pellets.

Now, at forty-one, Ronnie spends her days in a geriatric hospital, then sleeps in a bed in her father's room. Her father is one of the lucky ones since he is able to room with family. In most cases, the facility pairs one bedridden patient—man or woman—with a more mobile resident who can still use the bathroom on his or her own. This way, the ambulatory patient can have an ostensibly private bathroom. It might almost seem like a luxury: their own soap and teeth in a glass on the sink shelf, no danger of personal items being jumbled, and a somewhat smaller chance of theft.

Still, as always, she's doing what comes next, the next thing that has to be done. Ronnie curbs herself from wondering what she could've been doing if she wasn't changing soiled hospital beds, spoon-feeding pureed baby food into pink toothless ninety-year-old mouths, or wheeling withered bodies into showers meant to accommodate both an occupied wheelchair and one or two plastic-capped nurse aides. Reminding herself that she chose her sentence—not this exact outcome—to doggedly follow the life her parents started, Ronnie is always doing what's next, the next thing that has to be done.

It's actually a decent facility. The shape of an X, four long wings radiate from a central area with lobby, receptionist, gift shop, hair dresser and barber, recreation room, dining hall, nursing stations—one for each wing—and an abundance of genuine tropical foliage kept alive and robust by a two-woman enterprise that visits every other day to water and prune and, due to artificial light in the hospital, rotate certain plants with fresh ones from the showroom. A local grade school class painted several wall-sized murals of a rain forest, each mural complete with curling vines, purple snakes, bunches of bananas, monkeys, butterflies, and huge orange orchids. To complete the tropical atmosphere, there's also an aviary, a real one, filled with cockatoos, Amazon parrots, and even a macaw. The birds belong to a Dictionary Valley pet shop. The owner stops by before opening in the morning and after closing in the afternoon to replenish the feed and clean the aviary or to replace a bird that's been sold. It's a good thing the residents have to be up at five in the morning for breakfast service because that's when the birds start screaming.

Outside, it's still Dictionary Valley, Southern California, thousands of miles from the tropics. Sturdy, scrubby Bermuda lawn between most of the wings, and rows of drought-resistant mock-orange shrubs along the stucco walls, under the windows beside the sidewalks. At the end each wing, glass doors lead to small concrete patios with benches. All except the Medicare wing where the glass door at the end of that wing is kept locked and chained because it's the door closest to a tumbleweedy gorge with a small creek at the bottom. Migrant workers sometimes come up from the gorge. A landscape company, which not infrequently hires migrants, runs mowers over the yellow-green grass once a week, year round, and trims the bushes once a month. A sprinkling system clicks on only at night, one A.M., every other day. Sometimes, if she catches one of the landscapers, and if he speaks some English or understands her hand motions, Ronnie can get them to turn the sprinklers off when rain is expected, and they will usually leave it off for several days afterwards. Needless watering makes her pulse hot, her head throbbing to the rhythm of the Rain Birds. And when rain is pattering from the eaves and her father stirs in his bed, she half expects him to slip from the blankets and shuffle to the door, pulling on a robe, to go down to the basement and turn off the automatic watering timers.

A week before they both have to leave the hospital, Ronnie is tending to business as usual, up before the birds scream, so she's dressed, her father washed and clothed by the time she must begin tending to eight other patients assigned to her. In the smaller hours before the aviary wakes, the night still sounds like Dictionary Valley, especially with the window open: a breeze rattling thick, oily eucalyptus leaves, a lonely dog barking, bray of a backyard pet donkey, crow of a rooster long before dawn. Until the shrieks of the birds become part of the daily institutional white noise. At the first screech her father covers his ears with his hands. Actually one hand and the other wrist, because the curled arm has a hand he can't much control.

Before opening their door, Ronnie cooks orange potpourri on a hotplate, tinting the air with thin acrid citrus. Her olfactory senses haven't been totally cauterized; the odor in the hall and other rooms does jostle her, but gently, every morning. The smell is pure institution: oatmeal and coffee, disinfectant, permanent-wave chemicals, a thin fume of dust leaked from heavy duty janitorial vacuums (with a trace of oil from their motors), recycled air, and, on occasion, bodily fluids.

The residents need to be roused from their beds, helped to the bathroom or supervised in the use of toilet chairs or bedpans. Then, they must be washed, dressed, assisted into their wheelchairs, handed their walkers, or propped slightly upright in bed. Then Ronnie must fetch breakfast trays for those who can't or won't go to the dining hall. Those who can't go need to be spoon-fed. Those who won't go must eat from rolling table-trays in their rooms. The dining hall can be a rough neighborhood. The ownership of a particular place at a specific table has evolved into a part of the residents' customary code. Newcomers are educated with shouts, curses, and sometimes a blow to the head with a cane or serving tray. In fact Ronnie began wearing spandex bike pants under her nurse aide dress because one old man who's been known to swing a fist also pinches butts. With the spandex, he isn't able to get a hold of any flesh and his fingers slide over the surface, snapping together with nothing between them. He hasn't yet started trying to pinch above or below the spandex, but even so, Ronnie is far too agile with quick reactions, even though she never played schoolyard dodging games—in fact never went to school, instead was home-schooled by her mother whose death became Ronnie's high school graduation.

She doesn't presume the old man's intentions have anything to do with his attraction to beauty. She hasn't been young for a long time.

Although her body is in good shape, not fat, still muscled from the natural work on the farmstead, the rest—her skin and face—she can tell, is ravaged. And she's going bald, has been since her early thirties. Would her brother be going bald now? He would be thirty-nine. She shampoos and dries her hair in front of the mirror in the bathroom she shares with her father, sometimes wondering: is she going bald *for* her brother, because he can't?

After breakfast, bedpans need be washed and replaced and laundry needs to be gathered and put in the cloth bin on wheels parked in the hall. Residents need to be sent to daily engagements, which include: bingo or beauty shop or doctor's appointments, or "social time" in the lobby where they watch staff and nurses come and go. This is when Ronnie has time to begin packing, dividing things into a pile for the Salvation Army and another pile consisting of whatever necessary items will fit into the canvas rucksack, deep-pocketed hunting vest and hand-made pushcart that she'd salvaged from the estate sale. Her father is able to walk although one leg drags; it's possible he could even main-tain a pace wearing the faintly blood-stained hunting vest packed with toiletries and undergarments. He also hears, but she hasn't yet told him that the hospital is turning one hundred percent private, eliminating the Medicare beds. Six months ago one of the administrators told her they would help her make other arrangements, the most likely facility being the VA hospital. Ronnie had said, "I'll get back to you when I decide what's best for my father," but never had gotten back to the administrator, who likewise never again inquired. Today she'll give notice of her departure to her nurse supervisor.

She also now knows her father can converse more extensively than brief questions and one-word answers. Proof had come a while after the administrator's offer of relocation assistance, and just before Ronnie's subsequent decision last week. The television on her father's nightstand was turned on. He had woken from his after-lunch nap, was propped up in his bed wearing, as usual, sweatpants, a sweater and slippers. Ronnie had just retrieved his undershirts from the laundry before they could be stolen, and was putting them into his drawer. The midday news reported the discovery of a decomposing body in a shallow grave somewhere in the county—she hadn't caught the location: canyon, ditch, pasture, hill-side, dry river bottom, or backyard.

The sound on the television was abruptly louder, the reporter's voice suddenly broadcasting on a blaring electronic buzz, when her father mumbled, "It ain't he."

Then everything had quieted again. Except her heartbeat. Only if her father has a lucid memory, and only if he's willing to exercise it, can she have her questions answered or acquire some measure of absolution, but—another pact with herself—*he* had to be first to bring it up.

"Who, Dad?" Already knowing who.

"Our brother. I hear her. Still—know about her."

"I haven't forgotten either."

"They. Were too. Almost baby."

"You mean me? No, I wasn't too young. I remember some—"

"I do a— Tell *I will*. Say for me—when I tell *I will do*. Say it. "P—" He looks at Ronnie's mouth.

"A promise?"

"Promise. Promise our mother. To come back at."

"*My* mother. Your wife. Your pronouns are bad again today. Okay, where do you mean? Go back . . . *where?*"

But he'd fallen into silence again, eyes still open, magnified behind glasses that also reflected the flashing lights of the television.

A second dialogue had followed that same afternoon. She was in the next room feeding two invalid octogenarians, then returned to pick up her father's tray and said, "I wonder what those two geezers think about, lying there all day like two pieces of driftwood under sheets." Immediately she wondered why she would ask such a question of her father. As though in embarrassment, she'd busied herself with his tray, sponging his table, tugging the cuffs of his sweatpants down to cover his white, chalky ankles.

He hadn't mustered a direct answer, but her father had responded: "Before sun. At—the place. No—blue, yellow, green. Say it." Again, his eyes on her mouth.

"Color."

"Color. No color out. Air is clean through. The—wet place. Say for me."

"Pond?"

"No. But okay. Thing like a pond. Blue below sun. Everything is—like sleep. But not-sleep."

"Rest."

"Birds on rest. Before sun. Mockings. Meadows."

"Mockingbirds and meadowlarks."

"Shake our f—"

"Feathers."

"Yes, and calm and no noise. We do there to. Bang. Gun for dumb."

"For dove. Hunt for dove."

"Dove. Dove wings make—" His lips and tongue produce a soft trill. "Whistle."

"Wh— Wings whistle when . . . flee— Go in air."

"Fly."

"Fly from field. Where we feed."

"*They* feed. We don't eat in fields." Then, her hands still on his ankles, she'd settled to her knees and looked into his blurry eyes. "Dad, what are you thinking about? Is this because you remembered Chad earlier?"

"Maybe shouldn't. Go do with the kids. So little. Like baby."

"But you had to take us hunting if you wanted Mom with you to raise your limit."

"Four people—all us—the people— Us eat. Only do—bang. Say for?"

"Shoot."

"Shoot. Just shoot what they—do at dinner."

"Eat. *We* just shot what *we* could eat. Except . . . that time Mom shot the hawk. Remember? It scared us."

"Our sister crying. Everyone crying. Hang on mom, waaa waaa. Someone. A person had to do it. We . . . they . . . Too much a baby to . . . rem-ber . . . rem—"

"I think I *do* remember, Dad. Shooting the hawk . . . and . . . the pepper tree . . . And a lot of other things too. But I need your help to know for sure."

We screamed. Kept on screaming. Someone was screaming. Shoulders grasped and body shaken, STOP IT, STOP IT, then a dreadful silence, the sun growing hotter as the hole was dug in dry hard-packed dirt—the day our mother shot the hawk.

SOMEONE was screaming. But was it the same someone and the same screaming? The same savage sound and same raw throat.

Also the familiar awful silence. Chad lay on the hard-baked ground below the huge pepper tree with slippery but flaky, easily peeled bark where our father had built our tree house. Really just a platform bordered by eight-by-two-inch boards as edges, like curbs. No ladder necessary to climb up there because the crotch of the tree was low enough, the branches fat enough to make natural steps to the trap-door hole in the floor of the platform—enough room on the landing to spread two sleeping bags, but, to keep dirty shoes off the bedding, little space for walking except acrobatic balancing, tight-rope style, on the two-inch-wide wooden edges of the platform's imaginary walls.

An initial reprimand—for pushing him from the tree or at least not watching him or not protecting him to keep him from falling—could've been a slapped face or at least a wrist shackled in a big, tight fist, and dragged along, also crying, to the car, to be alone in the back seat for a violent ride, presumably to the hospital, but, with continuous hysterics, it almost seems maybe the car didn't stop until once again in the driveway. And for days, possibly weeks, didn't our father stay out in the gardens longer, later, even after dark, chest grunting with each drop of the pick-ax or heft of the shovel, then finally come in dirtier than usual?

We screamed. Kept on screaming. Weren't we screaming? He was four or five.

A mistake, an accident, a compound lapse. Doves don't ever glide—besides their feathers' telltale whistle, their continuous wing beat is a second giveaway. Prowling hawks sail on air currents, but this hawk wasn't gliding, not searching the ground for prey, beat his wing too swiftly, too regularly, too low to the ground, too similarly to the dove he may also, another time, have pursued. On immediate sight of a game bird—or when the guns were raised—instinctively, reflexively, those without guns were to let our knees buckle, crouch low to the ground, squat at our parents' feet, wait for the shots, this time a double crack from our mother's gun—hers alone—while our father shouted, No, AL, but too late. Perhaps only one of us made the misinformed recoil to squat at our mother's feet. Heart pounding at the appalling outlawed deed now done, to kill songbird or heron or raptor.

"WHY DID YOU—" our mother's voice resounds.

A misdemeanor, nothing more, a ticket, perhaps a small fine, none of that would undo the shot, best to bury the mistake, let coyote come sniffing and turn it to carrion. Or bury it deep enough so it's gone forever. Checking over shoulders, watching the bright, hot midday frontage road for the county sheriff or game warden or some kind of official, none of which had ever actually been seen on or near any hunting site. Ten o'clock sun flaring, ninety degrees already, only sticks and pocket knives for digging, for cutting the clay, only hands for scooping, it seemed the hole would never be deep enough, would take forever to excavate.

But who was screaming? Wasn't someone screaming? Would the mockingbirds learn and imitate this sound as song?

HOW COULD YOU—WHY DID YOU—?

MOMMY—

SHUT UP, STOP IT!

His limp body scooped up the way we would lift a dead cottontail with one hand—or was he screaming too?

"Dad, why did we— Why did *she* stop hunting?"

"Laws for shoot. Got different. Could only gun for bird. In—other place. Other country."

"Mexico."

"Yes and he stayed. Back with sister—you."

"You mean *she* did. Chad wasn't . . . when you hunted in Mexico. Mom stayed home with me. Your pronouns are awful today. But why did she stop going with you?"

"Danger."

"How was Mexico dangerous? Like disease or the water?"

"Want you on home. Always."

"I guess she got her wish."

"He—our mother— Hard to say you. Sad person. Even if on ax— Word for thing not did right. Ax—"

"Accident."

"Ax-dent. Even that. She just couldn't—couldn't not think on. F— Couldn't— Like look above. Say it?"

"Forgive?"

"Forgive? Maybe. No. For—"

"Forget?"

"Maybe that's right. He—our mother—was not be his-self. Never the same."

"It *was* an accident, Dad. I swear it was. Did you think I'd do it on purpose?"

His eyes, confused, bewildered, focused on hers. She sighed. "Sorry," she said, standing, "Why don't you take a walk before bedtime?"

"Please. Help me. To give back." His good hand clutched her smock. "To do it. To come. Back at—the place. I promise. Our mother. I *will* take back. Then I. Can't never did it."

"Sure, Dad," turning away, gently removing his hand from her smock, "we have nowhere else to go. Maybe I need to go back with you. Maybe it's what we should do next."

It took another couple of days, with no further substantial exchanges of conversation, for Ronnie to decide: that's exactly what they'll do, right away, as soon as they leave the hospital. If he is ever going to be able to remember anything, tell her anything, share anything, then finally resolve anything, perhaps he needs to be stimulated by the real sights, the sounds, the smells that can arouse a memory. So if doing whatever he promised her mother will serve to invigorate his recollection, she'll help him do it, maybe just consider it another part of *her* atonement to do so—if indeed she still owes reparation. Or if, in fact, she ever owed. Maybe if she knew for sure, either way, she wouldn't need to go back, unless it would count as a final stage of her redemption. But as long as he's alive, if his willingness to think, to dredge-up, is revived, then she has a chance to get free of it, the doubt, the guilt. She *might* discover the assumptions she's carried since she was seven are true and therefore her choice of atonement has been just—and perhaps he'll say he knows she's done as much as humanly possible to make it right. *Or* the memories of a seven-year-old will be proven as undependable as her most churlish bitter moments try to suggest—and in that case she'll simply put aside her decades-old guilt and finally have a life. She can't remember permitting herself to imagine an if-then string, but now all of *this* one depends on his ability to remember lucidly, and to communicate what he knows, and it could be the places—the old farmstead plus the marsh fields and back country canyons they hunted and gleaned—that will stimulate him to make the effort.

From sometime in late summer, through fall and into early winter—this was hunting season for dove, quail, duck and cottontail rabbit. All were plentiful, and legal to hunt in undeveloped parts of the county. Our father would scout terrain outside Dictionary Valley, looking for good places to hunt, often finding caches just as valuable. One site was in the Tijuana River valley. There was nothing but waist-high parched vegetation, sandy arroyos, native barrel cactus and century plant, fragrant sage and ocotillo and anise, coyote and foxes, rabbits, snakes, hawks, owls, meadowlark, roadrunners, horned toads, wasps and tarantulas. On this hunting ground, our father came across an abandoned farm. Rusted equipment—an old well-pump, a hand plow—a dead falling-down tree near a house foundation, and one lone live fig tree. While we played below, he climbed the low, thick branches and filled a bucket with ripe figs. Always had a bucket in the trunk, with other necessary tools to keep at hand.

With cuttings from that tree, our father eventually established several fig trees on our property, then grafted them with branches from other varieties— three different types that ripened different months—and we had as many ripe figs as we could want. But back when any trees on our farmstead were mere sticks, this tree was like an island paradise in the brown chaparral. In addition to the fruit, there were bugs and lizards to catch, old tools to pretend to use, a house foundation to pretend to be building. We were the only people on the face of the earth, in a pristine prairie of brown, waving grasses interrupted only by the dusty dark green dome of the old fig tree, no sound but the mournful cry of doves, intricate piping of meadowlark, rustle of mice, wind chime of rattling leaves or creaking branches.

Probably sixty miles north of the old fig tree, where the original El Camino Real was two parallel ruts going up a hill—almost invisible in weeds and non-native mustard, descendants of the trail of seeds left by Father Serra—our father found huge beaver tail cacti bearing fruits called nopales or cactus apples. The growth our father located had been eaten bald to head level by cattle who free-ranged in the area. He harvested as many cactus apples as he could bring home. After the thick cactus skin is cut away, cactus apples are about the size of a small fist and extremely juicy. A little like watermelon but with pleasant differences: the flesh is not as mealy, the seeds just chewy bumps, a deeper, brighter flavor. Our father also cut several lobes from the cacti and planted them on our property. In time they became as huge and gnarled as the eighty-year-old stand he'd found. Part of an impenetrable barrier on the southern property line.

Still in North County, but further east, away from the coast, where the droughty foothills begin, our father found an abandoned grove of walnut trees. Another hunting trip had us knee-deep in wild oats and buckwheat, picking up the walnuts our father shook from the trees, the black, leathery outer casing still wrapping the light brown shells. We brought home several full burlap bags, then helped to shuck the nutmeats which would be frozen for year-round use in brownies, cookies, salads, and candy.

Back down south, he looked for hunting areas in the vicinity of a farm-packing warehouse and loading dock where local truck-farmers brought produce to be shipped to grocery stores. Behind the dock they dumped rejects. From piles over eight feet high, we salvaged boxes of culled celery—taking only the hearts from the waste the farmers had cast out. There were also loose tomatoes scattered all over the ground—fully ripe, not squashed but unable to travel to a store without bruising. In a huge caldron on a Coleman stove outside, our parents turned boxes of tomatoes into jars of tomato sauce. Near the produce dock, we discovered a trash dump. Perhaps an unofficial landfill used by the few local residents, perhaps a site where migrant farm workers had been encamped. While our parents sorted through tomatoes, we picked up soda bottles. By the time we finished, we had several boxes of those as well, some needing to be scrubbed with bottle brushes at home, but at a nickel each, we had almost four dollars.

It was when our mother joined our father hunting, when we were two and four, that they began bringing us along. Partly to expose us to the philosophy: shooting was something you did with concern for safety as well as preservation of the terrain, including mindfulness of game limits and which birds were strictly off-limits. And it was an activity you did as calmly and quietly as possible, except for the report of the shotguns. Partly also to teach us the techniques: we padded softly in their footsteps, trained to stay behind them, to stop and squat down as soon as we heard the whistle of dove wings, so our parents could raise and aim their firearms and follow the flock in their sights, in a complete circle, over our heads, and pull off the four shots allowed them by two double-barrel shotguns.

The practical reason for taking us hunting was that we were the bird dogs. Dogs qualified to not only find the downed game, but to first locate and collect the spent shells which could be refilled at home. While still the only people on the face of this terrain, we did occasionally find other shells and picked them up too; sometimes our father could reload more shells than he'd spent. After gathering up the four shells, after tramping into the underbrush to where our conditioned eyes had marked the exact spot the game had fallen, we decapitated and drained blood from the bodies before the retrieve was completed and the headless bird slipped into the back flap of our father's hunting vest.

Slow-cooked in a wine sauce, the little bodies stayed whole but melted apart when touched. The dark meat slid easily from the fragile bones, drumsticks smaller than a toothpick, wings the size of bobby pins. We ate with our hands, licking our fingers, sucked the tiny skeletons dry. Quail—the same size as dove but all white meat—was fried with oregano. Cottontail rabbit was stewed with tomatoes. Sometimes our teeth hit shattered bone and we would stop chewing, feel with lips and tongue or use a finger to locate the tiny shot pellet that had been embedded in the muscle.

But the entire activity—being pulled from sleep hours before dawn . . . the tranquil, liquid chill before sunrise . . . the swell of dusty heat as soon as a September sun rose . . . the soft traipsing in our parents' footsteps . . . the retrieving, the decapitating, the de-feathering and dressing, the cooking, the dining—was not experienced without a twinge of . . . not guilt, not exactly. Maybe some sort of contrite sigh. Helping our parents hunt, breeding domestic rabbits for their meat, seeing adolescent roosters go into the burlap bag . . . there was always some trepidation during the volatile flash of death.

Chapter Two

All along the synopsis has been that Chad died after a fall from the pepper tree. A summation pieced together, inferred, fathomed, possibly remembered, but never spoken. Nobody ever said otherwise. He disappears from memory around that time. And the family changed so much with its number reduced by one. Mother in her room, perhaps days, weeks, months, the muffled sounds of writhing grief. Then her face a swollen, pallid mask, her colorless eyes lost far inside her head, when she came out to prepare a meal, to wash the dishes, to preserve sliced peaches or whole green plums . . . or were baskets of fruit left to rot, picked by father but untended by mother? Is there any recollection of a thick, fruity smell of wine, or, in the hazy hot band of sunlight across the kitchen, gnats and fruit flies hovering like floating dust? Their dead bodies needing to be sponged off the counter in the morning.

Slices of remembered conversation are run over and over, nearly chanted, nearly turned to verse, to rhyme, to lore . . .

Why did you . . . Why didn't you . . . Oh no oh no oh no, no, no, NO . . .

We'll survive.

No, we're not losing both of them.

How long, Alicia?

Until . . . until I say.

We'll get through this, Alicia.

You should've . . . You could've . . . You're supposed to . . . watch out for him . . . your fault . . . oh why oh why, please, no, please . . .

Al, don't make her pay for this.

All that remains of context is vaguely attached details, a slammed door, squeak of mattress and rustle of sheets, rattle of chain as he sat alone on the swing set outside the basement door, her voice raw and frightened or low and tentative on the verge of another session of sequestered weeping, her silhouette almost lost in a billow of steam rising from a pot of pasta dumped into a colander in the sink, water running down the inside of the window as though rain fell indoors.

All leading to a self-damning life decision made by a seven-year-old? No, the decision does have a specific circumstance. There is no memory of either parent ever saying "he died" or "he's dead." Just, "he's gone, Chad's gone. Do you understand?" Out by the rabbit hutches with Dad. He's raking and raking. A soaker bubbles under the fig tree, but dust rises from the hard baked ground where he rakes, causing eyes to water, drawing a sneeze from him, and he stops to blow his nose, a painful bleat like a chicken when it's caught by a leg and the water's boiling and the burlap bag's already bloody.

"Dad, when will mommy stop crying?"

Red bandanna he used for his nose wadded and stuffed back in a pocket. "She has a big . . . hurt . . . like a sore you can't see. She might not ever stop wanting to cry, but after a while you won't see it anymore."

". . . what if Chad and me—"

"Chad's not coming back, Ronnie. He won't be here to play with you. He won't be growing up. We can always remember him, but we have to . . ."

"Have to what, Dad?"

"Help your mother."

Why did you . . . Why didn't you . . . Oh no oh no oh no, no, no, NO . . . We're not losing both of them. . . until I say. You should've . . . You could've . . . You're supposed to . . . watch out for him . . . your fault . . . oh why oh why, please, no, please . . . We'll get through this, Alicia, we'll survive, don't make her pay for this.

"Dad, what if I—"

"What you can do is be a good girl, help your mother with the housework and chores, do what needs to be done, be there for her all the time, every day, help her . . ."

So the surrender is made. And a decision to make no more decisions, at least none that would lead to a new life growing away from the one, his, that won't ever be lived. Go ahead, if it's what your mother wants—go ahead and pay for this.

The parrots are mostly quiet, rustling and muttering softly, as she leads her father down the dim hallway then through the lobby. He's wearing the stiff, canvas hunting vest. Soap, toothpaste, sunscreen lotion, disposable razors, and shampoo in the side pockets. Underwear, socks, and undershirts in the big game pouch in back—the bottom tinted with a faint dark discoloration of blood, but there's little danger of stains transferring to the white cotton. The vest is slightly pungent, but the smell difficult to identify. Some strange mixture of mildew, army tent, and feral feathers.

Ronnie wheels the handcart and wears the army-surplus rucksack. The shotgun stands upright in the cart, in the middle, other possessions packed around it, the whole bundle covered with a raincoat to disguise the protruding barrel of the gun. From the kitchen she's procured a few bananas, a loaf of bread, peanut butter which she had to transfer from a huge tub into an emptied lotion bottle, and a jumbo can of chicken sandwich spread—it was the smallest of any of the canned goods. From a supply closet she took three rolls of toilet paper, from the laundry a few hand towels. There's no official way to requisition anything, and nowhere to leave any money, but in their room she's left a clock and nite-light which she'd purchased when they'd moved in.

Yesterday was the barber's day—an older guy with a one-man shop in Dictionary Valley who's contracted to come to the hospital once a month. He goes room-to-room to trim the scanty hairs on the heads of every male resident who can't leave his bed, then uses the hair stylist's chair in the facility's beauty shop to do the other men, who usually sit silently, gripping the arm rests, staring transfixed into the mirror for the entire ten minutes the haircut takes. Although she ordinarily took her father to sit in the chair, yesterday she made sure their room number was on the barber's room-visit list. When he arrived, Ronnie shut the door, and asked that he shave her father's hair down to a half-inch stubble, then had the barber do hers. She requested that no hair be over an inch long, but shorter around the ears.

They leave before daybreak. Any later, some bustling nurse or administrator might want to summon a cab for them, might call them back for some regulatory physical exam before hospital discharge. Were there any discharge papers she was supposed to receive? She never asked, merely informed them, someone, a social worker she believes, that she and her father would be leaving on this date and that all necessary arrangements had been made. Last night at the front desk, she'd paid for two bus passes: one senior, one adult.

Arriving at the battered wooden bus stop bench—down the street from the hospital, on the corner where Santa Rosa becomes Central Avenue—Ronnie gasps lightly to herself, nearly a laugh, turns to her father and says, "I guess I should've asked a little sooner, Dad, where do you want to go first?"

"At our—place."

"Home? Really?"

Well, it's the easiest thing from here. They are in the south end of Dictionary Valley, and it only takes one north-bound bus to get near their old farmstead on Hannigan Hill, named for the first owner of a home site there.

Dictionary Valley, twenty miles east of San Diego, was named during the Depression. Before that it was part of the Rancho Santa Rosa, a Spanish land grant bequeathed to some old conquistador in exchange for either killing or converting natives—or perhaps for agreeing to be governor of California—who then died or abdicated and fled back to Spain, the grant of thousands of acres of land forgotten in a trunk, written somewhere in a ledger, or possibly a pittance of rent paid yearly for the right to grow grapes or olive trees near the sad little creek—a collection of scanty rainwater from the rocky hills, nearly dry all summer—that bisected the thirsty, treeless valley.

When California became part of Mexico, then thirty years later a territory of the United States, there was some quandary and disagreement over what would happen to the immense ranchos granted to noble families and the Franciscan mission by decree of Spanish royalty. After all the negotiating and stipulating, many of the huge ranchos remained, titled to those who could most convincingly prove their rightful ownership and land boundaries. The rest of unclaimed California was eventually divided, on a grid, into homestead farm sites to be claimed by citizens of the United States. Eventually owners of ranchos, frustrated by their inability to make a profit on the sometimes inhospitable semi-arid topography, followed suit and began to divide and sell their property as well. It wasn't only small farmers who took advantage of the availability of inexpensive land in California. At the end of the 19th century, a reference book publisher from the East had accumulated all the sites in what would become Dictionary Valley and its surrounding low hills. It's possible the publisher never saw the sage-and-scrub terrain he possessed, or maybe on a jaunt to Yosemite and the Grand Canyon he briefly visited his rancho in Southern California. Perhaps he was bitterly disappointed. Most of his holding remained desolate and unused for several decades. The publisher, needing to sell his product more than he needed his piece of droughty Southern California, assisted his salesmen by providing them an incentive to offer their customers: buy a dictionary and get a home site in California; buy a set of encyclopedias and get a small farmstead. Slowly, a few of the new dictionary-owners began to trickle into California to start life over on their recently acquired acreage. Unfortunately, not only was there little water, but most of the land on hillsides didn't even have the potential for procuring water by digging a well. A few dusty ranches were established, some abandoned, and much of the rest of the land, still divided into untouched home sites and farmsteads, remained in its new owners' names long after the cheaply-made dictionaries had disintegrated, the deeds passed down to children or lost to unpaid taxes, until after World War II had helped turn San Diego into a city, and an influx of new roads, water and sewer lines, electricity, and telephone wires plugged Dictionary Valley into the postwar boom. Families began to sell the old farmsteads and home sites—some to large tract developers, but budding developers who dared to speculate were usually more interested in parcels closer to the coast. Most sites in Dictionary Valley sold individually to people like Ronnie's father, a groundskeeper at the fairgrounds. Even with a wife, toddler and new infant, he'd still been able to save enough from each payday to take advantage of a dip in real estate prices in the early sixties, and bought the farmstead—mostly undeveloped land with just a house, overlooking Dictionary Valley.

Ronnie's rendition of history—both national and local, not just the state and city, but the county, the east county, and the chronicle of Dictionary Valley itself—was part of the home-schooling planned and carried out by her mother.

The farmstead is a triangular plot occupying a quarter of the rounded crest of Hannigan Hill. The bus will only get them to the bottom of the hill, with a mile left to walk by a county road that winds up the more-developed north side of the hill, then dips down below the fat part of the farmstead on the south side. The house is up near the top of the triangle, at the tip of a private dead-end lane that splits off the county road. It's shorter to hike from the bus stop up the south side of Hannigan Hill. It isn't overly steep, although there aren't any switchback trails, just a faint rocky path heading almost directly up the grade until it hits the back-yards of new houses built over the past twenty years along the road where it cuts below the farmstead's three acres. Ronnie still considers them new, although the houses have long since sank their roots and became a suburban, landscaped establishment, with fences separating green lawns, paved pool decks and redwood gazebos from the brown scrubby rocky hill slope where, in the years before these houses arrived, fires would regularly roar up the grade, stopped by the road before reaching the farmstead.

She hides the handcart near the bottom of the hill under a laurel sumac bush. Despite the dragging leg, and the bad hand clutching the edge of the hunting vest—not likely to let go—her father tips his face up, squinting against the light sky above the hill, and sets his boots almost sturdily onto the rocky trail, one above the other. Finally, after floundering once on loose rocks—lurching forward, catching himself with the good hand against a boulder while Ronnie catches his belt loop and holds him upright from behind—he begins hiking with eyes trained down to watch the set of each boot.

Negotiating through the backyards of the houses is not difficult since many have motor homes or boats stored beside the property—outside the fences, on cement slab driveways with road access. Ronnie and her father pass single file between a Winnebago and a satellite dish and emerge on the side of the county road across from a graded dirt leeway over a buried aqueduct that runs up one side of the farmstead. It had been called Roadrunner Road because it's where they most often saw roadrunners—running, frozen, running again—and her mother had said that this was the original road that roadrunners ran on, and was why they were called roadrunners.

From the leeway, the row of now gigantic nopale cactus hides the nethermost rock retaining walls that form the many rock-walled terraces of crop-growing tracts.

From the level parcel around the house, down to the pepper tree in the middle of the wide end of the triangular acreage, the farmstead had at first embodied the natural continuous slope of Hannigan Hill. Two circular looping paths ran down the hill and finally met three acres below at a second slightly level place where the pepper tree grew. A professional broke up the granite bedrock with dynamite. Then our father, with a wheelbarrow, made piles of broken granite pieces anywhere from head-size to bigger than we were if we crouched and curled into a ball. Lesser rocks and pieces went into our small plastic buckets for us to carry and dump just off the property line.

Over the next ten years, our father mixed cement with a hoe, then—using those piles of rocks and boulders—pieced together thick walls. Some walls as low as two feet, others as high as six or seven. He saved aside any rocks with flat edges to eventually become the top layers of the walls—wide enough that he could walk along the top like a path on the outside edge of the terrace formed by each wall. The terraces staggered, some twenty feet wide, others more like fifty, the two dirt paths remaining between them, running down-hill, with access to each terrace. We pressed our handprints or scratched our names into a smooth patch of wet cement our father prepared at the comple-

tion of each wall, but most of the frozen placards only contain one name and one hand, growing slightly bigger with each wall.

As they get closer to the property line—wading off the leeway through knee-high brush, not knowing if a wasp nest waits underfoot—Ronnie has to hold the hunting vest to keep her father from striding toward the place where there used to be an opening onto the property, between the nopale and an ancient avocado tree that stopped bearing fruit thirty years ago. They had used the opening to bring bundles of weeds, leaves, branches, and one-season vegetable plants gone past their prime—tomatoes, peppers, eggplant, beans, zucchini—to throw onto the extensive mulch pile just over the property line. She can see from here that a gate has been erected across that opening, and the gate-builder obviously had considered the nopale to still be enough of a fence on one side. But the avocado tree is gone and a real fence now stretches up the properly line on the other side.

"Kneel down, Dad."

"What why?"

"To rest a minute."

"Do to the house. To rest. Almost to lunch."

"It's not our house anymore. And it's only nine. Are you hungry?"

"Shouldn't to do work after— Shouldn't to work under we eat—b— Say it."

"Before breakfast. I know. I'm sorry." She fishes in the rucksack, without taking it off—arms reaching up and behind her head—breaks off a banana, snaps the stem and pulls the peel halfway down before handing the fruit to her father.

The nopale has been growing, unpruned, for several years, even before the estate sale. There'd been so much other basic upkeep to maintain the place at a minimally functional level. Most of the lower growth is as woody as a tree trunk. A crop of cactus apples is rotting, drying, and dropping off.

Her father finishes the banana, holds the peel out in his palm. "Eat. The worms."

"*Feed* the worms. But I'm sure the new people got rid of the worm bed."

He looks at the peel, then tosses it under the jungle of nopale, where the oldest fallen lobes and rotting fruit are already thick, soggy, and humid.

"Yeah, worms could live there too, but we'd never be able to get in there and dig them out when we needed them."

Her father reaches to a lobe, scrapes a white fungus with his thumbnail then rubs the powdery white stuff between his thumb and finger, inspecting it closely. He had always been vigilant in his effort to control fungus on the nopale.

Why did he want to come here? Surely not to satisfy himself on the place's upkeep—it was sold over two years ago and already, even from this limited vantage point, obvious changes are evident. But change had always been continual, if gradual, even while they lived here. Vegetable beds had to be rotated, new rock walls constructed, certain trees would die or do poorly because of light or soil conditions then come back and thrive when relocated. Of course some trees were removed for other reasons—a dead ash, several un-grafted avocado, and the pepper tree, which used to monopolize an area right in front of them, through the dense nopale. After the tree was gone, including the stump, her father had remade the area into an asparagus patch. Asparagus can only be harvested during a short season in the spring, but must remain in the ground, undisturbed, year round. The ground may not be tilled or turned over or the perennial roots will be destroyed. A perfect place for consecrated ground.

Is that why they're here?

Just do the next thing. Do the next thing. No planning further ahead of that. Doesn't mean there's never a moment when decisions don't have to be made: When something happens, you decide what to do next and you do it. Something breaks, something wears out, someone dies, someone gets sick, decide what to do and do it, but lay no groundwork, no plans, no preparation for a different future life beyond what you need to do now.

That was your choice. Because Chad had no life either. Your atonement. Already too late to change it, even when . . .

The tree proves incapable of killing a second child. At any opportunity when there are no more chores—no more weeds in the vegetable beds to pull then lug off the property, no more zucchini to grate like cheese for loaves of sweet bread, no more eggplant and tomatoes and summer squash and eggs to pull in the wagon door-to-door to other houses spread far apart on Hannigan Hill, to sell for nickels or dimes that go into the jar on the windowsill for buying chicken scratch and rabbit food—whenever a tired, drained but less-frequently weeping mother says "go play for a while," the pepper tree is visited, called on for testimony. And the tree that once was so deftly climbed is now made of greased glass. Bruised hip, sprained elbow, bumped head, blackened eye, and maybe an involuntary outcry, but no tears.

What's wrong with her, does she need glasses?

She's probably growing too fast, a clumsy age.

She's only clumsy around that tree.

Not an attempt to achieve death, but to prove culpability in one. But proof was not to be met, no matter how many times the seven- or eight-year-old body hit the hard ground. And then the tree was gone—neither re-sprouting nor decaying into dirt—leaving only a tendril of dormant doubt beneath the surface.

"Dad, do you remember cutting down our tree house?"

"Poison to the tump."

"*Sssss*tump."

"Stump. Poison. Or little trees. Would get up. All under—beside—across. The new bed."

"That's not what I asked. But okay . . . yeah, I remember, you wouldn't let me near the stump after you drilled the holes."

"And our brother. Always bad into things."

"*My* brother. But Chad wasn't . . . here . . . when you took the tree down."

"Promised our mother. Next thing to do."

She snaps a straight barb, as long as a needle, off a nopale lobe. From somewhere on the farmstead a faint thumping, the heartbeat sound of a boombox, skate wheels on concrete and a tiny dog's cheerful yapping. Elsewhere: a siren down in Dictionary Valley, a mockingbird sings a telephone's jingle. The tickle Ronnie feels is not sweat but an ant walking down her arm. She cuts it in half with a fingernail. Perhaps the other scouts, sensing a cohort's invisible blood, will come swarming to carry him back to the nest as food for the larvae.

In the soft sand under our boots, in sifted patches around the shallow gullies where we sometimes took cover to wait for doves to land at water holes, tiny perfectly conical funnels dotted the surface—the residences of ant lions. Childhood home and food trap in one, for larva of what would become a doodlebug. The knobby creature hides under the surface, movement of legs causes a funnel of the finest grains of sand to form over where it lies. When a wandering ant falls into the funnel, it can't escape—minuscule granules on the deftly engineered sides fall away under its feet. Vibrations alert the ant lion who bursts forth, ambushes the struggling ant and pulls him under.

Our father began to bring an emptied flat plant box, originally delivered with seedlings from a nursery to the fairgrounds. Palms starting six-inches on either side of the ant lion funnels, he cupped deep handfuls of sand and emptied them into the flat box. So we brought ant lions back to the farmstead, each hunting trip brought another two or three feet of larva-filled sand. The funnels began to appear then rapidly proliferate in loose dirt between the house foundation and the first terrace, around the side and back of the house. As he built the rock walls and filled the new terraces with fill-dirt then top-soil, our father instructed us to scoop a few funnels here and there and bring them to a lower terrace. In years to come the sandy soil around the garden beds would support an army of ant control, thus reducing the number of aphids the ants brought to farm like cattle on the juicy green stems of bell pepper and broccoli.

The largest of the terraced produce beds has been turned into a built-in pool with a concrete deck. The buyers had made the sale contingent on a geologist-engineer's determination that such an improvement would be feasible. That's where the throb of music is coming from now, the in-line wheels on pavement, the splash of bodies hitting water, and now other voices, boys, the haunt of familiar coarse laughter, recurrent vulgar utterances used for any exclamation of disgust or accomplishment or joy.

"All your work, just for someone to turn into a playground and ruin everything." Ronnie uses the nopale spine to pry a dormant garden snail from the base of the cactus.

Her father, slow to answer even before the strokes, studies her. Bird-calls, both melodic and harsh, both shrill and undertoned, from scrub jay, sparrow and mockingbird, come from the direction of the old fig trees, the pomegranate and quince.

Certain large cultivated terraces were for seasonal produce, like the large plots required for squash, pumpkins and zucchini vines to tumble and tangle from mounds, spreading freely over the ground. Other beds held permanent strawberry, raspberry and boysenberry patches, plus rows of fruit trees, at least one from every variety that didn't require a frost. Pomegranate, three kinds of fig, apricot, peach, nectarine, banana, loquat, quince, two kinds of plum, more than one variety of orange—bearing at different times of the year—tangerine, lemon, lime, grapefruit, persimmon, and of course the old avocado and olive trees already on the farmstead when we arrived. Our father studied books from the library and assembled an olive processing system in the base-ment in cauldrons made of crockery.

Because the house was built on a gradual grade, the basement was not a true basement. It consisted of the area beneath the back part of the house, entered at ground level through a regular-sized door, no steps to go down. It had a dirt floor and a ceiling that was the raw underside of the living room and bedrooms. The further back into the basement we went, the more stooped over we stood. Way back there was where the rabbit skins dried, stretched whole and inside-out on wire frames. In the front part of the basement our father had workbenches made of old bedroom bureaus with drawers for hand tools, plus baby food jars of screws and nails, boxes of used hinges and drawer handles, door knobs, brackets, light fixtures, faucets, plumbing fixtures, fuses, wall sockets, wheels and coasters, corks, washers, locks, door stops, sandpaper, paint brushes, and other miscellaneous hardware, anything still usable that he'd found, and some things he'd had to purchase like caulk and paint. The walls of the basement held the bigger gardening tools—shovels, picks, cultivators, rakes, hoes, saws, pruning and lopping sheers, ladders, post-hole diggers, and spading forks hung alongside a wire-door wine cabinet holding dusty bottles of homemade root beer, vinegar, and pomegranate liquor. One of the workbenches was the station for our incubator and hatchling coop. When we needed new poultry stock, the hens could hatch their own eggs, but the Asian quail refused to brood, so their eggs were collected then incubated—but had a very low hatching rate in the incubator where the humidity and heat were not perfectly comparable to a bird's breast. We discovered a small bantam hen could hatch almost all the quail eggs she was given to brood, but then she killed half of them by accident. The black-and-yellow quail hatchlings seemed no bigger than bumblebees, blowing like a swarm close to the ground, staying like a skirt around the hen. But when she tried to teach them to scratch for food, her big feet kicked the quail chicks out behind her like gravel. So after the hen hatched the quail, they had to be taken from her and put into the light-bulb warmed brooder our father had made.

The house already had a front and back lawn, like green pools in the brown chaparral of the original property. The back lawn was on the same lower level as the basement, but the front lawn was six to eight feet higher. We only had rabbits, chickens and domestic quail, no bigger livestock. They were kept in a side yard adjacent to the back lawn, enclosed by eugenia hedges. The bushes, if left to outgrow their hedge contour, produced red berries, the shape of apples but the size of a fingernail, which we picked, then our father ground in his fruit press, and our mother turned the juice into jelly.

Inside the eugenia yard, the chickens and quail were in side-by-side coops, like walk-in aviaries. The birds lived on the hard-packed ground, ran from feeder to feeder, scratched and bathed in dust, dozed in the dappled sunlight or in the nest boxes built into the side of the coop so the eggs could be collected from the outside. Sparkling in the dirt on the floor of the coops were crushed oyster and mussel shells.

In the same side yard, five rabbit hutches—for one buck, three does, and an empty hutch for a growing litter—were suspended off the ground and shaded by a grape arbor. Underneath the hutches our father built a low rock-

wall border so the nitrogen-rich manure was contained. This was where we raised worms for fresh water fishing.

At one time the eugenia side yard held another type of agriculture—four bee hives sat behind the hutches, mounted on the top edge of the tallest of our father's rock walls, so the bees came and went from the white, wooden hives directly out over the tops of trees growing on the terrace below, pomegranate and quince. The bees were eventually moved over an acre away, to the middle of the farmstead, not just so they'd have access to more of the flower-bearing fruit and vegetables, but also because one time after the hives had been disturbed and honey taken, the angry bees had executed retaliation on the closest living things they found. The rabbits, trapped in wire hitches, had been stung in any vulnerable place the bees could get to, mostly inside their ears. Bees had swarmed into the long, blood-gorged pink ears, stinging and dying, while still more arrived with fresh stingers, ultimately killing all four adult rabbits.

"They—" His voice nearly startles her. "The people who go all here. Our people. F—"

"Family."

"Family. Live good. Us all. Except—"

The loose cactus thorn still in her fingers. "Dad, I know we probably haven't talked about it for thirty years. I know we never really talked about it. But . . . do you think you can?" With the needle, she catches a layer of skin on the ball of her thumb, passes it through only a fraction of an inch. The sting is more than it should be, as though the nopale thorns are poisoned.

"No—person can hear. No person hears how I think many much. How much many time . . ."

"How you think *what*, Dad, *what* do you think about, please . . . *please*, dammit."

Her father picks up a years-old avocado leaf, crumples it to dust in his fist, gazing up, as though blind. In slanted sunrays, Ronnie can see streaks and finger smudges on his glasses.

"I'm sorry, Dad," taking his glasses off to clean them with a shirt tail between finger and still-throbbing thumb.

The grape arbor, like the wooden frame of a small shed, was also our only slaughterhouse. In the overhead beam two rusty hooks held two leather thongs tied into slipknots. Nothing else was evident until the day came to dress eight-week-old rabbits.

The materials to be gathered started with two large plastic buckets—used originally as milk containers in the cattle barn at the county fair—one half-filled with salted water, the other empty and placed below the two leather slipknots. Then there were the hammer and two knives, one a meat knife from the kitchen collection that could cut bone, the other a smaller and sharper hunting knife. In the basement we needed to remove the dried rabbit skins from the previous slaughtering, store them in dry paper grocery bags, and bring the stretching wires—similar to two-foot safety-pins—out to the grape arbor. From the house, a sauce pan and two rubber aprons.

Our father required one assistant for the slaughtering. One at a time, the assistant handed a young rabbit to him, then immediately reached up to hold open the leather slip-knot while he, supporting the rabbit by the skin on the back of its neck, raised the rabbit to head level and inserted a back foot into the slip-knot which the assistant tightened between the toes and the hock. Then the other foot was similarly fastened into the other slip-knot. When our father released the rabbit, it hung upside-down and usually was immobilized without a struggle, just stretched out facing the ground like a pelt already. Our father gently tugged the ears down, exposing a pink tint of skin through a whorl in fine white hair on the back of the rabbit's head—the target for the hammer which the assistant was to have handed to him by this time. One crack at the base of the skull was all that was necessary, most times successfully clean and quick, and the rabbit hung limp, the hammer handed to the assistant who was, simultaneously, passing over the bigger knife. His hands still holding the ears down, one more quick motion of his right hand, the head was off, dropped into the empty bucket, and the blood drained, spattering the white sides of the bucket, a few droplets hitting our father's rubber apron as the body twitched briefly.

Sometimes, at least one per litter, a rabbit would kick a leg free, if the knot hadn't been tightened enough, or, worse yet, the rabbit would move just before the blow of the hammer and not die with the single blow, but start to scream—the death cry. Our father would grunt, an inaudible curse, raise the hammer again, one hand still occupied in attempting to restrain the kicking rabbit, holding its head still by the ears, the assistant replacing the free foot into the slipknot, leaving room for the swing of the hammer.

Once it succumbed, the rabbit hung headless over the bloody bucket, and our father needed the smaller knife handed to him. He cut the hide to the bone all the way around each leg, above the hock, peeled it down each leg, then slipped the knife between hide and meat through the crotch and sliced the skin open there, so the hide had become a dress rather than pants. Our father gripped the hide and peeled it off whole, in one motion, like removing a sweatshirt, until it was a glistening skin sack lined with fur, attached only at the wrists of the front feet. It usually popped free by itself, leaving the front paws, like the back feet, still covered with white fur, the rest of the body now nude muscle. The assistant had the stretching wires ready, held the two sides close together, almost parallel, slipped it into the hide until the coiled end poked out the neck hole, then released the sprung sides and the hide was stretched tight and suspended on a nail off to the side. By this time our father had opened the body cavity and scraped the viscera into the bucket, separating out the liver and still-beating heart which he held out toward the assistant who should already have one of the two sauce pans ready to receive the edible organs. That was it, the body was ready to be released from the leather thongs and slipped into the fresh salted water.

After the entire rabbit litter was done, the carcasses would be washed again then dried, the pieces cut apart—legs, backs, thighs, almost the same as a chicken—packaged and frozen.

Although we sometimes helped defeather them, our father dressed all birds, including dove and quail, without our assistance—mostly still in the hunting fields where he would bury the viscera. Poultry chicks can be sexed, so it wasn't often we had adolescent roosters to butcher. But the diminutive domestic quail, kept for eggs only, couldn't be sexed as chicks, so the males were left alone to thrive, mating and eating as they pleased, without worry.

"Okay, Dad, what did you want to do here—do you want to get any closer, do you remember exactly where you—where he . . . is?"

He puts his glasses back on by himself. "Everything is—not same. Say for me."

"Different."

"Different. The place when I give our sister—no, our mother. The ashes. Out to there. The place. Everything so different. But the iris. Still flowers. Still there."

"What are you talking about? Please, Dad, try to think."

"At where they. Used to come with guns. I give iris bulbs. That's how I knew. At where to come. I promised our. Mother."

"I know, but what did you promise?"

"Get there. And hunt him. Make her home."

"*Him* or *her?*"

"Her—*boy*. I come to give him out."

"*Get* him out? Is that why we're here? Doesn't he *belong* here? Shouldn't he stay *here?*"

"Yes. They. All our people. Family. *Us.* Live here."

"So let's leave him here."

"That's what I told him. Our mother."

"*Her*, not him. *My* mother. *What* did you tell her? What are you saying—why did mom want you to move him away from *here?*"

"Promised I'd come. Give his baby *out*. The boy. But didn't never. So instead give her—the ashes. There to him. Long way ago. At least make them. Together. Out at *there*."

"Dad, which one are you talking about? Did you or didn't you bury Chad's ashes *here?*"

"*No*. I have to come. To the place. The place for shooting. To that *place* so to give her—my brother. *Both* of them. *Get* both of them out. Before I go behind here. Give us all home."

"Your pronouns and verbs are so screwy. You're saying you put both their ashes out somewhere where we used to hunt?"

"Yes, that. And I promised—mother. I'd get—boy. Carry her behind— Not behind—*back*. Back home."

"*Damn*." A whisper. They'll have to come back. First go find wherever he'd scattered her mother's ashes, one of the old hunting sites. It's apparently also where Chad's ashes were taken years earlier—and then had her mother changed her mind? And he'd made some promise about bringing Chad home. It's going to be anywhere from ten to fifty miles from here, and no telling what's there now. And what then?— find the spot, bring a token cupful of dirt back to the farmstead? Help him honor his postponed obligation, with the hope it'll rouse him to tell her more about what had happened? If not, just add fulfilling his promise to her obligation.

The terrace holding the pool and deck is a plane not much more than ten feet higher than where Ronnie and her father are kneeling outside the nopale, but is at least fifty yards away up the hill. Through fissures of light between the cactus lobes, Ronnie can see two or three adult-sized adolescent males, one with entire head shaved except the ponytail that grows from his crown, a style used by that robed, san- daled, tambourine-shaking sect. But this cult is marked by a different uniform—their huge feet having mutated into plastic prostheses with a line of wheels fused into the soles. Like some sort of ritualistic sport, they skate around the pool deck in opposite directions, trying to push each other into the pool as they pass, usually succeeding, bellowing *fuck*, then skating off the edge to crash into the water on their own after successfully vanquishing another.

"Come on, then, let's go," she shrugs the rucksack higher onto her shoulders, still squatting. "Maybe it was for the best, if *that's* what little boys will turn into," immediately wanting to bite the words back into her mouth. Somewhere a bird sees no need to stop performing his trilled three-note boast.

But her father hasn't seemed to notice her impertinence. He's standing, his back to the nopale, looking out over Dictionary Valley. "He— no, our mother said. A baby can't. Be stay so long. From home."

"Okay, I said we'd do whatever it takes. But, Dad, why did you say you wanted to come here first?"

"My sh—shave. Need for dig."

"Your shovel? Dammit, Dad, you thought we'd drag a shovel along with us?"

"Army shovel."

"And what would make you think it's here? Dad, we *sold* everything. None of your shovels or anything else is even *here* anymore."

"In the—box—under car. Say for? T—"

"Trunk."

"Shovel lives in trunk in car."

"*Dammit*, Dad, we don't have a car, can't you remember *anything*?"

The riot of birdsong has snapped off. Buzzing nearby, a tiny helicopter, a blue-bodied dragonfly hovers briefly, alights on a nopale lobe, then vanishes. Her father's breath rasps.

"Hey, dude, there's some sorta like dirtbag over there taking a piss!"

"Hey you, bum, homeless asshole, this is private property."

"Go piss at the fucking bus stop with your slimebag friends."

"Go on, get lost, I'll send my fucking attack dog."

"*Dude*, like this little yapping wuss would do anything."

"Shut up, dude."

"You better run, dirtbag, *run*!"

A stone sizzles through tumbleweeds beside Ronnie, another several pop against the nopale lobes.

"Come on, Dad, run, *hurry*!"

A rock, making a lucky ricochet to get all the way through the nopale, taps against the ankle of her boot. It's a white quartz landscaping rock. Another plops against the stiff back of her father's hunting vest. Her father covers the back of his head with his good hand, taking precarious half-running steps with one leg, the other dragging and swinging, thrashing through the several yards of weeds hiding loose rocks or wasp nests or snakes. It's Ronnie, passing him, who nearly pitches herself into the weeds on her face. Finally, on the gravel leeway, she turns and catches her father, her two palms on his chest on either side of where his bad hand is clutching a fistful of his own shirt. "Okay, wait, we don't have to slide down the whole hill."

Her father spits into the dirt. "*Shanes.*"

"No, Dad it's not—" She steps back.. "*Oh*, that's right, a whole pack of Shanes."

"Where's. The—shoot?"

"Gun. At the bottom of the hill. Come on."

Her father only slips once—stepping down from the paved road's shoulder to pass between the houses, gravel gives way, he staggers and knocks his forehead on the lip of the satellite dish. When they reach the handcart at the bottom of the hill, Ronnie dabs the already-dried trickle of blood with a piece of toilet paper.

Chapter Three

Downtown in a little over an hour by city bus. Ronnie spreads a slice of bread with peanut butter, her father eats, dozes some, wakes to stare at people on the sidewalk whenever the bus slows at a light or stops to exchange passengers. Then Ronnie leaves her hunting-vested father in the library with a Zane Grey novel and plastic-covered gardening and outdoor magazines she selects from the periodical rack. Signs in the library forbid its use for sleeping by the homeless. Not only the odor and snores, but the duffle bags or grocery sacks, layers of ragged coats or fatigues no matter the weather, and the use of newspapers as drapes to block fluorescent light, will alert librarians to route them out and send them away. Her father doesn't smell, his hair and scalp are clean, only the bulky, blood-stained, fatigue-colored, underwear-stuffed hunting vest suggests his transience. So she has to take the handcart with her, several blocks away, to the county administration building and the department of records, then must leave the handcart behind an empty security guard station because taking the gun through the metal detector would likely elicit too many questions.

Of birth records, she finds only one, hers, Veronica Tattori. Her father and mother weren't born in San Diego County, not even in California. In this category, births, their names only appear once, as her parents. Chad could've been adopted. Adoption records would be sealed, wouldn't be considered county business. But Ronnie remembers photographs of her pregnant mother, leaning over to put her distended belly into toddler Ronnie's arms like a beach ball. They might've used the gestation as a first home-schooling lesson on reproduction. Ronnie can't remember when she *didn't* know that you put the doe in with the buck, observe the mounting, the agitation, the fall, and a month later, almost exactly, the fertilized doe constructs a nest of straw and her own softest fur, then delivers the litter of finger-sized, blind, pink, hairless, practically-still-fetal offspring. Ronnie knows her imagination never ventured to draw a picture of her parents engaged in similar behavior. She can't recall any distinct shift from ignorance to procreative knowledge. It was like the history or mathematics or geography her mother taught her, mornings at home—human reproduction was information without personal participation. Never having set foot in a schoolyard bustling with the heated bodies of jostling children, half of them male; never having known a boy older than the four or five-year-old Chad, never having had daily contact with testosterone-impelled adolescent youth, she's known only her father, and old men, and now he's one and the same.

And what's the point in this particular strain of lament? Too many other things she's never done, and who can weigh one as more considerable than another? She never took a test, never wrote a term paper, never sent an application to any college, never joined scouts or soccer or band. Didn't ever have a part-time job flipping hamburgers or scooping ice cream. Never danced under black lights or a disco glitter-ball, never waved a pompom, never lay on the floor with her feet against the wall twirling the phone cord around one finger and pressing the receiver to her face, never rode in a fast convertible. No softball teams, no summer camp, no cap-and-gown, no new workplace wardrobe, no first car nor first apartment, no girls' night out, no wedding showers, never a bridesmaid.

No need to examine county marriage and divorce inventories, she turns her attention to deaths. Tattori, Alicia Elizabeth. b. 4/10/32 d. 6/15/73 Cause of death: accidental drowning. No news here. Ronnie was seventeen and, the day before, had been told her home schooling was complete.

But, again, no Chad in this category. No *Chadwick Keith*. Would've said *b. 1962*, maybe 61. The month? She might remember a Halloween party, just the two of them plus parents—but was it for a birthday? They wore costumes and rang doorbells at least once, collecting lollipops and peanuts from the few houses on Hannigan Hill. She'd never done so alone. So what? She can remember making ice cream in July and roasting chestnuts in the fireplace in January, neither necessarily signifies a birthday. What about the tree house—was that a special gift, like for a birthday? Her father had taken time he could've spent building rock walls or cultivating vegetable beds or netting fruit trees, to instead scrounge scrap lumber from two new houses being built on the county road a mile away, then allowed more time to assemble the tree house platform. So the tree house itself could've been a celebration of Chad's birth—the epitome of a rockabye-baby cradle in the tree top? Which doesn't answer what month the tree house was built. Six months of the year were hunting season, not much spare time there. Of the other six, three, in the summer, saw fishing take priority, clamming could start in late November and continue through February, also the season for leafy produce, lettuce, broccoli, cabbage. There's no dormant winter in Southern California where a father repairs tools and whittles toys.

Anyway what difference what month Chad might've been born? He's not on microfiche nor microfilm here. No birth, no death, as though the tragedy has been erased. Her father is right, no one knows he ever existed.

After their hasty descent down the side of Hannigan Hill, on their way back to the bus stop, she'd thought aloud: "Before we go traipsing all over the county, I should put our papers in a safe place."

"Too many. Stuff."

"I know, you always thought we brought too much." She'd thought the handcart might rattle itself to pieces rolling over the dirt roadside on Central Avenue. "But I'm only talking about some papers, birth certificates, your Army discharge papers, social security stuff. Maybe I'll get us a safe deposit box. I hope we got all the stuff out of the house. Did you know we don't have a birth certificate for Chad?"

"Can't prove she—the boy. Born. Or not live."

"What's that supposed to mean?"

No answer. So she'd taken the long detour to the downtown office of records before doing their banking business.

At a drug store between the county building and the library, she buys two maps, City of San Diego together with East County—which contains Dictionary Valley—and a map of North County which includes the fairgrounds, lagoons, coastal sloughs, and inland rolling hills and flatlands now burgeoning with housing developments and growing cities no longer small enough to call towns or suburbs.

After sliding the worn manila folder of papers into the safe drawer, she pins the key at the bottom of the game pouch on the back of the hunting vest. She'll need to restock their cash, although hesitates to carry more than twenty dollars, so she picks up a list of branch locations. The estate sale two years ago, auctioning the land and house and most of the contents, netted enough to eliminate the hospital debt from her father's treatment in an emergency room, three days in intensive care, and over two weeks on the ward. But she has been able to save some every month from her nurse-aide checks, after paying the part of her father's monthly bill not covered by Medicare.

Although Ronnie expects to find him sleeping where she left him, he's not asleep and not at the table where the magazines and Zane Gray novel are spread in a fan around where he'd been. He's not far away, though, on a vinyl bench in the video section watching a PBS *Nova* about the formation and drift of the continents. A tap on his shoulder and he follows her back to the table where she spreads both maps. She's also taken every individual bus schedule from the rack in the library foyer.

"Help me, Dad. Where did we used to hunt? And which is the one you want to—need to go back to?"

In the chair beside her, elbows on the table, his face barely six inches above the map, leaning so far over the table his butt lifts off the seat, with one finger he traces interstate 805 down to the border. The freeway probably wasn't yet constructed when they hunted in the South Bay.

"Dad. . . ?"

His finger returns north on 805 then veers onto an even newer expressway, the South Bay freeway, which heads east before it curves gently to the north and slices through Dictionary Valley.

"No, Dad . . ."

But his finger jumps from the freeway, crosses the reservoir, stops, traces the name of a planned community. "What's this thing?"

"Something called Sunnyside. Looks like all houses now." The streets and tiny printed names entwine and circle each other like a thumbprint. "Did we hunt there?"

"Not anymore."

"Well we can't go back *there*, Dad, what're we gonna do, walk into someone's living room or bedroom and say I used to hunt here—"

"*Not* at here."

"Okay, keep looking."

"Figs." He points to a thin black line crossing a white two-inch expanse of map, just above the border, Dairy Mart Road, no other roads, no names of communities, no little schoolhouse markers, no shopping centers, just the blue line of the Tijuana River. "Under at river."

"I don't remember rivers where we hunted. Maybe little creeks."

"It gives wet. The people are every time. Have to save. Everyone. And they every time. Come back inside. Give wet again. And their. Animals. Flying horses."

"You mean where they lifted the horses out with helicopters that time the Tijuana River flooded? Is that where you want to go first?"

"That one gives wet. *Floods*. No one should. Have there. Morons. Keep coming there."

"So you're saying that's *not* where you went with Mom's and . . . the . . . ashes?"

"At the wet. But not at the flood."

"God, Dad, just tell me *where*."

"I do with gun. All over. Everywhere. Wherever birds."

"Do we have to remember and find each one so you can say *not there*?"

"Maybe. You— Someone can. Say it for me."

"Someone—you mean *me*. I don't know where you took her ashes. You didn't take me with you."

Her father has yet to take his eyes from the map. His finger re-enters the interstate. "North." He runs out of map at the top edge. Ronnie pulls the North County map over the city map, slides it under her father's eyes. "Still here." His finger stops.

"Dad, that's the fairgrounds, where you worked. We didn't hunt there."

It housed the county fair for three weeks a year, horse racing for two months, a weekend dog show here, gun show there, boy scout jamboree, rodeo, go cart races; but for months at a time, five-days a week, the fairgrounds were peopled only by the skeleton grounds crew, landscaping and building maintenance. Our father did any of everything, from painting the ticket booths to driving a golf cart from planter to planter down the midway to till each with a handful of fertilizer. He sloshed buckets of disinfectant in the restrooms, changed light bulbs in the exhibition hall ceiling from atop a two-story ladder, used a weed-whacker on dandelions growing around the foundation of the cattle barns, oiled the motor that ran the pump in the fountain in the racetrack paddock area, replaced belts in the ventilating fans in the poultry building. When the winter flats of pansies arrived from the nursery, he spent days on hands and knees, ripping the tangled roots apart and pressing each baby plant into topsoil he'd already raked onto an ornamental embankment or in the vast flower bed surrounding the pond on the racetrack's infield.

During the county fair, our father continued to work days, invisibly behind-the-scenes. Emptied trash cans filled with half-eaten sticky buns, popcorn, gnawed corn cobs, lemonade cups, soggy portions of corndogs, greasy paper plates stained with ketchup. Replenished toilet paper in restrooms. Changed dead bulbs in the strings of lights crisscrossing the midway. Clocked out then worked another shift as night gateman at the secondary entrance near the stock barns, taking tickets, stamping hands, waving through exhibitors' vehicles. During his break, he went to the cattle barn. The cows being displayed by local dairies—Holsteins, Golden Guernseys, Brown Swiss, Jerseys—had to be milked twice a day. Being the best of the best, high-profile advertising models for commercial dairies, the sleek, well-groomed cows poured forth rivers of rich, creamy milk. Small sample cupfuls were handed out during the day at the fair, the rest usually discharged down the drain. Unhomogenized, unpasteurized, the milk could not be sold. But our father brought home gallon jugs every night when he left the fairgrounds at midnight. By morning when we came out for breakfast, cream would be thick at the top of the jug.

Behind the restrooms and flower show, there was a small garden of trees, a few eucalyptus, Brazilian pepper, purple-flowered jacaranda. The square area was blocked off on two sides by eugenia hedges, a shade cloth stretched above the tops of the smaller trees, holes provided for the tall euca-lyptus to rise above, their leaves caught in the cloth netting before they landed on the picnic tables arranged in the shade on raked sandstone. When we went to the fair with our mother once a year, our first stop was always the picnic area where our mother would put our basket of egg salad, toma-toes, peaches, oatmeal cookies, and thermos of lemonade on a table in the shade, reserving the table for suppertime when our father had an hour between his shift as groundskeeper and his stint as gatekeeper. On either side of our mother, we visited merri-go-rounds and hobby show exhibits, home-grown vegetables and homemade pies, hucksters selling knives, har-monicas, and magic fry pans, and game booths with huge multicolored stuffed animals swinging high over our heads. Then did we really walk past the booths of fried everything—zucchini strips, cheese, onion rings, dough-nut holes—without a twinge? Once after eating our sandwiches, Chad was up from the table, his cookie likely still in his fist, drawn to one of the trees by another three-year-old running circles around the trunk. After a brief peek-a-boo race, Chad said to the other child, now whacking the tree trunk with a stick, "This is my dad's fair."

Other than recognizing an approaching season—dove, rabbit, duck, shellfish, winter produce, spring buds needing protection, summer fruit to preserve, autumn pruning and mulching, trout season, the next high tide, the next forecasted rain or dry Santa Ana wind—Ronnie can't recall looking into the future with either anticipation or curiosity over what changes might await her there, nor with concern over how she would prepare for or build toward another life. Now looking ahead with design was a difficult custom to suddenly be capable of.

On another bus heading north, Ronnie tries but has trouble push-ing her thoughts forward to next week or next month, let alone an eventual time when she'll be living in an apartment somewhere, hearing a phone ring through one wall, a stereo pulsate through another, planting her father in front of a television while she's out to work for whatever kind of employer will find her skilled enough. Isn't that the only feasible forecast, after they're done doing whatever it is they're doing? She clasps her hands in her lap to prevent herself from using nails and teeth to peel pieces of cuticle from her fingertips.

"Dad, we went north, but now we have to decide a good place to get off the bus."

"Okay." He lifts his head as though waking up.

"Remember where Mom shot the hawk? Wasn't that a place we used a lot? It's the only place I even remember. Probably because of that hawk. I remember that."

"Never did on bus."

"I know but this time we had to."

"Getting late. Best in the early. Under sun."

"We just need to find the place. Let's find the hawk place. Was it near one of these lagoons in North County? Wasn't that your favorite hunting place? But, near a lagoon, wouldn't that one flood too?"

"Ocean . . . In—place. Not bay. In—"

"I don't know."

"Salty wet get *in*. Like river in going back. In—"

"Inlet?"

"*Inlet*. Inlet fill and un-fill—"

"Empties."

"Empties on tide. La— Lagoons don't never. Overfl— Flood."

"Overflow."

"Salty mash too."

"Marsh."

"Marsh. For ducks. The rest of ground dry. Dove."

"But the map shows four or five lagoons up the coast in North County. Which one was it?"

"Some place is it. Key land."

"What are you talking about? There are no keys on this coast."

"Keesland. Needland. Keenland. Kaneen—"

"Dad, whatever you're babbling . . . never mind . . . try to think—"

"Person has cattle. She own cattle. Cows want. Leaf, grass. All plants. Eat every. But must give wet."

"Must *have* water. And. . . ? Go on."

"Place where wet—water. Is above ocean. A place. Es— No salty water. Duck. Br—like duck, br— You say."

"Brant."

"Brant. Dove. Quail. Rabbit. All in one place. Es— You say it." He stares at her mouth.

"I don't know."

"Es— Fresh wet. Near before ocean. Wait. Es— *Estuary*."

"Good for you. How did we get there? Can you remember?"

"Camino Real. Many good. Place can shoot. Get north as far. As clock gives us. Then work down. Toward home."

"We don't live down there anymore. We don't live anywhere anymore."

Probably our most game-rich hunting area was just off the seaside freeway in North County where several lagoons carve into coastal lowlands, meeting small creeks, creating marshes and, slightly further inland, dry washes and small orange sandstone gorges. It was private property where the landowner ran cattle, so the small creek making its way toward the ocean had been blocked in several places with dirt dams, creating watering holes. In an arid region, water attracts birds—especially dove who feed in grain fields and on the seeds left behind after cattle forage. Lowland but not flat— stubby sandstone bluffs and gullies, slightly higher plateaus, partitioned by clusters of huge eucalyptus trees imported fifty to seventy-five years before. Dry, steppe bushes—fennel, tumbleweed, buckwheat, wild oats, chamise, sage—and familiar sandy watersheds, bristly sand grass where grasshoppers flew in front of each footstep. We found snakeskins and weathered, bleached seashells. The whole tract was crisscrossed by cattle trails, dotted with parched cattle droppings. We never saw the cattle. But once we found a desert tortoise crossing the dirt road we used to get onto the property. Our father put the tortoise in the car, left all the windows open, and after the morning hunt, we took the tortoise home. Our father drilled a small hole in the back of his shell, attached a fishing leader, and used his strongest fishing line to tether the tortoise in the front yard where he could enjoy the lawn when the sprinklers came on and then burrow under the jade bushes. We fed him lettuce and sometimes fresh figs. But, despite the constant availability and variety of food, the tortoise broke his tether and found freedom again on the undeveloped south side of our farmstead's hill in Dictionary Valley.

There's a grocery store and strip mall where the bus stops at the corner of El Camino and La Costa. But the stores are not at street level, they're part way up a hill—a sharply sloped landscaped embankment—with the backs of the buildings and their signs looking out over the street toward the ocean. It takes a while to get her father up and into the aisle, put her rucksack on her back and lift the handcart from the empty seat in front of them. A group of men waits, standing close behind her. Two kids with skateboards go out the side door.

From where the bus drops them, they can either walk to the corner, turn right, go uphill on the sidewalk half a block, turn right again and enter the strip mall. Or they can hike straight up the landscaped embankment on a narrow dirt path worn through the ground cover by many short-cutters. A small, low sign beside a sprinkler head in the landscaping groundcover says *Auga Impura, No Tomar*. The group of men who'd been crowding behind her in the bus choose to go single file up the dirt path. Three Mexican men with a fourth who's head-and-shoulders taller, all wearing worn jeans, t-shirts, and flannel jackets. The Mexicans wear Dodgers baseball caps, their thick black hair dented in back by the hats. The fourth man has long dirty-brownish hair in a ponytail and carries two plastic water jugs. The teenagers lounge on the bus stop bench and light cigarettes. Their pants are longer than shorts and shorter than jeans, huge barrel-wide leg holes with their bare shins sticking out and immense high-top sneakers on their feet.

Ronnie and her father use the sidewalk. It takes awhile. Her father is clearly tired. She's wondering if she could rig a bicycle so he could sit behind her on the back without her worrying too much that he'd fall off.

Outside the grocery store, beside the phony fireplace logs and drinking water dispensers, there are two tables with umbrellas, as though the grocery store is also a French cafe. Her father, as if given an unspoken direction, sits and waits there while Ronnie goes in to get fried chicken and potato salad at the grocery's deli counter. They stay at the table to eat. It's around three in the afternoon. The teenage boys from the bus have attracted another one riding a tiny bicycle the size a clown might use, and the three are on the asphalt in front of the store using the concrete curbs and parking bumpers for skateboard tricks. Several cars, backing out of parking slots, have to jerk to a halt as a skateboarder or bicycle suddenly whizzes behind them. The parking lot echoes the crack of board against concrete, the shouts of the riders—*Dude! Dream on. Like hell. Fuckin' awesome!*—now also car horns and the boys' surly curses in response.

The migrants come out of the store, each with two bulging sacks. It's easy to identify milk, juice, bread, bananas, a cantaloupe and head of lettuce, in addition to the bumps of miscellaneous cans and boxes. Ronnie's father bites the meat off a drumstick, his eye on the skateboarding boys. "Many Shanes," he mutters.

"Everywhere you look," Ronnie answers. The potato salad is so goopy, there's probably more mayonnaise than potatoes. "Hey, Dad. . . ? Why didn't Chad have a birth certificate?"

"One thing. More thing. Doing many things."

"What does that mean? You were too busy?"

"She came at our place. Born. On—at—stove—? sink—?"

"In the kitchen? Didn't Mom have a doctor?"

"Just we there. Who else to hear?"

"But there's also no death cer—"

The store's automatic door opens for a man in a red coat. He cups his hands to his mouth and shouts, "Hey, fellows, no skateboarding allowed here, please leave the parking lot, it's dangerous, someone's going to get hurt." He's ignored, finally bellows, "Hey, you boys, *hey!*"

"Dude, it's a free country," one boy yells.

"Not on private property."

"Fuck you."

"You can say that to the cops." The red-coated man retreats into the store. A security guard is strolling from the other end of the lot where there's a row of smaller shops. As Ronnie stands to bundle the bones and trash from the table, the long-haired migrant comes over to use the drinking water machine, and the boys roll right past the table in the car exit lane, standing upright on their boards, the bicyclist following, insolently disregarding a car that's forced to inch slowly behind them. As they head out of the parking lot, their smirks are aimed at Ronnie, at her father, at the man filling his water jugs. The bicyclist sneers "get a job" over his shoulder.

The bank next door has its own parking lot, ringed by narrow ribbons of sparse landscaping—hard raked dirt sustaining typical mock-orange shrubs and medium-sized heavily-pruned eucalyptus trees. On one side of the building, a wider bed of dirt with winter pansies and heavenly bamboo, backed-dropped by a waist-high hedge and the windowless, doorless side wall. The drive-through lane emerges on this side of the bank; the entrance is on the opposite side.

"We have wheels, so we'll drive through, okay Dad?"

"For why?"

"Money, for a motel tonight. Maybe three nights. Think two or three days will be enough?"

"For some things. Never plenty. For something else."

"For what *you* want to do. To find the place you want to find and do whatever you have to do there."

"I said at him. Promise. I will come."

"Her. You promised *her*."

"Yes. Her."

Midway across the bank parking lot, she spots the three boys in a far corner sitting on a curb in the spotted, flickering shade of one of the larger trees, their feet on their skateboards in the gutter. The bicycle lying on its side, crushing a couple of shrubs.

Just before the drive-through lane makes a left turn toward the back of the building, a big convex mirror mounted high on the corner provides a darkly distorted, far-away view of what lies ahead. One car is idling in the narrow lane. An arm reaches from the window to touch buttons on the bank machine. The drive-through is almost a tunnel—asphalt lane, stucco bank wall, stucco overhang, and on the other side of the car, a shoulder-high stucco wall including pillars that support the overhang. The wall separates the drive-through corridor from the same landscaped embankment sliding downhill to the bus stop on El Camino Real.

After the car drives on, Ronnie moves forward, leaves the handcart in the middle of the lane. On some silent cue her father's hand replaces hers on the handle and he stays behind as she steps to the ATM machine. The wallet is three layers down, canvas pants on top, jeans under that, then spandex bicycle shorts with a hip pocket holding her billfold. Three nights in a transient motel, can't be more than $90 for two, plus food—she decides on $120. While the machine seems to count bills—humming and whining, like a discussion behind the wall regarding whether or not to give her that much cash—her father also makes a noise, a startled grunt. The handcart clattering to its side as he falls and cries out once more—and for a second, less than that, waiting mesmerized for the thick stack of bills to shoot from the machine, Ronnie's heart flies, a hot flash of freedom: Another stroke? But he'd taken his medication that morning. Her short flight already over, a brick wall slams into her from the rear, the machine spits the money, a hand not hers grabs it, her arms pinned behind her back, another hot hand over her mouth, too many hands to count, the wallet pried from her fingers.

"Welcome to the neighborhood."

"Time to pay taxes, bitch."

"Dude, bring'er over here."

"How do we even know it's a girl?"

"Being ugly's no excuse, man."

"See if she has anything else." Knapsack ripped from her back.

"I'm not touching her stinking shit." The knapsack kicked into the lane where her father, on hands and knees, struggles to get up, one foot under the handcart as though the cart weighs enough to pin him down. Then she's seeing only a blur of concrete and bare moving legs and big athletic shoes and the hedge and the wall of the building down where it meets dirt. She's on the ground, half in the bushes, between the wall and the hedge's lowest branches, bushtits fleeing shrub-to-shrub in a twittering panic of tiny flickers and flutters.

"Fucking Christ she's fucking biting me."

"Stuff something in her mouth."

"What, man?"

"Shit, your dick, asshole."

"With those teeth?"

"Christ, look where we are, someone's gonna come."

"Yeah, like *you*, dude."

"*Me*—why not you?"

"Sonofabitch she's strong, *hold* her, dude, I can't get my pen out."

"Maybe it ain't even a *she*."

"Like, then, find *out*."

"How?"

"Dude, didn't you take sex ed 101?"

"She's like, wearing fifty-million fucking pairs of pants."

"There—*tits*, it's a bitch all right."

"Call those tits?"

"Like I said, ugly's no excuse."

"Suck it, dude."

"Get outta the fucking way, man, she's getting her passport."

Her two sweatshirts and two t-shirts bunched over her face, twisted elastic bra strap across her eyes and nose, a pair of hard knees on either side of her head, something cool touches her chest, sharp scent of ink, between collarbone and breasts a line crosses her sternum, then two circles dip around and back up, circling each breast like wire rims of a bra, below that another line and a spot, then another line parallel with a cross. A boy muttering "bitch, bitch, bitch," as though to a tune. A hand digging, burrowing beneath her waistband, drilling its way toward her crotch.

"Dude, get her fucking pants off, I'm almost done up here."

"There's, like, what the fuck—bicycle pants, I'll never get these fuckers off."

"You fucking give up too easy, dude."

"Then *you* fuck her, I'm not getting her AIDS."

"Then fuck her with something else."

"I can't let go've her fucking legs, she's like *bionic*, dude."

"I'll get her, go ahead, man, *rip* them, where's your knife?"

There's another voice that nobody's listening to, not even Ronnie it seems, until she realizes it's herself who hasn't shut up the whole time, *No . . . No . . . No . . . No . . .* biting the hand that periodically attempts to cover her mouth, *No . . . No . . . No . . .* heaving her entire torso right then left then back again despite the 150 pounds sitting on her head and another 150 on her knees, *No . . . No . . . No . . . No . . .* wrenching hands and arms free from a vice-grip and flailing not with fists but bared claws until he crushes her wrists together in one fist again, *No . . . No . . . No . . .* her throat growing more and more raw but the voice remaining strident, fueled more by feral dread than pain. A death cry. Frightening enough to recognize it's herself she hears in abject, brute panic, even more horrifying to suddenly grasp there's another word she's yelling.

Mommy . . . Mommy . . .

Something familiar, as though she's cried like this before. But before the impulse is answered, her remaining senses come blasting back. The abrasive hard dirt and little pebbles and sticks scouring her back, skin of her arms twisted from front to back, the harsh sour smell of her own savage sweat, silvery bright taste of blood in her mouth, a car horn down on El Camino Real, tiny shout of the guy hawking papers at the traffic light. The voice becomes louder, but her own now obliterating everything else, and when at once, simultaneously, she is released, she's already, immediately on her feet as though she was a rat trap they'd been holding open, as though a *crack* when they release her, and the trap snaps shut empty, is the kind of detonation ending all other noise.

The long-haired migrant is beside her, holding a knife. The boys six feet away, a semi-circle, a stand-off, the migrant with a switchblade, but there're three of them. The migrant's Mexican companions have not accompanied him into the bank's drive-through.

"What're you gonna do, dude, tell our parents?"

"Who'll believe a stinking homeless fucker like you?"

"No one'll even miss you if we kick your ass."

"*Gun!*"

Even before the boys' rubber soles slap asphalt, after they burst in three directions through the landscaping, Ronnie is instantaneously crouching, fingers in her ears but eyes up to locate where the game falls.

"Hey there," the ponytail guy is practically crooning, the first she hears his voice "it's okay, old man, it's over, they're gone now. I owe you one."

Her father, shotgun raised, stands amid the contents of the handcart that he'd had to empty in order to liberate the gun.

It's not until they're a mile east on La Costa Avenue—the four-lane road that crosses El Camino at the light, pushing uphill, above and parallel to a creek bed golf course—that Ronnie sorts through what she's been told by the ponytailed migrant whose name is Adrian. About a quarter mile ago the four men had turned off La Costa to cut through a residential tract. The canyon where they make their camp is that direction, over a hill developed with houses, just past an elementary school, an untouched hillside sloping down toward a dry rainwash arroyo. Ronnie and her father—now with no money, no bank card to access cash, no identification of any kind with which to obtain another bank card until she can get back to the safe deposit box downtown—are on their way toward a different place to camp, recommended by the ponytailed guy as safer because it's farther from work areas therefore not populated by worker camps. It's beside a creek, though the water might not be drinkable. He'd attached one of his water jugs to her handcart before he and his companions had crossed La Costa to make their way home. Just up ahead, he'd instructed, about a mile and a half, take the second left, downhill, it'll look like nothing but condos and apartments clustered around the end of one of the golf course fairways, but just keep going, there'll be a cul-de-sac where the road ends but there's a chained-off utility vehicle route that runs steep downhill—go past the no trespassing sign, down the hill to the creek. If the water's high it'll be flowing over the service road, but don't cross, take the trail to the right on this side of the creek. If you go left, you'll be on the golf course in less than a quarter mile, the creek cuts through the golf course, creating lawn-bordered ponds so that mallards, egrets, and great blue herons will be part of the golf resort's milieu. That's what he'd said, *milieu*.

Off the service road to the right, though—he'd said—as it progresses east, there's a sheer, rocky ravine where the creek comes down. Actually it's in the midst of a housing development, but the houses are far above on the bluffs, with the creek way down below in the gorge, the sides of the canyon too steep to build on. The houses way up there look out over the golf course to the ocean, but right on the other side of their backyard fences, the natural canyon plunges almost straight downhill into the undeveloped ravine. Don't go too far into it, he'd said, you don't need to go far to feel it's like natural wilderness. Closer to the service road, the water is slower and spreads out in a pool with reeds and mud hens, towhees making nests underneath last season's fallen fennel with last year's dried grasses snarled in the stocks. Likewise, for people, crawl under the low laurel sumac bushes and it's a natural tent. Perfect camping place, he said, except too far from work and the bus to be practical for us. Meaning himself and his three friends and others like them.

She's still hearing her voice calling for her mother, a sound at once so utterly foreign and terrifyingly familiar.

The three Mexicans had reappeared immediately after the boys had fled, the sounds of skateboards and curses still clattering and hooting from the parking lot on the other side of the building. With plastic grocery sacks still dangling, one from each hand, the Mexicans had come from the dark drive-through entry lane, as though they'd been waiting there for their turn at the ATM. These're good guys, the ponytail explained, but they stay clear of those kids, there's been trouble, a lot of trouble, and, naturally, migrants like these guys can't go to the police. But *you* can, he'd said, do you want to call the police?

"No, I can't. My father. They'd take my father."

The tall ponytailed migrant didn't ask her why. The three Mexicans spoke in Spanish and he'd answered with much shorter sentences. "I just told them your father won't shoot," he'd said.

"The shotgun's not even loaded."

"You can imagine how they get jumpy about people with guns, but they're more leery of those kids than an old man with a shotgun." Some kids from around here, he'd explained, have made it a sport to harass migrant workers. Harass isn't even the word for it anymore, considering they've stolen food, money, watches, shoes, anything they can force a Latino to hand over. Plus there's scuttlebutt that they'd taken potshots, sniper-style, at men on their way to work in the flower fields; that they'd written vulgarities on people's bodies with ink that requires gasoline to wash off; that they'd driven past the roadside meeting places where contractors and landscapers pick-up day-laborers, one kid hanging out the car window with a baseball bat, trying to get a crack at the closest head; that they've got some secret white-middleclass-kid club where they "keep score of how many wetbacks they get," variable points earned for various infractions. Word's out to stick in groups of three, preferably four or more. There's even been farfetched hearsay of some rapes, of both men and women, with broomsticks or flashlights, one story had them attempting to castrate a worker they found waiting alone for a ride—rumors, he said, which seem *somewhat* more credible now, although that last one was still a stretch.

Do the workers also scream for their extinct mothers, a sound suburban mockingbirds will mimic in calls to their mates, or does their fear of deportation keep them silent throughout?

At some point, while reloading the handcart, cleaning bits of gravel from a scrape on her father's elbow, or during the slow trudge up La Costa Avenue before the four men turned off—she could tell her father's pace was significantly delaying the migrants' usual trip home—the tall ponytailed guy, Adrian (she should remember to use his name) explained how he'd come to live and work with the Mexican migrants. He'd been a college student, probably ten years ago, doing field work on the native geology, flora and fauna in coastal scrub. Then he'd switched his major to cultural geography, a comparative study of the migrants and the nomadic indigenous people who'd populated this terrain hundreds of years ago. To really know something, you had to live it, not just watch it, he'd said. Hadn't gotten very far with the thesis, but had never left the life, he was one of them now.

As they get nearer to the right turn downhill, the sidewalk levels off. Even though they don't stop, it feels like resting to no longer be lugging everything uphill. The handcart became heavier with the addition of the water jug. When the ponytail—Adrian—had noticed no blankets in the handcart, just the one raincoat wrapped around the protruding barrel of the shotgun, he'd taken off his jacket and instructed his companions to do likewise, and had tied the bundle of four jackets to the side of the cart. She doesn't need to be told that it gets to below forty degrees out here at night, especially in the deep canyons; even lower next month, there'll be frost.

"Return them when you get some blankets," he'd said.

At the bottom of the short hill, two level blocks of apartment or condo complexes, each with a gate into some kind of courtyard, sometimes a pool that's centered in the complex of doors like a fountain at the center of a mission's courtyard. There are still some empty lots between developments, green with thick new weed growth this time of year, taller anise and mustard at the property lines where the once-a-year tractor mower doesn't reach. And at the end of the street, a cul-de-sac circle of road, a for-sale sign on the last green, graded lot, and a cyclone fence with a chained-off opening big enough for a truck. From there, as Adrian had described, a cruder stretch of asphalt pours once again downhill, but at a steeper angle than would be suitable for any residential street. Their footsteps fall heavily as they make their way down into the gully, leaning backwards, the handcart now no longer being pulled but held back to keep it from pushing them downhill too quickly. The vegetation here has not been graded. Laurel sumac and lemonade berry bushes are thick and head-high. At the bottom, sycamore line the banks of the creek.

As Adrian had predicted, the creek runs over the pavement. The running water spreads out to about twenty feet across and several inches deep as it crosses the asphalt in a smooth liquid sheet. The service road acting partly as a dam, a small quiet pool of water has collected to the right, the shallow flow of water passing over the asphalt is like spillover on a tiny reservoir. On the other side of the creek, the service road makes a beeline straight up the opposite side of the gully to another housing tract up above.

The path off the road, running beside the creek east through the gully, is hard mud, not too slippery, with little litter, although if the creek had been higher in the past week or two, that would explain the absence of cans and papers. Dog footprints are pressed into the mud at creek's edge. Tall reeds circle the pool, a higher clump of green cattails near the center where a pair of mud hens glide silently, hardly creating a ripple.

Not more than twenty yards from the road, still beside the pool, Ronnie stops. Dusk is quickly falling. She removes her rucksack, takes the hunting vest from her father's back and replaces it with one of the migrant's jackets. Her father moves away, several steps up the side of the gully then to the far side of a clump of lupine threaded with dry reeds from last year's wet season. There, she knows, he's peeing.

She'll need to do likewise, but doesn't until she's dragged the handcart and rucksack under the biggest laurel sumac, spread the raincoat over the hard dirt, helped her father to lie down and covered him with the remaining jackets. He sleeps almost immediately.

For this she didn't need Adrian's instruction, she's always known the sumac bushes grow like tents, the thick gray-green leaves mostly on the outside. Underneath the branches there's a hollow shell, a low cave, a fort, dark enough even grassy weeds won't grow. Standing outside, she can hear her father's slow, sleeping breath, but she can't see him. On this side, the bush's most recent growth reaches upright, each shoot supporting a Christmastree-shaped cluster of tiny colorless nodules—the flowers. When they turn to seed, they don't change shape but darken to rust then black-brown clumps of seeds, favorites of sparrow, bushtit, mockingbird, and phoebe. Not only drought-resistant but fire defiant as well. When wildfires blacken entire canyons and hills, the roots of the sumac remain intact, not reliant on foliage for nutrients, feeding on the carbon remains of other vegetation. With root systems already completely developed, they can rapidly restore themselves. Often the first signs of life on a blackened hill are the shoots of laurel sumac pushing through the sooty skeletons of their former bodies.

The silence of twilight is like the relief of a fading headache. The ground is dark, the sky still slate. In the open, on a hill slope of sprouting wild oats, Ronnie lifts her t-shirt and sweatshirts; pushes down her canvas pants and jeans and spandex bicycle shorts, past her knees, to her ankles, frees one foot in order to spread her legs. Her pale body visible against the dusk, and she sees the letters, fat black ink on her skin, the *T C H* across her stomach and hips. And she feels, once again, the loops of the *B* circling her breasts, the dot of the *I* boring into her ribs. A brutal shudder, a silent shatter, something breaks, hot urine streams down her legs and tears down her cheeks, but no sound this time. Except a rustle of mice, hush of the creek, whisper of leaves. The mournful murmur of roosting dove, or an owl. The cry of a hawk. Or *is* that her voice again?

At what point did the earsplitting chaos start? Certainly not before our knees buckled to squat below the line of fire, the reflex so quick, so instinctive, impossible to say for sure which came first—the motion of our mother's gun being raised or the children hitting the dust at the sound or sight of game.

A mistake, an accident. The kestrel, smallest native falcon, doesn't have wings like fanned fingers. Its wings are pointed, like the dove. But such definite differences—without the dove's heavy-bodied silhouette, without the rhythmic wing beat and whistle of feather or the burst of feather-flutter when quail break from cover. The kestrel can hover, rise like a helicopter, while the dove must take flight gradually like a bulky jet from a runway. Who could've made such a misjudgment?

Call it simultaneous—crouch down, knees hit the dust, fingers in ears, head up, the report from our mother's gun, our father's shout, and the screaming.

MOMMY—

SHUT UP, SHUT UP, WHY DID YOU—HOW COULD YOU—

QUIET, AL, HUSH UP, RONNIE—

MOMMY—

The vast, arid bottomland could hardly be touched, let alone filled, offered no resistance to our voices, just sucked the sound out of us and dispersed it. But whose voice cried for our mother? Chad, there and not there. Chad's red, wrenched face.

When did the noise end? Where was Chad?

The hawk was dead. Hooked bill flopped down against speckled breast. We dug, with boot heels, sticks, fingernails, the butts of shotguns. Suddenly the vast field existed only beneath our hands, the hard yellow earth, woody root of sage, a tiny snake who'd burrowed into sandstone. Where was Chad? Wasn't he here and there, always in the way, holding the dead hawk up by its wings—making it fly, dip and soar over our heads as we dug—and impersonating the CAW CAW of its cry?

Chapter Four

In five days their food is gone and she hasn't yet returned the jackets to the migrants. She's busied herself at making a camp with the least possible discernible evidence that they're here, including the sound of her voice. No excuse for further crying, no occasion for laughter, and few reasons for words. Surprisingly, a need for dialogue is even more scarce than in the hospital, which adhered to a regular schedule, so simple memorization removed most of the necessity for conversation. Here the routine is even more basic, like instinct; they perform inherent roles. She imagines they're like human forms before the development of language. Perhaps she'll ask Adrian, when she sees him, when she returns the jackets, if the indigenous people who'd lived here centuries ago were here from primitive times, before spoken language existed.

Her father has collected rocks, using his good hand and the forearm of the bad side to lift and carry each stone, the size of a small head, to build a fire pit against a boulder that bulges two feet out of the ground as a backstop. But they didn't start a fire until they'd eaten all the chicken spread, so they can use the can to boil water. He collects wood. Some of what he gathers are pieces of board fence that must've been washed down the gully during a flood, a few are half burnt branches left over from the last wildfire that scoured the gorge. His best find is a long-discarded skeletal Christmas tree. They only burn a fire around noon, and he continually fans the smoke so it dissipates instead of rising in a traceable column. And only to heat water to wash with, once a day, then she hangs the wet hospital towels on branches to dry during the warm afternoon. Every morning her father finds at least one better rock, replaces one in the fire pit—rocks starting to fit like puzzle pieces, some with flat tops, so the cans of water don't have to sit in ashes to heat.

The closest houses, actually apartments, are barely a hundred yards away. But at night a caterwaul of coyotes careens through the gorge. The housing developments are clustered like barnacles on the hills, street and porch lights and neon from the community's gas stations and fast-food prevent the unusually clear sky from being ablaze with stars. If the low coastal overcast would start rolling in again in late afternoon, a little of the day's warmth would stay close to the ground. But the cloud-less sky allows the day's heat to lift and completely disperse, so Ronnie and her father sleep in a knot, dressed in everything they own, under a patchwork of jackets that smell faintly of tobacco smoke and male sweat.

Almost every morning, from a different direction at varying distances, a car alarm begins to sound, early, sometimes before dawn, like an alarm clock for anyone sleeping in nearby bushes. It's not long after, as though standing in line to take a turn, car doors slam, engines start—some de-manding a long hoarse warm-up. A few habitually backfire, which Ronnie mistook for guns the first morning and, in sleep-sluggish panic, jerked herself into consciousness to make sure the shotgun was still concealed overhead in the lowest branches of the sumac, a camouflaged gun rack.

Early one morning in the last five, from one of the developments on the hills above the gully, a repeating mechanical horn followed by loud clangs of metal, the reverberation of diesel engine, again the beep-ing, the clanging, the roar of diesel. As recognition dawned, Ronnie was awake, lacing her boots, crawling out of the bush, discerning the direction of the racket, then running up the steep asphalt work road. Unmistakably, the noise was refuse trucks working their way through housing developments. So it was trash day. Adrian had advised her to find out when trash day was, to get out early and peruse the receptacles pulled out onto the sidewalks. She chose a few plastic laundry baskets, a ripped flannel shirt, a few more cans and plastic water bottles from the recycle bins, a rusted highchair with attached tray that can be used as a shelf or table, and a crumpled wad of painter's tarps that practically cracked when she flattened them at the campsite. They'll repel water when it rains and can be used as blankets, so the jackets can now be returned to Adrian and his friends.

She doesn't know how much Adrian saw between the moment he came upon the scene behind the bank, and the next instant when, suddenly released, in a single motion, she'd covered herself and gotten to her feet. She's not worried about what her father might've seen—he'd been empty-ing the handcart to get at the shotgun. And he hadn't been close enough to look over the boys' shoulders. And he might not've even understood what was going on. But it took her two days to realize Adrian had said writing on bodies was only a rumor.

It was while scrubbing her skin with gasoline—which she'd siphoned from an old truck into one of the new plastic jugs the night after trash day, taking only enough to wash with—that she'd suddenly grasped how Adrian had referred to the indelible ink as hearsay. She'd washed the same night she took the gasoline, using the bottom end of a sleeve ripped from the flannel shirt she'd found, then rinsing herself in the brittle-cold creek water. Perhaps, when she visited them, she should tell Adrian and the migrants that it wasn't just exaggerated gossip, it was true, so the rest of what they'd heard, all or most, could be true too.

Adrian will likely be amazed how much she's completed in five days. The last essential task she's accomplished is to get a bicycle. It actually does seem overly serendipitous—buying a bicycle was one reason she went out to try to procure work in the first place, but she ended up just working for the bicycle, therefore thankfully skipping over the need to somehow locate a used bike, get to where it is and pay for it.

Her attempts had been tentative at first: going back up to the main road, to where there are houses instead of apartment complexes, to knock on doors and inquire about doing yard work. The first two houses had mounted machine-made placards beside their doorbells, *No Trabajo*. From other doors women peered suspiciously at what must be an unusual sight on their front porches, a ragamuffin middle-age woman with sun-toughened skin and short-cropped thinning hair, accompanied by a feeble-looking vacant old man, asking for work as gardeners. Several just issued a blunt *no thanks*, one offered that her husband took care of picking up wetbacks down at the Home Builders hardware store.

Ronnie had almost skipped the payoff house entirely. The house it-self was barely visible—a long driveway dropped downhill from the busy main road. From the sidewalk, Ronnie could only see the garage, the door open, displaying a car-sized hole vacant in the center of a tangled layer of stowed junk. But the reason she'd almost passed the house by was not just the crammed garage but the strip of cultivated earth that ran downhill beside the driveway, supporting some healthy weeds and a thin row of dwarf citrus trees, a grape arbor, cherry tomatoes competing be-tween the trees and stunted squash vines spilling over onto the asphalt. Not only was this startlingly different from the other houses—whose yards were a variation of iceplant groundcover, some kind of boxwood hedges, perhaps a rose garden or rows of teatree bushes, and strategically placed trees. But even more unusual about this house was the woman moving slowly beside the pathetic strip of agriculture. She wore a full-length skirt covered almost completely by a pinafore apron, with a babushka covering her pinned-up hair. The woman had a basket on her arm, a few tomatoes nestled in it. But as Ronnie watched from the street, the woman occupied herself mostly with lifting the citrus leaves to inspect the undersides.

"Pest," her father had uttered. "Fly—"

"Yes, whitefly, she'll have to spray." Then Ronnie had spotted a bicycle tire poking out between two trashcans amid the garage's junk, remnants of every usable thing that would pass through a household. "I wonder if she knows what to do."

"Tomatoes are. Good now," her father noted, "Can't spray they. So take—like for wash—for wash plate."

"Detergent?"

"Need more and more—on clock. Hours."

Ronnie had nodded and proceeded down the driveway. She wasn't sure the woman understood everything she said, thought perhaps there was a language barrier but wasn't sure which language, except she knew it wasn't Spanish. Apparently the woman did understand, when Ronnie pointed to the bicycle, then lifted a leaf on the tangerine tree they stood closest to, wiped her thumb through the debris left by the whitefly, and said "I'll do this for the bicycle" in as many variations as she could conceive. After the woman had nodded, it took another several minutes to ask for rags, a bucket and dish detergent. The woman seemed unwilling to go get these common things from her kitchen. Finally in a dusty wooden cupboard in the back of the garage—the only place it seemed anything was actually put away—behind the snail bait and coffee cans of used corks, the woman pulled forth not only liquid detergent but Ronnie spotted powdered insecticide. Leaf by leaf, it took Ronnie and her father half a day to clean the dwarf trees of whitefly and sprinkle the power in the dirt around the trunks, knowing of course the whitefly would not be eradicated, but it would take awhile to reinfest to this level. They left leading the bicycle up the driveway. It was a women's single-gear bike, rusted fenders and spokes, a basket on the handlebars and two more baskets over the rear tire. "I ride," the woman had said, "before car. For store."

Actually feeling buoyed, Ronnie allowed herself to imagine how surprised Adrian likely would be at the upturn in her miserable circumstances since the first time they'd trudged the now familiar uphill sidewalk. Had Adrian perhaps put a sympathetic hand on her numb shoulder? Had he really ever expected to see the four jackets again?

She's so focused on modifying the bike, which has to be done before she can balance her father on the back and go anywhere, she's forgotten she's hungry. They ate a few winter tangerines yesterday while working on the Bohemian woman's strip of trees, but their bread is gone, the chicken spread long gone, the peanut butter gone, the bananas gone.

"Suppertime."

"I know, Dad."

"Plenty for dove. And duck. Put some of those—things from gun— to shoot. Put in gun."

"I don't think that's a good idea. Anyway, we don't have any shells."

"Own some. At store. We still need. A sh—shave.

"You need to shave?"

"No. Dig. Spoon? No. What is it?"

"A shovel."

"Yes, please."

Ronnie stands. She's been trying to fashion a saddle type thing, made from part of a painter's tarp, that would cover the two baskets on the back fender and furnish a place for her father to ride behind while she pedals. But there's still nothing to actually sit on except the thin, rusty fender itself. "I'll ride down to the grocery store and get something to eat, can you stay here alone?" Maybe she can also find some kind of produce box to use on the bike's fender.

"Danger. Down at there."

"I'll be careful. I have the bike now."

"Give the gun. Along you."

"I can't take a shotgun to a grocery store, Dad, what do you think, that I'll stick-up the deli for some chicken and home fries?"

Her father is waving a towel in the faint plume of smoke made by his noon fire, watching water simmer, just about to boil. His face impassive, fixed, his beard a week old, a white haze over his sunken cheeks. He might not say another word for a day and a half. What does he ponder or visualize or contemplate during the day-long stretches of silence? Does he imagine Chad at various stages of growing up, ten, twelve, sixteen? Or just images of Chad at five and younger? Are there gaps in his memory, or just trouble bringing images to words? Surprising enough that he remembers the incident at the grocery store, now almost a week ago. Even more surprisingly, he has more to say.

"I wear you."

"That doesn't make sense, dad."

"I wear you," he repeats, this time pointing to his ear. "Cry."

"What're you talking about?"

"You never. Cry. About our mother. When he dr— In water, the sea."

"Because *she*—*my* mother—drowned on purpose."

"Never talk. That."

"Okay I won't, but you know it."

"His—her. Heart was. Sick."

"So was everyone's."

"How much mile beside . . . we, this place, and sea?"

"How far to the coast? I don't know. Not far."

Water hisses in the fire. Ronnie's father uses a green branch to scrape the burning sticks away from the cans of water, then drops a few handfuls of dirt on the scant flames.

"I'll need some of that now, to wash my hair," Ronnie says. "Then, while I'm gone, please please please promise to stay right here, in fact stay under the bush where we sleep. If anyone comes around, don't make any noise. Just take a nap, okay?" She takes his glasses from his face, cleans them, then hands them back to him and watches, silently counting to herself, the entire fifteen seconds it takes for him to get the glasses back on.

The beach—like all family outings—it seems we were the only people in sight. Which couldn't've been true.

There were no spontaneous trips to the beach. Our father planned trips by referring to a tide schedule. We only went on days when the tide would be ebbed in the morning and then flowing in the afternoon and evening. Fish feed during a flowing tide.

Morning at the beach was always overcast and chilly. We kept our sweatshirts over our swimsuits and kept our sneakers on our bare feet—at least until after we'd unloaded and carried the gear precariously down over huge pieces of scrap concrete with dangerous rusty rebar jutting from them, piled just off the road to protect the old state highway from high water. We had our choice of sand space and fire rings, we spread our towels and planted one old beach umbrella—its most useful function was for spotting our campsite from where we played in the skirt of perpetually wet sand and lips of gentle foam-edged water which were the last exhausted gasp of formerly powerful waves. We set about making things in the sand, like bathtubs, drip castles, moats and volcanoes. Our mother eventually taught us to overcome our fear of the cold, turbulent Pacific surf.

Meanwhile our father began gathering bait. He never used store-bought bait. He used what the fish might naturally be eating—sand crabs, the ones who'd recently molted so their shells were soft. The wet sand at water's edge was etched with the inverted V's of thousands of sand crab tentacles. Shaped like a beetle, sand crabs burrow backwards into wet sand at the waterline and leave their two antenna on the surface of the sand, gathering microscopic pieces of food as the waves lick their feathery tentacles. Our father had a special sieve he'd made from carpenter's cloth, shaped like a mini bulldozer with the shovel part curved inward instead of outward. Standing up to his ankles in the surf, he pulled the crab net against the movement of the waves, digging it down about two inches, first when the wave came in, and then again as the water drew back. Under the water, he twisted his heels into the sand to keep his balance against the force of the wave that filled the net with swirling, muddy sand-water. Then he stood with his back to the ocean, waves crashing against his calves, held the net up against his waist and picked through the crabs, discarding all but those with soft shells. A crab might only have a soft shell for a day or two after molting. On any given day the crabs he discarded might've been soft the day before or would be soft tomorrow.

We also dug for crabs, with our hands. There weren't many seashells to collect, no rock crabs or tide pools, but there were always thousands of sand crabs. We searched for the huge ones, then kept them as pets in the moats around our castles, digging them up and watching them burrow down out of sight over and over. We found the big females—carefully lifted the protective flap under their bellies to see the glop of bright orange eggs. We never touched the eggs themselves. All were granted freedom when we left.

After a picnic lunch of cucumber-and-cheese or peanut butter sandwiches, peaches or nectarines, sandy cookies, and lemonade, when the tide turned in the afternoon, our father, and sometimes our mother too, would begin to fish in the surf.

Our father would wade into the surf up to his waist, twist so his shoulders were facing the sand, likewise cock the long pole that direction, then he used legs, body, arms and the leverage of the pole to cast the weight and the two baited hooks as far out into the surf as possible. With the reel still open, he backed up, running, into shallower water, closed the reel, kept the line taught, and waited. When he felt a hit, he jerked the tip of the pole back to set the *hook, then began reeling in. Unlike lake or river fishing, there's no feel of a fish fighting, so he didn't know if he'd felt a bite or if the hook hit seaweed. Probably less than half the times our father set the hook and reeled in, there was a fish on one of the hooks. Rarely he caught a small sand shark and released it. Most of the time the catch was perch, and on special occasions when the corbina were running, he would get those too.*

When we got tired of digging holes or covering ourselves with sand, we would stand beside our father, waiting for him jerk the rod and set the hook, anticipating what he might reel in. He let us hold the pole ourselves, helping us reel in when we hooked a choice hunk of kelp.

Through the afternoon, twilight and evening, our father continued fishing as long as the fishing was good—sometimes as long as the tide continued to come in. We repeatedly moved our towels and beach bags, books and shoes farther and farther east, toward that scrap-concrete breakwater. Our mother would hold a beach towel around us while we squirmed out of damp, sandy swimsuits and put old sweatsuits on over our bare salty skin. As the sun went down and the coastal layer moved back in, we made a fire, roasted marshmallows, sang songs our mother taught us, and even cooked some of the fish, wrapped in foil and placed on the embers. Over the thunder of the surf, we couldn't hear so much as a giggle from other parties, no radios thumping, no shouts or dogs barking. The roar of water was rhythmic and constant. Gulls continued to call in twilight. Later the snap of the fire, the pop of dried kelp floats bursting open after we threw into the embers, our mother's voice singing or reading from TREASURE ISLAND *or* GULLIVER'S TRAVELS*—these were the only nearby sounds, under the surging of waves.*

Sometimes our father would fish until an especially high tide would start swamping up over the dry sand right to the edge of the fire rings. We would scramble to rescue our belongings and our mother would call, "Honey, yoo hoo!"

Coasting down La Costa Avenue beside the traffic, the wind chills her head while it dries her hair. The four jackets are stuffed into the bike's fender-baskets and the empty water jug secured with one of the sleeves through its handle. No danger of anything being stolen while she's in the store; with no money, she's only planning to scrounge around the back of the store, and manages to pack up a dozen slightly bruised apples, a limp head of lettuce, a few slightly shriveled potatoes, and four dented cans of something with the paper labels torn off. She hides everything under the jackets in the baskets, moving the water jug to the front basket.

She's quickly flushed and warm pedaling back up La Costa, thankful she decided while getting dressed that it likely wouldn't be necessary this time to armor herself with the several sweatshirts and layers of pants. She's worn the bicycle pants under jeans every day since making camp, but today just the khakis, wrinkled but cleaner because they'd originally been the second layer below the jeans.

The turn-off the four men had taken is a steep uphill grade. She walks the bike. Then that first road t-bones at the elementary school Adrian had described as the first landmark. Ronnie conceals the bike in a row of ten-speeds and mountain bikes locked to an iron frame, then walks silently, even keeping her slightly damp boot from squeaking, onto the blacktop play area to a drinking fountain and fills the water jug. Pedaling away with the sloshing water under her chin, she realizes it's her first time on a school campus.

The streets are completely developed and landscaped, house after house, yard after yard; and not a new development, the trees are mature, the hedges high and thick, some of the houses old enough to need paint and repair, other sporting a variety of additions and improvements. In other words, these streets, all draining north and northwest down toward La Costa Avenue, are not going to lead to an encampment any time soon. But one street turns to the south and quickly ends in a cul-de-sac overlooking a canyon, a *no-trespassing* sign planted just off a well-trod trail descending into the canyon brush. From the bank of the cul-de-sac, the hazy view over the canyon reveals the big Home Builders store down below on El Camino Real, and a vast gathering of stores across the street, skeletons of a housing development near the shopping center, and, due west, the tidal lagoon is not only visible but sends its marshy scent drifting on puffs of air currents.

At first she worries that his camp, if it ever was here, has been moved. But she can smell a faint trace of smoke and hears a dim sound of tinking and rustling. Then she sees through the slightly dusty glare, green canvas tarps draped over the domed tops of sumac bushes.

She walks the bike into the canyon because the dirt trail has a deep furrow down the middle. Rain runoff must enter the camp via the same path. In fact, when she arrives at the place where five or six laurel sumacs in a clump have all been draped with canvas tarps, someone has dug the runoff rut deeper, sent it straight through the camp and out the other side, and lined the edges with sandbags. A still-fragrant fire ring has been banked and hidden under branches cut from the sumacs, the waxy leaves still clinging, only slightly faded and shriveled compared to the leaves on living branches. But besides the faint scent of warm ashes, the camp is tinged with other odors, most especially a greasy smell of something having been cooked, and the slightest trace, on and off as the breeze puffs, of not just human waste but an outhouse that tries to kill the smell with chemicals and only creates a new type of stench.

The tinking sound she'd heard turns out to be a dog licking a fry pan—its tags clang against a metal rim—but the dog bolts as Ronnie steps into the camp, tail tucked and short hair raised in a ridge on its shoulder blade. It runs down a trail further into the canyon, then circles back around and ends up on the edge of the cul-de-sac above the camp where it turns and barks a few times before heading up the sidewalk through the streets with driveways, lawns and houses.

She tips the bike, squats beside it, and waits. It's probably between two and three o'clock. She left her watch with her father. It's all she has that anyone could want to steal, and not worth much, not a family heirloom or gift from her mother, just a drugstore Timex. Still, she took that precaution but didn't go so far as to bring the shotgun. Leaving both with her father who, after all, would be easier to steal from than she is. She grimaces slightly, knocking knuckles against her chin, and sighs. How long should she leave her father alone? When might these men return to their camp after work? The other day, a week ago, it had been before dusk. But wasn't that a Saturday? The day she and her father left the hospital. Only a week ago.

In alternating gentle gusts, the breeze carries the faint outhouse odor then the brackish lagoon, which must be much farther away, therefore its smell is actually stronger. On the map, some of the lagoons in the North County stretch a mile inland. This one, whose name she doesn't recall if she ever knew, reaches almost to El Camino Real, which runs parallel to the coast—the King's Highway, she remembers from her mother's schooling, the route Father Serra took on his way to establish the missions, each a day's trip apart. Measuring a day's trip by means of a passionate evangelist who probably had mules, not a day's trip according to a stroke-stricken old man. If she and her father had walked about a mile east on La Costa— from the grocery store and bank on the corner of El Camino—the answer to her father's question could either be that they're one mile from the ocean, if you count the lagoon as reaching the coast, or two miles, maybe two-and-a-half, if you only count waves hitting sand as the ocean. The creek she and her father are camped beside almost certainly must trickle into the lagoon, after doing its picturesque meander through the golf course, as Adrian described. Logically the golf course, separated from the lagoon by El Camino Real, must be planted in the middle of this area's most fertile basin, and the lagoon, on a low tide, one of the richest sources of food.

Clamming was not a summer beach trip—fresh shellfish can only be eaten in winter months. Besides that, the extreme low tides of winter are advantageous for harvesting clams from muddy sand that's usually under water. No licenses required, but there were mandated limits for quantity and size. Our father had a clam-sizer, a flat steel rectangle measuring device, like a broad ruler, with a series of holes ranging in sizes—for various size requirements designated by different jurisdictions. When a clam's size was in doubt, our father used the sizer—if the clam fit through the designated hole, it was too small and was left in the clam bed. Each time we went, we could harvest four limits. Sometimes Chad had to drop every clam he'd collected through the sizer and back into the mud. He made an explosion sound with his mouth every time a little clam plunked or plopped back into the muck. Our mother collected a double limit and let him pick half of hers as his, and let him carry them in his own bag. Once she let us mark our own clams with paint on the outside of their shells, red for mine and blue for us, so we would know when we ate our clams.

Our father filled jugs with sea water, then at home the clams were leached: in an aluminum tub he put them in the clean sea water with cornmeal, changing the water several times. The clams feed by filtering water, so as they fed on clean cornmeal and water, they extracted any sand they'd gathered from previous meals in muddy water. Most of the time, we ate clams raw on the half shell, sometimes in clam chowder or cioppino.

All tidal lands, up to the high tide mark, are public. But most of the clam beds are dead now. Right around the time of the drowning, it could've been a year or two before, the Los Angeles newspaper ran an article broadcasting the location of rich clam fields between Orange and San Diego Counties, encouraging people to come and get them. People did come. Whether or not they respected limits or size restrictions, the most harmful aspect of the deluge of clammers was that they didn't know how to take care of the clam beds after digging. They left their holes open, exposing the next generations of baby or immature clams to be consumed by sea gulls.

"Hello, look who's here."

Ronnie's head swims, blinded momentarily in colors and light, as she jumps to her feet too quickly. Adrian is standing in front of her, a fatigue jacket slung over one shoulder, water jug in his other hand.

"I . . . brought back your jackets and your other water bottle . . . filled."

"Keep it. I already had others. I pick up a gallon or two every day."

The three Mexican men are also in camp, seeming to move about cautiously as though not knowing what to do while she's there. One picks up the fry pan.

"A dog licked that," she blurts.

"Figures," Adrian says, then says something in Spanish to the man with the fry pan. "Neighborhood mutts have discovered us, like coyotes finding something dead. We can't keep food here anymore, just get a day's supply on the way home from work." The breeze blows a few light strands that have escaped his ponytail. She touches her own hair.

"I set up a camp," Ronnie starts, then pauses. "Can I . . . can I see how you do certain things?"

"Most things are pretty obvious." He kicks a sandbag beside his boots. "Collected these from alongside El Camino. Otherwise it rains and mud gushes into everything, our beds, our things, everything. These wouldn't be visible from a helicopter, everything else has to be camouflaged."

"Yes, I see the tarps over the bushes. Won't that kill them?"

"By the time these sumacs die we'll be long gone from here. I guess that's another way of saying we'll be gone before they die, but that's not why we'll be gone."

"Because you're hiding from something? Like those kids?"

"No. Work moves, we move. And those kids . . . well they're something to be cautious about, but it's not the biggest reason we hide the camp. We don't want another 1994. That's also why there's only four of us here." He begins to move further into to camp, slightly gesturing with the hand holding the water jug that she's welcome to follow him. One of the Mexicans is using a collapsible army shovel to scrape the banked sand and gravel from the fire pit. Another is still holding the fry pan, looking into it, then looking at Ronnie, as though still in slow motion because of her presence.

"Do they need me to leave so they can go to the bathroom or something?"

"We took care of that at the gas station on the corner."

"Don't you have a . . . place here too?"

"You smelled it, didn't you. Damn. I took some chemicals from the portapots in the field at work, but it doesn't kill the smell, just . . ."

"Replaces it."

He flashes her a smile then hangs his fatigue jacket on a sumac branch. "Here we are, home-sweet-home."

He's standing as though holding a door for her, so Ronnie crouches to look into the bush. The tarp draped over the outside doesn't allow much light into the bush, so it's much darker than her sleeping area is in the daytime. As her eyes adjust, she sees that the bush's underside is much more hollowed out than a natural sumac. It's because he has sawed or broken off any low branch that would've forced him to move around lower than hands-and-knees. In some of the space, he could maybe walk stooped over with knees half cocked. Two crushed cushions from an old armchair or sofa are placed end to end on the ground, a rolled sleeping bag on top of them. Beside the end of one cushion, a flat wooden vegetable crate is upside-down, making a bedside table which holds a book and a type of camping lantern that stands upright like a lamp. It's hooked to a car battery hidden under the vegetable crate.

"Comfy, huh?" he says, still standing behind her.

She backs out and stands again. "I haven't had time to find stuff like that."

"You'd be surprised, but don't get carried away—the longer you stay in one place, the more usable stuff you find, so the more you'll eventually lose." His face and neck have been slowly seared in the sun, the creases around his eyes are fans of lighter skin, and she can see inside his shirt collar the line separating sun-toughened leather from the rest. She could walk with him down El Camino Real and appear as though she's lived like him this way for years instead of days.

The Mexican men have begun to speak among themselves, the fire is going, one comes to hand Adrian a beer. "Want one?" Adrian asks Ronnie.

"No, thanks."

"Dinner?"

"I . . . My father . . ."

"Where is he?"

"Waiting. I left him. I have to get back to him with the food."

"At least take him some frijoles and tortillas."

"I have nothing to carry anything in."

"We'll just put it back in the can, save us the trouble of packing it to a dumpster." He calls in Spanish to the man who's holding the fry pan over the flame, stirring something.

"You bring all your trash out somewhere?"

"We do. Sort of my rule, you know, all those years studying the ecosystem. But also, every piece of litter is evidence. A can or bottle could shine in the sun, something they might look for from a chopper."

"Why're you more worried about helicopters than those boys?"

He begins to walk over to the fire pit, and Ronnie accompanies him, slightly following rather than being escorted. The fry pan holds a bubbling quantity of brown substance, smelling toasty and oily. Her stomach burns. One of the Mexicans is eating an orange, flinging the peels over one shoulder. They still talk quietly among themselves, but also, sometimes, seem to be listening to Adrian as he describes the huge twenty-year-old migrant camp, south of here near a creek in Mojado Valley, that was actually more like a little town with almost 400 dirt-floored shanties made of cast-off lumber, housing nearly two thousand people, including wives and kids; it had dirt roads big enough for cars, people kept chickens and goats and even pigs, there was a makeshift store and restaurant, the whole place had a name—El Rancho de Los Diablos—and the sum total was completely leveled by bulldozers in 1994.

Most residents—especially women and kids and the men who supported them, if they were legal—were relocated into alternate public housing. Some were deported. Some went back to Mexico voluntarily because they couldn't afford the rent, even shared quarters, in public housing. The leftovers, the unaccounted-for, the less-crucial cases for social workers are always single men, so as the big reshuffling took place, single men dispersed and disappeared into surrounding canyons, and now stay in much smaller camps, much less visible camps, much more mobile camps.

"There're always rumors it'll happen again," Adrian says, sort of nodding toward or with his companions, "even with camps as inconsequential as this one. I could argue to a city council or board of county supervisors that we don't cause any more dirt or damage than the native Indians who lived here, but it wouldn't get very far. If enough of an organized complaint gets aroused, they'll come looking for us."

Adrian goes to the fire, takes the fry pan from the man who's cooking, scrapes what looks like half the contents into the emptied frijole can, then stuffs some folded tortillas into the mouth of the can. The Mexican says something, looking into what's left of the frijoles, and Adrian answers, gesturing toward Ronnie, and the way the Mexicans look away make her think he's said something about the boys assaulting her.

As if confirming this suspicion, Adrian says, as he hands the hot can of frijoles to her, "I know it'll seem different from your perspective, but our problems with those boys are bigger than just getting robbed or hurt. People—the neighborhood residents—don't like their precious kids getting into trouble, and it's a hell of a lot easier to blame their shenanigans on us being here than to admit their cherished babies are pathologic savages. So if rumors about the kids' activities get too loud, that's when they'll send in the helicopters."

Ronnie, turning away, pauses, then says, "There's no way *I* could make a rumor louder."

"I wasn't accusing you—"

"I'm just telling you. My father and I . . . we'll be finished and out of this area in . . . I hope another week, maybe two, god I hope it's not three . . ."

"Finished?"

"It's just . . . don't ask. Some weird family business." She stands the bicycle up and tucks the can of frijoles upright in one of the baskets.

"Well, weird families are nothing new. But if you need anything, say the word."

"Here are your jackets. I'm sorry I . . . couldn't wash them."

"There's a laundromat down by the grocery store." He takes the bundle of jackets, then extracts one. "Hey, keep mine, I have another."

Taking the jacket back, she flinches, probably visibly, when her fingers accidentally touch his wrist. He's so much taller, she can see a scar under his chin. Somehow he shaves often enough, so do his friends, although two of them have mustaches. Considering asking if he has a spare razor, instead she says. "What did you use to saw branches out of the bush?"

"Here, I'll loan it to you."

The tool turns out to be one of the blades on his Swiss Army knife. She stands holding it after he's put it into her palm. "This is valuable. I'll return it right away."

"That's okay. Whenever you can, don't rush."

"Well, I may coming this way this week. We're . . ." Her fingers slowly curl around the army knife, she slips it into a front pocket. "Maybe you can tell me . . . we're looking for a place where we used to hunt, in the sixties there was a lagoon, but not as big as the one right over here . . . and on the same land, a creek dammed up for water holes, and a rancher had cattle there."

He's nodding, his clear eyes looking lighter, brighter in his buckskin face. The loose strands of hair blow across his face and he brushes them back. "I'd guess it was Kneenan's land. He and his sons owned land all over this area, even some of what's now the business district on El Camino."

"You mean, the place I'm looking for might be underneath a lot of stores and streets?"

He smiles, his eyes darken and deepen. "I doubt it, if you say there was a lagoon. Sounds like lowland. There's another lagoon three miles south and another about ten or fifteen miles north."

"Yeah I knew there were several up this way."

"But just ride south down El Camino, about a mile, and look at the mini malls, look at the signs at the entrances."

"Why?"

"You'll see." He smiles again and steps back from the path to make room for her bike, raises a hand, then turns to join his friends for dinner.

It's gotten late. But as soon as she reaches the top of the dirt path and is back on asphalt, she can fly through the streets back to La Costa Avenue, then she's only a little way from the downhill turn toward the creek in the gully.

The camp is very quiet, even more invisible than Adrian's, naturally, because there's no tarp over the bush. The creek tinkles quietly entering the placid pool. She can smell mud and wet grasses and the husky scent of the laurel sumac. But there's no sound of her father's heavy breathing coming from under the bush. His improved, enlarged fire ring is cold.

"Dad?" Her heartbeat is in her throat. "Dad!"

"Yeah!" he answers, bushes rustle, he approaches on the path that runs along the creek into the gorge, boots muddy, one leg—the weak one—wet almost to the knee. His good hand is holding a long stick, a branch from a sycamore with all the smaller twigs cleaned off it. Clutched in his weak fist is another thin branch, this one shorter with a forked stock and a few leaves still attached. Threaded by the gills onto the forked stick are two little fishes.

"Dad . . . how did you catch these?"

"Watched to see—some gackle."

"Tackle? Where?"

"Hooks and line. Caught at trees. Branches."

The two bluegill are no more than seven inches. Her father isn't smiling, but she doesn't know if he would be if he could.

Family vacation was the same event every year, two weeks right before hunting season started in September, before we were born and for seven years in a row afterwards. Our parents packed up the station wagon and a handmade trailer and drove eight hours to a high desert town in the eastern Sierra. In the mountains above town, there were rustic campsites and a creek rushing down from the glacier. The state of California stocks the Sierra creeks with rainbow trout, while brown trout—originally from Europe—now live as though indigenous in streams and lakes all over the Sierra. Here our father taught us fresh water river fishing.

Although our mother packed and brought boxes of canned and dried provisions, most of our dinners and half our breakfasts at camp were fried trout. So a cast iron skillet was necessary equipment, as were metal washtubs for giving baths to toddlers who daily masked faces with dirt and woodsmoke; buckets and jugs so our father could hike up the mountain and bring back fresh spring water; several sizes of saws and two axes so our father could keep firewood supplied; fishing poles and enough tackle for us to lose plenty of hooks; enough socks, underwear, sweatshirts, jeans, flannel shirts, tennis shoes and boots so we could fall into the river several times daily; an old canvas wall tent with wooden poles from army surplus; a sheet of stainless steel for pancakes; sleeping bags and Coleman lanterns and flashlights; a first aid kit, and two or three worn-out decks of playing cards.

Vacation was not a time of relaxation. Packing the trailer took them all night before we left in the small hours of the morning. Then it was not all fishing and hiking, but pitching heavy tents and digging rain trenches, gutting fish, cooking and cleaning up, chopping logs he dragged back to camp, packing water down from the mountain springs—three gallons on his back and one in each arm. And he worked with the river—carried big rocks into the cold, quick water, some nearly boulders, laid them across, side by side, just to slow or break a current in certain areas, to make trout pools, or places for fishermen to stand or cross to an opposite bank. He fished early mornings, then again at dusk, working both sides of the river. After he'd limited-out, he returned with his catch, gutted and cleaned them, then took us back out for our turns, giving our mother a chance to fish in a rare hour of solitude. He would hook a fish then thrust the pole into our hands to land it. Often a wordless struggle, except a sharp exhale or grunt in his chest when we artlessly flung the fish out of the water backwards over our heads, tangling fish, line and pole in heavy brush.

We were taught not to dump the fish guts into the water, not to throw empty bait cups, or anything else, into the river. We picked up other people's junk when we found it on the riverbank or could reach it in the water. Eventually we completely stocked our own tackle box with the hooks, weights, leaders, lures, bobbers, flies, and tools left behind by more reckless fishermen.

A few times each camping trip, our father made pancakes on the sheet of shiny metal over a fire pit built with rocks, like the walls at home, so everything was exactly level. He poured big perfectly round pancakes, nothing fancy. Standing in the firelight in a gray sweatsuit, the bowl of batter in one hand, *spatula in the other, the blood of a fish still on his arm from the morning's catch, he made pancakes without smiling. On a big rock between two trees, we wore out the knees of our jeans, got sap in our hair. It smelled thick and piney, turned black and tacky, and later he would have to use gasoline to scrub it off. He walked back and forth, past the rock, gathering dry grease-wood for kindling, a red bandanna around his forehead. We played with kids from other campsites and glanced up at him as he passed, but never shouted, "Hey Dad!" nor waved, and one little girl said, "I'm afraid of that Indian." Later we pushed her off the rock and our father sent us to our tent.*

In the daytime, the tent was a hot musty canvass-smelling place with musty bedrolls providing no cushion between us and the hard ground, and gigantic ants would creep across bare shins. Our angry boots kicked dust from the old sleeping bags. But at night, before sleep, the sleeping bags were warm cottony nests, the tent flickered with our flashlights, the canvas walls secure against the black night—out there where the roar of the river seemed louder when we couldn't see the water. With her own flashlight on the page of a book, our mother read to us—THE WATER BABIES, THE YEARLING, JUST SO STORIES. By the time we were five and seven we could read, although official home-schooling hadn't yet begun. So sometimes our mother lay on Chad's bedroll, her face in the dark but her glasses glinting, and he kneeled between us, book on his knees, flashlight in one hand, and he read aloud from his favorite, THE STORY OF A FIERCE, BAD RABBIT. When a hunter shoots the bad rabbit, all that's left on the bench where he'd been sitting is his fluffy tail.

His sticky fingers tore a corner from a page. He'd forgotten to wash after eating roasted marshmallows from the ends of green willow boughs. She had already dipped a cloth into one of the buckets of water always simmering on the back of the fire, had scrubbed sugar and cinder from our mouths and hands, but then before our last trip to the outhouse, he'd been pinching the end of the willow stick to get more charred marshmallow. When we came back, zigging our flashlight beams like fireflies on the trail—familiar by day, strange as a moonscape at night—she was pouring water from the cold bucket over the embers, the plume of smoke seemed light in the night, and the hiss like a long sigh.

"Hear the fire's breath?" she said.

"Fires don't breathe!"

"Yes it does, just like you, fire needs air, and it breathes out the same as you." She handed us our toothbrushes already loaded with paste, and she held a tin cup with cold water to dip them into. "Fire eats like you do too—it eats wood. And when you go to the outhouse, your body gets rid of what it didn't

need, just like the fire leaves behind the ashes. It can grow from a little fire to a big one, and it can make baby fires. All the same as a living thing. So is fire alive?"

We stared at the fire pit, a dark puddle of smoking slush. Chad seemed to have forgotten that he was holding his toothbrush, upside-down now, the paste fell to his boot. "It's dead NOW," he said. Then he put his lit flashlight under his chin to make a monster face. "Daddy brings it back to life in the morning."

"That's right," she said, holding his wrist and aiming his toothbrush into the tin cup. "It's just gone to sleep, just like you're going to do."

Chapter Five

With bugs and worms, he's been catching four or five bluegill every evening, and they cook on banked embers, folded inside discarded foil burger wrappers that Ronnie has smoothed flat, rinsed and dried. And in three days they still haven't gone to find the hunting site.

She's been sawing branches underneath their sumac. Now they can sit upright inside. A few times, especially on Saturday or during the evening, she squats behind her father with her arms around him, close together in the bush, keeping quiet and watching out as a neighborhood resident comes into the gully to walk a dog, or kids—not the bad ones—arrive with fishing poles but end up just floating trash in the creek, sending messages downstream in paper cups, or looking for frogs. One boy kicks at the rocks in the fire pit, breaking most of it apart. Her father spends several hours rebuilding it, half-burying some of the rocks so the foundation is sturdier, then finding several new flat-sided rocks in the creek so he can make a higher level shelf at the back of the fire pit against the boulder—where a fry pan could cook something, if they had a fry pan.

Saturday night it rains. They bring as many as possible of their belongings with them under the painters' tarps inside the sumac bush, but not much is spared from the damp. She wraps the shotgun in her father's sweatpants. The rain is steady, sometimes a deluge, then dying back to drizzle before picking up again. The creek rises, moves quicker, and in the morning a mound of white foam is growing where the water slides over the asphalt access road and splashes into the pool on the other side.

"Don't go fishing today, Dad. The mud's slippery, and this water could be bad."

He doesn't answer. He's dressed, but even the driest clothes are slightly clammy. He's sitting on a rock with arms crossed over his chest, hands gripping shirt material on opposite arms, chin tucked. The last two mornings he'd immediately begun fumbling with his fishing line even before eating the half apple she'd placed on the baby highchair table. But his fishing line, so laboriously wound around a stick—weak hand gripping the stick and good hand wrapping the string, in excruci-ating slow motion, while Ronnie stared as though transfixed by the rhythm—remains where he'd put it yesterday, cradled in a low sumac branch along with the Starbucks cup he'd found for keeping worms, which the rain has tipped sideways. She can see the cup's mud-streaked inside is now empty of his painstakingly gathered bait.

"What's the matter, Dad?"

He's either trying to speak or just grunting an answer. Or maybe he remains silent and what she thinks she hears is a car's gear shift and whine of acceleration way up on La Costa Avenue.

"Are you cold?"

This time he answers, opening his mouth first, closing it, open again, tongue appearing on his lower lip, then slowly, "Maybe."

"You don't know?"

"Wait awhile."

"For what?"

"Will get— Be okay."

She looks at the bicycle, still outlined in water, clear droplets hanging from handlebars and horizontal spokes. A brief crack of sun through the clouds, now moving swiftly east, lights up the beads hanging everywhere, from blades of grass to the rusty baby highchair, from sagging tufts of foxtails to the empty food cans turned upside-down in a row beside the fire pit.

"You always do this when you're sick." She moves to him, boots squishing in mud. "You've got to tell me." One hand on his forehead, then both hands on his cheeks. He's warm. "Dad, I've got to fix a dry place for you to lie down and sleep." She presses her hands to his thighs to feel how damp his trousers are, then down to his ankles and finds his socks are more than just damp. "Did you put yesterday's socks on again? We'll have to keep a fire going for awhile to dry out these clothes, do we have enough wood or is it wet too? Stay here for a sec." Moving toward his woodpile, each footstep makes a kissing sound, her boots feel twice as heavy with an inch of mud clinging to the soles. "I guess we're still not going anywhere for awhile."

She'd already been aware, had lain awake reminding herself that as soon as they finish their business, the next undertaking will be to start a new life, and—despite the temporary financial impediment—they are slowly getting closer. She knows she could do it all in a day, two days, it would be done. Then she'll have to make plans, a plan that carries further ahead than a week or two. But for the first time she's met someone else. Not that she hadn't ever met people or talked to them—store clerks, relatives of patients at the hospital, the meter reader and refuse collectors, they'd needed a plumber once or twice. But this was different, he was almost a peer, a colleague, possibly a friend, friends who lend helping hands back and forth, whenever needed, plus conversation, a continuing discourse about . . . well, *any*thing. But could he, or would any of that still be available after she helps her father finish his promise? After she finds the spot where the ashes are, or *were*—because with rain like this, even if only occasionally, any human ashes are long since washed away— and ceremoniously, if not literally, carries her mother's and brother's essences back to the farmstead. Then, whether or not her father's memory is exorcised enough, whether or not he provides her a coherent narrative, whether or not he gives any intimation that she's now paid enough—or even if she somehow discovers that her lifelong gesture of atonement had been to no purpose—*after* completing the ritual, when she turns to the business of starting over, Adrian will remain here, in his world. Unlikely their paths would ever cross again. So she has no plans to make the excursion to the hunting ground this day, nor the next, no intention of going anywhere for awhile. But why say it as she had, with impatience, to her father whose illness now prevents progress—why put the delay on him?

"It's okay, Dad, don't worry about it, let's just get you feeling better."

A fire on Sunday is not a good idea, but can't be avoided. She finds the driest twigs under the wood pile, surrounds the little flame with bigger pieces of wood so they'll dry out before being added to the fire. She sits him on a flattened piece of cardboard beside the fire pit and hangs the damp clothes over the baby highchair, the bicycle, and the handcart, all pulled close around the still feeble fire. The tarps are stinking even more of paint solvents because they're wet, so for the first time, she drapes them over the outside of their sumac bush, hoping for some muted sun to make them less heavy and funky. The tan, paint-mottled tarps are highly visible, like ship's sails, and can't stay that way for too long. Inside the bush, she removes her sweatshirt which has stayed fairly dry because she'd worn Adrian's jacket all night. She replaces Adrian's jacket over her bra and bare skin before emerging again from the sumac and putting her sweatshirt onto her father, in the same manner she used to dress some of the other residents at the hospital, but never her father. First each sleeve is threaded onto an arm, then the garment's body bunched in two hands all the way to the neck hole so the whole garment at once can be maneuvered over the patient's head and unrolled down to cover the patient's torso.

The sweatshirt is not too tight on him, although she wonders if she should've removed his own damp shirt first. Her arms still draped over his shoulders as she pauses to think, holding him for a moment to see if he's shivering, a rock the size of a golf ball rolls into the camp, stopping when it hits a bicycle tire. Ronnie whirls, grasping the zippered front of the jacket over her heart.

"I didn't want to scare you," Adrian says, emerging from the muddy trail beside the creek. He stops to scrape his boots on a rock. "It's a signal we use, rolling a rock into camp, to keep each other from being startled, to let anyone in camp know that if they hear someone approaching, not to be alarmed and react . . . you know, to not do something like run or hide or . . . shoot someone."

"You thought I would shoot you?"

"Just being careful," he grins.

"Did you come for your jacket? I . . ." Her hand slips from where it was clutching the zipper. "I can give it to you in a minute, I was just . . . I mean I'll have to change."

"No, no that's okay, not why I'm here. Keep it as long as you need it. I see you got a little wet last night. Everything okay?"

"I guess so. It's hard to keep going down there for food because I . . ." She looks at her father. "He's not feeling well this morning."

"What's the problem?"

"Feverish. Lethargic."

As Adrian comes around the fire where he can see Ronnie's father from the front, her father raises his head, makes a move as though to stand, but then stays on the ground, and says, "What's this person?"

"A friend, Dad, don't you remember him?"

"Adrian DeLeon," Adrian extends his hand, but instead of a handshake he squeezes her father's shoulder. Ronnie's father hadn't reached for a handshake anyway. "We'll get you feeling better, Mr. . . I'm sorry, what's his name?"

"Enzo Tattori."

"Excuse me again, but . . . ," straightening and looking at her over her father's head, "do I even know *your* name?"

"I don't know. Ronnie. Veronica." She finds her hand once again clutching the jacket, up near her throat. "I guess introducing myself isn't one of my best skills. And here I am calling you a friend. Sorry if I was being . . ."

"Well, we met under less than ideal circumstances."

"She's not Chad," her father says.

"No, Dad, *his* name is Adrian."

"She could get. Like Chad. A man."

"No, Dad, Chad was . . . wouldn't be as tall—" Her face burns. "But— How would we know what he would look like, how tall, how—"

Adrian laughs, looks up as a pair of quacking, fast-flying mallards dart past overhead, angling for a landing several hundred yards down-stream, probably on the golf course. "Just a second, I'll be right back." Stepping carefully so his boots don't splat mud, he leaves the campsite, but isn't going the way he came—he heads further up the creek, then turns away from the creek up the side of the canyon, around another clump of sumacs and out of sight.

He's right, he isn't gone for more than five minutes, but Ronnie has time to duck into the bush. She puts Adrian's Swiss Army knife in her pocket then replaces Adrian's jacket with her other sweatshirt, which is just at the turning-point from damp to dry so it's chilly, not quite a com-fort against her skin. The warm, soft flannel inside Adrian's jacket now smells of her body instead of his.

As she squats behind her father to drape the jacket on his shoulders, her father immediately leans back against her, practically falling asleep as soon as his body finds hers for support.

"Here, let's make him some tea with this." Adrian is returning, hold-ing sprigs of gray-green.

"Sage?" She straightens and steadies her father, then stands.

"Hey, that's good. Most people just call it brush or weeds."

"But it's for seasoning." Still, dutifully, she's holding out a can to catch the leaves as he crumbles them off the twigs. Between thumb and forefinger, he mangles the foliage—she doesn't have to ask why—to help release more of the pith as the water boils.

"We've gotten kind of narrow-minded about how to use things like this. No offense or anything." He takes the water jug she's holding out for him, pours the can half full. "I know herbal healing's gotten a bad reputation from being touted by new-age crystal worshipers," he says while nestling the can into the fire. Standing again, he looks around, chooses one of the pieces of board fence her father has gathered, props it against a rock and stomps to crack the wood. Soon the fire is actually producing some heat.

"I was afraid of making too much smoke and the flame being too visible on a weekend when these people around here are home," she says.

"Can't be helped right now, but if you can splurge at all, get yourself some charcoal, you know for bar-be-cues. And he needs a blanket."

"We've been using the tarps." She feels like she's been anchored, just watching, inefficient and incompetent. "Maybe they're dry now."

"Wait, get him to drink the tea, can I borrow your bicycle?"

"Help yourself, but—"

"I'll be right back. Get him to drink the tea." His grin once again folds the pale streaks around his eyes inside coppery-leather creases. His jeans do the opposite, hiding the darker blue denim inside faded creases. Especially where his legs and body meet.

When the tea is simmering, the can is too hot to hold, so she wraps it in one of the hospital towels, puts it in her father's hand, then once again crouches behind him, her hand over his on the can, brings it toward his mouth but lets him put the can to his lips and sip by himself. She only reminds him to continue raising the can. The tea smells, obviously, sagey, the way the undeveloped hillside around their farmstead would smell as a hot day emerged from a dewy morning.

Down where the pepper tree grew was the last part of the farmstead to be developed. At the lowest part of our acreage, just above the property line— marked intermittently with piles of rocks waiting to be made into walls—the tree stood in a small clearing, but just past it, going ever so slightly downhill, the native brush began. Our father had blazed trails into the brush, mostly on back-and-forth trips carrying armloads of pulled weeds and pruned trees or bushes, things that would take forever to mulch. He left mounds of botanic debris on the hillside which, in years-to-come, was itself buried in new growth of buckwheat, wild mustard, fennel, sagebrush, various grasses, and tangled wild cucumber vine. Nearby, not directly under the tree, our father had made a fire ring where sometimes he burned dry leaves shed by an old ash near the house that he would someday, long after the pepper tree, chop down. Occasionally we were allowed to use the fire ring to cook biscuits on sticks for an outdoor breakfast after we'd spent a night "camping" in a floorless pup-tent.

In the summer, anticipating a real camping trip awaiting us in late August, we often played at camping, raking smooth the dirt under the pepper tree, outlining a campsite in baseball-sized rocks, and laying sticks for a fire we never lit in the fire pit. We created the same useful things our mother did at "real" camp, like a tripod washstand made from stalks of bamboo

81

*lashed together like a teepee so a pan of water could be held in the three-
armed nest above where the three sticks are bound. And we gathered food:
going from bush to bush, we crumbled dry, red buckwheat flowers into our
mess-kit pans, stripped sage from twigs, cut fennel like celery stalks then
sliced it with our jackknives into bite-sized disks, and cut the prickly wild
cucumber open to extract the large wet seeds. Chad would eat anything he
was told to put in his mouth.*

"Bitter," her father mutters.

"I'll bet it is," she agrees softly.

It takes until the tea is gone, until her father is dozing curled on his
side on the cardboard in front of the fire, until the fire has almost gone
out and Ronnie finally dares to add more wood then stands fanning the
smoke with Adrian's jacket, before Adrian comes back, again rolling a
rock into camp before he emerges on the trail.

"I can't see smoke, but can smell the fire," he says. "Maybe we should
let it go now." He has a big shopping bag from which he removes a
thermal blanket, brand new, in a plastic zippered case. "Although, with
the rain, no one'll be out. It'll be extra quiet too. You'll learn to appreciate
the rain. No one mowing a lawn, no one outside with a radio." Again
Ronnie is rooted, watching without helping as Adrian hands her the shopping bag and the zippered case then wraps her father in the blanket,
waking him enough to get the blanket under as well as over him. When
mourning doves call she instinctively lifts her eyes to locate them. Her
father sighs.

"What store could you go to so close?" she finally asks.

"There's one of those outlet places down in that strip mall, just a
small one and mostly junk, but they do have linens, discontinued stuff,
hence the putrid color. And," again the grin that lightens his almost
gaunt face with a flash of white teeth, "A few of the women who work
there, they know me. I had them give me the biggest shopping bag—
it'll come in handy for waterproofing."

Women there know him. Suddenly she finds it difficult to look at his
face. Folding the bag carefully, slipping it inside the zippered case, she's also
seeking to steady her heartbeat, trying to swallow the sudden and confus-
ing hot bitterness in her own stomach, which isn't as soothing as the acrid
tea has obviously been for her father. "Thank you," she murmurs. Her
father's slow breathing, not quite a rasp, blends with the steady rush of the
creek. Adrian is folding his jacket and tucking it under her father's head.
The rest of her father is wrapped in mauve. "We'll pay you back."

"No need."

"But we will. Or *I* will. Can I . . . can you possibly help me get a job where you work?"

"It's not necessary."

"It is for us." She finally raises her chin and looks at him again. "You've helped us, we can't do much to return the favors. But I know about farm work. And I can copy what everyone else is doing."

"Well . . . Work is a little more scarce this time of year. I do fill-in construction work. But maybe you can get hooked up with a landscaper's crew for a few days."

"That'll be fine. Tomorrow, if possible."

Adrian nods, his eyes serious. Then silence again, and neither of them is moving, just standing halfway facing each other, but also halfway at an angle, so both can look away, to the fire or the sleeping old man, or east toward the hillsides of the narrow canyon where a dull roar advises that the creek is gushing even faster up there before it levels out and passes them, muddy and roiled. Suddenly flustered, she looks around for a place to put the bags, finally stuffs them into the bicycle's basket, then moves to her father and puts a palm on his forehead. "He's better already."

"Good. It was likely nothing but a chill anyway. Glad I happened along."

Ravens not too far away, probably on the golf course, seem to be squabbling and muttering like chickens. "Here," she says abruptly, handing him the knife. "Thanks."

"No problem." The knife slips into his hand, then into his pocket. "I actually didn't really happen along." Grinning, he squats to sit on the ground, but stays on his heels, takes a stick and pokes it into the mud as though to measure the depth of topsoil the rain has soaked. "Wanted to see if you were still here. Thought you should know that the immediate community may be—well not *may be*, they *are*—getting a little hot for action about what they call *the illegal problem*. Seems some boys—care to guess which ones?—told their parents they were playing at the strip mall and were threatened with a gun. There's a renewed demand, you know letters to the editor and vocal parents at council meetings, to clean the back country of migrants."

Before she has an answer, the ravens erupt into a screaming fight, the pitch rising, until one voice is snuffed out as though someone's been killed. She watched them the other day, from some creek bed bushes at the edge of the golf course. The raven that sounds like it's been mortally wounded is a juvenile, out of the nest and as big as the adults, flying with them, but still being fed, still screaming and demanding its food. It shuts up abruptly when one of the parents rams something into its open mouth.

"It means everyone has to be a little more portable, ready to move," Adrian continues.

She looks down at the top of his head, his hair a little cleaner, still pulled back into a ponytail. "We weren't going to be here very long, but . . ." She pauses when he looks up, squinting against the overcast glare where the sun is trying to burn through. She swallows, then says, "I'm sorry. If there's trouble for you . . . we caused it."

"No, hey, I'm just here to make you aware, not to blame anyone."

"Maybe after we move on, things'll quiet down."

"Maybe. But it also occurred to me . . . those boys might focus their fun down to looking just for you. I doubt anyone's foiled their games as dramatically."

"It was *you* foiling their . . . game." Trying to sound casual but feeling herself flush, and the weakness that passes afterwards, from knees to stomach to arms. Still looking down at him, his creased brow, his eyes unashamed, his voice gentle.

"Even so . . . maybe the sooner you're out of here the better. For you, that is."

"We can't until . . . we've got that family business. And I need him to help me." Glances at her father, his face ashen with the dying fire no longer throwing flame-light onto it. "It's really *his* business."

Adrian leaves his twig pushed into the mud when he stands. Ronnie's no longer looking down at him but looking up. Is he a foot taller than she is? To talk eye-to-eye they'll have to both be squatting, or sitting together somewhere, or stretched out on their sides in a park with elbows on the grass and heads propped up on their hands. Again she feels the flush. Abruptly stammers, "We have to find . . . to go get . . . something . . . something he left somewhere . . . out there. Before she died, he promised her—my mother—he would, and it's my . . . obligation . . . to see it through."

"He scattered your mother's ashes and now wants them back?"

As though waiting for the chime of noon, the sun finally burns its way through directly overhead, and a mockingbird trills a long part-meadowlark part-sparrow assertion. "Not exactly, but—How did you know?"

"Last time you mentioned this family business, you asked about an old favorite hunting place. Put two and two with what you just said. It's not uncommon. People see their favorite places being wrecked and don't want their loved-ones out there anymore when it turns into a shopping center or amusement park."

"Well, it's . . . more than that."

He doesn't answer, smiles slightly—not the flashing grin—and shows he's ready to leave: glancing at her father, taking the knife out of his pocket and putting it back in, looking over his shoulder down the trail toward the asphalt.

"Could you . . . ," her voice cracks, she takes a breath. "Maybe, while he sleeps . . . Could you take me to the lagoon . . . this one right down here?"

"I thought you said you hunted near a different lagoon."

"It's possible . . . that maybe it wasn't." The lie is easier than it should've been. "Maybe it wouldn't hurt to check." Almost feels herself smiling.

"This golf course has been there almost forty years, when everything else around here really *was* the middle of nowhere. People may've been hunting, but not right *here*."

"Just to make sure . . ." Her voice is trailing away. The sense of a smile is already gone. "But not if you're too busy."

"No—no plans," he says, "but how long should you leave him alone?"

"I think he'll sleep a while. Let's move him inside the bush. And I'll get some of the other stuff out of sight too." She begins pulling a tarp from the sumac bush, rolling it loosely. Both tarps together and folded over once will make four layers, enough to keep her father off the mud, which isn't as deep under the bush.

"Do you really feel okay about leaving him?"

She turns, her arms full of the rolled tarp. "He's not so incapacitated that he'll walk into the creek and drown. He knows how to stay in and around a campsite, but if he feels better, he'll probably go fishing. He's not a dithering old fool who goes wandering off. He just doesn't talk much, stays inside his own head, his own thoughts, his own memories." Then, as though the long speech both jolts and saps her, Ronnie closes her mouth hard, looks away, tears stinging.

"Hey, sorry, that's great, I wasn't implying . . ." In his pause, would he be grinning boyishly or become sullen and chagrined and wishing he were elsewhere, anywhere else, away from her? "Okay, he'll probably be fine. But yeah let's move him inside." With a snap that sends the last few drops of water in a sparkling arc, Adrian whisks the second tarp off the bush. Ronnie crawls into the bush to spread one tarp, folded in half, then takes the second from Adrian who crouches and passes it to her in a jumbled ball rather than rolled. It takes a while to smooth it flat and fold it over on top of the first tarp. Meanwhile, his voice continues outside the bush, "Yeah, I try not to be too much of an alarmist, just take things as they come. I can handle the uncertainty when it comes to just me, but for new folks out here . . . But even on the chance those boys happen to be out hunting today, even on the chance they happen this way, even on the chance they find him, they likely wouldn't mess with him. After all, he's the one who had the gun." Ronnie is crawling out of the bush as Adrian finishes with, "They might throw rocks but probably wouldn't be writing any words on him."

On hands and knees, she freezes, momentarily stupefied, shoots a defenseless, naked glance up at him but can't see his face, backlit against the glaring haze. Is he trying to tell her that he saw it, the word looped around her breasts? Did he see them as she lay writhing, her head gripped between a boy's knees, legs shackled by another boy's hands, did he see them pancake flat, like two eggs not-too-fresh so the whites spread out thin and watery and the deflated yokes stare pale and unappetizing?

"I don't think he's even waking up," Adrian says, no evidence of prurience in his voice. He is crouching beside her father, supporting the top half of his body while the old man gets his feet under him, still wrapped in the mauve blanket. Ronnie has to move out of the way as Adrian helps her father stoop and stumble into the bush. By the time she comes back with the clothes that had been drying over the handcart and highchair, her father is once again sleeping on his side. "If those clothes are darker than this blanket, let's spread them over him so he's not as obvious."

With the highchair and her father's architectural rock fire pit the only visible remains of the campsite, they leave, walking the bike up the asphalt out of the gully. Then Ronnie sits on the seat, and Adrian pedals standing up in front of her. With both hands she holds the edges of the seat beneath her, instead of reaching forward for his waist—because he needs freedom to move up and down working the pedals, not because she's afraid. Would she feel ribs beneath the loose cotton shirt, close under the surface of what must be skin and muscle stretched taut on his toughened frame? She watches his lower back, the shirt whipping like a flag until his skin dampens with sweat and the cotton begins to stick. He doesn't need to pump, just stands on the pedals as they coast down La Costa. A bright knot in her stomach, in her chest, in her throat, shooting upward faster than mercury over a flame—she can feel her mouth grinning, her teeth meeting the cool rush of air, her lips and skin stretched tight, a frozen scream of ecstasy, of freedom, needing no sound to be heard inside her head.

We must've been seven and five, mere weeks before the pepper tree incident, our first (our last) allowance of an hour's freedom at the fair, a handful of dimes and a strip of tickets for rides. Our mother anxiously watching her preserves and jam being judged, our father at work on his shift, we promised to keep our hands joined, always ride together, and be on the merry-go-round, the one with all ponies that float up and down, at precisely 11 a.m. by the big clock tower and she would be there to wave. More than one kindly janitor, hawker, fairgoer with little ones of her own asked if we were lost, but with a certitude that it was our-dad's-fair, we answered only no, and continued down the midway. Past the souvenir sellers with invisible-dogs-on-a-leash, plastic swords, Chinese finger traps, pirate flags, pinwheels; past the fried zucchini and hot-dogs-on-sticks, cinnamon buns and grilled corn-on-the-cob; SLOWLY past the man with a flat cloth-covered board on an easel with little chameleon lizards in tiny collars and leashes each pinned to the board for sale. Then the banner stretched overhead announced the onset of the Fun Zone. Our private joke, hand-in-hand, to be sober and solemn as we walked the last few yards toward the banner, then as we passed underneath, smile gaily, laugh out loud—now we were to have fun!

Pudgy smiling airplanes that flew a head-high circle, bumperboats we could steer by ourselves (all four hands on our boat's one wheel), a colorful choo-choo on a round undulating track. We stopped between rides to let the blast of screams and roar of clickety wheels on the little portable roller coaster exhilarate our already rabbit-paced hearts. Ten-forty-five, tickets counted, enough for two on the merry-go-round and one on the roller coaster. Chad standing at the fence enclosing the track, aluminum poles like horse corrals, bossy voice telling him, "Put your hands there, both of them, DO NOT let go." Then the zinging thrill of the coaster's downhill plunge—the air-rushing, lips-grinning, teeth-rattling, everything-vibrating POP of sheer acceleration.

Afterwards, solid ground feels odd, walking away with knees wobbly and head swimming with lingering giddiness—there he was waiting, still gripping the aluminum fence rail with tiny hands that go only halfway round, beaming face scanning the buzzing group exiting the coaster cars.

And our mother never need know. Astride our fancy wooden ponies with flaring nostrils, windswept manes and dress-parade saddles, we only went around once before there she was, short curly hair blowing around, waving and smiling her upside-down smile. Big enough to ride the roller coaster, big enough to get down from a painted pony alone, but our mother unsnapped Chad from his safety strap and swung him free, then balanced him on one hip, dabbed at a smudge on his cheek with a napkin she wet with her tongue.

"Come on," she said, "I'll show you a surprise."

Our mother taking a little hand with each of hers, we maneuvered the crowd without being separated, Chad had to run to stay by her side, heading for the Domestic Arts building to see her blue ribbons for preserves and jams, blackberry from last year (this season's berries just in, new jam cooling at home but too late for a fair entry), strawberry, peach, quince sauce and whole apricots in quart jars.

On the way, cutting through a smaller building, a bluish glow from a black-walled anteroom draws us, all three, and we discover the tropical aquarium exhibit. The clearest of crystal water, sparkling with bubbles. The glinting silver schools of zebra fish and slow-moving ogling oscars. Red sword-tails constantly flitting close to their pot-bellied, pregnant mates. Clouds of blue-and-red neons turning together with innate precision. Busy green catfish scouring gravel bottoms and suckermouth algae-eaters clinging to the glass. Even red-spotted salamanders, thumbnail-sized yellow-and-black frogs, tiny wormy-looking black eels, and glassfish exposing their stomachs and skeletons and beating hearts through transparent skin.

So the idea is born: next year we would win a blue ribbon with our aquarium! Discovered abandoned in the basement when they bought the farmstead, given to us just recently to keep lizards or horned toads and one woebegone tarantula who wouldn't eat. Our mother agreed, but said ours should be a natural microcosm, a model of life in the creek at the bottom of Hannigan Hill. Chad cried because he wanted a red-spotted salamander, but our mother said something even better might live in Dictionary Valley's creek.

Adrian maneuvers through traffic stopped at the light on La Costa, waves to the guy selling newspapers at the corner, turns right and once again begins to pedal uphill on El Camino Real, crosses traffic for a left turn. Ronnie leans back out of the way as he twists his upper body to look backwards for cars before angling across the three lanes. The vigorous damp smell of his shirt and skin are dizzying. Another mile or so, slightly uphill, then gradually down, through a condo-and-palm encrusted residential area, until he veers into a small parking lot with a sign advertising exercise apparatus set at intervals around a jogging trail.

Ronnie pushes herself backwards off the bike while Adrian swings his leg over.

The dirt trail parallels the coast of the long, narrow lagoon, running east and west. The condos, separated from the lagoon by a eucalyptus grove, are new enough to have been built in the last twenty years. On the lagoon's opposite shore, a steep brushy hill is undeveloped, except La

Costa Road, at the foot of the hill running along the lagoon's edge. The trail is shaded by eucalyptus; bordered by tall and short marine grasses on the water side; beaver tail cactus and scrubby drought-resistant bushes on the other side; sage, mustard and low salt-marsh ground-cover on both sides. Ronnie and Adrian move along the trail without speaking, passing one jogger and one man and woman each wearing binoculars. The low-tide mud is streaked white with salt. Puffs of breeze alternate the scent of sage with salty marsh. White egret are bright spots here and there in the dark shallow water, a small flock of brown pelican floats near the middle, a great blue heron stays twenty yards ahead, lifting its awkward body in short flight every time they get too near. Wading peeps eye them carefully, lifting big cautious feet far out of the water. Mudhens scavenging in the muck move only a foot or two further into the water, then return to the foamy brine where the water daubs soundlessly, almost motionless against the silt shore. Gulls cry overhead. And doves. Ronnie can hear their plaintive calls. Then comes across them sunning themselves in a cactus and sage dotted clearing where the eucalyptus grove veers farther away from the shore. At first the doves just stand, then they take flight in an agitation of whistling wings.

"We *could've* hunted here," she breathes. "But . . . we didn't. For one thing, too many trees."

Adrian stops, leans the bike against a sign that's tilted like an easel with a picture display pointing out various features of a salt marsh habitat.

"And too near a big body of water," Ronnie continues softly, "the birds might fall in after being hit, and we didn't have a retriever . . . a dog, I mean."

"I thought you hunted near a lagoon." He picks a cluster of red berries from a head-high bush then bends to break some pieces off a ground-cover succulent-type plant.

"It was east of a lagoon, where the golf course would be in relation to this one. We would've been hunting on that golf course which you say has been here thirty, forty years. So it wasn't this lagoon."

"You know, I'm sure you're looking for San Elijo, it's a state park now, a designated wetland. I don't know why they chose Elijo instead of this one, except maybe the three bridges they built across the mouth of this one caused some problems with the tidal flow, and the number of eucalyptus here not only may hinder hunting, as you say, but of course aren't native. The railroad planted groves of them over a hundred years ago, and most of the ranchers speculated too, for railroad ties, but the wood's too soft."

"My mother taught me that! You mean it's true?"

"Why would your mother lie?" He grins and hands her the piece of plant he'd picked.

"What's this?"

"Taste it."

"You mean eat it?" But without hesitation she bites into a baby-finger-sized lobe. "It's okay, a little tart, but just a little, not much taste. What is it?"

"Picklewort. It's edible. We could take some back with us."

"I was going to ask you, after the sage tea this morning, if you knew of any other plants . . ."

He laughs. "Remember all my varied and unfinished college degrees. The ecosystem of the area came first, and it's only a little side trip from studying ecosystem to learning a little of the history, what indigenous people found useful. Which was pretty much everything. You know, the quintessential hunters and gatherers."

"We were sort of like that, in a way. My parents would've loved to know what you know. I wish I could've gone to school." The exposed eagerness in her own voice is suddenly almost as disconcerting as the thought that he may've witnessed her body struggling against the three boys.

"Never too late. All the adult education and community colleges around here have classes about local history and ecosystems, native flora and fauna, that sort of thing."

"No, I mean . . ." At the shoreline, three or four mallards erupt in a honking quarrel, then quiet down again, except one who continues its rhythmic quack for a while, each squawk a little quieter until it also stops. ". . . never mind." Ronnie walks several feet away, staring directly into flashing pieces of sunlight flickering through the trees, letting her eyes smart. Some kind of concrete platform, the top of a sewer conduit, has a decorated surface, a mosaic of rocks and a brass plaque in the shape of a fish saying, PLEASE TAKE CARE OF OUR BATIQUITOS LAGOON. She sits on the concrete, facing back toward Adrian. He's still standing in the same spot, staring down at the plants in his hands. The downhill bike ride has loosened more than just a few strands of his ponytail, and a zigzagging onshore breeze tousles his hair as though tenderly. Her hand on her own head, nothing feels gentle, not at all soft nor pliant, the short hairs sticky with salt, so, despite being thin, manage to feel matted. Suddenly ashamed of the shorn cut she'd wished for.

Adrian looks up, squinting, and approaches.

"I have a policy," he says. "I don't ask questions, you know, about anyone's personal life or their past. My friends and I don't have time, and usually don't have the energy, for emotional conversations. But I know, with other people who aren't living like me, it makes me seem like I don't care or I'm not interested." He sits beside her on the concrete, but because it's a disk, they face slightly away from each other. "Actually," he says, his voice lighter, "the former or amateur anthropologist in me is *always* interested in the various ways people live, from their versions of miserable adolescence to how their marriages break up."

Looking at the remaining piece of picklewort in her hand, she decides to put it in her mouth rather than drop it. "We should go back soon." But she stays frozen, as though mesmerized by the spot where her boots rest in the sand.

His hand appears in her field of vision, palm up, holding five or six red berries. "They taste like lemons. The first settlers called them lemonade berries."

It seems she stares at his hand without moving for minutes rather than seconds, then she slowly takes the berries, softly touching his palm with her fingertips. She eats the sour berries one at a time.

"I'm honored you trust me enough to eat whatever I hand to you." He laughs lightly then stands.

Nineteenth-century ranchers established eucalyptus groves as a potential crop, but around their haciendas or ranch houses they planted pepper trees. Left when the vast ranch spreads were subdivided—along with olive trees from both 100-year-old orchards and 200-year-old plantings by the missionaries—pepper and olive trees shaded houses in Dictionary Valley, while the tracts of eucalyptus remained as windbreaks, shaded parks, reminders of failed speculation and old property lines.

Our pepper tree was actually too far from the house to have been planted to shade a compound; and our house, built in 1927, too new to have been the center of one of the original homestead ranches. Perhaps our pepper tree was a lucky sprout that found enough water to grow to a sapling, and then a bigger and bigger tree, spreading wide and low. Or perhaps the original owners put it on the property line to shade a horse, goat or donkey corral, already long gone when our father found the property. The pepper tree was ours, for camping, for climbing and swinging, for our tree house hiding place for treasures. Not needing an electric pump

or heater, our natural aquarium took residence on the tree house plat-
form, despite our mother's caution that we would have to climb up with
every jug of water and jar of new tenants.

Three hours have passed by the time they return from the lagoon. Her
father is still inside the bush, awake, she can see him sitting up, moving
slightly. Adrian reminds her where to wait for work the next day, who to
ask for, what to say. He says he'll try to get word to a landscaper he knows
who hires help each day. He hands her the lemonade berries they picked
on the way out of the lagoon trail; first they'd put them in a big soda cup,
then they'd found a plastic grocery bag blowing on the road. Adrian's
shirt and hair are sweat-soaked, but he doesn't stay for more than a quick
drink of water. All she says is "Thanks," hoping it's enough.

Her father has only recently woken—must've lay still looking up into
the bush until he noticed the shotgun in its hiding place. She finds him
in the process of taking it apart, or trying to, with Ronnie's pocketknife
as a screwdriver. "Should be. Washed," he says as Ronnie extracts the gun
from his hands.

"I know, but I don't think I can put it back together myself."

"Still have to give my shove."

"Shove*l*. Okay. What do you expect me to do about it?"

"Ask him." His fever is gone. He prepares his line for fishing.

On the way into the gully with Adrian, the water roaring across the
asphalt service road and the growing mound of foam had reminded her
to ask: "Is it dangerous to eat fish from this water?" It was the first thing
she'd said since eating the berries from his hand at the lagoon.

"Depends on how long you expect to be eating them."

"What else lives in here?"

"Just about everything you'd expect, frogs, crawdads, waterbugs, little
fish, mosquito larvae."

"And this soap, or whatever it is, doesn't bother them?"

"A big rain like we had last night—or actually bigger is better—can
wash a lot of gunk out of the creek. Of course it all ends up in the lagoon.
That place looks almost stagnant, but the foam'll be carried off by and by."

The creek at the foot of Hannigan Hill was almost seasonal, fed by a
spring, but during the driest months, there wasn't enough to keep a trickle
of water moving from pool to pool. In the winter, the creek could swell

and swamp the small flood plain at the bottom of the hill. Never enough to irrigate the olive and lemon groves planted by ranchers after oats and wheat proved futile as well, the valley would've best been left as cattleland, but when the cattlemen's fencing wars of the 1860's were lost in court, and the expense of surrounding the vast ranches with barbed wire was too great, ranchers turned toward the type of agriculture that didn't need to be penned in nor rounded up. Lemons, mostly. There was even talk of re-naming Dictionary Valley: VISTA DE LEMÓN, view of lemons, or VALLE DE LIMÓN, valley of lemons. "What would you name the valley," our mother inquired, and Chad declared it should be Lemon Ice, because our father often squeezed the big, plentiful lemons from our tree and made us Italian fruit-ice in a hand-crank ice cream maker.

Although our formal home-schooling wasn't going to begin until mid-September, our mother likely regarded our summer aquarium as a part of our education. She had us build it from the bottom up—after our father took it to the fairgrounds workshop and sealed it so it held water again. So with rocks and gravel taken from the creek bed, from the dry high-water line, we laid out our floor plan. Then with gallon jars our father brought home from work—containers originally for bulk mustard, ketchup and rel-ish—we retrieved the ten gallons of creek water the tank would hold.

Each trip to the creek was at least a half mile hike down Hannigan Hill and another half mile back up. We could pause to set the jars down and rest once at Rocky Flats, a natural rock outcropping with narrow shady crevices to stow found treasures. The hillside's various trails, almost imperceptible, were primarily slides of loose rocks, sometimes switch-backing but most of the time nearly straight downhill. Chad couldn't carry a gallon of water, so on every trip down for water, we also caught something to live in the aquarium, and he carried a quart jar carefully in both hands. Our mother made nets from wire hangers and old nylon stockings which we'd never seen her wear. The live-bearing mosquito fish were easy to see and catch in nets, especially the big females, four times the size of the slim, flirting males. Water skating bugs and underwater swimming bugs and pollywogs could also be scooped from the water. Sometimes in clearer spots—like the biggest pool, Pollywog Sinkhole—we could see the crawdads venturing halfway from their rock crevices, or else we turned rocks, working in tandem, one of us tipping the rock, the other ready with a net to nab the suddenly vulnerable crawdad. We always replaced the rocks as our father had taught us. We looked for plants that grew in the water, but there weren't many. Chad even collected clumps of algae, although our mother said it would've likely grown on its own. And she also advised that the inhabitants could conceivably eat each other, and that it was okay.

Did our mother know about the clawed frogs when she predicted we would find something better than the red-spotted salamander or the miniature eels? One time, as a rock was lifted, there was a spurt of mud, as though an octopus was discovered living in our creek squirting ink to conceal its escape. Using our "flush-and-snare" teamwork, our biggest hanger-net was positioned to catch the backflow as the rock was tipped. When the net was lifted, dripping and choked with mud and algae, there, wriggling in the nylon, was a dark, slimy thing, with long legs and feet resembling a frog's, with a wedged-shaped head resembling a frog's, but so flat it was barely the thickness of one of our hands. It couldn't have sat up on its haunches like the tree or bull frogs we'd caught and played with at lakes and creeks in the mountains. In the jar, it hung with nose toward the surface and legs dangling down.

After inspecting the creature in the jar, our mother spent a Saturday morning with us at the library. Our father dropped us off on the way to a morning of fishing at the jetty, then picked us up on his way back. She told us when our home-schooling started in two months, we would do Saturdays at the library twice a month, to pick out our readers. While Chad was absorbed in an ocean of vivid children's books, our mother discovered that our star denizen of the aquarium was an African clawed frog, brought to this continent because its chemistry was supposed to provide a new pregnancy test, then also more specifically imported as an exotic pet. Neither idea caught on, and the frogs were released—accidentally or otherwise—into local streams and lakes where they established successful colonies, especially in California. She read from her notes as we finished the drive home in the fishy-smelling car. Clawed frogs—so called because of the claws on their hind feet—were from the only frog family with toenails and the only one wholly aquatic and tongueless. Willing to eat almost anything, alive or dead, but not in the usual frog way of a sticky long tongue torpedoing out to zap the unsuspecting. Indigenously inhabiting stagnant pools and backwaters that lay over a bed of deep mud, an environment often choked with organic matter, it was no wonder they'd thrived in Dictionary Valley creeks that were barely able to trickle through the summer.

When the station wagon returned home, we raced to climb the pepper tree to observe our exotic tenant with new enlightenment. He was still in the tank, but, except for the crawdad hiding in its rock cave, everything else had been eaten.

Death, in this way, was not a ghastly occurrence. Not any more than the doves we hunted or the rabbits we raised for slaughter.

But we needed new fish and pollywogs and waterbugs, then the clawed frog would have to live alone in one of the gallon jars, eating worms and grubs we would dig from the compost pile until our exhibit went to the fair next year. Once again, with arms wrapped around wide-mouth gallon containers and quart jars formerly packed with tomato sauce or sliced peaches, we made our way down the side of Hannigan Hill to Pollywog Sinkhole. Mid-summer, the rains long since over for the year, fully into fire season. Willowy green prickerbushes had turned into crackling brown tumbleweeds. Tilted seas of billowing verdant wild oats—distant relatives of the failed crops of early ranchers—were stiff and straw-colored, the papery hulls had split to display feathery groat. The supple vines of wild cucumber that had crawled over bushes and rock piles, carrying elegant white flower and odd prickly fruit, were now like dry snakeskin, with only the partial husks of fruit remaining after mice, rats, opossum, fox or raccoon had gnawed through the spiny skin and eaten the seeds. Only the barrel cactus, often lost under the dry grasses of the previous spring, and the sumac remained darkly, dusty green. High season for snakes to be sunning in open patches, especially the rocky slide we used for a trail. Just the previous spring, when we'd gone to collect eggs from nest boxes our father had devised—so the hens could enter from their yard, sit in the dark on cedar-chip nests and lay their eggs, and later we could come from the outside, lift a hinged lid and remove the eggs—we'd found, instead of the light brown or greenish eggs, a coiled king snake. More severe still was the story of our mother going to the rabbits to check a new brood, and discovering a rattlesnake oozing through the wire into the hutch. So, contorting to peer around the jars in our arms, we scanned the ground and stepped gingerly, even while the hill's incline hastened us unnaturally toward the bottom.

In the nearly stagnant pools, minnows, stocked by the county to control mosquito, still flourished, and many of the pollywogs, notably larger than our last harvest, were now sporting two hind legs. Among bugs there were still the aquatic underwater beetle with paddles on either side, the surface skater, and dragonfly larvae. With the containers full of our replacement aquarium population, plus a new supply of creek water, we began the more difficult expedition of climbing the hill back home.

The jars were heavy but also had to be carried with precaution that the contents didn't slosh back and forth too wildly and batter the fish and pollywogs. The rocks under our feet threatened to roll away and send us falling backwards, juggling glass and living cargo. Although we'd gone up and down the hill several times in the past two weeks—and uncountable times in the past year since Chad had been allowed to venture off the property, as long as he always did what he was told—sometimes the trail seemed to disappear and we had to decide which way to go, with UP always being the guiding factor. No doubt we'd never trekked down or up the hill on exactly the same route. Even if we had, there'd be no way to anticipate the misfortune that was actually more probable than an encounter with a snake— since snakes would at least try to avoid large mammals bearing down on them, would skulk off into the chaparral long before our feet crashed down on their bodies. Not so the wasps who built paper nests in the rocks.

Chad screamed. Not just once—the screams continued, pausing only for a new breath. And the two quart jars he was carrying were catapulted into the air before he ran, screaming, scrambling with hands and feet when he fell forward, ascending the hillside faster than either of us had ever managed.

"No, CHAD, WAIT, NO, WHAT'RE YOU DOING—NO!"

Most of the wasps had followed Chad up the hill, so it wasn't until the quart jars had landed—one out of sight, just a crunch out in the bushes; the other in plain sight, the jar like a cracked-open egg, its contents a wet spot on the rocks—that the fiery stingers found another pair of bare legs. And yet, it seemed, there was no second version of Chad's reckless dash up the hillside. Anchored for agonizing minutes, as though paralyzed by the stings, but it was probably mere seconds, staring at the bright silver flash of our biggest minnow—even reached to pick her up, but she flopped once, like a hooked trout on the Sierra creek bank, and landed in dirt, coating her like cement. Then the echo of Chad's screams, farther up the hill, and the remaining few wasps tirelessly stinging, broke the trance. Urged homeward again.

Our habitat of mud-dwellers would not be entered in the fair's tropical aquarium exhibit the next year—by late September the aquarium in the tree house had just dried dirt and algae clinging to its sides. By the time the entry deadline rolled around in the spring, our father had already chopped down and cut up the pepper tree, and our mother never again exhibited her jams and preserves.

Chapter Six

For three days, since Monday, they've only seen their campsite in darkness. Who knew if during the day packs of neighborhood dogs or after-school kids on bicycles or foraging coyotes or scavenging raccoons or opossum with kits weren't ripping apart the stowed gear and stashed supplies, scattering items from creek to the hillside, or somehow carting everything away. But each evening when they return, long after dusk, the stuff waits untouched in the quiet cold. After crawling into the bush and burrowing under the painter's tarp, they eat whatever Ronnie has saved from lunch and go to sleep. Before dawn they'll have to be up to wash and dress and get back on the bicycle to get to the rear corner of the Home Builders parking lot and catch their ride to a new worksite.

Usually Ronnie's father is up even earlier, makes a slow fire and cooks a small bluegill which he then cuts in half—thumb of his bad hand pinning the gutted head to a small water-worn board, dull knife in his good hand, shaking slightly, making a mangled cut lengthwise down the spine. But Ronnie declines the half he offers her, a pile of cooked skin and flaking white meat and bones sticking through which barely cover half his palm. "You eat it, I'm fine until lunch."

On the way to the hardware store, a shortcut on a dirt path behind some houses, she'll pick oranges from a tree that has branches out-spread across a backyard fence, recalling the sign her father had her make when she was eight or ten, on a shiny piece of cardboard he'd brought from the fairgrounds, with *Gun and Knife Show* and an arrow on one side. On the blank side she'd printed *please don't pick this fruit* with blue paint left over from the shutters, then nailed the cardboard to a stick and pounded it under the tangerine tree which stood closest to the end of the driveway where the county refuse collectors turned their truck around at the end of the dead end lane.

The first day she'd stood at the edge of the small group of men who gather every day in the parking lot. Most of them sit or stand on the curb, some squat between the landscaping bushes or beside trees barely taller than a man, and the men themselves barely taller than Ronnie. Those that have come by bicycle chain their bikes to the fence surrounding the parking lot. Some wear boots, most have sneakers, a few have well-worn leather shoes which had maybe once been some kind of dress shoe. They wear jeans and t-shirts and open flannel shirts, some have jackets. Many will have already tied their jackets around their waists, the walk to the parking lot having warmed them. A few have mustaches but all have shaved as recently as that morning, their hair parted and combed. They hold plastic shopping bags, some drink from styrofoam cups of coffee. Other than her companion being an old man who slightly drags one leg and holds one arm close to his body as though clutching something precious, other than the nagging suspicion that her hair may be standing on end from riding the bike downhill before the creek water she rubs into her scalp has dried, Ronnie does not look out of place. That first morning, she didn't see Adrian but did spot two of the men he shares camp with. They met her eyes, said something to each other, then slowly, while still engaged in some slight conversation together, without obviously walking toward her, they moved closer. With the thin, rusty chain that had come wrapped around her bike's seat, and the flimsy lock with tiny key that had been almost rusted into the key slot, Ronnie attached her bike at the end of the row against the fence.

Every day just after dawn, trucks—from small pick-ups to larger stake beds towing tree-chipping machines—turn into the parking lot, drive to the back corner, and pull up to the gathering of men. One of the men goes to the open driver's window, then that one man will get into the cab of the truck, or he'll turn and beckon to one or two others and they'll climb into the truckbed. The trucks idle quietly, the men converse quietly, the employers speak through their windows so no one but the man standing outside can hear. But that first day, a dirt bike motorcycle entered the parking lot and accelerated toward the back, breaking the relative hush that Ronnie had already recognized as customary.

The driver was helmeted, a huge bug eye turned toward Ronnie as the motorcycle slowed beside her, but the rider on the back, with a gypsy-style bandanna protecting his head, was Adrian.

"Hey!" his mouth moved around the word, but was still overwhelmed by the idling engine. Ronnie stepped closer. "Stay near Manuel," Adrian shouted, "the guy who picks him up will take you too. It's a landscaper. Sprinkler systems."

The bike careened forward, like a high-strung horse lurching then being reined in, and Adrian moved naturally with the motion. His legs outlining the driver's were longer, his thigh muscles obviously flexing and shifting, his pelvis the supple center of balance that kept his head and body floating above the turbulence. The motorcycle circled and pulled up again, facing the opposite direction. Without adjusting his legs or putting a foot to the ground, Adrian leaned backwards, one hand braced on the seat behind himself, looking at her. Had he asked something requiring an answer?

"Where are you going?" Ronnie asked.

"Construction site job I picked up, it'll last me a while."

The bug head swiveled back, checking to see how far Ronnie was from the wheels, then the bike blasted off, lifting the front wheel slightly from the asphalt, Adrian's body now thrusting forward, one hand still holding the seat behind himself, the other raised in a long graceful wave before the bike made a turn and Adrian leaned into the curve.

Allowed one question and she'd wasted it on some kind of plaintive weirdness, but hadn't thought to ask if the landscaper expected her to be a man or a woman, or if he knew her father was to come along.

Both questions were answered eventually, as the landscaper, who hadn't shaved that morning, flicked his cigarette out his truck's window, looked Ronnie up and down and informed her he would pay her twenty-five dollars a day. "I pay the guys forty," he'd admitted. "They work like mules, I mean that in a good way, they work hard. But they're *guys*, you know, I don't know if you'll have the same . . ."

"I have my father with me," she'd said.

"Yeah? Adrian didn't say anything about an old man."

"He'll help, but you can just pay me."

"Think the two of you'll be the same as one guy?" he'd asked, but hadn't waited for an answer, put the truck in gear and motioned her toward the back where Manuel was already seated among the PVC pipes and bags of topsoil. The landscaper had still paid her the twenty-five dollars. Of course how could he have known what her father contributed; he'd left them at the site then didn't pick them up until after five. Manuel had worked there the previous day, so no instructions were necessary from the landscaper. And, with a glance, Ronnie understood the work—the new sprinkling system was marked off aboveground with stakes and string. They dug the trenches, setting aside the pieces of lawn to be plugged back in when they finished. They sawed and fitted the PVC, attached the sprinkler heads, filled the trenches, replaced the turf, raked the surface to remove the leftover loose soil, used a heavy roller to remove bumps and restore the turf's level surface, hosed down the lawn, the driveway and sidewalks to remove the mud, then swept the excess water toward the drains. Ronnie's father was never without a tool in his good hand or awkwardly clutched in both, a spading fork, a rake, a broom. He didn't get to have one of the shovels, but held a trowel for a long time. Ronnie didn't bother to try to notice how much he was accomplishing or not. He was never in Manuel's way.

The second and third days another sprinkling system from the beginning, tear out the old and install the new, the landscaper there long enough at the end of the day to attach the electronic timer and test the system. Ronnie can tell, from the calls he takes and makes from a phone not much bigger than a pocketknife, that the rest of the landscaper's day is spent dropping other workers at other sites, then visiting new clients to discuss what the job will be, make plans and buy the necessary supplies, and get a signed job order. She listens and watches, an idea slowly germinating—she knows what it is, but as though she doesn't want to think the actual words: Why couldn't she do what he does? *Someday*, is all she'll let herself think, then doesn't let the rest completely formulate.

Traveling to the first jobs had been a blur of turning this way and that through sidewalked neighborhoods lined with eucalyptus, palm, sycamore, and tall, square eugenia hedges. But today it's too familiar, as though he's driving Ronnie and her father back to their camp. Then he turns from La Costa down a driveway that slopes at least thirty degrees and stops at a level place with a house, garage, lawn and pool. Behind the house there's another grade, much sharper, iceplant-covered to prevent erosion, with the golf course at the bottom. Standing on the lawn scanning the golf course view while the landscaper and home owner discuss the day's work, Ronnie can look past the end of the golf course's uniform greenness into the indistinct brownish haze of weeds and rocks, to the area where she and her father had been sleeping only hours before.

The recent rainwater that has run down the driveway isn't going down the drain, so the level part of the driveway is flooded. Under the lawn is where the drainage pipe is located. It's supposed to empty halfway down the iceplant embankment, so they'll be digging up the lawn and replacing the clogged pipes. Similar to a sprinkler system except bigger, the trench will go down at least a foot, the pipes at least six-inches across. Heavier, harder work, and in the last two days Ronnie has eaten only a few oranges, some picklewort and shriveling berries, a few pieces of bread, and half a small fish she hadn't been able to say no to this morning.

At lunch, in what has become almost routine, Manuel abruptly stops at noon and sits on an unaffected part of the lawn, takes a sandwich from his grocery sack, fills his plastic water bottle from the hose. Close enough to not seem that either is ostracizing the other, far enough apart that neither group is attempting to dine together, Ronnie and her father like-wise sit, facing each other. She knows Manuel watches her peel the two oranges. His sack is still making crinkley sounds as he takes items from it. Maybe tortillas rolled together, a package of store-bought cookies, maybe a cold baked potato wrapped in foil. She's seen him have any of these.

"Hey," he says.

Ronnie looks up, putting a peeled and sectioned orange in her father's bad hand so he can use his good hand to take the segments to his mouth. Manuel's hand is also extended toward her, offering a portion of his sandwich which he's broken in half.

"Okay," Manuel says, extending his hand further. "Okay." He glances at her father who's seated so his back is mostly toward Manuel so he can't see the sandwich. "Para tu Papá."

"Thanks." She takes the sandwich, slightly squished from how he's broken it in half, fried zucchini inside a crusty roll, the oil has seeped half an inch into the bread on both sides. Her father, like a dog, stares at the sandwich without looking back at the man who has given it to them. Ronnie takes a bite, doesn't stop to chew before taking another, then hands the rest to her father. She chews while looking at the remaining orange in her hands in her lap, scoring the skin with one fingernail, then digging in and starting to remove the peel. "Gracias," she says, softer, after swallowing.

"Okay," Manuel replies. His water bottle sloshes as he drinks.

"Are we living. To here?" Ronnie's father asks.

"This is someone else's house." She glances at Manuel, ready to smile as though sharing her father's bewildered question, but he's taking a bite of his sandwich, eyes closed.

"Here," her father repeats. "At out in this place."

"Oh. No, not forever. For a while though. Until I can get back down-town to the bank."

Her father chews, looking away as though satisfied or perhaps forget-ting what he's asked, but Ronnie continues, "But I've been thinking—

before going all the way back downtown, we could make a little money to save, without having the pay rent. Just, at least, until we finish . . . you know your . . . our family business." She watches her father's teeth bite into the sandwich and pull a translucent, oily slice of zucchini from between the crusty bread. With his good hand he catches the zucchini against his chin and pushes it into his mouth. Ronnie takes the remaining stumps of the roll and puts them into her own mouth, trying to squeeze out and taste the oil before swallowing.

"Hay una fiesta," Manuel says suddenly, crunching his grocery sack and other wrappings into a ball.

"Where?" Ronnie stretches her neck to peer past her father down to the golf course.

"Domingo. En el parque." He gestures vaguely northeast while Ronnie digs backwards for the Spanish lessons her mother included in home schooling. A Spanish-English dictionary between them on the kitchen table, together they'd bent over the pages, her mother's loose curls tickling Ronnie's cheek, the air washed by the sharp scent of lemon or vinegar her mother used to rinse hair after a shampoo. As though singing or reciting a poem, her mother's tranquil voice read the lists of colors and kinds of clothing, names of months and holidays, types of jobs, subjects in school, varieties of vegetables, and irregular verbs conjugated in a chart. Then Ronnie and her mother made flashcards with a packet of blank index cards, Ronnie wrote nouns and verbs on one side, passing them to her mother who looked up the Spanish word to write on the back. Often in a steamy kitchen while jars of applesauce or whole apricots were processing on the stove, Ronnie's mother wiped her face on her apron, flattening sweated tendrils of hair to her forehead and temples; then, this time sitting across from each other at the table, Ronnie's mother held the cards up, English word facing out, and after Ronnie said the Spanish, her mother repeated it, not correcting her accent, just acknowledging, agreeing, maybe even learning at the same time.

"Adrian dijo que vengan a comir. Hay mucha comida."

"Adrian? What about him?" She knew he was talking to her like a child, and she still wasn't getting it. With her mother, they'd probably both been speaking like children, memorizing and reciting verses together, forgetting to think the meanings, lulled and allayed by the timbre of their feathery voices echoing in unison, the same way they had years earlier with three voices, Chad wedged between them on the sofa with a rhyme book.

"Adrian dijo que vengan a comir. Fiesta grande para la Dia de Gracias. En el parque . . . próximo a la Canón Cajon."

"Um . . . que? Que es? In El Cajon? Why would Adrian want me to go to El Cajon?"

"Canón . . . canón. . . uh . . . la garganta . . ."

"Gorge," Ronnie's father says.

"You understand him, Dad? I think Adrian wants me to meet him somewhere? But I don't know any gorge except Mission Gorge. That's not very close to here. Are you sure it wasn't Mission Valley? Or Mission *Bay*? Maybe he means the lagoon—are you sure you understood him? Maybe Adrian wants me to meet him at the lagoon?" She points west, toward the lagoon, looking at Manuel.

"No," smiling, he points east again. "Una parque pequeno."

"Miserable place. That bay," Ronnie's father says. "The kids. They say do us to beach with no waves."

If the beach afforded us opportunities to grub around in an alternate ecosystem—playing with whatever living things were to be found there—it also held terror. The waves. Out there the cold water heaved in angry humps, then rage crested and they broke open with a roar, standing up at the height of fury, crashing forward, boiling, churning, vehement, and vicious. Our mother, without hesitation, would run without stopping through loose, dry warm sand, all the way from the towels and umbrella, down into the ocean, still running, splashing through water that reached ankles, then calves, then knees, then waist. Then she would dive forward and swim and be lost to us, just a white plastic cap bobbing helplessly in front of a monster wave just beginning to rear up in front of her. Her head would vanish just as the breaker crested, and we couldn't see her again until after the white frothing wave had moved forward enough, had shrunk enough, and her head would once again be bobbling just in front of the next brute. Sometimes she went into the surf with a canvas air mattress upon which she rode the enraged wave all the way back to where we played. Water dripping from nose and elbows, streaming from her plastic cap, she ran back into the fray. Even after being accustomed to her disappearance in the surf, this was when we played with trepidation, often looking over our shoulders, because we knew, eventually, it would be our turn. Once every trip to the beach she would come out of the waves and, like a sea serpent, swoop down on us, snatch up one or the other, then return back to the ocean with a screaming, kicking child.

She never let go of us, but took us with her as she plunged beneath each roiling wave just before it broke. When we bobbed back up on the other side, we re-filled our lungs and resumed wailing. Our mother snorted, laughed and said, "What's the matter with you?" but carried us all the way back to the towels where she wrapped our still furious bodies and rubbed the sun-warmed, rough material against our chilly skin.

The bay was, indeed, worthless, there being no fishing allowed, there being no sand crabs at the surfline. There being, in fact, no surfline, just cool timid ripples patting the manmade shore where too many children ran with brightly colored plastic pails and useless plastic shovels. But it also held no promise that we would be taken against our will into cold breakers.

Our mother's strategy ended, finally, with success. One day we laughed with her and said, "Let's go back in." Impossible to remember the exact moment when, in this case, screaming turned to joy. But memory is sure it was the day we buried our mother in the sand. She was helping us make a sandcastle, customary every beach day. But no fairyland for a princess waiting to be rescued, with towers constructed from pail-shaped pillars of wet sand. Ours were always more medieval, a muddy brackish pond surrounded by dozens of lopsided, leaning, twisting, needle-thin spires. Drip-castles, she called them, showing us how to take palmfuls of the loosest mud, more water than sand, then hold our hands like we were milking a cow, only upside-down, so the dribbles of wet sand dripped from our pursed fingertips. The sand-filled droplets hit, splatted and hardened, each followed by another and another, and a distorted steeple grew. The pond and its peculiar landscape then became home to our day's collection of sand crabs.

But this day as we began to dig the hole that would be our gothic city's pond, we asked her if we could instead bury her and surround her head with drip-castles. We wanted to do it vertically, have her climb feet first down into a hole, then let us push the sand in around her. We'd seen some teenage boys do this to a friend on a previous beach trip. But she suggested we bury her to her waist as she sat with legs extended in a shallower, scooped-out hole, and we could build a race car around her. After she helped us dig the trench and sat down in it, she was still able to help us scoop the sand into mounds over her legs, then she fashioned the steering wheel and dashboard in front of herself while we smoothed the sand into a chassis and molded four wheels. The car, a long cylinder extending in front of and behind her, was then adorned with a single drip-castle hood ornament.

After we laughed and shrieked, dancing around her for a while, looking for our father to come see what we'd made (but he was waist deep in the surf, fishing), our mother said the race car driver had finished the race and needed to climb out of the car. First she flexed her knees and cracks formed in the car's long hood, then she raised her hips and stood, and the vision of the car broke *apart, crumbled into sand, with us helping it to dissolve, kicking and stomping the wheels and what had been the rear chassis.*

"I have to wash off, who's coming with me!" she cried, and our shrieks of pleasure turned into another kind of scream. Did people up and down the beach turn to see if children were being attacked by sharks, beaten by bullies, had cut their feet on buried glass or burned them on buried hot coals?

This day with superhuman strength she captured BOTH of us, one in each arm, and still was able to run then crash into the surf, still upright on her feet, plunging onward, somehow shifting us—the five-year-old held in her arms and the seven-year-old riding her back, clutching her around the neck. "Not so tight," she'd occasionally say upon surfacing from a plunge underneath a cresting wave. Her voice calm and normal despite the crying children, despite the turbulent surf, despite the constant roar of water. That must've been part of what quelled us. Plus we must've finally noticed the rhythm, the cadence, that when the terrible wave stood up in front of us, instead of trying to escape by going over the top, we submerged underwater, did the very thing we feared the wave was trying to do to us. And under there with our strong mother's body to hold onto, the water wasn't a tornado of agitation, not at all, almost the opposite. It pressed or pulled firmly one way then the other, but the roar was muffled, there was no crest to shatter, no foaming tumult. We floated in saline silence, could even open our eyes and see thousands of tiny bubbles sparkling underwater, like swimming among stars in a greenish sky. When we rose again and broke the surface, the vanquished wave was past us, on its way to the beach, fuming that it hadn't even so much as disturbed us with its fury.

"Wait til' we tell your father," our mother boasted, bracing us, one on each hip. Then halfway back to the beach, she released us to swim back by ourselves.

The first day, after lunch, when Manuel had stood and gone toward the front door of the house, he'd turned halfway there and beckoned Ronnie to follow. He'd nodded her to go forward ahead of him and said "el tocado," then pantomimed washing his hands. Now Ronnie already knows that's what they do before going back to work. Manuel rings the bell, and when a teenage girl answers the door—saying into a cordless phone, "just a second," after she's already eye-to-eye with the three people on the porch—Ronnie asks, "May we use the restroom?" But she doesn't go first. She sends her father, and whispers, "Wash your face, and use soap," then when he returns, the front of his shirt more than a little damp, she gestures for Manuel to go before her. He gestures in return for her to go, but she shakes her head. She has to go in last so she can clean up the water her father will have splashed over the countertop or dribbled on the floor as he groped for a towel, and she'll have to neaten towels he may have left wadded on the sinkshelf or trailing off the towel rack almost to the floor.

They've finished, and the sky's gone completely dark, but the landscaper hasn't yet returned to pick them up. Ronnie and her father could easily walk back to their campsite, but the landscaper pays her cash at the end of each day. They've not only replaced all the sod and hosed the mud off the lawn and driveway, but they've swept the asphalt and raked the grass to make it stand upright again, and, even if they could still see, there's nothing more they can do but wait for the truck to return. Her father's stomach is softly growling. Sitting on the lawn, in a dry spot they hadn't dug up or hosed down, under a ficus tree, each of them leaning their spine against one of the three low trunks, she can hear cellophane crinkle, then Manuel taps her arm with a sandwich cookie. "Gracias," Ronnie murmurs, passing the cookie on to her father. "I need a day to go to the store myself."

"Donde está tu casa?" Manuel asks.

"Our house? Um . . . We no have un, I mean, una casa. Um . . . No Casa."

"Por qué?"

"Um . . . we sold it? Um . . . sorry, I don't know how to say it." A lot more than that she can't explain. Like why she's done everything backwards, couldn't even think enough ahead to secure and pay for a weekly apartment before leaving the hospital. Like why traipsing around in dry salt marshes seems more important than making sure her father has a warm bed, food in his stomach, clean clothes and, for that matter, a simple roof. Like why with *her* making the decisions, they haven't even gotten to the arroyo hunting ground yet, her whole plan sidetracked in a stupid second of carelessness. But of course Manuel knows that part. How about trying to explain why her father's son wasn't the one now making the plans and giving instructions, why he hadn't ever become the new owner of their farmstead on Hanigan Hill, or why he wasn't even here to help them dig up other people's lawns. But of course, if Chad were here, there'd be no need to traipse around salt marshes or any other kind of field. And if she could explain why, maybe she wouldn't be here either.

Her body startles when her father says, "Tell her. Ate our own. Land." His voice garbled from disuse. He clears his throat, coughs and spits.

"What do you mean?"

"F— Eat own. Work own. Fame? F—" Staring at her mouth, "Say it."

"Farm?"

"Ours. She asked to know. *Tell* her. Everything. Did ourself. Plant. Animal. Everything the people—us—need. Alone. No other people. Come do *our* work."

"I'm not going to say that, even if I could. It would sound like an insult."

On her other side, Manuel softly crunches a cookie. She can feel night dampness begin to make her jeans clammy.

"No insult. Everyone should do own place. Work at her own—things. Grow what to eat. Not sit in the night. Waiting. Someone else to take up. To carry home."

"I'm sure he'll be here soon, Dad."

"Maybe she can. Give a shovel."

"Dad, it's *he*—"

Like the sound of a hoard of buzzing insects, lights mounted on the garage roof suddenly come on, white light, blindingly bright, illuminating the whole driveway like arena lights, like on Friday nights when, from their living room windows, they could see the high school stadium ablaze down in Dictionary Valley. The buzzing fades behind the heartbeat of portable music, the pulse of a ball bounced on pavement, the beat and scrape of big sneakers, the rasp of coarse laughter and howled words. "Shhhh, Dad," Ronnie whispers, although her father has already gone silent. She and Manuel barely glance at each other. In identical positions, side by side, Ronnie and Manuel squat on their heels, keeping their butts off the damp grass—Ronnie's father will have a wet spot she'll have to dry over the fire before sleep tonight—knees close to their chins, hands cupping kneecaps. Manuel rests his forehead on his knuckles. Ronnie, breasts pressed to her thighs, continues staring out of the darkness at the figures flickering in the strange brightness, a pool of light that doesn't bleed, as though the darkness she sits within is a closet she can hide inside. She can't tell if they are the same boys. It would be too big a coincidence. But they are boys anyway.

Yellow headlights finally come down the driveway, flashing a beam across the lawn and ficus tree—Ronnie's father holds up one hand, Ronnie ducks, Manuel freezes—then the spotlight is past, the truck parks between them and the boys, engine idling, headlights cutting a swath to the house's front door. A tone in the truck sounds rhythmically when the landscaper opens the door, leaves it open, and meets the house's owner who has come out the front door and is following the headlight beam down the walk. Manuel nudges Ronnie, she hooks a hand in her father's elbow, and the three of them slip into the truck bed—Manuel goes first then helps Ronnie's father up. They settle against the truck's stake bed side, their backs to the boys, but the throb of music, bouncing ball and heavy feet never pause. Ronnie lets a breath out slowly, unable to recall how long she'd been holding it.

It's uphill, almost the entire way, to the neighborhood park where volunteers of some social agency have put out their annual Thanksgiving dinner for migrant workers. Spread on five end-to-end picnic tables, steaming mass-quantity industrial food in stainless-steel pans—identical to the hospital kitchen's fare—is augmented by a cauldron of corn-on-the-cob, pans of chili rellenos and tamales and beans and aromatic seasoned rice, bowls of cut tomatoes and cucumbers, sliced avocados, green and red salsa, baskets of fried pork rind, and stacks of hot, soft corn tortillas. There are pickled carrots, salted prunes, sautéed peppers, and baskets of pastries similar to the ones her father would buy on the way home from a hunting trip into Mexico, fragrantly bready and only barely sweet. Two trashcans are filled with ice and packed with sodas.

Besides the picnic tables spread with paper tablecloths depicting smiling turkeys and garlands of red and orange leaves, a large area is cordoned off with streamers of orange and yellow crepe paper. Bouquets of red and yellow balloons tied to trees or signposts blow in the breeze like flags. And, dangling from ropes suspended between trees, two piñatas bob and turn in slow circles—one a many-pointed star, the other a smiling black-and-red bull with gold streamers flowing from its horns. Bouncy music with trumpets, occasionally a male voice singing in Spanish, is piping through loud speakers resembling megaphones, the sound scratchy and muffled, but buoyant. The people gathering under the trees can't help but nod their heads or bob their shoulders back and forth. Many of the men from the hardware store parking lot, plus others she doesn't recognize, are already there, all dressed in their jeans, boots, t-shirts and flannel shirts, but there are also women in long skirts, toddlers and small children dressed as though for church in stiff peticoated dresses or little ties and v-necked sweaters, and a few boys anywhere from eleven to fifteen, dressed much like the men but their t-shirts are huge, billowing down to their knees.

The day after their late job, Manuel had handed Ronnie a note when she arrived at the parking lot. Written on an envelope, it was from Adrian and said, *Manuel said he tried to invite you to the picnic but thinks you didn't understand him. Sunday at La Costa Canyon Park, straight up La Costa then the first left. Come and eat all the grub you want.*

On a residential street winding on the rim of a canyon, the small park takes up three or four lots and butts up against the steep canyon slope, a chain link fence blocking access. Down in the brown, rocky canyon, unmistakable darker green foliage indicates a hidden creek—the same creek that passes quietly beside Ronnie's camp. As the ravine stretches north from her camp, it narrows to a thinner chasm. Houses ring the canyon's rim, on hills that have been bulldozed into flat layers.

After parking the bike and slowly leading her father down a meandering sidewalk past the decorated tables, Ronnie starts to direct him toward a concrete bench, but becomes aware of the children, playing on painted hobby horses mounted in a sandbox and a dome-shaped jungle gym, who momentarily pause their games to stare. It's not necessarily the children's gawking that causes Ronnie to continue down the path, but her father's unabashed gaping back at them. An observer would think they were two different species who'd never before seen one another. Ronnie sees Adrian in a group of men standing near the chain link fence, as though their hours spent leaning against the fence around the hardware store parking lot have caused them to gravitate to this fence as well.

"Hi," Adrian smiles as they approach. Beside him, Manuel grins, abashed and almost blushing. "You and your dad want a beer?" Ronnie notices they all have beer. Her father is already reaching out for a bottle, which Adrian takes from a grocery sack on the ground by the fence. As he passes the bottle to Ronnie's father, Adrian says, "We're tightening our ball—I mean, getting up our courage to go down into Box Canyon." He extends a bottle toward Ronnie as well, but she doesn't take it She's never had beer, except the root beer her father made in the basement. "Rumor is they're going to dynamite it soon, so it might be our last chance."

"What is it? I mean, why—"

"At the end of this canyon there's a vertical rock gorge with a pond at the bottom. The creek makes a waterfall down the rock walls going into the pond, then empties out of the pond and continues through this ravine . . . all the way to where you've been staying. It's pretty awesome. You'd never know these hills would have this little Shangri-la hidden away here." He lifts his bottle to his lips. Wearing short sleeves on a crisp day, but his ruddy skin looks warm.

"What're you going to do there?"

"See it one more time. Maybe take a dive. I've never had the resolve before, three or four people have been killed jumping off the rock walls toward the pool. I'm not even sure how deep the pool is, but apparently a few guys have missed the water completely. That's why they're supposedly going to blow it up. Someone owns it and they can't keep the riff-raff out, and people get hurt. It's like an urban legend—well, suburban legend, I guess—but this one's true. I've seen it. Wanna come with us?"

"My father couldn't possibly hike down there."

"He can stay here, he won't wander out of the park will he?"

"He's not *senile*. He's just . . ."

"Sorry, I didn't mean . . . But hey, he can sit here in the sun and eat all he wants for a change. How's he been feeling?"

"He likes working, but . . . it's strange for him when it's not his own property."

"Yeah, well . . ." Adrian gazes away, drinks again. "Don't know of many societies where everyone gets to own land, he was lucky he had his day, I'll bet he hired his share of wetbacks."

"No, he never did," she answers simply. Adrian still doesn't look back at her, drinking more frequently from his bottle which looks empty or almost empty. "Did I say something wrong?"

He lowers his face, his gaze returns from the distance, the film of ice melts from his eyes, a look that makes Ronnie's knees and gut hot. "Where did you come from?" he says softly.

In her peripheral vision, Ronnie can see Manuel look down, turn slowly away, then back up as though trying to leave without being noticed. In the background soft laughter and conversations in Spanish. White popcorn clouds skate across the sky, blot the sun momentarily and the air turns chilly.

"What do you mean?" she asks.

"It's like you were kept on some kind of survivalist commune."

"We weren't survivalists. I saw them on TV. I don't understand what you're saying."

"I'd love to hear about your life. That's all."

"There's not much to tell."

"Okay." He's still holding the unopened bottle she'd never taken from him. "I'll just wait 'til you're ready. Want a beer?"

"No thanks, I don't . . . Okay."

After the first half of the bottle, the hot looseness in her knees seems it'll be permanent and her head may as well be one of the meringue clouds circling the sky. She does leave her father at a picnic table where some older women are playing cards, puts a plate piled with food in front of him. The women, their black hair streaked gray, look up and smile, nodding, when Adrian says something to them. One has a gold front tooth that glints in a ray of sun as she grins and answers.

After climbing over a chained gate, they're heading single-file down the canyon on a zigzagging trail, sometimes barely discernible in the grasses, last year's dry stocks mixed with new green growth. Besides Adrian and Ronnie, four of the other men, including Manuel, are along on the excursion. Hopefully there'll still be food left by the time they return, as Adrian had promised when she'd slipped a tortilla from the stack with one hand and took a pastry from a platter with the other. They all drink from the bottles they're carrying, and Adrian has an extra six-pack. Ronnie's halfway through her second-ever beer. The man in front suddenly stops, pointing down into the canyon, saying something to the men behind him. Even if she could understand Spanish, Ronnie might not have been able to hear everything. A breeze seems to carry his voice in another direction. She can't see anything unusual down where he's pointing, a hillside spread evenly with grasses and green tumbleweeds, dotted with laurel sumac, a few rock formations that make lookout ledges.

"He knew someone who lived there for a while," Adrian says from behind her. The line starts moving again down the trail. "He thought he could still see some of the plastic shelter."

"You mean those tatters caught on a branch?"

"Yeah, you can buy those big sheets of plastic at Home Builders, if you need any more waterproofing."

"The guy must've lived just up the creek from where we are."

"Actually this is about a mile up the creek from you. Way too far in to be close to work, but it's starting to look good again. Bulldozer rumors never really go away, but recently have heated up. Especially with the community getting wind of the 'encounters'—that's what it's called when someone gets robbed or harassed—between those groups of kids and ag-workers."

"Bulldozers could easily get to where I am," Ronnie says. "That service road, that's what it's for I assume."

"Well, not specifically, but it sure does give them access to you. I assumed you'd just be temporary when I recommended it."

"Yeah, I hope." It's difficult to throw conversation over her shoulder. She tries to turn and walk backwards. "How do you—" She stumbles, Adrian reaches to catch her wrist but she's already regained balance, turns back around. Someone's giggling. "How do—" Like sentinels just off the trail, phoebes perch on the thinnest tops of fennel bushes then dart into the air for gnats and flies and return to another perch further down the trail. Regaining her breath, "How do you hear all these things—bulldozers coming, what the community talks about, who gets robbed or . . . beat up. . .?" Suddenly realizing the giggling has been her own. Her telltale heartbeat thuds hot.

"I guess my ear's always to the ground. Either that or I'm nosy! Actually a lot of the guys come to tell me what they hear, I guess they think I can do things they can't. Like go to the police or the city council. By now, because so many people come to me, they know I can tell them what else I've heard, sort of verify certain rumors, keep them updated, like I'm radio-free ag-worker."

"Do you tell people about . . ." Her free hand moves involuntarily to her chest—as though the chip and trill of a towhee in a nearby lupine actually comes from her ribcage—her other fist tight on the beer bottle, quickly lifts the bottle for another swallow, the harsh liquid getting warmer, not as fizzy, but still spreads lava down her throat. Adrian is behind her. She flashes a glimpse over her shoulder.

"About what?" he says.

Ronnie glances behind herself again, looks longer, but just for one or two steps, and her hand no longer on her chest.

"Oh," he says. "No. Not really. I mean . . . only as much as I had to in order to make sure people watch out where they go and keep someone else with them."

The men on the trail in front of her have been walking faster so a gap has opened up between Ronnie and Manuel. They're nearing the tangle of higher, denser bushes and straggly trees clustered near the creek. The hillsides are much steeper, the canyon a definite V, the houses at the crest at least a hundred yards up. Manuel and the others are disappearing into a dark crack between bushes as the trail now runs right alongside the creek. Bushtits and finches flee the bushes, twittering alarm, as the men advance into the thicket. "This would certainly be safe," Ronnie says.

"Too far from work but maybe I'll retire here," Adrian answers with a chuckle.

"It wouldn't take that long to hike up the trail to the park, then take the road to work . . . or wherever."

"But getting supplies down here would be a bitch—"

Ronnie flinches, finds her jaw clenched, lifts her eyes to watch a pair of mockingbirds chase and harass a raven.

"Sorry," he says, softly, "Anyway, I probably *will* have to look for a new place, but this ain't it. Probably have to push further north, closer to Pendleton."

"What if—" She stops before ducking into the shady part of the trail through the bushes. "What if they just bulldozed one big camp—maybe they'd think they got it all and not bother looking for any more little ones, like yours."

Adrian holds a branch aside so she won't have to duck as low. "Well, they did feel satisfied for a while after they dismantled Los Diablos."

On the other side of the bushes, the terrain is suddenly rocky, with sage and grass poking through fissures. Burned skeletons of bushes and trees attest to a recent fire. Then the canyon ends. The other men have already arrived at a place where the two hillsides on either side of the creek have abruptly met, forming a craggy pocket protecting a deep-looking, nearly black pool. On three sides of the water, sheer granite walls rise up probably a hundred feet. The creek, still swollen from recent rain, swashes down the lips and ledges of one stone face, not a true water-fall but a river running straight downhill over rocks, splashing into the pool at the bottom. A skinny sycamore tree, nearly stripped of branches, leans out over the pool from one side, its trunk growing from a crack in the steep rock. A ratty rope secured to the tree near the top, dotted with knots and frayed ends where it has been broken and tied together, dangles over the pool. Bottles and cans, plastic bags and cellophane wrappers, a few tires and abandoned shoes are scattered, even caught in branches. A withered leather belt flutters from a twig, hung there as though in a dressing room. And on the rock faces of the box canyon, words Ronnie can't read have been painted, some with fancy lettering, fat and white with black outlines, words overlaying words, but she can only recognize a few letters, mostly S, T, and P.

"Beautiful, huh?" Adrian says.

"But it's wrecked. How do they get up there to write, anyway?"

"Just pretend you're discovering the ancient cave writing of the Kumeyaay people. Here,"—he picks up a triangular plastic box that once held a store-bought sandwich—"One of their cooking vessels, this one used for frogs and crickets, or maybe for snakes, little baby snakes cooked tender so you can just pull the spine from your mouth all sucked clean of meat."

The other men are standing in a group, talking and laughing softly, then one takes the empty bottles from the others and comes toward Adrian. It's Manuel. He and Ronnie exchange bashful smiles, then he drops the empties in Adrian's sack and pulls out three full bottles.

"Last one?" Adrian offers her another beer.

"No you take it."

"We'll share." He holds her bottle steady, his fingers wrapped on top of Ronnie's around the glass, as he pours half the new bottle into hers. His vivid eyes concentrate on the yellow liquid as though performing the final phase of a scientific experiment. "Hey, how about you take a swing out over the pond?"

Drinking, Ronnie turns to gaze at the tree. It's almost a snag, which, in swamps or meadows are preferred perches of raptors, providing them unobstructed views of terrain, but here in this crevice canyon it wouldn't be as serviceable. Still gazing up, she startles at the coincidence of a hawk soaring above the granite walls, but it's actually another raven. The twitters of sparrows cease, as though they also mistook the shadow for a hawk.

"What's the matter, you never climbed a tree before? C'mon, I'll give you a boost."

"No, I—"

"Hey, c'mon, have some fun, you're too good at saying no."

She turns toward him. Her face feels like a mask, the kind with only eye holes, no mouth and no expression.

"Oh jeez, I'm sorry. God, again. I'm sorry. I keep stepping in it, don't I?"

"I've climbed trees." The sparrows begin twittering again, first one, then several more. Behind her, a resonant plunk and spatter—one of the other men has tossed a rock into the pond. "And I've been the one who wouldn't take no for an answer."

A hot night in July, a bed just a griddle sheathed by thin cotton, no need for covers, every flaming welt throbbing in rhythm, no breeze through the open window to soothe fevered skin, but one or two shrieking mosquitoes found a rent in the screen, and if Chad was suffering the same distress, it was apt punishment for spattering our water and mud creatures across the hot, dry hillside that afternoon. His legs pokadotted with pink calamine, he'd gone to bed still sniveling, our mother beside him in the dark, singing a camp song, OH DEAR WHAT CAN THE MATTER BE or WHERE HAVE ALL THE FLOWERS GONE or KUMBAYA.

Someone's laughing, Lord, Kumbaya
Someone's laughing, Lord, Kumbaya
Meanwhile the soft, wet bodies of minnows and pollywogs, fragile water skaters, slick-skinned frogs, even an armored crawdad, had been coated in dry dirt or impaled on prickerbushes, slapped against rocks, their mouths opening and closing, their moist flesh growing sticky, then withered, then brittle.

The flopping of weary tails slowing, growing heavy with sand, abraded by grit, liquid eyes filmed over with dust, ants swarming over their bodies and tearing off pieces of them while they continued to gasp silently for breath.

Someone's crying, Lord, Kumbaya

Someone's crying, Lord, Kumbaya

Something Chad didn't even know, while our mother ministered him in a cool bath: down in the tree house, our clawed frog, hungry again, went hunting. Slipped out of the gallon jar, found nothing but dry boards, tiny curled parched peppertree leaves, the dust from the bottoms of our sneakers. Slithered to the edge and could go no farther, turned to dead leather jammed nose-first into a corner of the platform.

Oh dear, what can the matter be?

Johnny's too long at the fair.

Probably, after Chad finally drifted off, our mother came to sing in my stifling room, but fitful sticky sleep prevented me from knowing.

A new venture for the new day, tears forgotten, he scratched at his legs and was ready for the next scheme. In the tree house, with coffee can pails with wire handles our father had made, we harvested clumps of pepper growing in our tree. Like miniature clusters of grapes, each peppercorn encased with a papery husk of bright red—rubbing them between our palms we would remove the stems and red paper, eventually have pails of peppercorns to dry then test in pepper-grinders. Our mother would exclaim with round eyes and mouth, use our pepper in rabbit stew or spaghetti sauce, perhaps then we would sell some door-to-door to other homes on Hannigan Hill.

We'd picked all the clumps we could reach from the platform and from the sturdy thick branches we could sit astride like horses. The rest of the peppers were higher. We could reach a few more by standing on the 2x4 border of our platform, hold the tree's trunk and balance on our toes, extend the free hand up to the tips of the graceful willowy branches laden with ripening pepper.

Chad said shake the tree and he would pick them up from the ground.

They won't fall that way, only dead leaves. Come on, stand up on the railing. It's easy.

Did Chad actually say no? He didn't dare.

So, balanced like tightrope walkers, we walked the rail, only four inches higher than the platform, but at the outer edges, allowing us a means to lean way out, grab at the furthest branches. A droning fly, smelling the stagnant aquarium, smelling sweat, circled, buzzed, homed in, and with a thin squeal, the two bigger feet landed back on the platform, arms waving the pest away.

What happened? he asked. What is it?

Here come the wasps, Chad, the wasps, they're here, they found you again!

Screaming long before he fell, batting his face, releasing the tree trunk to flail with both arms, screaming, screaming, nothing stinging, nothing assailing him, arms not waving in attempted flight but to ward off the phantom hoard of angry stingers.

Most of the broken-off branches have left enough of a stump for her to climb the skinny sycamore with relative ease, gripping with her knees. The coarse bark rasps against her palms and fingers even though her hands are callused. The tree is at an arching angle, out over the water, so when she gets to about four feet from where the end of the rope is tied, she's also close enough to the upper third of the dangling part to reach out and gather the rope in. Then she slides partway down the tree again, so she's still eight or ten feet off the ground, but now has the rope with her. Gripping as tightly as she can above one of the knots, she kicks away from the tree and swings out over the dark, motionless water. The men laugh and cheer, words of encouragement she doesn't understand. When she swings back to the tree she wraps her legs around the trunk, then immediately releases herself for another swing out over the water. A scrub jay lands near the top of the sycamore, screeches, then flies away. The third time back to the tree, Ronnie lifts her legs and hits the trunk with the bottoms of her boots, lets her legs coil then kicks off from the trunk to make her next outward swing even faster. The rope is abrasive against her palms, but a hot lump in her stomach and chill in her neck urge her to kick off the tree three or four more times.

From out over the water, she calls "How do I stop?"

"Just let go and land on your feet."

"Are you kidding?"

"I'll catch you." And he does, just before she lets go of the rope, and her body slips feet-first through his hands, her boots hit the ground on either side of his, she catches herself against his chest, his body bracing against the jolt of her landing, her hands on his shoulders, and his arms are around her, but then they're not anymore, and they're all on their way back up the trail toward the park, from somewhere far away the jay screeching again, up close the empty bottles tinking in the plastic bag Adrian carries.

. . . leaving only the whisper of sand pushed aside, pebbles rolling, the silent effort to muffle a grunt or moan beneath soft but heavy breathing . . . the clink of shovel on rock . . .

Chad holding a dead hawk up by its wings—making it fly, dip and soar over our heads as we dig—impersonating the CAW CAW of its cry.

A mistake, an accident.

Our knees buckle to squat below the line of fire, the reflex so quick, so instinctive, impossible to say for sure which came first—the motion of our mother's gun being raised or the children hitting the dust at the sound or sight of game.

Call it simultaneous—crouch down, knees hit the dust, fingers in ears, head up, the report from our mother's gun, our father's shout, and the screaming.

MOMMY—
SHUT UP, SHUT UP, WHY DID YOU—HOW COULD YOU—
QUIET, AL, HUSH UP, RONNIE—
MOMMY—

Nothing would undo the shot, best to bury the mistake . . . deep enough so it's gone forever . . . only sticks and pocket knives for digging, for cutting the clay, only hands for scooping, it seemed the hole would never be deep enough, would take forever . . .

We dug, with boot heels, sticks, fingernails, the butts of shotguns. Suddenly the vast field existed only beneath our hands . . .

The vast, arid bottomland could hardly be touched, let alone filled, offered no resistance to our voices, just sucked the sound out of us and dispersed it, leaving only the whisper of sand pushed aside, pebbles rolling, the silent effort to muffle a grunt of voice or moan beneath soft but heavy breathing, the clink of shovel on rock.

Chapter Seven

After lukewarm turkey and sweet potatoes, tamales and rice, chili rellenos and stuffing, her father is dozing at the concrete picnic table, his back bowed, his chin on his chest.

But Ronnie, her stomach aching, her head still light, is being blindfolded and spun around, hearing herself laughing, saying "*wait*!" Adrian's voice laughing too, telling her, "Life's too short to wait, and parties are even shorter," and "If you wait too long, someone else will crack it open," pressing a plastic baseball bat into her hands. The music as dizzy as she is, bouncing, going round and round, she staggers—giggling in her pounding stomach, sucking back hiccups—three or four people clapping in rhythm, voices calling something like *ya! ya!* Adrian's voice easily located in the noise, also calling, "to your left, swing, swing *now*!" She swings the bat and reels, stumbles, hitting nothing, holds the bat out and makes a slow circle, but touches nothing, startles when big hands land on her shoulders, but knows immediately they're his, and he turns her, steadies her, whispers hot against her ear, "five feet straight ahead, then swing."

She's already watched some of the kids, the littlest ones, without the blindfold, one at a time go at the other piñata, hitting at it with the bat while someone raised and lowered the swinging red-and-black bull to evade their efforts. Then the bigger kids, old enough to be blindfolded, skillfully got themselves close enough, unfazed by having been spun to confuse them, to make them dizzy and undo their sense of direction. They flailed rapidly, even viciously with the bat and damaged then cracked the cardboard and paper piñata while the rest of the screaming kids dove beneath to scoop up candy and plastic toys.

Several people are singing and clapping with the music, another chorus wails *ohhhh* every time she swings the bat, counting her swings, *quatro, cinco, seis* . . . But she never connects, and finally he catches her again, the bat lifted from her hands and he holds her shoulders to stop her, then reaches behind to untie the blindfold. She's breathing hard like she's been running, raises her spinning gaze to his face and crinkled eyes. "I missed!"

"You missed big time, you weren't even close."

"Wow, but I was dizzy, I couldn't tell where it was."

"Yeah, maybe you should'a tried before the three beers." Laughing again, "You're a lightweight, girl." He's guiding her to the table where her father sleeps.

"Three? Oh my—" She sits and lands hard on the bench because she hadn't judged how far down it was. Her teeth clack together. Adrian sits on her other side, extends his arms along the tabletop behind them, one hand once again holding a bottle. She doesn't know where he picked it up, nor where he got the soda he hands to her. Ronnie takes a deep breath, then feels herself sag comfortably when she exhales. The soda can is cold. Her father wakes, but without a startle, merely opens his eyes and raises his head. Ronnie opens the soda and hands it to him.

"I've got to clear my head before I try to ride my bike."

Another child is batting at the piñata, a girl around seven or eight. After reaching up for every swing, she reaches behind herself to tug her skirt below her bottom.

"Here, this'll make you see straight." Adrian passes her a dish of what look like hoarhound candy, but the shapes are more irregular, more like elongated raisins covered in something white and crusty.

"What is it?"

"Saliditos. Salted prunes. Guaranteed to make you sit up and fly straight. Puckers your mouth so tight you won't be able to close your eyes for a week."

The taste is indeed pure salt, chewy salt, a little sour, but without the olive-oily taste of her father's salt-cured olives. She gasps, takes the soda can from her father and washes her mouth, gulps down several swallows.

"Good, I wanted to make you drink some of that. You're drunk and you're going to be hung over tomorrow—dehydrated." After putting the dish back on the table behind himself, he replaces his arms along the edge of the table, one right behind her shoulders, but not touching her.

"I'll buy. More," Ronnie's father says. He struggles to stand, and together, both Ronnie and Adrian push him upright, without either of them getting up from the bench."

"Do you need help, Dad?"

"Someone over there will fill a plate for him."

Dragging his foot a little more, as he does just after waking, her father hobbles along the line of tables, one hand reaching out as though to use the tables as a handrail, but he never actually does touch or lean on one.

"A lot different from our old family Thanksgivings," Ronnie says.

"What was that like?"

"Well, just the four of . . . Just us. But pretty traditional. A few times my dad bought a turkey chick in the spring then killed and dressed it for Thanksgiving. Or we might've had one of our chickens that turned out to be a rooster by accident. Sometimes duck. Once a pheasant he'd gotten on a hunting trip."

He sips his beer. "I have news for you, that's not all that traditional."

"But . . . nothing like this."

Another sip. He's holding his beer in the hand that's farthest from her—his arm extended behind her back doesn't move. "I don't think this is like traditional family Thanksgiving for anyone here."

"I know, they don't have Thanksgiving in Mexico, I didn't mean . . ." She blows out another deep breath, picks at the tab on the soda can. Her stomach is swimming a little uncomfortably. Screams and cheers as someone cracks the piñata. Then, almost immediately, a child is crying. "What about your family?" she asks.

"What do you mean?"

"What kind of Thanksgiving did you have?"

"Actually I'm half Mexican."

"So you didn't have Thanksgiving, I guess." The circle tab breaks off the top of the soda can. She pushes it up to the first knuckle of her index finger.

"No, I'm sorry. That's misleading. It's actually a mess. My Mexican half is from Spanish blood, they always held themselves apart, wanting to believe themselves more European than Mexican. At least that's what I suppose, I don't really know. It was completely unacknowledged in my house, being half Mexican. Maybe that's why I've chosen this life, I've wanted a heritage besides the conquistadores."

"But this isn't the only kind of Mexican life."

"I know. But this is the life I've adopted. I said it was a mess. I meant what the hell I'm doing. I call it my heritage but I didn't go looking for it, just stumbled over it while researching native plants. But now I say it's a habit I can't break, I say they need me, I say now that I'm here and have seen how they live, it's my obligation not to leave them. But am I doing anything *for* them?"

Ronnie leans back, turning to look behind Adrian down the row of tables to see how her father is doing. Her shoulders brush Adrian's arm. "I know about habits you can't break," she says suddenly.

"How long has it been just the two of you?"

"It's . . . well, a long time." Her father is on his way back, a plate held in his good hand and balanced on top of his bad fist. She can smell the spicy tamale sauce.

"Do you remember your mother?" He removes his arm from behind her, leans forward, holding the beer in both hands, dangling between his knees.

"Oh, yes. I was around eighteen when she . . ." Ronnie turns sideways, swings one leg over so she's straddling the bench, takes her father's plate and puts in on the table while he grunts with the effort of sliding himself onto the bench on the other side of the table. The music is turned up and several men begin dancing with some of the youngest children. Some of them pick the children up and swing them around off the ground. Most bend over, dancing at the toddler's level, letting the kid kick and twirl uninhibited. Others, forming a circle around them, clap and call out what must be ribbing and cheers. Still sideways, her back to Adrian, halfway facing her father, she says, "When I was a teenager, I had fantasies about sitting with my mother on the sofa, leaning against her, telling her how I felt about . . . everything . . . about not going to school . . . not knowing other kids . . . And about how I felt so guilty . . . I mean, about things I'd done wrong, or how sorry I was." She swallows, staring straight ahead, any lingering dizziness rising away from her like steam. "But I never did."

"I'm sorry." His bottle clinks onto the concrete tabletop, sounding empty now. "But," he brushes something off her shoulder, or maybe just touches her, "—not to be mercilessly blunt or anything—whose fault was that?"

"Both." Her voice with hard edges.

After the last unit test from Advanced Algebra, *after the last two-page report on the last chapter of* Peoples of the World, *after the final list of "questions for discussion" on the cold war in the history book called* We, The People, *she'd closed the cover. Stacked the books in the center of the kitchen table. "These can go back where they came from"—she'd prowled library sales— "when you have children, there'll be newer texts. You'll learn all over again, like I did with you." Her smile had always been the kind where the corners tighten and go down instead of up, but it had long ago ceased to seem happy.*

"But we're done. You've finished high school." Sweeping hair from your eyes, tucking it behind your ear, her hand lingering on the side of your head—your graduation cap.

The next day, after breakfast, a present on the kitchen table where the books had always been. An a.m. radio equipped to also pick up National Weather Service broadcasts and warnings, and a new swimsuit, a black one-piece, like the kind she'd always had, the kind she'd worn in college on the swim team, a racer's suit. First day of summer, June 21st, Dad loading his surf-fishing gear into the station wagon, Mom making egg-salad sandwiches, wrapping whole-wheat brownies in wax paper, filling a thermos with lemonade homemade from the single enthusiastic tree that left a dozen lemons a day on the lawn-clipping mulch around its trunk, like eggs in a nest box. Three towels, sweatshirts and jeans, firewood, ball caps with the fairgrounds logo on the front, and the air mattress—patched in a few places, smelling of salt from a thousand voyages in the frothy surf.

A chilly day, at first, the coastal stratum lingering until after noon, until after Dad finished gathering bait. The low tide turned, and he began fishing. The expanse of glistening sand at least twenty yards down to the water line—he was way out there, in water that swelled and drained from ankle to waist-deep. The low tide had been an extreme one, giving Dad hours of fishing time as it came back in. Mom in a sweatshirt sitting upright on her towel for hours, dragging a stick through the thick loose sand, staring out to sea. No thought that she might ask you about plans, a career, or where the husband would come from to supply the grandchildren who would receive the passed-down education.

She said, The sun'll come through soon.

Finally.

A man and woman walked slowly along the damp sand, footprints melting behind them, the man's trousers rolled up to show chalk-white ankles, the woman in a skirt, holding her sandals. You'd always imagined these would be visitors from some land-locked state, their first view of the ocean, their first dip of a pallid toe into primal saline.

Your father won't come back for lunch. Be sure to save him a sandwich. I can wait.

Don't go hungry.

Three little children, genders unknown, all wearing fat padded swimsuit bottoms over diapers and carrying colored pails and shovels, screaming and running from the mild lip of water that spread up over the sand then re-treated. The children followed the line of water as it pulled back out, then squealed and ran away from the next. She must have seen them.

I did my best.

You should've been a teacher.

I was.

I meant—

She looked at you, a long look.

What?

Nothing, she smiled, just noticing you grew up. Gazed back toward the bright hazy sky, the greenish ocean, the breakers that seemed so far out but slowly getting nearer. The three children, by now, happily wet to the waist and on their knees digging muddy holes, one stood to peer into the heavy, drooping diaper-pants.

You grumble: Kids are never cold.

She shed her sweatshirt, stood, arched her back with hands pressed just above her buttocks, then bent over forward with hands dangling, spread her feet and lunged sideways, slowly, one knee bent then the other, stretching cool muscles, recognizable gestures. Took the mattress under one arm.

I'm going in.

I'll come too.

You said you were cold.

No, I was talking about those—

Smiling again, she reached down to lift the ponytail that would be would cut off the next day. She wagged it playfully, remarking, It's almost blond at the very tip, a real California girl.

Even you knew not many California girls in the seventies wore one-piece black racing suits, had unshaved legs, cleaned perch and wrapped the guts in used wax paper from lunch's sandwiches.

It was a long walk down to the waterline. Mattress held with both hands above her head, then when the water was calf-deep, she flung the mattress in front and dove onto it, kicking her feet and padding with her arms, raising the front edge like the prow of a rowboat to go up and over each advancing wave.

You didn't even notice how long she'd been gone until your father came in from fishing, the waterline had moved half the distance closer. Instead of saving him a sandwich, the two of you ate, saving hers. You wouldn't know until long after dark—the Coast Guard helicopter moving slowly up and down the beach, white spotlight sweeping the surf—that earlier in the afternoon the mattress had come ashore a hundred yards down the beach. But her body didn't return to the beach for several days, and then Dad went alone to identify and claim it, and he went alone to spread the ashes. Not back into the ocean—when asked, he said no, but never said where.

Shadows longer and air much chillier, Ronnie is holding her father's empty paper plate to keep it from blowing off the table, tells him to go use the restroom. "Take some napkins, Dad, and wash." She collects plates, empty cans, wadded napkins. Adrian could go join the knot of his buddies regathering beside the fence—everyone seems reluctant to depart and conclude the party—but he remains, perhaps drowsy, on the bench with table behind him, legs stretched out, arms once again extended on either side of himself along the tabletop. "I'll . . . uh . . . be right back." Adrian's eyes seem closed, but he smiles, possibly a reply.

The bike, with water bottles tied to the handle bars, is leaning against a Brazilian peppertree near to the closest trash can, likewise chained to the tree. Only diligent landscaping keeps the tree from creating a jungle forest of peppertree bushes sprouting from the underground snarl of roots that cause earthquake ripples in the ground where no grass grows around the trunk. As she fumbles to untie the bottles, fingers still clumsy with beer, an eruption of voices, just a few at first, like the deceptively gradual swell of a building wave. People start to look, start to stir, start to pull in one direction, a slow migration of motion, until, like the wave's crest, all at once the voices become outcries of hostility, clamors that precede a skirmish, and the calling of children's names. Motion becomes fast and embroiled, focused yet chaotic, people running and shouting, beer cans hurled, sticks brandished, the fence rattles, a child cries—the whole event mere seconds, not much longer. Two boys fly past the street-edge of the park going downhill on bikes, shouting curses over their shoulders. Then they stop at the far corner of the park, turn to howl a last clearly audible warning, *You're toast you old beaner, you're fucked, you bought your ticket to greaser-hell.*

The party participants are returning, some muttering, some speaking with more excitement, one with an arm around Ronnie's father, another holding her father's wrist and raising his bad arm like the winner of a prizefight. Adrian is among the group coming back toward the tables.

"What did he do, what happened?" Ronnie hurries toward them, a water bottle in each hand, bulging out over her knuckles like boxing gloves.

"He's a hero!" From behind, Adrian wraps his arms around Ronnie's father's ribcage, lifts him a few inches off the ground then sets him back down. Ronnie's father grins, his eyes ablaze, looking at Adrian who comes alongside and hooks an arm around Ronnie's father's neck.

"Those boys were hassling one of the little girls on the playground. For all we know they were trying to lure her out of the park."

Several men and some women are trying to come close and stroke or pat Ronnie's father's arms and shoulders, and they're all saying something, all in Spanish, pattering so quickly she can't pick out any words, making it more difficult to hear Adrian continuing, "Your dad was yelling *Shame, shame.* Who knows what might've happened, maybe nothing, maybe . . . but your old dad sounded the alarm."

"What I think he was saying, he was calling them Shane—"

"They want to know your father's name. They're going to want to thank him."

"It's the name of a boy who used to— Wait, so what those kids said, that threat, they were saying that *to* my father?"

"Your father's name is Shane?"

"*No*! Enzo. But . . . Did they threaten my father?"

"Who? They want to thank him. They're calling him Padrino." Adrian moves her father close to a bench and her father sits, still grinning, gazing at Adrian.

"*No*," she says, "those boys, that gang, didn't you hear them? They threatened him."

"Nothing new there. We'd all probably better move outta this immediate area."

"But they meant him, they specifically meant *him*, and what'll I do if . . ."

After several more pats on her father's back and pumps of his hand, most everyone has begun to wander away, packing their belongings, preparing to depart. The truck that brought the industrial charity meal has already picked up and left. The music shuts off abruptly when someone unplugs the speakers and begins winding up the cords. Adrian listens to one of his friends, not Manuel—one of the others—then says, "So, *Shanes*, that's the name of this bicycle-whiteboy gang? How does your father know that? Have you had a run-in with these same kids before they— before they robbed you at the bank?"

"No, we just . . ."

"Shane. She chased the men. Working our street." Her father completes an answer while Ronnie falters.

Monday, Tuesday and Wednesday, Ronnie and Manuel and Ronnie's father work three different jobs, two sprinkler systems, one re-sodding.

They seldom attempt conversation, but both smile when a transition phase of the job or a spontaneous moment of rest gives rise to an exchange of affirmative glances between allies. Monday, after getting into the truckbed, Manuel had softly punched Ronnie's father on the upper arm with a closed fist, and said "*campeón*." All three evenings, upon returning to their camp—when Ronnie expects to encounter a gasoline-soaked smoldering mess or merely tatters of their former shelter, with bicycle tracks crisscrossing the mud beside the creek—instead they find something has been left for them, a stack of tortillas wrapped in a dishtowel, four grapefruit, a plastic bag of peanuts in shells, a worn but mostly clean hand-woven blanket.

Thursday, Ronnie arrives at the Home Builders store when the doors open at six, then uses the previous two-days of pay to purchase two rolls of black plastic sheeting, twenty-four metal fenceposts, three rolls of duct tape, and bungies of various sizes. Unless the job today extends as late as 7:30 or 8:00, she has plans to make an extra trip to the grocery store this evening, after leaving her father in camp, and collect cardboard boxes.

Her scheme has come over her quickly and with persistence, joining, even embellishing nightly visions of courageous self-protection when the boys return (or slight variations when, instead, she's rescued by . . . someone else). The planned project is also absorbing enough to almost overshadow other night-thoughts—those of a new future life, including her father's improved body and spirit, when, together, they finally resolve her familial status, and after that formalize her vocation as a landscaper, maybe someday with her own business, even eventually buy another plot of ground—distant reveries that have jostled her sleepless brain for an hour or two after lying down in the sumac bush. The new plan is much more immediate, therefore easier to entertain, to bring into focus.

Even though, by the time she makes three trips to carry her purchases to the end of the parking lot where she left her father to wait with the men who will give him a doughnut and share their coffee, it's later than usual, Manuel is still not there. Ronnie rests her bags on the curb, beside the pile of metal fence posts. She hopes the landscaper will bring them in his truck all the way to their camp.

The men seem to be lining up, some digging into the pockets of their jeans. Then she notices the motorcycle with bug-headed driver idling in a car stall. The bug head swivels backwards, looking toward congregating men, tips down while one hand fiddles with something near the engine, then returns to midline to stare forward, the engine revving. The string of men is becoming a cluster, circling someone, and the someone is Adrian. Each man is handing him money.

"What's going on?" she asks her father as she wipes crumbs from his face with the bottom of his sweatshirt.

"Did you buy. The—thing. The tool. Sh— Shovel?"

"*Dad*, what's going on over there?"

"A person. Died."

"Really? Oh god—Wait here." She hurries over to Adrian. The men are casually dispersing, returning to the places where they wait for trucks to pull up and take them to work. Adrian looks up from straightening the bills in his hand as Ronnie approaches.

"Hey," he says, barely smiling. "Some bad news. You may not have any work for a while."

"Where's Manuel?"

"He's going back to Mexico for a while—I'm going now to meet him at the bus depot. Just heard yesterday about his cousins. Manuel's been expecting them for over a month, but they hadn't shown up. The three of them were going to go north to the Central Valley where some of the produce ranches have bunkhouses. Apparently when they came across, they were dropped off by a coyote and were waiting for another ride that never showed up, somewhere southwest of El Centro. Border patrol found them last week in the desert, completely mummified."

"Oh no . . ." her breath escapes with the words. "Here." She has a five dollar bill and some change left over after her purchases.

"No, I just said you may not be working for a while. Lee—your land-scaper—he got two other guys. The first guy he asked had a buddy so he took them both. I'm real sorry, but looks like you're odd man—or woman—out."

"Take it, please, and tell him . . . tell Manuel . . . he was nice and we were like partners. That sounds dumb."

Adrian looks at the folded bill pinched between her thumb and fingers, his face drawn, eyes grave. Then he takes it. "I'll think of something, compañera. He admires your tenacity."

"He said that?"

"I know what he meant. I better go. Sorry about the job. Maybe I can turn something else up, I'll keep my ears open."

"I'll come see you. I have something to tell you anyway."

With another sad smile and a wave, he turns toward the motor-cycle, mounts it, his body accepts the jolt of acceleration then joins the motion, and they are gone.

By Sunday, when she'll see Adrian again, when she'll go to his camp to ask about Manuel, and to tell Adrian her plan to build her own camp into a visible target for county officials to dismantle, by Sunday most of her new simulated camp will be finished.

She's yet to see any vehicle use the strip of asphalt painted straight down the slope of one hill, through the creek and back up the other side where there's a locked chain hanging across the pavement. At its lowest point, the road foundation was built above creek-level, but the engineers must have intended for the current to flow across the road, because where the pavement runs under the creek, it changes to concrete there, not asphalt. Concrete weathers better, isn't as porous. Where the creek approaches, the road foundation is protected from erosion with a solid bank of cement, a mini dam, thus creating the pool spreading in front of Ronnie's camp. On the other side, the road's foundation of bedrock is visible—it was built up with boulders and some hunks of cement from something that was demolished. The water, flowing smoothly over the road—eight to ten inches deep just after the rainstorm but down to about four now—cascades down the short drop over the rocks and jagged pieces that used to be something else.

The canyon, the locked service road, the pool, the creek have mostly drawn dog walkers, but also kids with fishing poles, even some adults with younger kids looking for frogs and tadpoles. Their old campsite was not just off the service road—about twenty yards upriver—but the new camp is even further back into the canyon crevice. Not as far as the tattered remains she'd seen from the path on the way to the Box Canyon waterfall, but another twenty or thirty yards further in from where they are, because as much as it'll be a target for county officials to bulldoze, Ronnie and her father will still need to stay here for a while. She hasn't yet collected enough money for a deposit on an apartment—and no more coming in has presented a problem she's tried not to think about. In fact lately she hasn't done much—make that hasn't done anything—toward accomplishing her father's promise. How long will it take, a day . . . at most two? After finishing it, she could take a day to go back downtown, get her paperwork from the safe deposit drawer and get her money from the bank. So if she's purposely stalling, is it only because of Adrian, because how will she ever see him again after the mission is completed?

Just do what comes next. Somewhere along the line, after her mother's death, she'd realized her mother must have mapped her schooling, which had started the Autumn after she turned seven, so she would finish the advanced algebra book, the history book, the science book, and all the others, at about the time public schools would let out, the summer after her eighteenth birthday. Even while she works— pounding fenceposts to support cardboard walls, strapping cardboard in place around 45-degree angles with bungies stretched from post-to-post-to-post, cutting plastic sheeting, taping it to walls and ceilings— she's not sure she can duplicate her mother's adept timing, but she'll try: She'll build a migrant camp. Not a huge one, but something that could hold five to eight men. Something a group of seasonal agriculture workers would be trying to keep hidden in this canyon. Something that *can* be kept hidden during the time Ronnie and her father still need to live here. Something a little safer, because of its size and the appearance that many more live here than just Ronnie and her father, so even if the boys on bicycles discover her here, they may be less likely to storm in. Maybe they'd throw rocks. Maybe Ronnie should get some shotgun shells, but she doesn't know if the gun's in good working condition anymore—she's tried to keep it dry, but it can't help but get dirty. Anyway, after building the new camp, she'll get more work and continue saving. Adrian told her that down on the coast road, the old highway that runs past the beach where years ago her family had fished, there are motels converted into apartments with weekly rents. He'd been telling her how lots of the guys who wait for jobs at the hardware store live in those places, although with rent to pay it's more difficult for them to send money home. Likewise she could save a lot, as long as they live out here, then a one-room place in an old motel a few miles from here could be her next step, or call it the *first* step—after she finally takes her father back to where the ashes are, then takes the ashes to the farmstead fifty miles south in Dictionary Valley. And now, if her timing is good, taking that step will be an appropriately apocalyptic turning-point: she won't help her father fulfill the unfinished family history until they're ready to make the move to an apartment motel, because that's also when county officials will be tipped-off about the good-sized migrant camp in the canyon right below all those houses— the same migrants, the anonymous informant will infer, who've been having skirmishes with local boys, and someone's going to be hurt if the camp isn't wiped out and the migrants forced to live elsewhere. So the camp she's building will be sacrificed. After that, *because* of that, Adrian won't have to move. The county will assume a menacing nest was cleaned-out, so won't bother to look for the smaller, insignificant two- and three-man camps. And after that? How long does it take to start a landscaping business? Would Adrian someday work for her? But like building a rock wall in your sleep, there's never a place for a last rock, you just keep lifting and fitting and lifting and fitting and there's always another rock and always another place for it, another layer, so when her thoughts get that far, she snaps back to what comes next, do what's next, do what's next, until she has four cardboard and plastic shelters, about four-by-four feet, clustered around a new rock fire pit that her father has spent these days constructing—even carrying some of the rocks from the old campsite—in a small clearing between two laurel sumac bushes and a lemonade berry, beside the creek where the water runs a little quicker than the pool where they used to be. On the other side of the creek, a hill slope of buckwheat, green tumbleweed and wild oats, so steep she can't see the houses at the top.

Your father would've worked with the same blind focus, do-what's-next, do-what's-next, not for inability to look forward but an unwillingness to look back. Just do what's next until the job is done, and after that another job, and another. First use the tree house platform to reach and saw through the biggest branches. So when the large branches are severed and all leaf-bearing tendrils and branches have been removed the tree house platform looks like a small piece of flat board being held in a half-open hand, the newly stumped branches like the ends of fingers extending up and around the wood. Now the platform itself would be destroyed, knocked free of the limbs with a hammer, broken pieces of two by four and one by eight with bent protruding nails flung from the shorn tree, landing softly in the nest of leafy shoots and off-shoots, with more of the thick branches to follow. Quickly the whole thing becoming a stump surrounded by logs, piles of thinner leafy branches, and broken lumber. Too dangerous to allow a child to stand below and watch. The logs would be stacked to dry and cure before use in the fireplace, the lumber cleared of nails and likewise stacked for firewood, the leafy tips dragged away and piled where they would rot to mulch on the hillside below the property. The stump would be shorn down so it was only inches from the ground, then holes drilled all over its surface and poison poured into each hole, so in another year or maybe two, the trunk itself would have died and rotted in its place, while the new asparagus bed flourished around it, hiding it from view.

He started taking the tree down long after summer tomatoes had been canned, both as sauce and stewed whole; after strawberries, too many to eat fresh, were turned to preserves; likewise boysenberries, plums, peaches, and apricots—the latter two also preserved whole or in halves; after summer turned the corner to September, the hottest month, and September wore slowly toward October. And wouldn't that have been the same fall your mother started lessons at the kitchen table after breakfast of fresh figs in milk and toast with jam?

Fill in the blanks . . .

P _ A C H . . . 'E' for peach
B _ A T . . . 'O' for boat
B _ A C H . . . 'E' for beach

While the worksheet she'd made was completed, she drew a picture of the rule: WHEN TWO VOWELS GO WALKING, THE FIRST ONE DOES THE TALKING. An O and an E with legs and arms, each with a walking stick and backpack, the O with a round open mouth and a cartoon bubble above its animated eyes, saying, "You be quiet and listen!"

With the start of formal home-school, Chad gone, no more plans for aquarium habitats, for blue ribbons from the fair—you joined them just doing what was next. Each day's arithmetic or reading task was what came next, and the next day's assignment would follow, would be marked in a book after your mother cleared away your empty plate and bowl. So no need even to look ahead to tomorrow or that afternoon, schoolwork would be placed in front of you, and you would do it—not ever stopping to daydream, certainly never about the pleasure of spending a Saturday dove hunting when the weekend came around.

A mistake, an accident.

Our knees buckled to squat below the line of fire, the reflex so quick, so instinctive, impossible to say for sure which came first—the motion of our mother's gun being raised or the children hitting the dust at the sound or sight of game.

. . . crouch down, knees hit the dust, fingers in ears, head up, the report from our mother's gun, our father's shout, and the screaming.

MOMMY—

SHUT UP, SHUT UP, WHY DID YOU—HOW COULD YOU—

QUIET, AL, HUSH UP, RONNIE—

MOMMY—

Chad holding a dead hawk up by its wings—making it fly, dip and soar over our heads as we dig—impersonating the CAW CAW of its cry.

Hunting season opens in September. You can't remember bird-dogging without Chad. You would've been too young to leave at home alone. Your father's hunting junkets to Mexico began years later. Did your father go si-

lently to the lagoon by himself, bring home only one limit of birds? Would that cause him to go more often, weekday afternoons after a day's work at the fairground, or did he go both Saturday and Sunday, hunting faster and quieter, without the burden of children in tow, bag his limit in a matter of hours and return home with enough daylight left to till garden areas for winter produce, to add another layer to a rock wall terrace in-progress, to strip the remaining now-rotting fruit from the summer producers and prune as necessary, to weed between rows of raspberries where the plants, thinking ahead, have sent their shoots for next year's crop?

Four days, the new, bigger camp, tucked in the brush fifty yards upcreek from the service road, is finished. Three empty shelters to stow their gear—which would easily fit into one—and the fourth for Ronnie and her father to sleep, the old painter's tarp becomes lining under their bedroll made of the blanket Adrian bought and the one they'd received as a gift. The baby high chair, sitting near the new bigger fire pit, now organizes her father's fishing equipment—hook points pricked into the old vinyl seat, bobbers lined up on the tray, the sapling poles leaning upright against the seat back. He's found enough fishing line for Ronnie to lash together a tripod of thin branches, which could hold a bowl of warm water for washing, if she can find a bowl. One thing she has found is a mayonnaise jar with a lid, lying in the gutter after trash day. Perfect for collecting ashes, or dirt that's pretending to be ashes. She washes the jar and lets it dry then stashes it with the gun in a shelter.

Friday she lets a visible plume of smoke trail into the sky in daylight, observes it from the service road, beside where the creek pours over. Then stops to watch it again from the top of the hill at the chain link fence, and again from the sidewalk on La Costa Avenue. From that far it could be from a chimney. A person would have to be thinking, planning to find a migrant camp then deliberately track the smoke to investigate its origin.

Sunday they've exhausted their stores of food, have eaten the last of the tortillas, biting around spots of mold that appeared after five days. With some of the money she has left, she'll have to get more, but will also scrounge what she can from behind the grocery store. On the dirt trail she used to use on her way to the hardware store, she'll pick from the orange trees that have stretched branches over backyard fences. That's also close to Adrian's camp.

She tells her father she needs room on the bike for supplies and he'll have to stay in camp. Please stay close. Stay inside if you can. Take a nap or be real quiet. Even though her father would not be shouting or talking out loud to himself, or to her absence, or to phantom memories, she knows she shouldn't be leaving him alone on a weekend day when he could be discovered by anything from a nature-lover walking a dog to marauding adolescent boys still holding their latest grudge. Adrian said they should stay at least in pairs; she should take her father along, although his company didn't deter the pack of boys the first time. Not until they saw the gun. Her father doesn't know that Ronnie moved the shotgun from its former location in the branches of the old laurel sumac to a new hiding place inside one of the empty shelters, wrapped in some leftover plastic, wedged between the cardboard wall and two of the fenceposts, so it just looks like the last extra end of plastic that's been tucked under the cardboard and rolled up inside the shelter. So she can't leave him alone for long. And *she'll* only be alone until she gets to Adrian's site. From there, perhaps he'll accompany her to the store and help her carry provisions back so he can see her new ruse encampment.

While checking the visibility of her campfire smoke, her bathwater was heating in the industrial-sized chicken-spread can she'd brought from the hospital. Every other day she uses a little toothpaste and her toothbrush to continue to scrub at the last traces of ink she thinks she can still see just above her breasts and around her navel. From her ribcage down to her slightly protruding hipbones, her body is flat, partially a hollowness from eating so little, but also tight with muscle. Her canvas pants fold over at the fly where she cinches her belt to keep the pants from falling down. Every three or four days she shaves her father's face, but the plastic razors are getting rusty. She hasn't been using them on herself so they'll last longer, but today quickly scrapes the hair from her armpits and soothes the nicks and burns with a drop of sunscreen under each arm. After washing, she rinses out the underwear she wore the last two days and hangs it inside a sumac bush to dry, empties the water and refills the can to heat some for her father. She tells him to douse the fire when he's done and leaves him to do his own morning bathing.

Picking oranges from someone else's tree is one thing at first light on a weekday morning. Sunday at eleven is a different world. People are outside in the yard, and Ronnie only manages to surreptitiously pick two oranges without shaking the branch, but the rest of the fruit is too high. If she leaps for more, not only will her arm and maybe even her head pop up above the fence, but the branch will bow down when she lands, then spring back up after the fruit is released, certainly enough for the newspaper reader on the patio to notice his tree suddenly dancing when there's not a whisper of breeze to encourage it to sway.

So two oranges, filled water bottles, that's all she has as she arrives at the viewpoint over the hardware store, at the erosion trail running downhill to Adrian's camp. A few dogs are barking in backyards on the cul-de-sac behind her. The bounce of a ball is several houses away up the street. Closer than that, the equally rhythmic snip of pruning sheers. But Ronnie would be not visible from any of the houses because she's behind an old brown van parked on the cul-de-sac, on the end where there is no house, where a low wooden fence with light-reflectors prohibits cars from progressing onto a parallel-rut vehicle trail which stays high on the canyon rim and veers north, away from the furrowed path leading down to where Adrian's camp is hidden. The van's bumper is rusty and its muffler is dangling, tied to the van's underside with string. She can hear a phone ringing in the closest house. Across the street, someone calls out a window, admonishing one of the barking dogs, but the dog only stops for a few seconds, its voice a high-pitched yap. Ronnie locks her bike to the wooden barrier. While threading the chain through her spokes, her heart leaps for a second when a man emerges from the back of the van, leaving the van's two back doors open. The inside is bare metal, as though burned out, and Ronnie can smell a condensed odor of bodies that have sweat in there. The man glances at Ronnie, then stands looking down the erosion trail toward the camp. He's wearing dirty polyester pants and a sweatshirt, a mustache that covers his mouth, and a cowboy hat with curved brim that almost covers his eyes. He's tall, rawboned and lanky with a small pot belly. She thinks he's not Mexican, but maybe he's come with news from Manuel, maybe he brought Manuel back to California, maybe he came to collect the rest of Manuel's belongings, if there was anything worth sending someone to pick up.

"Do you know Adrian and the guys down there?" she asks. The man doesn't answer, or she doesn't hear him. He moves forward, closer to the beginning of the trail, as though for a better view, then starts waving one arm in a gesture urging someone to hurry. Two women come into view, advancing up the trail. Neither is under thirty, maybe close to Ronnie's age, but both are dressed in tight cutoff shorts and platform high-heeled clog shoes with straps around their ankles. One has a long t-shirt knotted at her waist, her hair bleached blond with a tint of black at the roots. The other wears a short thin-strapped lacy tank top, her black hair dry and bushy with reddish highlights. Both have heavy thighs and big bosoms, smeary thick makeup caking their eyes and blood-dark lipstick. They're clutching each other as they make their way up the trail, their awkward shoes faltering on the dirt path.

"Hurry the hell up," the man says when they get close enough to hear his tight mean voice, not speaking very loud, "we have three more stops today."

Just when Ronnie thinks the phone might still be ringing behind her, she realizes the sound is now a mockingbird, perched on a weathervane.

The two women are speaking in Spanish. The man ignores them, either not understanding or uninterested in what they're saying, and they don't seem to care or notice that he's ignoring them. They board the van at the rear and the man closes the doors.

"What're'ya staring at?" The man suddenly slings words at Ronnie. She feels her jaw snap shut, whisks her eyes away from him, heads toward the dirt trail. "You're twenty minutes too late," the man smirks. "Honey catches them flies." His chuckle turns into coarse coughing, then the cab door of the van slams and the engine starts.

Her blood is hot in her face, pounding in her ears and throat. The sputtering and clanking rattle of the van, chugging out of the cul-de-sac, could be her bones collapsing from underneath her as she crumples, as she feels she might, or she might be rippling in a wisp of ocean breeze like a limp flag, teetering instead of standing on the top edge of the downhill dirt trail, perhaps powerless to take a first step, let alone tip forward to let gravity pull her feet quicker and quicker toward the camp. Repeated deep breaths leave her lightheaded, spots of bright color blot her eyesight.

But she finally does step forward, almost falls on some loose pebbles, opens her eyes, bats away the bleary wet blindfold, proceeds carefully, head down, eyes on the ground. A mutter of voices stops her. A low cadence of something she can't understand, then *huh*? Then "Ronnie?"

She raises her eyes. One of Adrian's friends—his name, she thinks, is Hernando—in boots and jeans but shirtless, faces her, squatting, a bucket between his knees, shaving lather on half his face, a not-too-clean towel in one hand and razor in the other. The other man has his back to her but is turning toward her as she looks up. It's Adrian. His hair is wet. He's combing and gathering it, fastening the rubber band to the ponytail. He says, "Hey, what happened to rolling a rock into camp so we know someone's coming?"

"I—" Her voice is a sticky noise in her throat.

"How long have you been there?"

"I . . . don't know. I guess I—"

"Yeah, jeez, sorry, but you caught us at sort of an . . . awkward moment. Is anything wrong?" He's fully dressed, but instead of the usual t-shirt is wearing a blue button-up shirt, long sleeves rolled to mid-forearm, top two buttons unfastened, the cotton's perfect-sky color crisp against his ruddy skin. "We're . . . Nando has to catch the bus to Baja, and I'm going to visit my parents. Our once-a-month homage to family."

The other man scrapes the razor across his face, swirls it in the bucket, returns the razor to his face, using fingers to tell him where his mustache is while he traces around it with the razor.

Adrian clears his throat, then says, "We're running a little late."

"Why didn't you just get a ride from . . . those . . ."

"Ronnie . . ."

The razor taps against the side of the bucket. The man's face now buried in his towel. The breeze they catch from the lagoon picks up a little, but it carries the smell of toilet chemicals. An old newspaper page skitters over the ground until Adrian steps on it. She's not looking at Adrian's face. He's wearing tennis shoes today instead of boots.

Somewhere up the hill a lawn mower is started. And as though the ignition also revved her voice, "Do your parents buy you shoes so you can save *your* money for—"

"Come on, Ronnie." The crumpled newspaper in his fist. He stuffs it into a plastic grocery sack hanging from one of the bushes, half full of other trash. The other man stands, holding the bucket, turns away and heads down hill out of camp to dump the frothy water. "You can't be . . . I mean, this is awkward, let's just . . ."

"I have to go. Sorry I . . ."

"Wait, I'll walk out with you—"

" . . . disturbed you."

"Wait."

"No, it's okay . . . no . . . never mind . . ." She's running back up the trail. Trips once and catches herself with one hand, pain zinging through her wrist, but her feet collect underneath herself again and keep going. Only when she gets to the bike, her wrist throbbing, does she brush away dirt and pebbles and a few stickers stuck to abrasions on her palm. Instead of using the dirt trail behind the houses, she rides the bike on the road out of the cul-de-sac, pedals without gliding, breathing hard then harder until there's a little sound of her voice at the bottom of each breath, grunting with each pump of the pedals, knees hitting the water jugs tied to the handlebars, fleeing through the neighborhood streets where each coffee-drinking lawn-waterer or flower-snipper or patio-sweeper looks straight at her but none waves or says good morning.

She doesn't get off the bike until she's beside the creek on the service road. A pair of mallards are standing on the muddy bank where their old camp had been. Iridescent male and brown-streaked female, they ease into the water as she gets near them. Approaching the encampment on the creekside path, she can still smell the fire she'd doused before leaving, now a cold ashy scent. Her breathing has slowed some by the time she enters the square of shelters. Her father's feet and lower legs protrude from their sleeping shelter, but not because he's reclining. Soles of his boots on the ground, knees bent, he's sitting inside the shelter but has scooted forward so his hands and lap, in the doorway opening, are in light, and with his good hand he's working at unsnarling a tangle of fishing line. With her pocketknife, Ronnie cuts one of the oranges in half, then one of the halves into quarters, offers the quarters to her father, who looks up without reaching and says, "Busy now." She places the quarters on his lap, under the snarl of line, then holds the remaining orange half to her face and forcefully scrapes the pulp with her teeth, smashing the fruit against her cheeks and chin, eyes closed, tears dripping past her nose and mixing salt with the citrus acid which also stings in the scrapes on her palm.

"What did you take? What more? A shave?" her father says.

"No, I didn't get a shovel. Just water." When he doesn't respond she continues, "We'll both go again tomorrow when everyone's at work. Then we need to . . . just go do what we came here to do."

"And come home."

"*Go* home. Well . . . *find* a home."

He stops unsnarling to slowly wind the newly freed line onto a small piece of wood where a scanty layer of line is already wound, not very tight nor smooth.

Slowly Ronnie's knees buckle and she sinks to the dirt in front of her father in the doorway of the shelter. "I should thank you, Dad, for protecting me . . . all my life . . . from . . . unnecessary garbage like . . . you know, so much useless . . . dumb . . . *shit*."

"Soap your. Face. Bad talk. Young lady."

"Oh Dad, I'm no young lady, *look* at me." Fists clenched, one still holding the orange half, juice dripping down her arm. "You should know what I am, you and mom helped fix it so I wouldn't be *any-thing!*" Abruptly she snatches the wooden spool of fishing line from her father. His hands jerk up toward his face, quivering. "Did you ever stop to think maybe I wanted to go to school, to college, have a career, do something *else?* Maybe even have . . . *friends?* Maybe I wanted more than to just take care of your little farm and then take care of you until I was too old for any life of my own, did you ever consider that maybe I was only trying to make up for . . ."

"Our mother. Took you. Brought you. No . . . teach. *Taught* you—"

"*My* mother. She was *my* mother. And *what* did she teach me? That everything I needed was at home with my parents? That everything I would need to know I already knew by the time I was eighteen? That I wouldn't even need a *mother* any more after that? What did *I* know? *You* could've suggested I leave, do something for myself, why didn't you *make* me go? *Push* me out? It had damn well been long *enough.* Did you *want* me to feel guilty the rest of my life . . . because it ensured I'd never leave you?" She throws the spool of fishing line, but it's too light to go far. It pulls the attached snarl of line from his lap, a rusty hook at the end flicking briefly between their faces, her father's eyes following it like a dog's. Then his eyes rise when the pair of mallards fly past, low, following the creek, quacking with their wing beat. "Okay, I'm guilty, is that what you've been waiting for me to say all these years? Okay, I killed him, or I caused it—all of it, and all of *this*, living in the dirt and weeds, planning to collect ashes that aren't there anymore . . . and should never have been there in the first place. Considering all that, why should anything that happens *today* feel so damn bad?"

Her father leans forward, groping with one hand, finally uses Ronnie's shoulder to get himself upright. He retrieves the spool of line, holds up the snarl until he locates the dangling hook, pinches it between thumb and forefinger of his good hand, then, laboring, breathing hard, he fastens the hook to the pocket of his flannel shirt, with his teeth clips the line about six inches from the hook, then clips the line coming out of the other side of the snarl. In all it takes him three or four minutes. He shuffles away to bury the snarl in the fire pit—where it'll melt as soon as a fire is started—then, his back to Ronnie, says, "Us—all us—always do what must do." Only then does she let her forehead fall against her clenched fists, let her shoulders heave, let her eyes get hot and wet and her mouth stretch into grimace no one sees. The orange falls to the dust at her feet.

It doesn't last long. Her father clears his throat. He says, "Ronnie." Then she feels him touch her head, maybe just two fingers, timid in her short, thinning hair.

She looks up and rocks backwards onto her butt on the ground, and doing so moves her head out of his reach. "Okay, Dad, if it's easier to keep facing the same old misery . . . if we just go do it, go do whatever you think we have to do, whatever you promised to do . . . *Then* can we. . . ? I don't know . . . *what* should we do then?"

"They—We always do. We come *up*. We always . . ."

"Don't say survive."

It was a game like Simon Says, but it was also like training Pavlov's dog. The whole family out on the back bottom part of the farmstead, each parent with a shotgun and wearing their hunting vests, we were around two and almost five, giggling and jostling to follow the funny rules. Rules that had us making sure we were always behind our parents, always facing their backs, never beside, never EVER in front of them. They walked side by side down Roadrunner Road, simulating a morning hunt, with us in tow, and when they turned one way or the other, we skittered to remain behind them, and our mother chanted a rhyme,

> *wherever we go, we stay behind*
> *whatever we do, make not a sound*
> *when the guns go up, we hit the ground*

That meant when they raised the shotguns, taking aim at a flying dove or quail blasting out of the underbrush, we were to immediately drop in our tracks and stay down so our parents would be able to swing all the way around with guns raised, keeping aim and taking all four shots as birds flew past from front to rear or circled around us.

"Ronnie, make sure he knows this, make sure he gets down, I'm not going to be able to turn around to check."

After four shots—we counted them off—we were instructed to wait until the guns were cocked open and our parents reloading, only then were we to gather up the four shells then venture out into the field, wherever the birds had gone down, and, right there, dead or alive, hold the body with one hand, fingers of the other hand in a ring around the neck, pop the head off and drain most of the blood. After decapitating and draining, we were to return and slip the bird into a pouch at the backs of the hunting vests, then remain back there where the vests would slowly begin to bulge, where a stain of blood would begin to grow at the bottom. For each bird we put into the vests, we put a pebble in the pocket of our jeans, so they could keep count easier, without unloading the birds from the vests, until a limit of pebbles was counted, the day's hunt completed.

"Whoever puts the bird into the vest picks up the pebble, not both of you," our mother warned. "Ronnie, make sure he understands."

On the day we practiced, when they raised the shotguns—our mother called out "down!" and we squatted—our father tossed two or three beanbags made of orphan socks. "Watch the birds that drop," he tutored, "your mother and I have to keep aiming at the ones still flying." And our mother voiced the four mock shots, "Pow, pow, pow . . . POW." When they cocked the guns open, we took off into the brush and tumbleweeds to see who could find the most beanbags and therefore win the most pebbles. If one of us forgot and started to stand too quickly, getting a head start, our mother never missed the call: "No, you're out, you don't get to go for the bird this time."

We had to practice longer than the time it took for them to explain the rules, because we had to remember the rules over a span of hours, when we got hot or bored, when we got tired or hungry, when our mother stopped reminding us to squat down, we still had to remember: THE GUNS GO UP, WE HIT THE GROUND, THE GUNS GO UP, WE HIT THE GROUND. Until—well-rehearsed choreography, everything in perfect synchronization—when on a real hunt, our response was as automatic as snapping a fishing rod back when the fish strikes or hitting the brake when the light turns red. Repetition perfected our stimulus-response: eventually our response to hit the ground was no longer triggered by the raising of guns, but by the whistle of the dove's wings that sounded just before the guns went up.

A mistake, an accident.

Our knees buckled to squat below the line of fire, the reflex so quick, so instinctive, impossible to say for sure which came first—the motion of our mother's gun being raised or the children hitting the dust at the sound or sight of game.

Chapter Eight

She doesn't dream very often, not that she remembers. Sleep is either thick, mute and stupid, or thin and imbued with sounds and smells hovering in the living world, mixing her rest with cognizant reality, like a wary animal. But if she dreams, as in an alternate, colorful, breathless adventure unrelated to waking life, she's not sure. There have been a few murky night-heavy episodes where Chad is alive, has been alive all these years but she just failed to notice that he was never gone, and no one bothered to inform her, and now, even though she still doesn't see him, still doesn't know how he looks as a man, it's the knowledge suddenly thrust upon her: that he's alive and living, as always, on the farmstead, so she needs to make up for over three decades of neglect, of not setting his place at the table nor offering to share a can of soda, failing to wash and fold his clothes, and not making him a cake for his birthday. She doesn't wake in a cold sweat nor wondering where she is, although once—she doesn't remember if it was before or after they'd left the farmstead—her heart did hammer her awake when she saw the splash of something falling into a clear pool, and she immediately dove in, knowing what it was and meaning to fish him out. He'd be light enough and she was strong, but when she went under and opened her eyes, the clearer-than-air water in the pool was miles and miles deep, and she could see forever down into the crystalline liquid where a five-year-old Chad was dropping like a stone, already hundreds of yards down, moving silently and swiftly, dwindling, receding, while her adult body floated at the surface, unable to dive down as fast as he sank, and no underwater scream, not even so much as a bubble escaped her lips.

A failed rescuer, and now she dreams of being rescued, although she seems to be fully awake. While walking her bike up the steepest incline on La Costa Avenue or still waiting for work until noon at the hardware store parking lot—after most of the others who would earn nothing that day have already drifted away—she's entranced, a few flickering seconds at a time, by sensations of herself being carried in strong arms, the hot breath of his exertion and alarm gasped against the side of her face, or maybe she's carried on his back knapsack-style the way she used to carry Chad when they were five and seven. By now their sizes would be reversed, her head only reaching his shoulder, easy for him to hoist her and run, her cheek tucked against the back of his neck or chin hooked over his shoulder, his hair whipping in her face, saving her from she's not sure what—flood, fire, earthquake, enlarging hoards of kids with bats and bikes, the bulldozers that he forewarned will eventually plow their spindly, broken possessions into the ground.

But not all her time seated on the parking lot's asphalt curbing is spent in illusory flights to safety. She continues to arrive early because the men still share their breakfasts with her father, and she can tell he likes to stand among them, listening to their spare exchanges of words. Sometimes when a pickup idles for a moment while the driver speaks to a man outside his window, Ronnie's father will come close, put his hands on the edge of the truckbed and look inside, at the tools or bags of cement, bricks, paving stones, PVC or topsoil for the day's job. If he hasn't moved away by the time the chosen workers have climbed in back, the driver will slap his hand once or twice against the metal on the outside of the truck door, so her father will back away and the truck will pull out.

Meanwhile Ronnie sits and figures. She'll need to make back the money spent enlarging their decoy camp. Everyday admonishes herself for worrying about *that* when she could just abandon everything, go back downtown and get her own money from the bank. Then what, come back up *here* to get an apartment? Is this the only place to find one of those weekly-rate flats converted from rooms in an old motel, one room with kitchenette—it's a start, some place to use as an address so she can apply for more reliable work, maybe at a nursery or at the hardware store, another hospital job not beyond her willingness either, although that won't lead to anything bigger, more satisfying or with more potential. Amazing that her brain has started this habit of leaping so far ahead when she knows even the right to have fanciful thoughts— of a landscaping business or job at a wholesale nursery or flower farm, a small organic vegetable farm to supply local restaurants—has to wait for her to finish what she's started. And it all requires planning and timing: locate the hunting grounds and likely location where the ashes were scattered—probably do this in advance so everything can be put into motion at the point when the actual pilgrimage takes place, and that can't happen until she's gotten money for the apartment. But when all is ready—the money earned or retrieved, the location learned— somehow tip the authorities as to where they'll find a medium-sized migrant camp in a suburban canyon near La Costa Avenue. Who are the authorities and how to tip them is more groundwork to investigate in the meantime. But once accomplished, by the time the bulldozers roll in, she and her father can be halfway to the hunting site, or leaving the site already and on their way for the conclusive visit to Dictionary Valley. The newspaper or TV will report that an illegal camp was destroyed, so the community will stop buzzing and assume that since the nests have been wiped out, the pests who inhabit them will move on, move further north where they won't be a threat to developed neighborhoods. With the general assumption that the problem has once again been eradicated for a while, public attention will wane, and the immediate apprehension will be eased for anyone still living in a smaller camp, and that includes anyone in the only other camp Ronnie knows of. He'll feel freer to remain on his hillside, reading by flashlight under a sumac bush, cooking frijoles or re-warming take-out food over his campfire, washing his hair under a stream of water he pours from a plastic gallon jug . . . then entertaining guests . . . At one time, just last week she might've seen herself as one of his visitors, just stopping by the sheltered glow of his fire's embers at night, to sit and tell him of her progress, or hear whatever news he's gathered about the men he lives with, their families, and other families, or his own family, just to hear him tell her anything he knows. But after what she saw, then her foolish departure, how can she think she'd be a guest he'd welcome?

Three days she waits, sitting quietly, maybe too quietly, and is neither offered work, nor does she take any initiative, when a truck pulls in, to approach and ask. And by ten a.m. few trucks will come. Some of the men linger until noon. Most leave to wait elsewhere, on various secretly-designated street corners where homeowners who need hedges trimmed or brush cleared from backyard hillsides may stop to pick them up. Ronnie has her father back in their camp by noon. He snores softly inside their shelter, after eating an orange and a slice of bread. Another strangely idle time for her to sit and drift and give herself up to her recent exotic inclination to float down blurred, tangled paths of possible or even hardly imaginable future scenarios.

In a haze of sluggishness, amid irritable calls of ravens from treetops and low oink of mudhens somewhere in the creek, the constant riffle of water, the dull surf beat of traffic on La Costa Avenue, her father's placid snores, the faraway tinkle of telephones, thud of car doors, and boom of stereo, she picks up and holds onto the sound of the motorcycle and lets it make its way closer. Of course, the rescue won't be piggy-back on foot—she'll be pulled to the seat of the motorcycle behind him where she'll hold him round the waist with her arms and clutch his hips with her legs, moving as one body, dipping low around curves, crushed into his back and shoulders with forward momentum when the bike slows, his spine returns the urgent pressure against her body during sudden acceleration, the motor a high tight insect whine, dropping a pitch and rising again, their bodies bump slightly with each change of gear, change of pitch, eyes like slits against the wind or tucked down against his neck, his hair curling round her face like a cat's tail—

"Hey, Ronnie . . . you asleep?"

She hears his words seconds before her heart and body simultaneously leap. She scrambles off the boulder where she's been sprawled. Adrian is staring at the enlarged camp, the four black plastic shelters, the banked campfire in the rock wall fire pit.

"If I hadn't caught a whiff of smoke, I wouldn't've come in this far. I thought you'd packed up and gone. I didn't know you built up. What's going on?"

"I guess I wasn't asleep," she stammers, "I heard you coming." She blocks the glare with her hands, obstructing most of her view of him, except his feet. "What're you doing here? It's a work day."

"I took off at lunch, borrowed my friend's motorcycle. Wanted to tell you about another work opportunity, seasonal, some of the landscapers take on extra crews to put up people's Christmas decorations. Lee, the guy who hired you with Manuel, he'll take you on for these jobs stringing lights."

"How is Manuel, is he back yet?" Her cupped hands fall from around her eyes, but she's still not looking at him. Her gaze roams from her bike leaning against a sapling, to the shelter where her father sleeps, to the path Adrian had come in on quietly enough to catch her half-witted and lethargic at midday.

"No, unless he came across with more of his family, his nephews or cousin's kids, and went straight up into the Central Valley for winter produce." He moves away from her, closer to one of the empty shelters, puts a hand on a corner. They had seemed substantially better shelters than a bush, but now beside him appear smaller, more flimsy or shabby, the roof barely higher than his waist. "So, what's going on here. You sharing a camp?"

"No, it was part of a . . . plan . . . I guess."

"What plan?"

"Make my camp visible, so they'll bulldoze it, when they find it, and they won't go looking for . . . any others . . . yours." When he turns to face her and their eyes finally meet, it's almost palpable, something in her gut.

"Oh . . ." His throat moves. He turns away again and walks slowly between the shelters, his back to her. "How are they going to find it?"

"They will."

"Where's your dad?"

"Napping. Can't you hear him?"

"What have you been doing this week?"

"Besides planning?" She feels her wan smile. Adrian turns around, then smiles too. She realizes how completely somber he's been since waking her.

"Tell me about your plans."

With a hot rush of weakness, Ronnie suddenly sinks back onto the same boulder where she'd been dozing. "It's all gotten so complicated. We need food, we'll soon need warmer clothes, a real place to live. But look what I've been doing. Building . . . *this*." Her last words almost a cry. Then, softer, slower, "I still haven't finished the real reason we came up here. It should've taken two days, then we'd be back down in Dictionary Valley and find a place to live, a job, take care of him myself."

"You still going out to San Elijo Lagoon for your mother's ashes?" He comes closer, all the way to the boulder, kneels on the ground so their eyes are level.

If she fell forward and he caught her, she'd be in his arms. Her eyes drop, her breath catches. "I forgot I'd told you that."

"It's not every day a determined, invincible woman brings her old father out to live in a canyon on a quest to find her mother's burial spot."

"I . . ." It's hard to look away when their faces are so close. But he doesn't move, and his hazel-brown eyes, although still dispirited, don't waiver. "I . . . wish I could live up to that. I haven't really done right by his mission . . . and, I guess, his promise to her."

He stands, lifts each leg and stretches as though his knees have stiffened. "Do you realize how many times it's rained, dried up, rained again, even flooded in the past—how many years, a decade, two?"

"I'm sure his ambition to take them both home is mostly symbolic."

Surely he'd been about to move away, the impatient leaning gesture of someone who wants to leave—hands in his pockets, flicker of glance the direction of the trail back out to the service road—but in another second, although his body is half-turned away, his heavy eyes come back to her.

"*Both?*"

Still seated on the boulder, Ronnie draws her knees up to her chest, puts her forehead on her knees and words start to slip out like a breath she's been holding. "I always wondered why he took her ashes out there. Sure they hunted there, but we did so many other things, fishing, harvesting, clamming . . . why *there?*" Another breath, almost fluttering in unison with doves cooing somewhere up the hillside, until her heartbeat in her ears overtakes the rippling pulse. "But, just before we came up here, I think I found out it's where they'd taken my little brother's ashes, years before, and she'd always wanted to be with him again . . . or something like that. Some promise my father made to bring him home." She looks up, cool air splashing her face. "Still, why they took my brother out there is also . . . beyond me. He, my father, was never communicative about it . . . about my brother and . . . what happened, and by now . . ."

"Hey," his boots grind in the sand, turning suddenly toward her, "Let me take you out there, right now."

"I . . . but . . . it has to me and him . . . just us."

"I just mean to scout it out. I can get you there faster, on the motorcycle. Then when you take him, you'll know exactly where to go. We can pick up some food on the way back. We left him before, and this'll take less time—besides, it's safer, a weekday, and you've moved further in here, and people are a little afraid to come near these shelters, who knows what the barbaric wetback might do! What would your dad do if he woke up and you were gone?"

"Probably go fishing."

"Hey, I brought you a sack of potatoes. Could he start a fire and cook a spud?"

"Of course."

"Then, come on, let's go. I need to do something useful."

"What about your job?"

"Construction's iffy. They said maybe tomorrow. I've got some other stuff going on anyway."

Ronnie finishes retying her boots and stands. "Another job?"

Standing aside for her to proceed him down the trail, he says, "Call it an offer I have to think about. Get your jacket."

It's actually his jacket, and even with it on top of a sweatshirt and flannel shirt, even with the front of her body tight against the back of his, it's a frigid ride down to the first light at El Camino Real. He's brought the motorcycle owner's helmet and insisted she wear it, so her head's alone in muffled-motor white noise. But she can hear his voice when he turns his head, as they sit stopped at the light, his long legs extending left and right to plant his boots on the pavement on either side of the bike, holding the motorcycle upright with her still perched behind him, her feet still on the passenger foot rests, hands holding the edges of the seat. "Hold onto me," he calls. "Clasp your hands together around my waist, I don't want to hit a bump and have you go into orbit."

So she puts her arms around him, gingerly at first, as though trying not to touch him—one empty hand in a fist, the other in a fist around her own wrist—but the first acceleration of the bike away from the light, and a banking left turn onto El Camino, knocks her caution away. Equilibrium instinct allows her to clutch him tightly, her knotted hands against his belly just above his belt, and inside the helmet, she closes her eyes.

Blast of furious wind in our faces . . . our bodies locked together in runaway and turbulent acceleration . . . screaming or laughing or both at . . . the thrill of fear and freedom . . .

In Dictionary Valley, the county road that twined up one side of Hannigan Hill eventually passed below our farmstead's acreage on its way down the other side. On the populated north side of the hill, and near the rounded top, the road had several dead-end splinter turn-offs and long driveways, or loops of secondary road that broke off then rejoined. But in the segment of county road curving down the southern side of the hill, there were no houses and no driveways, so few cars that came up the hill ever went down the south side that way—there was no reason to, and, in fact, the road was not paved all the way down the hill, it became dirt and gravel about a half mile after skirting the bottom of our property. It was more considered a firebreak than a road to get anywhere.

Most fires started somewhere down the hill, sometimes all the way at the bottom—kids with firecrackers or cigarettes, making campfires, burning math tests, butts thrown from cars. At least once a year, what seemed a plague of crickets and grasshoppers began to flee past, a knee-high current of clicking, ticking, clacking, pelting our bare knees and arms, while we stood in hot breaths of localized gusts, whipped up by a brushfire billowing up the slope of the hill. Maybe once or twice our father stood ready with a hose to wet down the brush just off his land, but he never had to open the spigot. Fires were checked then snuffed by the road that circled the hill below our farmstead. So for us, the thrill was without trepidation. Besides the shrill drama as the fire whipped up wind and the wind filled with grasshoppers and crickets with snapping legs and papery wings, there was the possibility that lizards and king snakes would also take refuge on our cool lawn and therefore became easier to catch. There were the fire trucks, sirens piercing ever closer, crowding onto the county road below our property, then dozens of men in boots and thick yellow flak jackets swarming over the hillside. And the aftermath: just as nature planned it, when the matted covering was purged, giving new growth increased nutrients and plenty of space to spread roots and stalks . . . a season of two to three weeks when we could poke around in dirty ash to discover treasure—soda bottles worth ten cents or cat skulls or rusted pocket knives with blistered handles—previously hidden in the underbrush.

Just before the county road passed below the farmstead, it plunged into a steep slope. After that, what was left of the paved route began a gently inclined, long continuous right-hand curve around the shape of the hill. That part of the road was called Lakeview because there had once been a small pond at the foot of Hannigan Hill when ranchers had dammed the creek. But from our metal wagon poised at the top of the downhill slope, our only view was the dry wild oats and tumbleweeds, thick and tall, lining the road, and the ski jump of asphalt before us.

The wagon, chipped red-painted metal, was likely forgotten and left behind at the fairgrounds, at a 4-H or Future Farmer's booth—something they'd used to bring in equipment, the ranch sign, the grooming tools and buckets, the tethers and halters—then rescued by our father after the barns had emptied, brought home in the back of the station wagon, useful for hauling rocks although he also had a big old wheelbarrow. The wagon was never very workable on steep rocky or rutted paths, either on the farmstead or off, although it did find some use in carrying baskets and pails of harvested fruit, flat trays of strawberries and piles of big squash or pumpkins. When it sat idle, we claimed it for our own similar purposes, but putting ourselves in the wagon for an impetuous ride was always more enticing than giving our possessions utilitarian trips from here to there.

Chad sat in front, the wagon's pull-tongue extended back across his knees. We both held onto the handle, although little steering of the hard tiny wheels was even possible. Best to just use the tongue to keep the wheels going straight. Otherwise, a sharp turn, the wagon would tip, tumble, roll, spilling its contents—us—on rock-rough asphalt at a speed enough to flay a layer of skin.

And there were no brakes. So the one of us with longer legs sat straddling the wagon, knees bent over the sides and sneakers brushing the asphalt. Zinging vibrations from sand and pebbles sang through thin rubber soles, while bigger rumbling bumps were absorbed by the bones in our butts and the jounce of our heads and the clack of our teeth.

He wanted to stand up and do a circus balancing act while the wagon was being pulled back up the hill, but had to squat to keep from falling almost immediately, and was too heavy anyway. Commanded to get out, he lagged way behind, dragging a stick, the scratchy sound of him trudging the rest of the way up the hill persisting long after the wagon was poised and ready for another descent, until he chucked the stick and climbed in front again and shrilled, "Faster, this time, no feet!"

Not indulging him, nor obeying, maybe galvanized by or envious of his toddler fearlessness, the brakes were raised, but remained ready, hovering inches above the ground. Speed was immediate and violent, rumbling through us like underground thunder, like an earthquake. Screeching, laughing, our outcry lost in the whip of wind, the rattle of rusty axle, the clatter of hard plastic wheels. Our at-first jubilant screams muffled by the blurred tangle of dry grass extending up the hill on one side of the road, disappearing over the steep downhill slope on the road's other side. There may have been a moment when our voices stopped, when relative silence accompanied the sudden jerk of the wagon tongue, the abrupt change of direction, the lurch of the wagon, then the almost simultaneous termination of the wagon's motion while we continued pitching, falling, tumbling, flat out on the pavement, and maybe then our voices resumed.

He continued crying all the way home, lagging way behind at first, then was allowed to climb into the wagon and be pulled. He held his two scalped elbows in his scraped and pebble-imbedded palms, his skinned knees showed through asphalt-smeared rips in his jeans, his tears likely stung as they rolled down his raw cheek. We took the shortcut across the Dove Pot—the empty lot that would someday be Shane's house. Doves would sun themselves in the warm dirt between tumbleweeds and dry oats. Usually Chad pointed at them and said, "Pow pow." By the time we got to our own driveway his sobs were just a tired whimper punctuated by jerky hiccup breaths. Until our mother *came out the back door. Then his wail rose again, and by the time he'd scrambled from the wagon, she'd collected him in her arms. They sat together on the lawn, rocking, mother's humming and Chad's thin by-now imitation moan merging into a sorrowful duet.*

But perhaps the drone was the station wagon's idling engine and mother rocked silently, kneeling on the road in the spotlight shine of headlights, in her lap the head of a deer whose liquid eyes could not be soothed of fear and pain, its body nearly motionless, twitching, stretched out beside her, father helpless by the side of the road in pre-dawn darkness, no shotgun in his hands—it was a day fishing trip to the local mountains, no guns necessary. He held a flashlight . . . and a camping shovel.

The back seat of the station wagon had a sole occupant, the silent scene viewed through the windshield by an audience of one.

". . . what if he. . . ?" mother's voice strange and faraway, breaking and watery in a way her cooing comfort song never was. ". . . still alive. . . ?"

Did she bend to kiss the dying deer? No, it was Chad she kissed, on each elbow and each knee, the palms of his hands and his road-scoured baby-soft cheek, then led him away for a bath and first aid—fire red iodine and white gauze bandages, an oatmeal cookie and lemonade.

Later her ministrations were just as tender on the second set of flayed elbows and knees, her voice calm and earnest, not hard but also not a song, her face looking up from where she kneeled to clean sand from bloody shins, "You're old enough to have some sense about being careful. He's too young. A big girl should know when something is too dangerous."

Stopped at a light on El Camino Real where its six lanes across with a landscaped center divider, they're in the middle of an overrun business district—not individual street front shops but shopping centers and strip malls, both sides of each block housing a different cluster of franchise stores and restaurants, marquees on the street listing the facilities and services available in each. Adrian turns to shout over his left shoulder, "Remember the name I told you—the guy who owned the land where you hunted?"

She nods, realizes he can't see her head moving, calls "yes!"

He turns the other way, points toward the right, to the big corner of the intersection, a landscaped triangle showcasing an imitation Western covered wagon made of fiberglass, words painted on the side of the wagon, *Encinitas Or Bust*, and in much bigger letters on the wagon's cover: *Kneenan Plaza.*

"He had two sons, I think, they must've divided the land, sold it as commercial property. Probably made millions."

"So is it all . . ." *Gone?*

The motorcycle begins going forward again, accelerates through the intersection, the last malls and shopping centers are higher off the road, with longer driveway ramps to reach them, their parking lots not visible. El Camino also sweeps slightly uphill, now lined with willowy eucalyptus on an embankment topped by stucco walls retaining housing developments. On the downhill side, treed neighborhoods of houses turn to garden apartment complexes, a synagogue, a tennis club, an assisted-living residence house, a Christian learning center, a roadside vegetable farm and produce stand, a few old houses buried in foliage surrounded by small orchards of a dozen orange trees, a Greek church, a cactus garden surrounding a metal sculptor's studio—his name hanging from a ranch gate. And El Camino Real ends. It picks up somewhere else, chopped into segments the whole length of the state, at least as far as the missionaries got, but its original passage through these wetlands, through the lagoon, through certain parcels of private property is gone. Here El Camino hits a winding east-west crossroad—east into the foothills and a gentle curve west, under the coastal north-south freeway, then ending at the old seaside highway that's within high tide reach of the breakers.

Adrian follows the sweeping westward curve, goes slowly another fifty yards, pulls into a bicycle lane and lets the motorcycle idle. The street sign says *Manchester*. On this side of the road, a small new-looking community college, white stucco buildings, landscape-dotted parking lot, a clean new sidewalk. A little further west, beside the college, another small produce farm, this one about three acres of strawberry and lettuce rows sweeping gently up a hillside, with a fruit stand and espresso bar.

And there, across the road, on the south side, Manchester Road borders a long, shallow tidal basin. To the west, not very far, where the freeway crosses on pillars, the lowland is a lagoon extending a mile in from the ocean. But here, right here across the road from where they sit on the grumbling, vibrating motorcycle, the basin is coastal scrub bottom land, with the familiar mint-tinted and dusty green of brushwood, buckwheat, and fennel, dry gray of last year's grasses, purple status flowers, and wild mustard like a yellow mist floating among the thick chaparral. There's the tell-tale thickening and darkening—coyote brush, juniper, sumac, lupine—concealing a zigzagging creek. Lone islands of occasional gnarled pine, wax myrtle, the crown of a small palm, huge three-in-a-row eucalyptus—foreign and too-geometric, but still seeming as native and natural as the salt grass and yucca.

After a few tucks pass going west on Manchester, Adrian swings the motorcycle across the road to the wider shoulder directly alongside the lowland. In fact the wide shoulder funnels into what looks like a dirt road that had once gone onto the property, perhaps to a wooden farmhouse, but is now a footpath, a chain barring vehicles, and a sign giving it all a name: *San Elijo Ecological Preserve*. The gently meandering dirt road almost seems to divide the basin, the west side more of a slough, to the east the higher-and-drier coastal thicket, one-time range land, but all of it still a watershed, a creek's final terrain before reaching the ocean, first carving a bed through sandstone, then spreading out in the slough to trickle shiny trails across sand bars and mud flats, before it oozes into the lagoon below the freeway. This close, she can see remnants of barbed wire fences tangled in the salty chaparral, orange dirt paths that become miniature Grand Canyon gullies carved in sandstone. *A slightly higher level clearing where several more eucalyptus trees grow in a half circle where the station wagon had been parked when we arrived before daybreak—we kneeled there in the dirt and sorted spent shells we'd collected, by size and color, while our parents feathered and dressed the dove, lay the naked birds on crushed ice in a cooler, dug a hole for entrails, let the breeze scatter the feathers.*

Near a patch of tall cord grass—likely a pool where the creek is obstructed—the bobbing white hat of a birdwatcher pauses when he stops to raise his binoculars. Peeps and shorebirds flit in the brush. A low flying egret unfolds its legs and lands. A hawk glides softly overhead.

"Do you want to walk in a ways?" Adrian asks.

She shakes her head. Again remembers he can't see the gesture, says "no." It's a cracked whisper. Clears her throat. "Not yet."

If the landscaper is going to regret hiring a middle-aged woman and her slow-of-speech half-lame father for one of his efficient holiday-decoration crews—each crew expected to finish three to six houses a day—it won't be because her father is barely dexterous enough to unpackage a string of lights and obviously can't climb the trees or roofs. It would be because, at first, Ronnie is useless, like a halfwit standing and staring, mouth dry, palms damp. Her father immediately plunges into the boxes of decorations and begins testing each individual string of lights in an electrical socket to make sure all the bulbs are working, even though the lights aren't the same kind as the big colored glass bulbs he used to hang from the rain gutter of their house, but tiny inch-long plastic pin-prick lights, mostly white, and if one isn't working it certainly won't matter when they're eventually wound like candycane stripes up palm trunks, are encrusted in square-cut hedges, outline the major branches in pruned Brazilian peppers, become a blizzard of white stars in thick head-high junipers, or delineate each line of the roof and eaves, the windows, arched doorways and porch pillars in tiny lights, some that hang in a fringe to look like icicles. Besides the strings of lights, there are cutouts of Christmas characters or images, outlined in lights, some hauled out of homeowners' garages, some brought by the landscaper, rented for the season. These only require being set up on the lawn, the light wire unrolled, secured and hidden and plugged into an outlet. Some of the places are apartment complexes or small condo clusters which are the landscaper's regular weekly maintenance customers. For these they erect conical tree-shapes of lights on the flat roofs, or stars mounted on tall poles, a few have Santa and reindeer to suspend between buildings or on a thin framework of wire the crew has to construct on the roof just for this purpose. On condo balconies and patios or through the windows, they see people staring at computer screens, talking on the phone, taking cookies from the oven, washing dogs and watering ferns, walking on treadmills or jumping on little trampolines, and dark-haired housekeepers polishing wooden furniture, cleaning kitchen sinks and counters, beating cobwebs from ceilings, coming outside to shake throw rugs. Phones ring and vacuum cleaners go on and off through the quiet mornings and into gradual afternoons.

It isn't insolence over the frivolous work that at first makes Ronnie slow to move, as though fighting through the thick fog of a sedative. It isn't even entirely because of her father's strange exuberance and authority, although it's that too. Standing below a tree keeping the cord of lights untangled as he passes it foot-by-foot up to where the little bulbs are being sewn into the branches, he says, "Watch out. The shoe," "Not good place," "That branch. Okay there," "Thin at here," and "knock that off." Mailmen or meter readers passing by, dog walkers, utility workers, plumbers, if they speak at all, speak to Ronnie's father, "Nice job," or "Looks good," and her father replies, "You bet." It's likely the crew doesn't regard nor understand his instructions and urgings, not because they speak Spanish—many speak a rapid-fire English too—but because he's an old man with raspy throat and stroke-slurred words, and also because—the detail that had stopped Ronnie so cold—because they are boys.

But isn't this what Adrian had been telling her?—just before the motorcycle buzzed away again up the steep service road and droned into the distance where she could still hear it changing gears on La Costa Avenue. The engine had already been roaring as he sat straddling the bike, and he'd been fitting the helmet over his own head, so it was hard to hear him—especially with the pressure of his back against her chest still recent enough to throb in her fingertips, and the brief odd exchange they'd just had at her campsite still reverberating, and both sensations vying to wrestle her entire meditative attention away from the enormous hush of the coastal lowland. Since his dark words in the campsite, he'd shifted to a less personal level, so it had been difficult to concentrate on him telling her more about the Christmas decoration job—something about kids. Had some vacantly ardent look on her face encouraged him to go on whitewashing the air between them with nonessential information which only now is registering in her consciousness? Most are local kids whose parents have green cards—they don't work full time, but get taken out of school a few weeks before their Christmas break for this seasonal work. Some of them will spend the summer traveling anywhere there's a crop to pick. The youngest, sometimes as young as eleven or twelve, are usually the ones who may not be in school much at all, are completely migratory, usually working in fields—green beans, Brussels sprouts, lettuce, cucumber, strawberry, watermelon and cantaloupe, citrus groves, peach orchards—all over the country. "Sorry," he'd said then. "I get on my soapbox about stuff like this."

When they'd left the watershed, he hadn't taken the same route back on El Camino Real, instead continued east on Manchester along the lowland's long rim. Further east, still part of the former coastal cattle ranch, the land began to rise in small knolls, but was no longer part of the protected preserve. None of the houses, horse ranches, landscaping companies, or Christmas tree farms had been there three decades ago. The far eastern end of the Kneenan ranch is now a cluster of restaurants, an upscale grocery store and small boutiques. There the bike had leaned into a long, sloping left turn, and she'd closed her eyes again, eventually realized her face, surrounded by the heavy helmet, was resting solidly against Adrian's shoulder. Had he rubbed that shoulder, stiff and sore from her deadweight head, when he'd walked in front of her on the trail into her campsite? Perhaps an apology forming in her mind, or an offer to massage the ache she'd caused, but that had been forgotten when her father had stood from where he'd been squatting at the campfire using his pocketknife to drag a potato from the hot ashes. In his eyes a strange light, startled or bewildered—had he stroked again?—but no, the hand holding the knife was his bad hand, and yet he'd put the blade cleanly into the potato's flesh and raised it when he'd turned, and he'd said, "Where do you kids. Come off to? I—" Then, his face falling back into itself, "No. He's not her."

The sparkling vibration remaining in Ronnie's body from the motorcycle had suddenly slowed to a hot, slow throb.

"Not who?" Adrian had asked softly, more to Ronnie than her father.

"Our brother."

"He means my brother."

Her father's hand resumed its tremor. The steaming potato, soft and cooked through, was in danger of falling from the knife, so Ronnie had stepped forward, used her shirttail as an oven mitt to slip the potato off the blade. She took one of the plastic plates she'd brought home from the picnic, put the potato there, removed the knife from her father's hand and cut the potato lengthwise, then, leaving the skin whole, chopped up the flesh with the knife and handed the plate and knife back to her father.

Then Adrian's voice had surprised her, not because he was still there, but his tone, dark and glum, "God, I'm sorry . . . its only me."

Ronnie had turned, without pausing to think had said, "He would've been proud if Chad turned out like you."

"Tell that to my parents."

This time Ronnie had no quick answer. She possibly stood bluntly gawking. Quickly enough, he'd smiled, dissipating his momentary gloom.

Since the boys can fearlessly scramble around on roofs and climb into trees and big hedges with far more nimbleness, and since her father's service feeding them the lights from sometimes-tangled spools means they don't have to come down as often, Ronnie is barely useful even as a ladder holder. She works alone setting up the lawn ornaments, winds garlands around colonial pillars, mounts big blinking Merry Christmas signs to fence gates and oversized wreaths on garage doors, stacks and puts away empty boxes. Between unshakable thoughts of the motorcycle ride with Adrian and the wetlands sanctuary that awaits her next sojourn, she barely has time to smile at her father's managerial posture. Then the boys' conversation rips into her preoccupation.

"You shoulda seen him, man, wettin' his pants when those skinheads at school tell him, hey beaner, I wanna see you eat your girlfriend's taco."

"Man, those bastards, they need some ed-u-*ca*tion."

"Yeah like he don' even have no girlfriend."

"He's waitin' for his step-sister to grow up."

"They know better than to mess with me, man, I'll harass their asses inside out."

"That's cuz you flashed a sign, they think you Los Hermanos, but yer tat's just drawn on with a pen, man."

"Hey my cousin drew it and he's in, I just ain't got my real one yet."

"L.H. don' want you—you spend the summer picking pickles in Iowa."

"Cucumbers, man, in *Ohio*, don' you know Iowa from Ohio?"

"Well you don' know a skateboarder from a skinhead."

"Hey, man, they started hanging with summa those GI Joe-jungleboot dudes."

"'Sides, you don't got no firepower."

"Those Shanes don' know that."

"They say they gonna send a message back to ole Me-he-co."

"Mí papa me dijo que no les hable a los Shanes."

"Tú Papa es un chickenshit, all he sez is *sí señor, sí señor*."

"Fuck you, man."

Later, waiting for their ride to the next location, they're all sitting on the front lawn, all facing the same direction, in two rows as though assigned seats. The sun is at their backs and their shadows are a row of black upper-body cutouts spread in front of each of them. Ronnie's father leans on her shoulder and dozes. When his deep breaths turn to soft snoring, the two boys closest to Ronnie snicker, so she looks at them and smiles, taking the opportunity to say, "Hey, who are the Shanes?"

"Just some kids, my old man calls 'em that."

She doesn't look directly at the boys, plucks at the grass between her boot heels and asks, "Are they really . . . dangerous?"

"I dunno, man."

"They talk like they badass skinhead enforcers."

"They just anglo wannabe-vatos."

"Like wiggers?" Ronnie asks.

"Huh? Who?"

"Never mind."

One of the earliest glimpses of Shane: a boy of eight or nine wearing a baseball uniform, swinging a bat in his yard, hitting the tips of new-growth branches drooping down from a jacaranda tree. He kicked his glove across the lawn when his mother came out and told him it was time to go. He didn't want to play, it was only a practice game, it didn't count, he wanted to go to Danny's house and play computer Star Trek.

You're on a team, his mother stated, loud enough to hear from the kitchen sink. Shane turned his back, lashing at the young green leaves.

His logic: It's just a practice game, I'll only play like two innings, it's dumb.

And his mother's: Is this how you treat your team? Is this teamwork?

The sun glinting on the window and the boy moving in and out of the tree's shadow.

There were two kids who, at one point, might've become our friends. For awhile our father had another hunting partner, a man who also worked at the fairgrounds. They would go hunting together a few hours after work on weekdays. This co-worker fellow-hunter had children, a girl and boy, whose ages staggered ours: the boy older than Chad, the other girl the oldest of all. It could've been a family friendship, with shared picnics, beach days and camping trips. But with just one episode together, they've all remained strangers to stare at from behind our parents. Memory wants to put the woman in a white shirtdress with gingham apron, the girl in pigtails and bangs, pedal-pusher jeans, but of course this is from our father's black-and-white TV, from Sunday evening programs we were allowed to watch, Lassie and My Friend Flicka and The Wonderful World of Disney.

There were bees swarming in the hedge in this man's back yard and, since our father kept hives, he asked our father to come get the swarm.

We knew a little about bees, and, sometime later, learned that honeybee colonies—which are cooperative familial groups of one egg-laying queen, thousands of sterile female workers, and a few male drones (produced only when necessary, then killed)—occasionally need to split the family due to overpopulation. When this happens, the workers allow one of the royal larvae to hatch into a new queen and they also bring several of the drone larvae to maturity. The new queen fights with the old one to see which will have to leave the established hive. Then the exiled queen, along with the drones and a healthy percentage of the workers, venture out to seek a new residence. The exodus is called swarming.

Out in the world, while scouts are searching for a location to settle the new colony, the queen mates with the drones and they die. She stores their sperm in her body and won't ever need to mate again, even though she'll lay the equivalent of her body weight in eggs every day for the rest of her life, producing thousands of progeny, creating her entire colony.

Meanwhile the rest of the workers tightly envelop the queen, and not just by flying orbits around her. Impelled by an urge to stay close to her, they mob her, pile onto her and then onto each other, as though each fights for a turn to get to the center of the mass and touch her, thousands of bees forming a big buzzing orb of bodies. That's the swarm, and it can even fly that way—a confused jumbled cloud, denser in the middle where the queen is hidden, seeming to roll through the air. As soon as it can, the swarm lands the queen in a bush or sometimes in the eaves of a house, still waiting to move into a new hive. Thousands of workers continue to congregate around the queen, crowding their bodies close to where she is encapsulated in their center. Until a hive is established, that's all they care about. That's how people are able to cover themselves in bees or wear "bee beards" for world record books—somehow get the queen on their chin or head and the swarm will bury the person's face. While swarming, they won't sting, they won't fly away, they won't visit flowers, they won't eat. They will all die if they don't settle soon.

We already knew that unlike wasps, honeybees can only sting once. Their stingers are barbed, so after the bee stings, when she pulls away, the stinger is yanked from her body and left behind in whatever she stung. But when the stinger is torn from her body, it also tears away part of her abdomen, and she dies. Maybe that's why they don't want to sting when they swarm—they need every able-bodied worker to stay alive to set up the new hive.

Our father prepared and painted a new white wooden hive then inserted new frames of already-prepared honeycomb so the bees wouldn't have to waste time making the comb and could immediately begin to fill it with honey. He told our mother that Bill had asked him if he wanted to harvest the swarm and also suggested he bring the family along; they'd barbecue some quail. Our father put the empty hive in the back of the station wagon and we were not allowed to wear our regular play-clothes, instead pastel cotton shorts with elastic waistbands which we hated.

Despite a swarm being too stupefied to sting, our father wore his full bee suit: a safari helmet with netting attached to the brim that gathered with a drawstring around his neck, oilcloth jacket with elastic wristbands and heavy canvas gloves all the way to his elbows with elastic cuffs, two layers of jeans and tall rubber boots with a canvas draw-string cuff tightened just below his knees. The bees would still sting if they got trapped in his clothing or hair, he explained, which was also why we had to stay way back and watch him harvest the swarm from across the yard.

Our mother wanted to take Chad inside the people's house, but Chad said "no!" and swung his arms to keep her from catching onto his wrist. But still he stayed behind her, peering out at the other little boy as much as at our father enclosed in his bee suit like a man on the moon or deep sea diver. The man, in jeans and a fairgrounds workshirt, mentioned his son had been throwing rocks at the swarm and hadn't gotten stung. The boy was about five. He had a long stick and was poking a cat, tapping it, herding it, until the cat had enough and ran off. The girl may not have come outside. Chad looked around and likewise picked up a stick. Our mother tried to take it from him, but again he flounced away from her, just far enough that she couldn't reach, and she probably didn't want to flail around trying to catch him, with the other mother standing there too, all of us way across a big lawn from where our father was positioning the empty hive under the bush where the swarm was lodged. The two women stood shoulder-to-shoulder, shaded their eyes and watched the men. The other boy thwacked a tree trunk with his stick, Chad batted at tufts of grass with his. They never spoke to each other, they each stayed in a half-sphere closest to their own mother, but they circled, stalked, displayed like when we had two roosters in the chicken yard. The other boy put his hands on the grass and tried to kick his feet up into a handstand. Chad, staring unabashedly, dropped his stick and squatted, put his palms and top of his head down on the grass. He could only lift one leg at a time. "Do the wheelbarrow, Ronnie!" So we plowed a little circle around our mother with Chad walking on his hands as the wheelbarrow. But Chad kicked his legs free and wanted to get up when the other boy started picking berries off a eugenia hedge and throwing them at the doorway of a doghouse where an old dog was chained and sleeping in the dirt. The dog got up and woofed once. Our mother had used the berries from our eugenia hedges to make jam. He already had a handful of berries when she caught his arm and pulled him away from the hedge. He started to whimper, his little fist squishing the berries.

Our father cut the branch where the queen bee must've been perched under her hoards of guarding workers. Being moved, the swarm didn't stay in one solid mass, more like the condensed center of a hurricane, with dozens, even hundreds of bees shaken loose, circling, getting lost, desperately trying to stay with the swarm as my father dropped it into the hive. He called "Get in the house now," beginning to secure the lid and doorways, and all those bees who'd gotten confused and separated were zinging in bigger and wilder circles around the whole lawn area, searching for their queen and the rest of the swarm who were now closed and sealed in the wooden hive. So we ran.

The barbecue and anything afterwards is lost to memory. Perhaps too many bees still wandered the yard for us to return outside. Without a hive and queen, they would die, but it might take hours. The sealed hive was under a canvas tarp in the back of the station wagon. There were still a few loose ones who'd managed to follow the hive to the car. We spent the ride home opening windows, trying to chase the loose bees out. The buzzing coming from inside the hive under the tarp was like an army of chainsaws clearcutting a forest just up the block.

In fact, the barbecue must've been postponed—indefinitely, it turned out— because that night our mother made rabbit stew. It was simmering on the stove, nothing could be more sensually irresistible than a bubbling ragout of rabbit, onions, garlic and tomatoes with oregano, basil and Italian parsley. It pulled us to the house from late evening play, panting from a run up from the pepper tree, the back door banged shut behind us, our footsteps thumped through the laundry room, Chad bringing up the rear, our mother herded us to the bathroom to wash. When we returned there was something wrong with the stew. It frothed with white foam. Granules of white powder were spilled on the stovetop. Our mother followed the trail back to the washroom. The jumbo-sized laundry soap was open on the floor. Had he really taken a hand- ful of soap as he passed through and dropped it into the stew? He said the other boy told him to do it. What a lie, barely intelligible coming from his bawling face. But, while our father may have continued to hunt after work with the other man, we never saw those kids again.

Twenty years later, on a spring Sunday morning a boy comes out of his house next door with an Easter basket, suit too small already, one shirt tail untucked, two ends of a badly tied necktie making an upside-down V on his chest. He twirls in a circle with the basket at arm's length—like a sick-mak- ing ride at the fair, the basket whirling orbits tilted on its side, but the cen- trifugal force keeps his candy from flying out. One day he's a boy with an Easter basket, the next day he's . . . not.

Her father is fully asleep and lying on his back beside her. Their ride still hasn't come. She has balled up Adrian's jacket and eased it under her father's head. The lawn slopes a gradual decline toward the street, mak- ing the boys—a few also lying on their backs, arms flung over their eyes— seem to be waiting in two rows of bleacher seats, anticipating, but with- out much engrossment, whatever is supposed to occur on the street in front of them.

When it does happen, the audience of boys is no longer sluggish or bored. A car pulls into the driveway beside them. Probably it is when the passenger door opens and music flares out from the car's interior that those who are reclining rise to sit like the others, either propped back on their arms with elbows locked, or leaning forward, forearms braced on their knees, twiddling stems of grass in both hands hovering over their laps. Only Ronnie's father still sleeps, but under the music his droning snores can no longer be heard. A girl in a short white skirt and an armload of books is getting out of the car, gives only a fleeting glance at the boys on her front lawn, turns back to the car and bends to speak through the window. Her heart-shaped rear end swells toward the boys. Her head turns slightly and one eye peeks back over her shoulder, she shifts her weight but doesn't change her position.

It starts with one, under his breath—perhaps he means it to be out of earshot but his maturing voice is hard to control—possibly in Spanish, separate words indistinguishable to Ronnie, except at the end: " . . . cream puff hoochie mama . . ." But after that, there are no more words, just noises, whoops and chirps and clucks and trills. Ronnie can barely tell who's making which noise. They duck their faces, grinning, and punch or shove each other's shoulders. The two rows of boys stretch between Ronnie and the driveway where the girl's behind makes a hard-to-miss target. But their projectiles sound more like bird calls than either barbs or flattery. The girl glances over her shoulder once again, but doesn't stand upright and turn around until the second car pulls up to the curb at the street in front of the boys and the cat-calls snap off, leaving only the motorcycle-loud machine-gun detonation of the car's engine and the pulsing music.

Several things are happening at once: the first car begins to back out of the driveway, passing in front of the car at the curb, straightening its wheels, then accelerating and driving away. The girl, with a defiant look at the boys on the lawn, saunters toward the front door, leaves her books on a low decorative wall, and turns back to return down the driveway and gets into the back seat of the idling car at the curb. There are two boys in the car. The one on the passenger side has his window lowered halfway. His hair and eyebrows look very dark, almost wet, and his skin pasty, as though made-up. In fact his eyelashes, nostrils and lips seem unnaturally dark as well. Meanwhile Ronnie's father struggles slightly to sit, grabs the belt loop of the boy closest to himself to pull himself up.

"You missed a weed over there," the boy in the car says. Someone else laughs inside the car. "And when you're done here, you can trim the bushes in back, don't forget to sweep up all the clippings."

One of the boys on the lawn says something in Spanish. " . . . fucking puto estupuido . . ."

A car-crash boom—the driver has shot himself out his own window, slamming his palms on the roof of the car, now pointing a finger at the boys on the lawn, "If she tells me any one of you greasy burrito-dicks said anything to her, even if you spoke in mud-people grunts, you're gonna see a race war like you fucking never saw."

The boy beside Ronnie's father is about to jump up, fists clenched, maybe reaching for a knife in his pocket—he used it at lunch to open a package of cupcakes—but his leap is aborted, isn't anything more than a flinch, because Ronnie's father still has hold of his belt loop. Amazing how strong his grip.

Ronnie thinks the boy gesturing over the top of his car is one she's never seen before, with most of his head shaved Marine-style, a long mohawk slicked down and drawn straight back, presumably a ponytail hanging down his neck. Vaguely she can make out a tattoo of barbed wire around his throat. The graphic on his limp, dingy T-shirt is mostly obscured by the purple or black car. About half the boys on the lawn stare back at the car's driver, the rest focus on the grass between their sneakers. Then they seem to switch—those looking down raise their heads, the ones glaring allow their eyes to drift elsewhere. If they start to grin, they tuck their chins to their chests and aim their smirk to the ground. Any muttered words likewise die in the grass between their legs.

As the driver pulls himself back into the vibrating car, Ronnie's father leans heavily on one of her shoulders. She realizes he's standing up. He's also using the boy's shoulder for support on his other side.

"Dad . . . wait."

"Hey," the pallid-faced passenger boy says, "No one's afraid of you, old man, or your so-called gun. Yours is coming soon. We're waiting for you."

Ronnie's father raises a hand. Ronnie's heart is crashing, her mouth dry, her skin aflame, sweat breaking, she can already smell it. She's tugging on his pant leg, about to get up and tackle him back to the ground. But her father is looking behind the car . . . to the landscaper's truck pulling up to the curb. With a long scream of rubber on asphalt, a middle finger held aloft outside the window, the car lurches away into the street, narrowly missing another vehicle driving past, tires screech again, the car lurching side-to-side in its lane, then is gone around a curve.

Chapter Nine

The coyotes are rowdy again that night. An exhilarated chorus of laugh-yapping, howl-barking, whoop-yelping. And in the middle of their jubilant melee, the sheer scream of a cat. They could be tearing its soft body to ribbons ten yards away or a hundred. But how many cats will it take to satisfy the three or thirty coyotes in the pack prowling the gully? So many large wild canines, yet they vanish completely when daylight shrinks the canyons down to mere undeveloped strips of land lying useless between landscaped neighborhoods.

Her sleeping father breathes slowly, only a slight wet rattle. Ronnie is hungry. Or it could be overdue menstrual cramps. She can tell by the way her hips and elbows grind against the hard ground, she's lost enough weight that her cycle being late is no surprise, and its lateness not to be lamented. Obtaining and then disposing of sanitary napkins—what her mother used to call "commodities" during monthly trips to the discount store for paper goods and staples like flour and sugar—will just be another lifestyle adaptation, although she'll have to dig her sanitation pits deeper and dump down heavy rocks before filling in the dirt. It's how to go through a day's work without increasing her need to use a restroom more than once that will require some correction.

But she needs to be thinking. While she's working, whether for pay or daily camp upkeep, it's still difficult to push her mind onto other possibilities or ventures, and especially the if-then kind of planning. After half a lifetime of waiting for whatever happens before determining the best reaction, it seems imagining variations, let alone manipulating a desired outcome, requires a more agile mind, one that's not already occupied with banking embers for a smokeless fire or coiling white lights in a prickly juniper bush. Or menstrual cramps.

Tomorrow is—*today* will be Saturday, and she wants to get to Adrian's camp early, too early for any . . . other visitors. And before any neighborhood boys would be patrolling, either on bicycles or in cars. Telling Adrian about the scene yesterday is more than enough reason to visit, but she's also trying to decide whether or not to share her revelation, or if it wouldn't be so much of a revelation to him. That is, these suburban teenagers wouldn't have had much use for the original Shane, even if they were all the same age, but what would Shane be now, in his mid or late twenties? Maybe in jail by this point, but would he, by now, have traded his blond braided, beaded hair and baggy bright orange pants for a white-wall shaved head and military fatigue t-shirt and boots? He may have evolved from wigger to W.I.N. The boys she'd worked with today—*yesterday*—didn't know what the letters stood for, except the first one had to mean white and they guessed the last could be for nation.

"Indian?" one of the youngest boys had guessed.

"Estupido!" Another had thrown a crushed cola can at him.

Picking up and loading their ladders and empty boxes in the landscaper's truck, Ronnie said to one of the older boys, "I thought the kids that hassled everyone rode bikes and skateboards, not these . . ."

"Some of the ollie-nollies, the boarders, they joined up with these wanna-be skinheads, they all just posers."

So if yesterday's threat was just posturing, then nothing need change right away . . . except, what's the date, how long can the Christmas decorating jobs last, another couple of days? Shouldn't she ask Adrian what other kinds of work come up this time of year? And in the course of conversation mention to him the renewed menace, and that somehow her father has become infamous to the teenage thugs. Gauge Adrian's reaction to determine if she should have concern, then, if so, try to make prohibitive plans. Or hope he makes them for her? Since her scheme depends on the hearsay tension to be enough of an incentive for authorities to immediately demolish her camp after an anonymous complaint, wouldn't the plan be even more sure if there is an actual escalation in hostility? Or is this a time when waiting to see what happens really is the best strategy? But if the threat is real, shouldn't Adrian be told, since he knows how to spread the word quickly?

Finally it's light enough, meaning it's barely light, probably 6:30. It might take over an hour to get to Adrian's camp. She prods her father awake. "Go on to the bathroom. And take a can full of ashes from the fire pit. There's getting to be too many. Dig a hole and dump them in first."

"Where's our— Dig-tool?"

She sighs. "I haven't gotten you a shovel yet, Dad."

Out on the service road, Ronnie pauses, holding the bike upright beside her. On the other side of the bike, her father has one hand on the seat, as though helping to hold it up. The creek flows in a level ribbon, three-inches deep, across the asphalt, pours off the other side, like the smooth lip of a reservoir dam giving up an overflow, but in miniature. It hasn't rained down here since before she built the new camp. Early morning drizzle barely wets the top of the dust-dry dirt, and leaves no dampness at all under bushes. But with rain in the mountains last week, the creek has been flowing strongly enough to have washed a lot of the sudsy foam downstream. Just a few days ago the water running over the road was half a foot deep and moving too fast to risk stepping into it.

"We're going to try a shortcut," Ronnie says. "Get on the bike."

With her father on the seat and Ronnie holding the handlebars—her father gripping her right arm with both hands—Ronnie wades into the water, pushing the bike. The water doesn't manage to reach the tops of her boots, then she's on the other side, stops and her father gets off again. Over here on the other side of the creek, there's a dirt road that cuts off from the service road, not going upstream in the direction of their camp, but downstream through a thicket of bamboo, laurel, eucalyptus, sycamore and tall grass reeds. It doesn't go far. In less than fifty yards, the road comes out at an unofficial entry to the golf course where a paved path curves around on the outside of trimmed fairways and greens. Now pedaling the bike, her father riding on the rear, Ronnie follows the path, passing a golf cart with tools and a hose piled on the back, parked beside where two men are raking a sand pit. Both look up and nod as Ronnie rides by with her hand raised in greeting.

A raven is sitting on the grass just off the path. As they approach, it raises its head but doesn't fly away. When they get within six feet, the raven finally moves, begins to walk away toward some flowering shrubs. There are big knobby tumors on its toes. It walks awkwardly, pausing or falling every few steps, one wing opening as though to break a fall. Ronnie wonders if this is what an old raven looks like—is he old and sick and wondering why he's walking around on the ground, maybe thinking that tomorrow he'll feel better and fly away? From nearby trees, other ravens are calling encouragement, or jeering.

The golf course resort is at true sea level, spread out in the eastern end of a coastal watershed, bordered on the south by La Costa and on the west by El Camino Real. On the other side of El Camino is the first lagoon she visited with Adrian, the one she can smell from her camp on clear mornings with an offshore breeze. Instinctively Ronnie continues to choose the most westerly or southwesterly routes when the golf cart path branches, keeping the feel of La Costa Avenue humming above her on her left. The final fork in the path is obvious. The asphalt veering right winds between a small pond with spraying fountain and an embankment of red and white potted poinsettias imbedded in the ground, arranged to spell out the initials of the resort. But the left fork almost immediately becomes a dirt path leading across the creek to a long row of garages where golf carts are repaired and airport limos are parked. Dozens of coiled hoses are piled outside tool sheds, potted shrubs lined up between the outbuildings, and a fleet of groundskeeping carts sit in a row, each with a trashcan, several rakes, and a collection of hand tools on board. Broken branches and grass clippings are heaped up in big mulch piles. A few men in jeans, plaid shirts and ball caps are loading hoses or sprinklers or replacement shrubs onto one or two carts.

Her father says "Hey," but Ronnie doesn't answer. It's too hard to try to converse on a moving bicycle with her father behind her, but she's thinking they'd both like working here, always enough work, always another thing to take care of, and all these tools. That's probably what her father is trying to say—he's probably spotted a shovel.

Right after they pass the outbuildings and storage area, the dirt path climbs slightly uphill and meets La Costa Avenue, very near the turnoff through the residential area surrounding Adrian's canyon. The shortcut not only easier, but safer.

From well up the path from Adrian's camp, where she can see the tops of the bushes the men use but nothing else—no clothes drying, no smoke, and none of the occupants—Ronnie stops, lays the bike gently on one side, and tosses a handful of walnut-sized pebbles one at a time down the trail into the camp. Her father picks up several more rocks and hands them to her, but from the camp she hears a shout, "Hola!" The voice is familiar but she doesn't know for sure until she comes into the camp, and they are just getting up from rocks where they have been sitting sipping coffee from styrofoam cups from the deli counter at the grocery store— Adrian and Manuel.

Ronnie drops the rocks still in her hand and hurries toward them. "Manuel, when did you get back!"

"This morning," Adrian answers. "He knew better than to come blasting into camp at 6 a.m. Saturday without bringing coffee. Oh, uh . . . want some? I can pour some of mine—"

"No thanks," Ronnie says, realizing she's put a hand on Manuel's arm. She pulls in and crosses her arms on her stomach. At the same time her father has reached out with both hands toward Adrian to accept the offer of coffee. Adrian pours some of his coffee into a tin drinking cup then Manuel passes his coffee over too, to split the two cups three ways. Adrian's t-shirt is slightly too small. With his arms raised to pour the coffee, a shadow of his stomach shows above his jeans.

Manuel says something, looking at her father, then at her, then at Adrian, but Ronnie can only catch the words *Papa* and *héroe*.

"He asked how your father is, working hard? Still a hero?"

"As a matter of fact," Ronnie says, "it's probably gone to his head, how much he thinks he can do." Then, remembering her father not only understands some of what Manuel says in Spanish, but that she and Adrian are speaking in English, she adds, "Just kidding, Dad," and squeezes his arm.

"Say again?"

"Never mind."

Adrian's saying something in Spanish she doesn't catch, but it's got to be more than what she said. Her father gulps at his coffee.

"Y tú, Ronnie, como estás?"

"Okay. We've been working some and it hasn't rained. When are you coming back to work, Manuel?"

Manuel smiles, nods, then looks at Adrian, but instead of translating, Adrian says, "He's just back today, maybe he'll spend the night. Just came back up to pay back the guys who chipped in. He wants to stay home and help out his aunts. He's got a job in a tire factory."

Manuel asks something and Adrian answers. It's obvious, when he isn't talking to her, Manuel doesn't speak slowly and simplistic, doesn't separate all his words as though talking to a child. He takes a thin folded bundle of bills from his pocket. Adrian says "No," and Ronnie adds, "No, Manuel, you helped us out and I—" But Manuel extends a tenn dollar bill, shakes it a little when she doesn't reach for it.

"I only gave him five," Ronnie says softly, looking at Adrian.

Adrian says something and pushes Manuel's hand with the ten dollar bill back. Manuel shrugs and starts to put the bill away, then holds it out toward Adrian who says "No, man, forget it, okay?"

"What did you tell him I said?"

"I told him I already paid you back for him."

"But you didn't. I mean, I don't want you to."

"Forget it."

Ronnie's father sits down on one of the rocks where Adrian and Manuel had been sitting. A breeze shifts, carrying a smell like wet grass and earthworms and the odor of Adrian's sanitation chemicals. With a hand over his nose and mouth, Manuel says something, laughing, then drops his hand and finishes his coffee.

"Sorry," Adrian answers, seeming sheepish, but maybe just pretending.

"I'm glad you got a good job, Manuel, but . . ." she turns to Adrian, "tell him I wish we could work together again. He treated me so . . . well . . . tell him maybe he can come back when I've got my own landscaping company, he can be my . . . I don't know, my foreman."

"When'd you come up with these big plans?"

"I don't know, I . . . it's something I think I could do. I don't really want to keep living out here, hoping for work every day."

"You sound like my . . . actually you sound like him too." Adrian playfully kicks a foot out toward Manuel who jumps back, grinning. They exchange several quips in Spanish, then Adrian says, "Manuel's glad to be living at home again, even if he does have to share a bed with some of his cousins."

"We—us—doing to home too," Ronnie's father says. Adrian bends to take the empty tin cup from his hand.

"*Going* home. But not to stay, Dad, we can't live there."

"Why doesn't anyone think of where they *are* as home?" Adrian says, reaching to take Manuel's cup too, but Manuel holds it up indicating he still has coffee.

"Well, it's not much of a home, when you have to be careful of . . . so many things, . . . just being seen, for one thing . . . and when you have to keep picking up and moving . . ."

"That's the beauty of it." His eyes crinkle in a different kind of smile. Ronnie's empty stomach burns, but more a feathery than biting glow. Manuel, holding his cup in front of his face, looks down at his feet—dusty mock-leather shoes with rubber soles. "Nobody knows where you are unless you want them to know," Adrian continues.

"I . . . well . . . not a big benefit if there's no one . . . or very few people you'd want to not know . . . or to *know*. I mean . . . you know what I mean."

Is her father staring at her in astonishment, is her skin suddenly blotched pink? Manuel is saying something and Adrian swings a mock punch, softly smacking his fist into his own hand in front of Manuel's face. Again his shirt rides up and she can see a flash of his pale back. The hair on his arms stands out white against red-brown skin.

"What did he say?"

"Never mind, he's a wiseass."

"What?"

"He asked if he should leave us alone, but that's not a direct translation!"

"Oh—" She didn't mean any word to escape, but better a word than a grunt. She looks away, off toward the lagoon, still shrouded in a thin low fog. On the hillside, a flock of house sparrows descends from the nearest backyards where they've likely gorged themselves from a feeder. They vanish into a coyote bush then seem to light up the bush with the wind-chime sound of their simultaneous but individual songs.

"These kinds of translated conversations are difficult," Adrian says, "everyone feels too safe in their own language. Like this wiseass." Again the playful kick toward Manuel. "The translator's always in the middle, or in *trouble*."

"But the translator's not even translating . . . did you even tell him what I said?"

"About him working for you? You don't want me to say that. The gringo takes away his rancho but lets him stay on and work for him—or her—as foreman."

"*With* me. But . . . never mind, you don't understand."

"Yes I do. Have you considered anything like, I don't know, a collective or co-op?" He continues flashing his eyes between Ronnie and Manuel although he doesn't stop to use any Spanish.

"A. . . ? I guess not. What do you mean?"

"You know, like a bunch of people own the business. A business owned by everyone who works at it." Adrian goes a few feet to where a plastic grocery bag is tied to a branch. He deposits his styrofoam cup into it. "Maybe you don't realize how much money it would take to start a business, but by everyone owning it, you'd have a better chance of getting your start-up capital. Or . . . better yet . . . if it's a non-profit biz . . . say, started with a trust fund . . . then no one works *for* anyone . . . they all feel like they're working for themselves, or something that's *theirs*. Their work will *mean* more."

"I was just thinking of something I could do, something I could . . . want."

"I know, when you've had your own, it's hard to think of day labor as a good thing, without it leading *to* something." With both hands he smoothes all the loose hairs flying around his face back toward his ponytail—his shirt rides up—when he drops his hands the hairs fly again. "And I can't really claim to know their feelings about their work, since I don't have a family to care for. Even the guys without a wife and kids, they've all got family back home they're helping out. I don't know anyone who's just cut out on his own, just taking care of himself."

"Except you?"

"Wish I could say so." He looks at Manuel. "*He* knows this." Adrian says something in Spanish, Manuel smiles and nods, then Adrian goes on, "I'm a little bit subsidized from home . . . you know, sort of the opposite of everyone else out here, money flows the wrong way. And the natives are getting restless."

"Who, your parents?"

"Yeah, but that's my problem," he scratches his arm, "no big deal, I'll figure it out."

On infrequent winter rainy days, a card table held puzzles of old castles bought in the Salvation Army, homemade play-doh dyed red and blue with food coloring, watercolor paints in long tin boxes, a board game called SORRY! which our mother had since she was a girl, or popsicle-stick and glue-and-glitter crafts. But sometimes preparing a surprise for our mother demanded we bring our crafts to the pepper tree.

We had a bucket that our father gave us, a rust-leak in the bottom. A rope tied to the handle and the rope's other end wound around a branch just above the tree house platform. This allowed us to put paints and glue, paper and cardboard, popsicle sticks, buttons, seed-pods, seashells and other supplies into the bucket, then climb into the tree house and hoist the cargo up hand-over-hand. When our mother was unhappy, upset or aggravated with one or both of us, we made her gifts, our enterprise concealed in stealth, complete with hand-painted "Keep Out" sign dangling from the tree house, then the treasure smuggled under a sweatshirt into the house and hidden on her chair at the dining room table for her to discover when she finally sat down for supper.

It always worked. Her face, possibly somber or set, looking down as she approached her chair, would rise up, suddenly alight, opening like the dull red pomegranate skins that split in the sun when the seeds are ripe and juicy. Her eyebrows would be high on her brow, her eyes round, looking first at our father with a private laugh while she said "Grand!" Then her brown eyes would glitter at each of us, her face beaming, her mouth smiling upside-down red, holding our cheeks in both hands and kissing our noses.

We fixed surprises for our father sometimes, too, like when we raked the ground in front of the basement, clearing all twigs and pebbles off to the side, then outlined a path leading from the basement door with stones we'd painted white from a leftover can of house paint. None of the white stones was so big a five-year-old couldn't carry it, which meant some of them were no bigger than a fist. Our father exclaimed his appreciation, "Ho, looky here!" but kept tripping on the stones and eventually piled them off to one side and we took them to make paths down by the pepper tree.

For our mother we made candle-holders on cottage cheese box lids: glue a bottle cap upside down in the center of the lid to hold a candle, then affix seed-pods, acorns and small pine cones in a thick cluster around the bottle cap, hiding the Dairy's name printed on the lid. We decorated empty beer bottles with glitter and buttons. We likewise ornamented cleaned-out soup cans and made them into little plant pots—holes punched in the bottoms for drainage—then transplanted tiny barrel cacti we found growing on the hillside. Once there was a special gift—special because we needed our father's help to find us a suitable board for mounting a rainbow wreath and fix the back so she could hang it from a door. We must've been apologetic for something particularly astonishing, like maybe the time we were finishing our baths, one at a time, and getting ready for bed, then our mother would read to us on the sofa—we'd been hearing a chapter of OLE YELLER almost every evening. So, waiting for Chad, warm in pajamas beside Mom with the book, waiting for him to come out so the story could be continued . . . But before he appeared, a terrible smell wafted out from the bedroom hallway. Something burning. Something rotting. Something suddenly dead and putrid.

"What's that—" Our mother dropped the book face-down and lunged up from the sofa.

He was just two or three years old, still bare in his room, and noticed the heater, the old electric kind with glowing coils like red-hot springs side-by-side. There was one in the bathroom too, and we liked to make it spit by flicking our wet fingers at it when we were in the tub. So why not make this one spit and hiss too. Even though his fingers weren't wet, he aimed and peed into the coils, making them sizzle longer and louder than any flick of fingers ever had.

Would that have been the thing that prompted us to make the wreath? Our father's shotgun shell reloader could only reload the shells made from cardboard—they were always brick red, and after we collected them during a hunting trip, he took them all down to his workshop. But many of the other empty shells we found while hunting, dropped and left by other hunters, were the plastic kind, and they came in red, yellow, blue, and green. We picked those up too, and we could keep them. By gathering together all the plastic shells we'd collected from several trips, and gluing them—flat metal end down and tightly clustered together, inside a donut shape we drew on the board— we made a three-D colorful wreath to hang from the front door at Christmas.

But it also easily could've been any time we ripped holes in new jeans, when we didn't like the stuffed Pismo clams she'd spent all afternoon making, the time we played with the baby bunnies on the lawn and lost one, the time he threw soap in the stew, the time we wrote Mommy in black indelible ink on her canvas laundry cart and her ironing board cover. Or the day she shot the hawk—which happened because one of us had mistook it for a dove and squatted. It couldn't have been him because . . . wasn't he tramping along admiring the colored shells he had stuck on each finger? Ten of them, a rainbow of plastic finger-covers with metal tips. He wouldn't see any game, wouldn't know to duck. Our mother had said to make sure he knew. He was going to get in trouble for not paying attention. But the sudden squatting-down caused our mother to assume we saw game, so she spun, lifting her gun, and shot. A mistake, an accident.

Grocery shopping can wait for tomorrow, especially since her father will want to carry the shovel through the store with him today. He'd spotted it lying on the ground beside Adrian's fire pit, a collapsible army backpack shovel, a newer version than the one he used to keep in the station wagon tool compartment. Ronnie's father had struggled to push himself up from the rock where he sat. Before Ronnie could turn and help him, he was hastening toward the fire, his rush making his gait look even more lopsided.

"We do this," he'd said, squatting down, then slowly rising, holding the shovel.

"It's not ours."

"You can borrow it," Adrian said. "I can't believe you haven't had one all this time. What've you been using?"

"Cans. They work okay. We don't need to take your—"

"Yes, need," her father had said.

"Dad . . ." She'd moved toward the fire pit.

"Buy—?" He'd looked at Ronnie's mouth. "Say it? Give for it."

"He means trade," she'd murmured.

Behind her Adrian had said, "Well, okay, I'm up for a little barter. But, hmm, let's see, what've you got to trade?"

Manuel had laugh-spit a mouthful of coffee, and Adrian's eyes, when she turned to look at him, had been creased with a glinting grin that his mouth wasn't showing. But then his face cracked and the grin broke out all over. Once again she'd felt her face burn and stomach flare, sending a tingle through her guts down to her knees.

"Camp place. We come away. Then she move to be there," Ronnie's father had said, coming back around the fire pit with the shovel. "Better than at this place. Flat. Water to do fish."

"No, Dad, that won't work, after we leave, our camp will be . . . won't be there."

"Just borrow the shovel, okay? As long as you need it." Adrian's smile had become less brash and more amiable. He'd patted Ronnie's father on the back.

Because she leaves for the grocery store after nine—and golfers will already be spread, in groups of two, three or four, throughout the golf course—she can't take the shortcut, has to walk the bike up out of the gully and ride on the street. The temperature is in the upper fifties, but she's panting and perspiring by the time she reaches La Costa Avenue. As usual, when visiting the strip mall, she wears her spandex pants under her khakis, her t-shirt and flannel shirt both tucked into the spandex, then Adrian's jacket over the top. Sweat tickles between her breasts and she soaks it up by rubbing her fist over her heart. But the sweat dripping from her hair and trickling behind her ears, chills her then dries as the bike flies down La Costa Avenue. When clean, her hair—growing, but slowly—is downy and fly-away, like the head of a dandelion, or a dandelion with half its feathers already blown away. Now it'll be slightly stuck together and gamey, marking her, along with the layers of clothes, as someone to be watched and followed in the store.

There's no bike rack so she locks the bike to a dumpster behind the store. Since the rusty chain snapped some time last week—lock and chain dropping to the street as she rode, and she never found them—the only way to lock the bike is to tie it with a piece of rope with a knot so tight and complicated, hopefully no one will go through the trouble to untie it just to steal a rusty beat-up, gearless bicycle. If someone chooses to cut the rope—nothing she can do about that. She can only prevent a casual, easy theft.

She knows the store employees focus on her immediately, and there's almost always someone pretending to check stock high on a shelf at the end of whatever aisle she's on, which is mostly the produce area. Whenever she shops the produce man always seems to be replenishing the bananas and onions or re-straightening the pyramids of apples and pears. With a basket on one arm, she takes two large cans of beans, a small can of frijoles, pack of tortillas, six potatoes, a sack of carrots, four apples—her usual items and as much as the produce box on the back of the bike will hold without tipping.

Today she goes to the other side of the store, to a paper products aisle. Should she waste the money before her period starts, or should she gamble on the chance that it may never start, at least not before she gets her plan into motion, finishes her father's promise, then gets him and herself settled into at least a furnished room? But what are the consequences of wasting a few dollars? On the other hand, bloodying these tan trousers would be reason enough to abandon everything . . . *every*thing . . . including her father's promise and possible resolution to her obscure condemnation . . . and also including Adrian. Should she come this far and risk losing all of it because her body can't wait to howl at the moon?

She selects the smallest generic package of maxipads, and it's still bigger than the roll of toilet paper she also needs to squeeze into the bike's produce crate. The fancy new-style flat pads have smaller packages, but cost more. Then she notices the smallest packages—the tampons. She's never used one.

Mom?

Mommy?

Mom? What're those big pink boxes? Sometimes I see one in the bathroom cupboard too, what are they?

Not here, Ronnie, I'll tell you at home.

In the glare of the warehouse store, the buzz of fluorescent lights and drone of other shoppers and beeping of forklifts, she seems so far away, her face way up there, not looking down.

Then bedtime, Mom seated on the edge of the bed—not the regular habit anymore, a little over two years since Chad is gone, she's only here to say goodnight like this occasionally, her face often still wan, eyes no longer puffy and red but frequently dull, it seems the corners are downcast.

But when she's here, keep her talking as long as possible, it's so uncertain when she'll sit here like this again.

When you grow up, once a month you'll find blood in your underwear. You'll have to wear a pad to keep it from staining your pants.

Blood . . . why?

It's just . . . what happens.

Why?

To tell you that you're old enough to have babies. It's called your period.

Why period?

Because you bleed for a period of time.

How long?

About a week. When it happens, come tell me. I'll show you how to fix the pad to a belt.

Do you bleed?

Yes. You'll have your period until you're older . . . older than me.

Do you wear a pad?

Sometimes. I use something else that's for grown-ups. It goes inside.

Inside what?

Inside you.

The little package is tucked in with the toilet paper and tortillas in one plastic sack. Another sack for vegetables, a third for the cans. The bags are wedged into the produce crate on the back fender of the bike, handles tucked in, before Ronnie notices, as she squats to untie the knot, that her tires are flat. Both of them. She stands slowly, staring, swallows, and first sees that the bike's seat is gone, then spots the piece of paper folded and stuck between the spokes.

A car is passing behind her, heading out of the parking lot. She doesn't move until it is passed, trying to determine whether or not the car slows behind her, wondering if she hears the car's radio or her own heartbeat. But in another second, when she turns her head slightly and checks, the car, now waiting to turn onto La Costa, is a minivan and she can see the head of a small child in one rear window.

She can see the first word before unfolding the note. *Bitch.* A flare drills through her, leaving her own pulse thudding and sweat breaking in its wake. She can't make herself look directly at the paper, like an eclipse she knows will burn her eyes. She holds it near her waist, slightly away from herself, then glances down. *Bitch, we saw you ride this here, we'll watch you walk it back to your mud-people hole and know where you are.*

The paper in one fist, then into her pocket. Standing as though paralyzed, turned into a statue. Another car passes. Ronnie blinks. Her eyes are scratchy dry. Forces herself to move, to reach for the bike.

As though locating where the tires are punctured will help, she lifts the front of the bike off the ground so she can twirl the wheel and find the rupture. Two slits, six inches long, in two different places, likewise on the rear tire.

She can use the bike to walk the grocery bags home, but the tires can't be mended, especially not by tomorrow—they'll have to be replaced, and a new seat acquired—maybe she can get home quicker and quieter and less conspicuously on foot today, and worry about tomorrow's transportation afterwards.

But she does walk the bike out to La Costa Avenue, waits for a break in traffic big enough to push it slowly across the four lanes, then immediately heads down the dirt path toward the golf course's tool sheds, garages and storage buildings, hidden down below the road, and concealed from the resort itself by extra tall, extra thick reeds, grasses and cat-tails lining the banks of the creek after it leaves the fairways and greens, just before it dips under El Camino and empties into the lagoon. There, as far away from the grounds-keeper activity as she can, behind a pile of brush that even includes two brown Christmas trees from last year, she hides the bike, taking the produce box off the fender, carrying the box in both arms in front of herself, not because she needs it to carry the bags of food, but because she might need the box.

Other than a few groundskeepers' voices coming from a shed, the tink of a tool, the whirring of a small motor somewhere farther away, the whoosh of traffic up on the road, the area seems quiet, and quieter still as she nears the bridge that joins the dirt path to the paved golf cart trails snaking through the course. Somewhere ahead of her a golfer shouts, "Oh look, looka that." Another calls, "Your last stroke of incredible luck today." Their voices small and benign. The clock of a club hitting a ball. Hum of cart. Splash and quacking complaint of ducks retreating from their sunbathing on the creek's grassy bank as a pair of golfers gets too close.

But before crossing the bridge, Ronnie, already sweat-drenched, takes the grocery bags out of the box and leaves the box beside a trashcan. She rolls her pants up above the cuffs of her boots, freezing when something rustles in a large oleander bush just across the creek. She squats and lets her boots slide down the creek bank, which is steep but only a few feet high here beside the bridge. Then she rearranges the groceries, putting the vegetables in with the toilet paper and using the empty bag to double the sack holding the canned goods. The bush rustles again. Is the snap and tick too delicate to be a human, a boy? She glances behind her, up from the creek bed and up the watershed's embankment toward the road. From here not even the tops of passing cars are visible. Anyone could be up there, walking along the road, staying parallel with her. Could they see her if she can't see them?

What about the tampons?

She can imagine the potatoes and apples being thrown into the creek or launched onto the golf course. She can see the toilet paper being unfurled as a streamer through the pines and spruce that line the fairways. She can picture the cans being beaten with bats until they split like melons or skulls and their contents ooze and glisten in the winter sunshine. And during all of it, perhaps she would be free to run and would arrive panting, empty-handed, but still . . . intact, back at camp. But what if they found the tampons?

Under the bridge—just a narrow wooden arc spanning a ten-foot creek bed, and just wide enough for a pick-up truck—she reaches up to feel gingerly atop one of the support beams, then places the package there. She can come back tonight, retrieve both the wooden produce crate and the tampons, maybe even the disabled bicycle as well.

With thumbs hooked in the plastic loop handles and the sacks slung one over each shoulder, Ronnie walks with head ducked, eyes on her boots, along the muddy edge of the creek. It seems she holds her breath all the way until the creek veers away from the edge of the golf course, no longer parallel with the road up above, and begins to meander east through the landscaped fairways, greens and gardens. The landscapers have allowed the creek, in many places, to remain natural amid the pine and fir and eucalyptus trees, the flowering shrubs and beds of pansies. When tall grass gets too thick or the dense red-berried toyon or sage shrubs growing at the water's edge screen the entire stream bed like a canopy, and also in swampy places where the golf course lawn meets the riverbank, she has to skirt around the creek's foliage and walk up on the edge of a fairway, always checking first to see how far is the nearest group of golfers, squatting in a spot of concealed shade or behind a tree if they're close enough that she can hear specific words. She frequently pauses to turn and survey where she's come from, and to search the shady parklike areas under big trees that block the golf course from strings of condos built at sea level on the resort property. Bridges where the golf cart path crosses the water are too low for her to pass under, so she has to again venture onto the golf course until the riverbed once again allows at least a partially shrouded place to make progress. Bush tits and phoebes feeding in the dense growth along the creek flutter from bushes as Ronnie comes closer, alight further up the creek only to hasten away again as she slowly, softly approaches. Quacking ducks and grunting mud hens slip into the water. She flinches, turns and falls awkwardly to one knee, nearly dropping the bags, when a great blue heron breaks from its camouflage in the reeds and flies to the top of an old eucalyptus. When she looks up to watch the heron alight, she recognizes the continuous, it seems, melee in the air between treetops as ravens chase hawks and mockingbirds chase ravens. On numerous occasions she's seen hummingbirds chase birds of any size.

It seems much longer this way, following the branching stream, to reach the spot at the eastern end of the golf course where the dirt trail breaks off the paved cart path and plunges through the thicket of sycamore to the flooded service road where the creek riffles across asphalt. Ronnie uses the water-covered road to wash the mud from her boots—looking left and right up the pavement's slopes for the silhouettes of bikes—then moves quickly up the trail to the camp, doesn't stop or drop the plastic bags until she's inside the first shelter she comes to. An apple rolls out of a sack. Ronnie, crumpled so she's sitting on her boots, closes her eyes for a second, feeling the dampness from her boots seep into her pants. Then she settles again and sits on the ground, unties and removes her boots. Her socks are dry.

When she comes out of the shelter to put her boots near the fire pit, her father is returning with some fish he's cleaned at a spot upcreek, several yards from the bank, where he digs holes and buries the guts.

"Bread?" he asks.

"Yes, I got everything." She stands on a flattened clump of grass to keep her socks out of the dirt. "But I have to go back tonight, I left something on the golf course."

"Why?"

"Well . . . Dad, they wrecked the bike. I don't even know if I should go back and get it. And now they might know where we are."

"Who?"

"Those mean boys."

He looks down at the fish he still holds on a flattened waxy fast food bag. "Okay." He hands her the bag and fish, like a platter, and goes past her into the shelter where they sleep.

"Dad, didn't you hear what I said?"

There's no answer. She can hear him breathing, a slight whisper of plastic which could be him brushing against the wall as he sits. She hears scraping feet, a muted grunt or mutter, then a click, and another click, familiar sounds of the shotgun being broken open to load.

Only seen once, it was by far more beautiful than his. The breechblock and double-barrel were brushed steel instead of glossy blue-black. The forearm and stock made of blond wood with a visible swirly grain, even including a small reddish burl like a rose on one side. The pistol grip area was not yet worn shiny from the hand that would grasp there, both when the gun is carried up diagonally across the chest—muzzle up—while moving through brushy terrain, or when lifted and aimed at game. He was standing in their bedroom, just inside the door, and she stood in the hall facing him. Like two hunters who had met in the woods. But only one had a gun.

He'd been doing his hunting in Mexico for a few years. Each season, he borrowed or rented a tent trailer, drove down Friday afternoon, spent both Friday and Saturday nights, hunted Saturday and a half day on Sunday, returned late Sunday afternoon with two limits.

The bedroom behind him was dark, darker than the hall, lit only by a window veiled by a wisteria arbor. The new shotgun in his hands, between them, was practically in the doorway, could probably have been held up in the door frame by itself, butt propped against one jamb, muzzle braced against the other.

She said, "No. I can't. Please don't ask me."

"It's a long way down there, and uses up a whole weekend, seems such a waste if I can only get one limit per day." A pretty, almost resonant CLICK, *he broke the gun open, rubbed a finger inside the clean, smooth hole where a shot cartridge had never yet been loaded.*

"Why didn't you ask me before buying a new gun?"

"I bought it a while ago, but I've been waiting. I thought you'd change your mind, finally come with me again."

"I can't. I'm sorry Enzo."

"What about Ronnie?"

"We had this conversation five years ago. Nothing's changed."

"She's old enough for a license, it would raise my limit even if she didn't shoot."

"She'll stay home."

"We could all go together."

Hands tucked into her armpits, elbows drawn in tight like bird wings. Her body seemed to flicker like a magnified, distorted shadow of a candle flame. "We'll never all do anything together."

"Al . . . don't."

"I'm staying home. She'll stay with me. It's bad enough that you go. I can't tell you what to do, but . . ." Her face blotching, her throat strangling her voice, "I'm sorry, I'm sorry, nothing can change anything now." She pushed past him into the bedroom, then into their bathroom, the door closed, the water ran.

Click. The new shotgun was closed.

"Dad?"

"You never mind."

"I don't want to go. I'll stay here. So she won't cry."

Mom continued to prepare the dove and quail, the ducks and cottontail, but didn't she stop eating them? At those Sunday meals, didn't she only take helpings of fried squash flowers, green beans and eggplant parmesan? Was it just wild game or did she become purely vegetarian? And didn't she eventually even delegate the cooking of game, as soon as was feasible? She sat on the porch—reading or snapping beans or sewing buttons or sticking trading stamps—while the dove were browned in olive oil, then pressure-cooked, then simmered with stewed tomatoes, wine, garlic, parsley and basil.

During the meal, Dad would say, "It's good, Al."

No response, or she might ask how much longer the beans and snow peas would be in, or how many zucchini were ready for making breads and relish.

Kept her word, never hunted again, determined her own punishment, her sacrifice . . . for shooting a hawk . . . for killing the deer . . . or her odd expression of grief for all three . . .

And yet, when the pepper tree came down, while the chainsaw whirred and droned, she didn't stay in her bedroom ironing handkerchiefs or sorting laundry. Didn't she go down there to help bundle the leafy boughs and lug them off the property? In the new garden bed where the lethal tree had been, did she ever turn the untouched, untried loam with a hoe?

Never saw that new shotgun again.

He has insisted on carrying it with them since they lost the bike, won't even answer when Ronnie points out they have no shells.

They have to rise even earlier now, to be able to walk through the golf course then a mile down El Camino Real to the Home Builders store and arrive around 8 a.m. The first day without the bike, they'd stopped where she'd hidden it to assess the damage, but Ronnie decided buying new tires for the few days or weeks they would remain here prior to putting the plan into motion would be money up in smoke. But she also realizes her need for independent transportation won't disappear once they're in an apartment. She just doesn't know what to do with the damaged bike for now, so that first morning, while her father waited with the shotgun cradled in his arms, she'd put a few old brown Christmas trees over the bike, still hidden behind the big mound of boughs and brush piled there by the golf course groundskeepers.

That day she tried to ask one of the groundskeepers, before he left the tool shed and nursery with a cart of tools, how to go about getting a job like his tending the golf course. He'd looked at her solemnly, without impatience, but shook his head and said "No inglés." She'll have to come back with Adrian, she'll find a time Adrian is free, another day the unpredictable construction business leaves him available.

Just after dawn as they take the golf course short cut, there's little reason for concern or overactive imagination—it hardly seems that a boy would want to separate his vigorously growing body from his warm and slightly rank bedding, slink away from his sweet-smelling mother's fragrant coffee-and-cinnamon kitchen, mount his bike hours early for school, just to lay in wait for a gaunt, middle-aged woman in dull, baggy, soiled work clothes, and the slightly decrepit elderly companion she urges to hurry. That's Ronnie and her father the way she imagines they look if viewed through binoculars from a living room picture window overlooking the golf course, from a car pulled over to the curb up on La Costa Avenue, even from a camouflaged treetop blind.

But in the afternoon, when they can't cut through the golf course, when traffic is at its peak, when kids are plentiful on bicycles or skateboards or skates or on foot or in groups in cars, Ronnie asks the man who drives them from job to job to please drop her and her father at the road that turns off La Costa and bends down to the cul-de-sac above their gully, instead of bringing them back to the hardware store like the rest of the boys in their crew. If he has to pass by the turn-off on the way to the hardware store, he will stop to let them out. But a few days they'd had to accept making their way back to camp from the hardware store. There can't be more than another few days of work. She doesn't let herself ask why she accepts this risk, as she counts the remaining possible days they'll spend over two hours after dusk on roads and streets where every bike whizzing down the westward grade of La Costa Avenue might hold a volatile adolescent, where any car passing from the rear might produce a bat or board to crack against a pedestrian's head, where every lit window in every golf-course-view home and every resort-access condo and every ocean-vista townhouse could have binoculars tracing their progress then locating the secluded camp.

Her cramps fade and recede into the background like a dull backache. She doesn't go back for the tampons for several days. When she does, when she heads out of the shelter one night after nine, after stirring softly and putting her boots back on when she'd thought her father would be asleep, he startles her with a whisper, "*Hey.*" In the darkness, she can see him sliding the gun toward her. He had it lying beside him, as he has the past several nights, under his good hand as he sleeps.

"I don't want it, Dad, no one will be out, I'll be back—"

"Have it."

"It doesn't even have any shells."

"Looks good. To do it."

"Oh it looks grand all right." But she takes the gun rather than waste any more time resisting.

She meant to leave it hidden just outside camp, or maybe at the concealed entrance to the golf course, but, her attention waylaid by the nightsounds of frogs and crickets, of distant barking dogs and the muted mutter of televisions and radios, she's forgotten she still carries the gun until she's halfway through the golf course.

The tampon package is still stowed on the beam under the last bridge, slightly dusty but not damp. She stuffs it against her skin in the rear waistband of her pants, pulls her two shirts and one jacket down, and heads back toward camp, cutting directly across the grass of the open fairways. Without her father, she realizes she can hike twice as fast, her strides strong, long and swift. She breaks into a jog. The turf absorbs her footfall. She runs silently down the dark middle of the grass, striped with blacker patches where trees block the moonlight or porch lights from the fairway-view apartments. Runs fast, faster than she's run in it seems like forever, the way startled geese and ducks sprint on water, wings extended and flapping until they're airborne, Ronnie races with arms outspread. One hand still holding the shotgun.

When she stops beside a sand trap on the short, tight grass of a green, breath puffing, arms sagging, she feels the weight of the gun again.

Even though we never carried the shotguns, he gave us a gun safety lesson early that summer—the summer of our aquarium project for the next year's fair, the summer we learned to like going into the surf, the summer we got stung by wasps, the summer before home-schooling would start, the summer with the tree accident, Chad's last summer.

He gave us a lesson in gun safety, just one lesson.

In brushy or waist-high foliage, hold the gun in both hands, across the body, muzzle pointed diagonally up and away. In open terrain, tuck the stock under one arm, weight of the gun balanced in one hand holding the wooden forearm, muzzle pointed to the ground. He showed us how, from either of these two positions, the hunter could easily and smoothly lift the gun into shooting position, and of course when he did, our reflexes honed, we squatted and ducked, fingers in our ears to insulate the detonation. We laughed and he said, "You're not watching. Pay attention." He handed the gun to Chad. His little fist immediately wrapped on the pistol grip, his finger finding the trigger.

"No, never carry it with your hand on the trigger. Move your hand up to the breechblock."

Never wave the gun around, never use it as a walking stick, never run while carrying.

Was that also the same summer Chad played with a piece of Sierra driftwood from our mother's cactus garden as his gun? No. That time was a warm November. The driftwood had already sat in our mother's garden for several months before Chad decided it would be his gun. We must've found it, at camp, the summer before.

After a winter with a tremendous amount of snowfall, after a snowpack twice the normal size had melted, the resulting swollen river not only surged and overflowed its bed, overtook the campground areas and trails, washed out the bridges, and filled a small ravine with its new temporary breadth, it grew equally in ferocity, boiling in white eddies, rooster-tails and hummocks, plus the unseen demolition that occurs beneath the surface of the black ripple-topped rapids, pushed faster and faster by its own weight and momentum, digging up everything in its path as it ripped new riverbanks and crashed through new chutes and channels.

When the river withdrew back within its predictable banks for the summer, in the alluvium left behind, piled high twenty to fifty yards on either side—rocks and tree trunks and roots and gravel and brush and boulders and pieces of outhouses and picnic tables and thousands of sticks and branches scrubbed white resembling haystacks or beaver dams—we searched for luckystones. These were stones of any color that had a ring of another color making a complete orbit, from a small halo near the tip of an oblong stone to a complete circumference right in the middle of a head-sized rock. Some were gray-blue flecked with pinprick white stars, and the stripe a pure white. Some were pinkish red with a vein of dark brown. Some pale gray wrapped with a black ribbon.

We helped our mother gather luckystones of all shapes, colors and sizes for her cactus garden—a place on the property not outfitted with a watering system yet, therefore too dry to grow anything useful, already adorned with a cow skull we'd found while hunting. It was either our mother or Chad who found the golf ball-sized luckystone encased in a washed up pine root. Underground as a young tendril, the root had hit the buried rock, had swerved to avoid it but somehow ended up making a complete circuit around the rock before continuing on into deeper earth. So the rock was grasped by the root as though tied up in a knot or as though squeezed by a snake. As it grew wider, the root had begun to further embed the stone it held, and the supple tuber hardened. Now, the tree dead and uprooted, roots and branches alike smashed into firewood and driftwood, the section of root holding the rock was only as long our mother's arm. The whole thing had a slight boomerang bend—a longer, thinner length divided from a shorter, thicker section by the bulge where it held the luckystone.

Our mother brought the driftwood home with the other luckystones and put it in her cactus garden. But to Chad it soon became a shotgun, the wrapped stone was the breechblock and trigger area, the fatter end the stock, and the other end the muzzle. He lay his cheek against the wrapped stone, squinted one eye down the slightly knurly barrel. "P-kew! P-kew! Gottem! I shot a hawk—I got an eagle!"

Our mother repeatedly took the driftwood away and put it back into her garden. "I don't want you playing with this. Look, you broke the black rose and stepped on the jade plant. Stay out of this garden, both of you."

Meanwhile, being searched for something else—new shoestrings or a flyswatter to use in the tree house or old handkerchiefs for making flags—a linen closet had revealed two brand new, still-in-boxes, b-b air rifles. Chad didn't know about the air rifles, nor would he be told and ruin what was obviously meant as our Christmas surprise.

Then Chad went into the cactus garden again, and when our mother caught him with her driftwood, he was kneeling behind a rock pile, the gun propped on the rocks, protecting a fort under siege, "P-kew, blam, blam blam!" She pulled him up by one arm, her other hand landing several swats to his backside. "I asked you to stay out of that garden and leave this driftwood alone! What's the matter with you!"

"It's my gun, it's my gun," he wailed over and over, the words blubbered through tears and barely understandable, as she took the driftwood back for the final time. Chad trailed along behind, still crying, trying to hold onto the backs of her legs as she walked. She placed her feet carefully between specimens of succulent plants, then squatted and placed the driftwood where she

liked it, and Chad flung himself against her back, his arms around her waist, sobbing into her shirt. She was almost thrown forward onto her knees, but she reached behind herself, hooked an arm around him, and stood with Chad clinging to her back, probably neither of them realizing he was still repeating, "my gun, my gun." He seemed to half dangle, half ride on her back like a baby gorilla as she stepped out of her garden. Then she was able to swing him in front of herself like a pack she was shifting from her back, grip him with a hand in each armpit, and avoid getting struck by his angry kicking feet while she set him upright on the ground facing her. "Find somewhere else to play," she said, wiping his cheek with one thumb, then we followed her to the house where she gave us each an orange juice ice cube on a stick.

Sitting on the patio with our feet in the gutter as we sucked and licked our orange ice cubes, our mother back in the house checking the jars of apple sauce that were processing, a good opportunity to warn him: "Please, you have to be good, Chad, or you might not get any Christmas present this year."

But never saw those air rifles again either.

They catch her after dark in the cul-de-sac. Just before Ronnie and her father slip between the chained posts and no-trespassing sign blocking the steep service road from the cul-de-sac, four bikes swarm into the street from an apartment cluster driveway. Four seemingly identical, almost tiny bikes, the clown-sized, and four riders with flapping flannel shirts over huge billowing t-shirts, sack-like jeans with ragged cuffs dragging in the dirt as the bikes tilt, forming a carousel rotating around, closing in on Ronnie and her father. It's hard to look long at any one of them, hard to recognize, impossible to identify the shock of tattoo around a neck or menacing razor haircut and matching smutty eyes. She feels herself rotating also, but slower, keeping her back to an undefined center point, as though there's a solid pillar behind her, or as though she has a war-trained partner likewise keeping his back to hers, safekeeping each other from rear attack. In the dim streetlights, their mouths are dark grinning cracks. Their voices and laughter a dizzy dissonance. Rasp of sand under their tires, grind of heels on pavement, flap of their clothes, savage odor of their sweat . . . or is it her own?

"Hey bitch, who's gonna save you now?"

"Which one-a us you gonna shoot, old man?"

"Your own personal spin-the-bottle game, cunt, pick whicha us goes first."

"Where're your wetback friends?"

"No more mister-nice-guy."

"Homeless scumbag, dirty barfbag."

"Just die and make everyone happy."

"Come on, old man, you're the one with the gun."

"Who're you gonna shoot?"

"Shoulda paid attention to our *friendly* warning."

"Hey, let's hang her underwear on a stop sign."

"Advertise her services!"

"Then we need a *go* sign."

"A *bitch* sign."

"Come on, aim and shoot, aim and shoot, we'll give you the first one free."

"Bang bang, old geezer."

"Old fart."

The street below her feet is starting to spin faster than the circling boys. Her knees about to buckle, to allow her to crumple and surrender. She raises her queasy eyes, perhaps hoping the sky, the shadows of rain clouds blowing across and dim stars in between are too far away to be caught in the raging current, will hold still and hold her still.

Beside Ronnie, a sudden movement, her father holding the shotgun's pistol grip in both hands, thrusts his body forward, his weight lunging onto his good knee, jams the steel double-barrel in the front spokes of one bike. Simultaneously the jolt immediately takes her father to the ground—but he releases his grip on the gun and isn't dragged or rolled—and the bike's rear wheel somersaults up and over the now bent front wheel that's dragging the shotgun's muzzle, making sparks against the asphalt. And the kid's airborne, separated from his bike. He lands hands first, then his mouth and face on the street, a smack of sound that stays in Ronnie's head even after the hum and whiz of the other three sets of tires dwindle up the street, and the other boys' fleeing voices call back their final malice.

"Get ready for war, fucker."

"Your ass is grass, asshole."

"Crazy old fucker, next time *we'll* have the guns."

But all does not fade into an ordinary evening tranquility, leaving only her heartbeat and the rasp of her father's breathing as he labors to get up from the ground. The fallen boy is not unconscious. Through his cursing, she can't hear if he's crying. "Asshole fucker, crazy fucking lunatic, god-fucking-damn-you, bitch . . ." He's sitting up, his voice thick, warped and garbled, coming from behind one hand, blood spattered down his shirt, the other hand curled and held against his chest the same way Ronnie's father carries his bad hand. Ronnie pulls the shotgun from the bike's ruined front wheel. The dark wooden stock is scuffed and bright silver nicks and scrapes show on the blue-black twin barrels. The front aiming sight is broken off. Then her father is beside her, taking the gun. "Let's go, dad," she murmurs.

But her father is moving away from her, toward the boy. Now cradling his crumpled hand with his other arm, Ronnie can see raw, swollen bloody lips. An abrasion flames on one cheek. He's stopped cursing but continues stammering and moaning.

"The one's hurt," her father says. He looks up the street where the other three boys rode away, then up the driveway they had come from. "This person might go home at here," he says. He leans on the gun like a cane and bends to take hold of the boy's upper arm. The boy pulls his arm away, but her father grabs hold again. He doesn't really help the boy up, but the boy gets to his feet while Ronnie's father holds his arm.

While Ronnie is lifting the little bike by the crossbar to leave it on the sidewalk, she notices something in the gutter near where the boy fell. From her pocket she pulls one of the baggies she saved from the work crew's lunch trash, picks up a broken tooth from the street, wads it inside the plastic, then takes the boy's other arm. "No, Dad, you can't go to someone's door holding a gun. Go on. I'll catch up to you."

The boy rips his arm away from her as well, spits "bitch," but just like he had with her father, the second time she takes hold of him, he doesn't respond.

"Where do you live?"

"Bitch. My parents'll kick your ass."

But they are walking toward the apartment complex. As she starts up the driveway, he squirms his arm away from her again, this time not violently. Now he's crying for sure. Ronnie follows him through the parking lot, but she doesn't know why. When he turns down a row of apartments, each with a tiny patch of lawn, two-bush mock orange hedge and concrete walkway connecting their front doors to the main sidewalk, she takes his arm again and stops. When he stops beside her, sniffling, not looking at her, she presses into his palm the wadded piece of plastic that holds the broken tooth.

"Tell your parents they can come talk to us."

"Yeah they'll kick your butts."

"Well, you can tell them where to find us. . . A camp . . . down in the gully."

A misdemeanor, nothing more, a ticket, perhaps a small fine, but none of that would undo anything, best to bury the mistake, let coyote come sniffing and turn it to carrion. Or bury it deep enough so it's gone forever. Checking over shoulders, watching the bright, hot midday frontage road for the county sheriff or game warden or some kind of official, none of which had ever actually been seen on or near any hunting site. Ten o'clock sun flaring, ninety degrees already, only sticks and pocket knives for digging, for cutting the clay, only hands for scooping, it seemed the hole would never be deep enough, would take forever to excavate.

The vast, arid bottomland could hardly be touched, let alone filled, offered no resistance to our voices, just sucked the sound out of us and dispersed it, leaving only the whisper of sand pushed aside, pebbles rolling, the silent effort to muffle a grunt of voice or moan beneath soft but heavy breathing . . . the clink of shovel on rock.

Did we have a shovel? When did we get the shovel?

Chapter Ten

She can smell the campfire before arriving in the compound. Drawing near on the trail, smelling the fresh muddy creek bank, then seeing the twinkle of flames as she comes around the first black plastic shelter, the silhouette of her father in savory incense-scented smoke made from his greasewood kindling, her throat chokes up. Her gut is heavy, her knees once again jellied, her boots like concrete. Her unexpected adaptation—bending the ambush into part of her plan by confirming the location of the camp, even inviting a visit—has also hastened everything. The tip-off of authorities almost certainly now underway, they'll have to prepare to leave.

Inside the shelter where the food is stored, Ronnie counts remaining apples, potatoes and carrots, hanging in the grocery bags from the fence posts that also hold up the plastic walls. There's still a can of beans and a few tortillas, although a faint turquoise of mold is starting to tint the edges. She brings the remaining potato out to the fire, pierces it twice with her pocketknife, the second stab overlapping the first, so the puncture is the shape of an X.

"I already did one," her father says.

"I know. We have to use them up."

He looks at her through the blowing greasewood ash. His hair is being lifted by the same breeze, the longest white strands standing almost straight up, appearing to be part of the drifting smoke, as though when it clears, he'll be gone.

"We have to get ready to go, Dad."

"To where?"

"We're going to . . . *you* know . . . go do the thing you promised Mom." She squats and pushes the second potato into the ashes beside the one he'd buried there.

"Too dark later."

"We'll go first thing in the morning, before light. We need to get our stuff together."

"The shover."

Ronnie stands, glancing down at the shovel that's jabbed into the dirt and standing upright not far from the fire pit. "*Shovel.* Dad, when did you start always keeping a shovel with you, even in the car?"

"Teach to wear proper tool. Good to whatever happens."

"Yeah, well this one's not ours so we'll return it. We can only take what we can carry. We're not coming back here."

"Why?"

"We *hurt* him. That kid. We can't even say it's an accident. He'll tell his parents."

"Sorry. She was just a boy."

"He's a wild animal."

Chad lay on the hard-baked ground.

Our mother rocked silently, kneeling, in her lap the head of a deer whose liquid eyes could not be soothed of fear and pain, its body nearly motionless, twitching, stretched out beside her . . . father helpless. He held a camping shovel.

A mistake, an accident.

Our knees buckle to squat below the line of fire, the reflex so quick, so instinctive, impossible to say for sure which came first—the motion of our mother's gun being raised or the children hitting the dust at the sound or sight of game.

We screamed. Kept on screaming. SOMEONE was still screaming. But there was also an awful silence.

Chad lay on the hard-baked ground

His limp body scooped up the way we would lift a dead cottontail with one hand.

Chad holding a dead hawk up by its wings—making it fly, dip and soar over our heads as we dig—impersonating the CAW CAW of its cry.

—or was he screaming too?

He was tramping along admiring the colored shells he had stuck on each finger, ten of them, a rainbow of plastic finger-covers with metal tips. He wasn't paying attention . . .

Familiar screaming, throat peeled raw, shoulders grasped and body shaken, STOP IT, STOP IT, then that dreadful silence . . . again . . . sun growing hotter as the hole was dug in dry hard-packed clay. A mistake, an accident.

When they leave the camp at dawn, there are still tortillas and a can of beans in a grocery sack hanging in one of the shelters, two jugs of water on the ground beneath it, a roll of paper towels is tied to a bush at a convenient height, a bar of soap sits in an empty can in the tripod made of willow sticks, a torn towel hanging from one of the three sticks. Other empty cans of various sizes are stacked near the fire pit, the fishing-pole branch with line and hooks still attached leans against the outside wall of a shelter, the painter's tarp and two blankets are spread out—still rumpled from a night's sleep—on the floor inside two different shelters, her father's sweatpants hang from a fencepost above her bedding, her dirty khakis folded as though for a pillow, a pair of socks with threadbare heels are limp like snakeskins on the ground, the baby highchair has a torn shirt flung over the back and a plastic spoon on the tray. And, for the first time, Ronnie tells her father to not douse the fire, to leave it burning. She has no idea how soon a complaint will be filed with whatever office is authorized to receive it, nor how soon any kind of inspector will be sent to locate the illegal camp, but if it's today, the ashes might still be warm.

Her father is carrying the camping shovel and is once again wearing the hunting vest, pockets stuffed with their extra pairs of underwear. In one big pocket, Ronnie has slipped the tampon package, still unopened. In his pants pocket, he carries most of their money. Adrian's jacket tied around Ronnie's waist, spandex pants under her jeans, the denim stiff from being washed in the creek. She wears the rucksack and pulls the handcart, its skinny wheels shuddering and jiggling as they jolt over rocks and ruts.

Every day the creek has gone down, so the water pouring over the asphalt is now far below ankle-depth. Ronnie stops her father before crossing the water, pulls two wadded grocery bags from her pocket, and squats in front of him holding a bag open. Her father starts to shift his weight, shuffles his feet slightly, then finally shifts the shovel to his bad hand—clutches it under his arm—and puts his good hand on the top of Ronnie's head to steady himself. One at a time he lifts each foot and Ronnie pulls the plastic sacks over his boots then ties the handles around his ankles. Her father gathers the fat pockets of the vest into his arms with the shovel, holding everything against his body as he begins wading across the rill, as though he's fording a waist-high river. Ronnie lifts the loaded handcart in both arms, moving her head aside to avoid the shotgun, once again standing upright in the cart, but this time not wrapped in blankets.

Her father wants the plastic off his boots immediately on the other side, and Ronnie doesn't want the wet plastic back in her pockets, so she ties the bags to the handcart, then they head down the dirt road toward the entrance to the golf course. She can hear the big sprinklers clicking and spouting on the closest fairway. Above them, atop a sycamore, a mockingbird trills like a car alarm, then mimics a meadowlark. Ronnie looks up, trying to locate the bird. She hasn't seen or heard a real meadowlark in thirty years. Maybe the mockingbird's imitation is of a pet canary. Her father begins using the shovel as a walking stick. The metal blade crunches against the dirt path, causing shivers on Ronnie's neck with every step. Their progress seems slower than usual. Finally Ronnie takes the shovel from her father and he doesn't protest.

They can't cut across the grass because of the sprinklers, but on the paved golf cart path the handcart rolls better anyway. She wedges the shovel in beside the shotgun, careful to not break the clean, empty mayonnaise jar she's been saving.

The first explosion could've been a car backfiring. Ronnie and her father are rounding the edge of a green—artificial-looking short grass in the shape of a pond—and passing a sand trap, moving slowly, Ronnie staying a step behind her father. At the sound of the blast, her head jerks up, but her father continues methodically.

"Dad . . ."

Then the second detonation, followed by a third and fourth. When her father does pause and turn around, Ronnie realizes she's stopped and has her hands over her ears.

Several dogs immediately begin to bark. Someone shouts on the residential street near the cul-de-sac. Another shout. Maybe it's more than one voice. Then silence. Except the sprinklers. One by one, a few birds resume twittering.

"Look," Ronnie's father says.

Ronnie turns, lowering her hands from her ears. Just beginning to come into view over the tops of the trees that block the golf course from the ravine, puffs of black smoke are rising.

"Bombs?" Ronnie says softly. "Who would use bombs?"

A groundskeeper's cart is coming toward them on the path. Ronnie takes her father's arm and moves him aside. He's still watching the smoke which is now starting to dissipate a little. The groundskeeper parks the cart near the sand trap and gets out with a rake, but his eyes are also on the smoke. Then he turns to Ronnie and holds one hand out, palm up, a slight shrug of shoulder, eyebrows raised.

"Um . . . no sé," Ronnie says. "I don't know."

Her father looks at her. "Our fire," he says.

"No, Dad."

"It wasn't off."

The groundskeeper begins raking the sand trap.

"I know," Ronnie says, "but it was . . . never mind, let's just go. We don't even really know what . . . that was."

Their pace maddeningly slow, Ronnie counts two heartbeats for each step. By the time they go the length of the fairway and pass another groundskeeper dragging some auxiliary sprinklers to a dry spot near the next green, Ronnie sees people in backyards and on balconies that overlook the golf course, shading their eyes and looking east, in the direction of the gully. Ronnie glances over her shoulder. Instead of being completely thinned out and wafting away, the smoke has reformed into a column.

Another twenty or thirty plodding yards. She can see the first bridge up ahead. It's a little less than half way to the second bridge. Then they'll pass the outbuildings, go up the hill to La Costa Avenue, and it's almost another mile to Adrian's camp. Ronnie's father glances at a crumpled doughnut shop bag and coffee cup sitting atop a covered trash can beside the path. He continues another few feet, then stops. "Anything for eat?"

"We have to keep moving for now, Dad."

A woman jogger with a dog comes toward them down the middle of the path. The woman's eyes are raised over Ronnie's head, toward the east, toward the smoke. Ronnie's father says "'Morning." The dog's face is beaming and tail wagging, but the jogger never glances and yanks the dog away. Turning as the jogger passes, her father spots the smoke behind them. "Look."

"I know."

"Our fire."

"No, it's not that. Not without some help."

The thin wail of a siren approaches, growing louder.

"I thought something else would happen," Ronnie says. "But I guess they did it themselves. They didn't even tell their parents. They didn't even take the first step of what I thought would be the way it would happen." It was supposed to be official, done with bulldozers, and newsworthy because it ensured safety for the neighborhood. Of course, ironically, would also be safer for the other camps still hidden in the neighborhood. Would this work the same way?

Crossing the bridge, their boots softly thumping on the boards—three thuds and a scrape as Ronnie's father drags his bad foot. The fire truck, now up on La Costa, adds its horn to the siren. Another siren howls in the distance.

"But we can't change anything now," she says. "Come on, hurry if you can, we'll rest at Adrian's camp."

By the time they cross La Costa above the resort's maintenance buildings, no more sirens can be heard, but the smoke in the east is thicker and blacker, billowing like thunderheads but many times faster. Traffic is heavy, so she estimates they left camp about an hour ago. They lose time when they have to go down to the corner and cross at the light, but they might've waited the same amount of time hoping for a break in traffic long enough for her father to get across. When they head uphill through the neighborhood south of La Costa, the smoke in the eastern horizon is over their left shoulders. People coming out to their cars with briefcases or nylon backpacks and cups of coffee, pause while unlocking their doors to look at the darkened sky. Sunrise has been subdued, veiled, but without the silken refreshing and liquid-colored air if it were rain clouds gathering. A flock of starlings, changing shape as it moves overhead, crests the hill and descends into Adrian's canyon.

On the last road with sidewalk before they get to the canyon, they're on a slight downhill incline and the houses and trees behind them block most of the eastern sky. Her father is breathing with a grunt in his chest.

"Just a little farther, Dad. After we get to Adrian's, it's just down the hill the rest of the way, and out to El Camino to the bus stop."

Another siren is zinging in the valley on this side of the hill, coming toward them from the south on El Camino Real.

Nobody's in Adrian's camp, but she didn't really expect they would be. They would've left for work an hour ago. There's not even any scent of a fire, but likely Adrian doesn't make a fire every morning. He gets coffee at the grocery store, and why bother washing up before work, he can use hot water in the restroom at the Home Builders store in the afternoon. There's not even any smell of sanitation chemicals. Ronnie's father immediately sits on the same rock where he had rested the last time they were here. From here, down over the southwest side of this hill, only the topmost rounded parts of the smoke can be seen, but there's a strange eastern breeze, unlike the usual still morning air.

Ronnie parks the handcart outside the covered bush that serves as Adrian's tent. She takes off the rucksack and tosses it into the bush, then kneels and follows the rucksack into his tent. Perhaps he has a piece of paper and a pencil. The handcart outside will make it apparent she's been here, and probably even obvious enough that she's left the cart here while she has to attend to something—he may even figure out what—no need to leave a note about that. But she never did tell Adrian about being directly warned by the boys in the car, or the note left on her bike—and now their upgraded threats already acted out?

His scent rises from his bedroll the way a delicate scent of fire should've still hovered over his fire pit. She shoves the rucksack further into the bush, pushes it onto the sofa cushions that keep his bedroll from lying on the bare ground. She hesitates. Her father needs to rest. On the bedside crate, along with the camping lantern, there's a book and a toothbrush. A small plastic bottle of aspirin, the label nearly faded white—only four or five tablets still rattling in the bottom—a clean, folded pair of socks, and nail clipper. But no pencil. Wedged between the crate and one sofa cushion is a metal cash box. Ronnie slides it out. She sits on Adrian's bed with the box on her lap, but then picks up the book. It's about a man who walked the whole length of the Continental Divide. In a picture on the cover, he's carrying a pack three times the size of hers, but just wearing shorts and an undershirt, his arms and legs knotted with muscle, reddish-brown. Face hidden with a half-grown beard, it could be Adrian, but his hair is short and dark, and it's not Adrian's name on the book cover. She looks at the dark-haired man again. The photo too small to see his eyes beneath heavy black brows, a tint of gray or maybe streak of sunlight in his hair over his ear. Could Chad's name have been on this book? The type of unabashed adventurer who knows in his heart and bones that the world has something for him to find.

The metal box isn't locked. She knows he doesn't leave money in camp. He wouldn't leave anything valuable here. Perhaps a place to keep pencils and paper. Or it could be where his toothbrush is supposed to be, to keep ants from finding any sweet residue left on the bristles.

She's partly right—the box holds two candy bars.

MOMMY—

The vast, arid bottomland could hardly be touched, let alone filled, offered no resistance to our voices, just sucked the sound out of us and dispersed it.

But whose voice cried for our mother?

Chad, there and not there.

Chad's red, wrenched face.

The hawk was dead. Hooked bill flopped down against speckled breast. We dug, with boot heels, sticks, fingernails, the butts of shotguns. Suddenly the vast field existed only beneath our hands, the hard yellow earth, woody root of sage, a tiny snake who'd burrowed into sandstone. Wasn't Chad here and there, always in the way, holding the dead hawk up by its wings—making it fly, dip and soar over our heads as we dug—and impersonating the CAW CAW of its cry?

Yes . . . He WAS there.

Our mother brought chocolate when we hunted. Breakfast at 3 a.m. had been meager, a corn muffin and milk. Sleeping stomachs don't know what to do with a sudden load of food, might respond with sour nausea. But then by 9 a.m., a full three hours after sunrise, our empty bellies were wringing and pinching.

The same thing when we were roused so early to begin the drive to our summer camping vacation—by 9 a.m. it was time for a stop, we were roused a second time and treated to our once-a-year breakfast in a restaurant, pancakes and eggs and sausage. Always the same family coffee shop on the edge of the Mojave Desert, a blowzy waitress in tight synthetic dress, not so different from a nurse uniform except a stiff ruffle at the neckline, and Chad—our last time there?—boldly proclaiming as we left, "This is my favorite restaurant."

No restaurant for weekend hunting excursions, we would be home by noon. In the meantime, our mother had chocolate and little apples to quell our rumbling hunger at mid-morning.

But the day she shot the hawk, our mother forgot to give us our snack.
We looked at each other, wondering how to ask.

At home in the evenings, after supper, after baths, while our mother read
to us from BABAR THE ELEPHANT *or* THE STORY OF A FIERCE BAD RABBIT, *we*
sucked on hard candy, fruit or coffee flavor. Usually our father was ready
when we settled down with the book, came to the sofa with three wrapped
candies in his hand, or with the whole jar, giving it a shake as he extended it
for us to choose our flavor. Our mother would take one too, then read the first
few pages while rolling a butterscotch from side to side in her mouth, the
sweet yellow smell of it became part of the story. But if our father was preoc-
cupied in his den or reading a magazine or watching a cowboy show on TV,
Chad was the gallant one who went to him, before the story started, to say,
"Can I have a candy?"

Eventually, that day while our parents cleaned the birds—the legal yield—
we kneeled close to our mother, just slightly behind her. Usually we would be
off playing with our collection of empty shells, throwing them at each other,
picking them up again, trading for better colors, or off in a fifty-yard radius
searching for more shells or for snakeskins or tortoises.

But he WAS *there that day.*

In that case, was he the one screaming? Who was screaming? Was anyone
screaming?

Quietly kneeling close enough to be her shadow. The hawk already bur-
ied, our mother de-feathered while our father removed the viscera. Her hand
worked in repeated swift upward movements, and the sound was like ripping
cloth, a hundred simultaneous little pops as each feather came out of the skin.
Chad put his hand on her arm and she shook it off.

"Can we have a candy?"

"My hands are dirty."

He reached into her hunting vest, the side pocket where she didn't put
dead birds. "It's in here," he said. He fished out an apple for each of us, and
a bar of chocolate we would split. Her hand never stopped the rhythmic
ripping of feathers.

The candy energizes her father enough to finish the trip to the bus stop
on El Camino Real, across the street from the Home Builders store. Without the handcart and rucksack, Ronnie could've run down the hill and
caught an earlier bus, but for her father—once again lugging the shovel—
going downhill on the sandy trail is more difficult than climbing up, like
a horse that runs uphill but steps gingerly one foot at a time going down.

But at least she got him to leave the gun. When she'd come out of Adrian's tent with the candy, unwrapped one for him and told him they had to get going so they could catch 9:15 bus, he'd pushed himself up from the rock and went past her to the handcart, put the chocolate in his mouth and held it between his teeth while he went to work pulling the shovel from where it was wedged firmly in the cart.

"Dad, let's just leave that here."

"No. Wear it."

Another far-away siren was shrilling, a thin mosquito sound.

"It's not ours."

"Not doing to break it."

"Okay, don't make me end up carrying it."

He'd grunted an answer, finally freeing the shovel from the handcart. Then he'd begun working on freeing the shotgun.

"No, we can't take a gun on the bus. The shovel's bad enough."

"Bus?"

"Yes, I told you, we're taking the bus. It would take two days if we walked out there. Here, I'll make it a little easier for you." Ronnie took hold of the hunting vest by the collar and her father had automatically relaxed his arms and let her slip it from his back. She put the vest on herself. It hung down to mid-thigh, Adrian's jacket trailed below that like a skirt. From the handcart she took the mayonnaise jar, put it into the vest pocket where the tampons were, transferred the tampons to the handcart in the space left by the jar.

"That way," she'd directed her father out of the camp on the path that continues downhill. Before following him, Ronnie had glanced again to the east. The rising black cloud was blocking half the sky and she was starting to smell the ash of charred undergrowth.

The bus goes the length of this stretch of El Camino Real, out to the same place Ronnie and Adrian, on the motorcycle, paused before circling back. The bus will also circle and go back. The last stop is in front of the small, new college that seems to share a strange, too-clean-looking parking lot with a blindingly white Greek church with gold dome. Maybe it's the newness of all the white sidewalks and stucco, brilliant yellow parking lines and nearly shiny black asphalt, or maybe it's the thunderstorm-glow caused by the black cloud blocking the rising sun that makes the facilities on the north side of Manchester Road look surreal and cartoonish sitting across the street from the silent wetland. Dim, colors subtle and muted, nearly gloomy, the desolate wild region—marked by a wooden sign saying SAN ELIJO ECOLOGICAL PRESERVE—seems to be gearing up, bracing itself for what the dark light and strange breeze are threatening.

Traffic is backing up on Manchester before entering the freeway half a mile to the west, so it takes awhile, waiting for a break that never opens. Finally Ronnie forces approaching cars to wait because she prods her father to step into the lane, and, despite her earlier admonishment, she takes the shovel from him then holds his arm with her other hand, pulling him across the four lanes.

But on the other side, he takes the lead on the sandy trail where the sign marks an entry into the preserve. Leaving the roadside, the noise of engines, exhaust and car radios almost immediately becomes muffled, as though a protective dome hovers over the flood basin instead of the parasol of bleached sky and shreds of rainless cirrus clouds. The black cumulonimbus-shaped cloud rising in the east contains no moisture either. Ash, soot, slag, cinders. Black plastic sheeting, even enough to make four shelters, couldn't possibly make that much smoke. Gulls scream and fly toward the coast, but would they be screaming and flying even without the slowly boiling smog?

A woman with pastel jogging outfit is coming toward them, stops to aim bird-watching binoculars to the east, then continues approaching with the binoculars dangling from her neck, resting in the V of her unzipped jacket. She doesn't say anything when Ronnie's father passes her, but murmurs "Good morning" when Ronnie looks her in the eye. *On immediate sight of a game bird—or when the guns were raised—instinctively, reflexively, those without guns were to let our knees buckle, crouch low to the ground, squat at our parents' feet, wait for the shots. The birds would fall on either side of the trail, into the sage and scrub, and, hands over our ears, we marked the down spot with our eyes.*

This first stretch of trail is like a raised dirt viaduct, separating the tidal lagoon area from the flood basin, although the lagoon itself doesn't come lapping against this earthen dam of slightly elevated walkway. From a hunting perspective, the viaduct would separate the duck hunters from those pursuing dove and quail. And, as though for that very purpose, soon the trail forks, one branch heading southeast into the dry watershed terrain, the other fork bending westerly toward, then eventually around, the tidal lagoon . . . *carved into coastal lowlands, meeting small creeks, creating marshes and, slightly further inland, dry washes* . . . Ronnie's father, without pausing, takes the trail into the brushy watershed. . . *the tranquil, liquid chill before sunrise . . . the swell of dusty heat as soon as a September sun rose . . . the soft traipsing in our parents' footsteps . . . the retrieving, the decapitating, the de-feathering and dressing, the cooking, the dining . . . never without a twinge of . . .*

They're walking in deep sand, almost as deep as a beach, and the sparse vegetation is mostly buckwheat—brick-red seed clusters half gone and scattered—and patches of greygreen dry-marsh groundcover. The trail has a slight uphill grade. The ground becomes firmer, more like sandstone in spots, then back to loose sand, difficult to hike through. . . *we padded softly in their footsteps, trained to stay behind them, to stop and squat down as soon as we heard the whistle of dove wings, so our parents could raise and aim their firearms and follow the flock in their sights, in a complete circle, over our heads, and pull off the four shots allowed them by two double-barrel shotguns.*

Black sage seeds still cling to their stalks, and the terrain is starting to grow thick with evergreen chamise, the bush that when dead and dry becomes greasewood. On the hillsides in the distance, the chamise is even thicker, a blanket of juniper green layered with the darker, larger laurel and lemonade berry bushes, and colored with grayish sage, buckwheat and deer weed. And on the rims of the low bluffs in the distance, on a three-sided horizon, sizable houses draped and bordered with pruned, sculpted eucalyptus and pine.

"Dad, do you know where you're going?"

"Find her. Behind iris." He reaches to take the shovel back, so she hands it to him.

"This is the right place, isn't it? I mean, *this* is where you wanted to come? I never asked you if this was the place."

He doesn't answer. Or maybe a grunted assent she can't quite hear.

The trail crosses an oddly straight, slightly wider gravel road, cutting directly north to south across the flood basin, hidden by underbrush until they're directly upon it. But now it's clear the gravel road follows a line of six or seven telephone poles stringing wires across the shallow valley.

"Were these telephone poles always here?"

"Her house." Ronnie's father points northeast with the shovel to a half circle of three old, stocky pine trees, lowest branches blending with the thick chamise growing underneath.

It was private property where the landowner ran cattle, so the small creek making its way toward the ocean had been blocked in several places with dirt dams, creating watering holes. In an arid region, water attracts birds— especially dove who feed in grain fields and on the seeds left behind . . . When cattle ranged in this area, when her family hunted here, brush, grass and bushes wouldn't have been as thick, might not have grown at all because of the herd's constant foraging and trampling the vegetation as they foraged. Rabbit droppings dot the trail, occasionally the gnarled fur-and-grass scat of a fox or coyote, but no cow paddies drying in the sand between the flourishing scrub, layered with generations of stocks and dry branches from season upon season of undisturbed cycles. *After four shots, we were to wait until the guns were cocked open and our parents reloading, only then were we to gather up the four shells then venture out into the field, wherever the birds had gone down, and, right there, dead or alive, hold the body with one hand, fingers of the other hand in a ring around the neck, pop the head off and drain most of the blood. After decapitating and draining, we were to return and slip the bird into a pouch at the backs of the hunting vests, then remain back there where the vests would slowly begin to bulge, where a stain of blood would begin to grow at the bottom.*

The strange atmosphere is still whitewashed with the smothered sound of faraway surf, but it's probably the freeway she hears reverberating, about a mile away to the west, cutting between the never-dry lagoon and the marsh. She's not sure the surf can be heard from here, the ocean more like two miles away. But, pulsating within the freeway hum, a helicopter beats overhead, high up, making sweeping circles that will take it through the mounting bank of smoke in the eastern sky.

The thick-growth chaparral breaks open in patches—sand washes, grasses, or empty rocky runoff ditches with upright dried stocks of short-lifecycle wildflowers. Weeks of sun following the rain have brought the mustard to an unseasonal bloom, standing in shoulder height thickets all together, thousands of small yellow flowers making clouds of misty color that seem to hover above the barely visible, spidery and greenish skeletons of the plants.

Up ahead a very old eucalyptus stands alone in a field of withering grass. It's like a hunchback tree, with branches bowing over and leaves hanging to the ground, like a willow, so different from the elegant erect outlines of pruned trees. . . *our father came across an abandoned farm. Rusted equipment—an old well-pump, a hand plow—a dead falling-down tree near a house foundation, and one lone live fig tree. Back when any trees on our farmstead were mere sticks, this tree was like an island paradise in the brown chaparral . . .* All around the old eucalyptus, the grasses, maybe remnants of an old oat or wheat field, have been flattened by rain and wind, combed in one direction, parallel to the ground, a thick padding. It's been so dry since the last rain several weeks ago, the foxtails are already brown and gone to seed—there's more than one bloom-and-seed season per year, depending on when the rains come and how long they last. Half buried in the grass, in twos and threes and fours, old bricks still clinging together with mortar.

On the other side of the trail, there's a huge stand of fennel on a slightly higher knoll. *He was tramping along admiring the colored shells he had stuck on each finger, ten of them, a rainbow of plastic finger-covers . . . not paying attention.* The trail is moving slowly uphill between the lone eucalyptus in its grass bed and the forest of head-high fennel, up a very slight rise, then the path seems to disappear when the land sinks again. Ronnie starts to smell the ocean, and just past the hedge of fennel, the land rolls down to a subtly secluded salt marsh with a creek's slow rill running through it. Amid sites of dry salt sediment, patches of marsh grass form a textured design of varied heights and colors—dark cord grass, feathery salt cedar, brown cattails, pale salt grass—with a river of brighter green spongy groundcover and other currents of white sand running through and between the stands of grasses. The helicopter makes another pass, still circling overhead. Sparrows twitter, fluttering between clumps of brush. She has yet to see a single game bird. *When they raised the shot-guns, taking aim at a flying dove or quail blasting out of the underbrush, we were to immediately drop in our tracks and stay down so our parents would be able to swing all the way around with guns raised, keeping aim and taking all four shots as birds flew past from front to rear or circled around us. "Ronnie, make sure he knows this, make sure he gets down, I'm not going to be able to turn around to check."*

The trail skirts the salt marsh, goes around to the south, but still heading basically east, taking them closer to the edge of the basin that eases up the hillsides like the rim of a plate, not the sides of a bowl. All around as she turns, all the low hills surrounding this watershed valley are clustered with houses. In the middle of the basin, the salt marsh runs up against a small flat-topped hillock forested with a few more lone over-grown eucalyptus and several thick-trunked, untrimmed palms. . . *well-rehearsed choreography, everything in perfect synchronization, our response as automatic as snapping a fishing rod back when the fish strikes: eventually our response to hit the ground was no longer triggered by the raising of guns, but by the whistle of the dove's wings that sounded just before the guns went up.*

A low drone overhead—it's a thick-bottomed propeller plane, a tanker holding water in its bowels.

Still heading east, the trail ducks into a small eucalyptus grove, a shelterbelt, shady and thick with hedge-like acacias and wild cucumber vines wrapping piles of downed, dead branches, new green wild-flower shoots tangling with seasons-past dead leaves and stocks, a bower of boughs and twining branches above.

"I don't remember a forest like this," she mutters.

"These things. Go big too fast. Weeds. Roots do everywhere. Never wear one. At our place."

The trail is crossed by dry trenches made by rivulets carrying runoff down to the creek that winds through the middle of the watershed. It looks like a flood came through and deposited a lot of debris, but it's just from these easily hundred-year-old trees that are never pruned. Old growth drops off, becomes windfall, creates a lot of mulching litter on the ground.

"And long . . . time between . . . to do more . . . growing," his words come in puffs. "You had . . . too young . . . to remember . . . " a soft cough . . . "any things."

Ronnie stops. Looking out from the forest, through windows framed by gently blowing eucalyptus limbs. The upper part of the flood basin is light brown, pale green and hazy yellow with more stands of cattail reeds, mustard, lupine, sage, toyon, and the plentiful chamise, its leaves tiny and thick and tough like plastic. A shaggy sedge growing into immense tufts also produces seed-stocks of feathery plumes three times Ronnie's height—used as decorations in some of the houses where she's worked. When the bushes die off they become big mounds of dry grass that resemble a beaver home, out-of-place in the middle of a field or hillside. The kind of habitat where quail should cluster, but the dead haystacks don't rustle with a hidden covey. *When they raised the shotguns, taking aim at a flying dove or quail blasting out of the underbrush, we were to immediately drop in our tracks . . . Who could've made such a misjudgment? The reflex so quick, so instinctive, impossible to say for sure which came first—the motion of our mother's gun being raised or the children hitting the dust at the sound or sight of game.*

Suddenly they are at the end of the trail, with the sandy shoulder of a country road at their feet, and a sign announcing the eastern boundary of the San Elijo Preserve.

"Did too much," he says. "Take to go back."

"I thought you knew—"

"Came every place. To—do with eyes. To know right."

Her father comes back past her, going back on the same trail. He's got the shovel cradled in his weak arm, handle in his armpit, blade resting on his curled bad hand, the sharpened tip pointing toward the path in front of his feet. *In brushy or waist-high foliage, hold the gun in both hands, across the body, muzzle pointed diagonally up and away. In open terrain, tuck the stock under one arm, weight of the gun balanced in one hand holding the wooden forearm, muzzle pointed to the ground. He showed us how, from either of these two positions, the hunter could easily and smoothly lift the gun into shooting position, and of course when he did, our reflexes honed, we squatted and ducked, fingers in our ears to insulate the detonation.*

He stumbles over a downed eucalyptus trunk lying across the path, half-buried, left there to prevent the trail from eroding during drenching rains. But he catches himself before falling, and the shovel never moves from its place under his arm.

FINGERS IN EARS . . . How would a scream be heard—if it was him screaming? Difficult to hear any screams . . . except your own.

"Do with eyes. On ground. To hear iris." He's walking with a slight highstep, picking his feet up unusually high.

"What? Look for iris? Why?"

"I did do visit back. One time. And gave iris tubers."

"When? Did I come with you? Did mom?"

Ronnie and her father are starting to emerge from the grove, facing north-east where the big cloud of smoke is still thick and boiling black in the center, no longer upwelling in a column but rising like a huge dark planet. But even vaster is the brown of earlier smoke already settling over the whole sky as haze, slowly growing like a stain. The sun, a brighter spot shrouded in the smog, is approaching noon.

"Me only. Under he went in ocean." The tanker airplane rumbles overhead again.

"You mean . . . *after* she drowned . . . when you brought her ashes?"

No answer . . . *Shooting was something you did with concern for safety as well as preservation of the terrain, including mindfulness of game limits and which birds were strictly off-limits . . . and an activity you did as calmly and quietly as possible, except for the report of the shotguns.* Ronnie sniffs, but can't yet smell the fire, just the salt marsh, and only when a low puff of breeze sweeps past. Phoebes fly from the top of one spindly bush to the next. The creek is obscured, running down below the thicker vegetation that crowds close to water, may even be barely a dribble if the stream has fanned out into braided rills. She can now see that the palms on the small plateau above the salt marsh are planted in a straight line. One of the old eucalyptus is so shaggy and bowed, from a distance it looks like a pepper tree. *Chad lay on the hard-baked ground below . . .*

Then . . . who was screaming? Wasn't someone screaming. . . ?

Where the trail skirts the salt marsh, as though on a rim above a canyon, the closest plant growth is now low, almost all foxtail grass, and it's all going brown, again an unseasonal early-winter seeding, blown almost flat, deflated. Then they veer slightly west and back uphill toward the stand of fennel—a thicket that's oddly segregated from vast patches of wild mustard blooming in a layer all around the fennel stocks that rise well over Ronnie's head. The rhythm of their footsteps seems to be dragging, getting slower, heavier, as though they're moving through the gluey strain of a dream. Just after the path levels out, it goes into and through part of the fennel thicket. Entering the hedge is like hitting a wall of the fennel's fragrance—unrefined, wild, buzzing with bees, thinner and less sticky than the odor of candy licorice. She closes her eyes, dizzy for a second, then runs into her father who has stopped on the trail just after emerging from the fennel. He's gazing off the path toward his right, not at the black sky but at the rest of the dense copse of fennel—the majority of the thicket—that spreads out north of the trail. Behind them is the lone eucalyptus in the field of low seeding grasses and scattered bricks.

"That place," her father says.

"What?"

"I think . . . at here." He heads off the trail through a wide swath of shorter grass within the fennel thicket. In fact the fennel seems to grow on three sides of an open space, a meadow of waving grasses, almost the exact center of the entire watershed, ground that's higher than the lagoon or salt marsh or other lowland, so the creek isn't nearby nor would any rivulets run here if rains were heavy and the creek overflowed to find new channels. On this higher ground, dry except for what rain would fall here, the rubbery-stalked fennel is hardy enough to predominate.

"There." And he heavily drops to his knees.

. . . *instinctively, reflexively, those without guns were to let our knees buckle, crouch low to the ground, squat at our parents' feet, wait for the shots.*

But who was screaming? Wasn't someone screaming? Would the mockingbirds learn and imitate this sound as song?

"Here." His good hand brushing, almost caressing the stiff fan of gray-green leaves of an iris.

"You mean you found it—the spot you wanted?"

Still on his knees, he positions the blade of the shovel in front of the iris. "Dig."

"What for?"

"She's buried under. Here."

"You mean their ashes—scattered here." Ronnie pulls the jar from the vest pocket.

"No. She's at here."

"Her *ashes*."

"Our brother. Dig down to put here."

"No, we buried a hawk."

"Different time. The boy—buried under here."

"You *buried* him here?"

"We three. Mom, us."

. . . only sticks and pocket knives for digging, for cutting the clay, only hands for scooping . . . vast, arid bottomland could hardly be touched, let alone filled, offered no resistance to our voices, just sucked the sound out of us and dispersed it, leaving only the whisper of sand pushed aside, pebbles rolling, the silent effort to muffle a grunt of voice or moan beneath soft but heavy breathing, the clink of shovel on rock.

"Why? Why here?"

He takes the jar from her hand. "Dead. Nothing else. Could we do."

"But why *here*? Didn't he . . . die . . . at home?"

Leaning on the shovel, Ronnie's father pushes himself to his feet, then steps on the shovel with his bad foot, pushes at the hard soil and falls sideways, catches himself on one knee, good hand on the ground. He's grunting softly and breathing hard. . . *who was screaming? Wasn't someone screaming?* He struggles to his feet again, picks up the shovel, standing above Ronnie . . . *mother rocked silently, kneeling, in her lap the head of a deer whose liquid eyes could not be soothed of fear and pain, its body nearly motionless, twitching . . . father helpless. He held a camping shovel.*

He prepares again to dig. This time the blade goes in. Uproots the sod layer of dead grass. Exposes yellowish sandy loam.

"What *happened* here, Dad?"

"You don't re— You don't keep—don't hear . . . old times."

"I know, so *tell* me."

Panting harder. "It had . . . by mis—mis— Not anything on purpose."

A mistake, an accident.

. . . our knees buckled to squat below the line of fire, the reflex so quick, so instinctive, impossible to say for sure which came first—the motion of our mother's gun being raised or the children hitting the dust at the sound or sight of game. He was tramping along admiring the colored shells he had stuck on each finger, ten of them, a rainbow of plastic finger-covers with metal tips . . . not paying attention!

We screamed. Kept on screaming . . .

In front of Ronnie, the trench being dug by her father—slowly, tediously—expands and deepens. Every scrape of blade in sand, against hard-baked clay or sandstone, in dry rocky dirt choked with grassy roots, is a chill on her skin. Her own breath seems to rasp against her throat, but her mouth is closed. Her eyes dry and staring. Her arms leaden and motionless. Her heartbeat thick and queasy. *We screamed. Kept on screaming. Someone was screaming. Shoulders grasped and body shaken, STOP IT, STOP IT, then a dreadful silence, the sun growing hotter as the hole was dug in dry hard-packed dirt—the day our mother shot the hawk . . . wasn't the hole for the hawk? SOMEONE was screaming. But was it the same someone and the same screaming? The same savage sound . . . Chad lay on the hard-baked ground . . .*

Over and over, his dusty boot picks up so slowly, is set deliberately onto the tiny shovel, then the slow push of his leg, grind of metal in parched soil. Each time he lifts out mere cupfuls of sand and pebbles. Staring, Ronnie barely feels herself sinking, her knees hit softly on the dead foxtail grass beside the open furrow. *We dug, with boot heels, sticks, fingernails, the butts of shotguns. Suddenly the vast field existed only beneath our hands, the hard yellow earth, woody root of sage, a tiny snake who'd burrowed into sandstone. Where was Chad?*

. . . the clink of shovel on rock . . .

"Dad. . . ? When *did* you start always carrying the shovel in the car?" Each shovel-full poured delicately in a little pile, the little piles lined up around the outside of the trench. An inverted antlion colony. "Dad?"

"Good . . . tool . . . to keep . . . always beside . . ."

The shovel continues shaving the edges of the trench that's growing gradually wider as it becomes half-inch by half-inch deeper.

. . . here and there, always in the way, holding the dead hawk up by its wings—making it fly, dip and soar over our heads as we dug—and impersonating the CAW CAW of its cry.

"But Dad, the day mom shot the hawk and we buried it . . ." *. . . with boot heels, sticks, fingernails, the butts of . . .* The blade screeches against a buried rock, her hands fly to her ears. *But who was screaming? Wasn't someone screaming?* "Dad, we didn't use a shovel that day." *. . . leaving only the whisper of sand pushed aside . . . the clink of shovel on rock . . .* "We didn't *have* a shovel to bury the hawk, Dad. Did we?" Watching her father's hand brushing sandy dirt from the rock he's hit. "Dad?"

"There. No. Not it yet."

"Not what? *What* are you looking for?" Her hands now on the lip of the trench.

"Get behind."

His limp body scooped up the way we would lift a dead cottontail with one hand.

Fists clutched against her body, stares down and opens her hands to find two palmfuls of dirt.

The hawk was dead. Hooked bill flopped down against speckled breast.

The delicate smell of licorice fennel, of dust and scrub, the deeper earthy scent of the loam out of sight below countless plant lifecycles. Nothing pungent, nothing too thick or sour. No rotting mulch, scant fodder for worms or grubs to help break down into over-rich nutrients. The smell of humming bees, of thin quiet air, of clean seeds and tiny dry leaves in a slightly salty arid flood basin surrounded by roads and houses. SOMEONE *was still screaming. But there was also an awful silence.*

The shovel clinks. "There." He bends again, his hand in the dirt, digging down under something with one finger. No thought in her muscles to lean in and assist him. She can hear his fingernail scraping in hardened sand. Has to use the shovel again—places the blade precisely and works it in gingerly, uses it like a crowbar to ease the object from the hard-packed earth. The ground shifts and cracks appear then crumble all around where he's lifting it, something long, dirt-colored or dirt-crusted. He lays the shovel down beside himself, squatting, the thing across his knees, stringers of roots hanging from it, swinging clods of dirt dangling down.

"What is it?"

"Our mother's gun."

. . . crouch low to the ground, squat at our parents' feet, wait for the shots, this time a double crack from our mother's gun—hers alone—while our father shouted, No, AL, but too late. Perhaps only one of us made that second misinformed recoil to squat at our mother's feet . . . crouch down, knees hit the dust, fingers in ears, head up, the report from our mother's gun, our father's shout, and the screaming.

MOMMY—

SHUT UP, SHUT UP, WHY DID YOU—HOW COULD YOU—

QUIET, AL, HUSH UP, RONNIE—

MOMMY—

"Why . . . did she bury . . . her gun?"

"You. Too little. To know." Like defeathering a bird, he's pulling the dead roots from the rusted barrel. The thinner steel of the trigger area is heavily pitted, completely eaten through in spots, the trigger itself so skinny, it would likely crumble to dust if touched. The wooden stock is gone, long ago became a dark mulch spot in the yellow loam, then slowly leached away into the sandy sediments.

"But, Dad . . . I'm sure . . . Mom didn't bury her gun that day." Her voice as faltering as his, watching him brush soil and burnished rust powder from the corroded barrel with a single slow finger. "She didn't bury her gun when she shot the hawk." She's reaching for the oxidized gun lying across her father's knees, saying, "Why *would* she? She wasn't *that* upset. It wasn't . . ." He lifts the gun and hands it to her, her words still sputtering out, "Killing the hawk wasn't such a big deal. Was it?" Cool, slightly heavy, the muzzle packed with black dirt. Suddenly looks up at her father, awkwardly getting to his feet again, picking up the shovel. Her fists close on the gun, Ronnie's voice catching, ripping, "Shooting the hawk—it wasn't . . . *that* awful. Not *that* day—nothing was *that* awful that day. Chad was—playing. He was *playing. . . No one* screamed when she shot that hawk!"

The vast, arid bottomland could hardly be touched, let alone filled, offered no resistance to our voices, just sucked the sound out of us and dispersed it, leaving only the whisper of sand pushed aside, pebbles rolling, the silent effort to muffle a grunt of voice or moan beneath soft but heavy breathing, the clink of shovel on rock.

But he was here and there, always in the way, holding the dead hawk up by its wings—making it fly, dip and soar over our heads as we dug—and impersonating the CAW CAW of its cry.

The kestrel, smallest native falcon, doesn't have wings like fanned fingers. Its wings are pointed, like the dove. But such definite differences—without the dove's heavy-bodied silhouette, without the rhythmic wing beat and whistle of feather. Who could've made such a misjudgment? . . . impossible to say for sure which came first—the motion of our mother's gun being raised or the children hitting the dust at the sound or sight of game.

Bird coming in. We squatted. We hit the dirt. Sensing the motion behind her, she swung around and shot. A mistake, an accident—to kill songbird or heron or raptor.

Our mistake caused her accident. But—she shot the hawk the previous season, a full year before the other one . . . a repeated accident . . . when the same thing happened a second time.

Almost the same thing, a second time. The same mistake. A similar accident.

He was tramping along admiring the colored shells he had stuck on each finger, ten of them, a rainbow of plastic finger-covers with metal tips. Someone had to show him how he wasn't paying attention, how he was going to get into trouble, get US into trouble. So . . . only one of us made the second misinformed recoil: squatting at our mother's feet—knowing there was no game in sight.

Sensing the motion behind her, she swung around and shot.

"Where's the glass?" The shovel is motionless in his hands, the blade held level. It's right in front of her face. Then he shakes it, just a little, the way a prospector pans for gold, the way an archeologist sifts for . . .

On the blade, amid soil and dirt-covered pebbles, three small teeth, a piece of curved brown bone.

"*No!*" The thing in her hand falls to the sod. "*No!*" On her feet. "No . . . *no!*" Now eyes shut. Swinging her hands and arms wildly in front of herself as though waving off a swarm of bees.

"You won't. Know. Can't re—"

"Stop it. Stop *saying* that! Why do you keep *saying* that? I *do* remember."

. . . offered no resistance to our voices . . .

"He wished. For you just always. Didn't know. Can think something else, not this. And not never know this."

"*What?* Finish a sentence, dammit."

"He didn't. Want you to know. What he'd did. Done."

. . . Kept on screaming. Someone was screaming . . .

"What? What are you saying? What *who* did?"

. . . sucked the sound out of us and dispersed it.

"He—our mother—wished. Wished for you didn't know. And never knew. That he'd—What our mother *did*. Shooting the brother by mis—"

. . . the same savage sound and same raw throat.

"I HATE YOU!"

Chapter Eleven

Cries of sirens come from several directions, but are more remote than the drone and thump of helicopters overhead—more than one now, and another tanker plane, and, in an upshift of wind, the acrid taste of smoke and charred earth. Ronnie is panting at the bus stop. When the bus comes and she steps aboard, when the brakes sigh and the door is sucked softly closed—the usual sounds of daily transit as well as the extraordinary noise of emergency vehicles sealed outside—the throb of her father's voice, and her own, still pound in her head.

"He wished. Wished for you . . . not never know this. That he'd . . . What he'd did."

"*What?* Say a whole sentence, damn you."

"He didn't. Want you to know. What our mother did—"

"So it was better for me to think I'd done it *myself?* You *knew* I thought I'd done it. You *let* me think *I* did it."

"No. He want you never to think— When you eat guilt, he hear you were meaning . . . when you— You bend down, hand in ear, so our mother . . . think there have . . . game . . . birds in sight. So he— Bang. Just acc—mis— Say for me?"

Her scream—almost an hour ago, now at least two miles ago—might still be carrying, might still be shredding the hum of faraway traffic, the tanker planes, the white noise of the city, kept at a distance, surrounding them. *"Shut up. Why couldn't you just stay a senile old man?"*

People are moving away from her. Getting up to stand and wait near the rear door several stops early. An older heavy woman doesn't get up but pulls the end of a scarf across her nose and mouth. The bus is overheated, despite the door opening and closing. Ronnie's breathing eases, no longer panting. Now she can smell it too. Faintly it's dust and smoke, but also a more heady, almost sticky block of odor. Simultaneously crude, savage and dank, fetid. And it's coming from her. It is her.

The woman glares over the top of the gauzy lavender scarf she presses to her face. Ronnie looks down at her lap, moving slowly, unties the sleeves of Adrian's jacket tied around her waist under the hunting vest, then threads the jacket onto her arms over her sweatshirt, overlaps the two zippered edges across her chest, covering the vest. Crosses her arms, hunches her shoulders, leans forward. The spandex cuts tight into her gut.

It's not late enough for the bus to be full. It seems that no one is talking. The driver has a portable radio on the floor, attached with a bungie to the fare box. In a cyclone of static . . . *roughly a five hundred acres so far have burned* . . . a crackling voice informs . . . *as many as twenty hillside homes in La Costa* . . . probably reporting by telephone from one of the helicopters that can't be heard from inside the bus, but surely are still droning, orbiting overhead, making passes over the fire, dodging tanker planes, other news aircraft, the police choppers, circling wider and higher, just a faint thump and buzz as each vehicle passes over her father, out on the lagoon plateau, in lengthening shadows cast by the tall fennel, with his shovel and his irises and his son.

By the time she walks the trail from the hardware store up to Adrian's camp, it could be three, possibly even four o'clock. The daylight is dim but has been all day. Haze of smoke from the fire has grown enough, hour by hour, to accompany the sun east to west across the sky, and now continues to throw a dense curtain over what would soon have been clear rays of sunset.

The camp is cool and quiet. Her handcart and other belongings have not been moved. She does not go back under the bush into Adrian's sleeping quarters. Instead she sits on one of the big rocks beside a smaller bush where two gray socks are draped in a fork of branches. One of the socks has a threadbare heel with a small worn-away hole. She stares at it, imagining how, if she had a needle and thread, she would weave the thread through the remaining frayed mesh of the cotton, fabricating new material to cover the hole without a seam that might cause blisters. Eventually she can barely see the socks. Daylight is gone.

Ronnie shivers, startling herself out of the stupor. As darkness and chill drop heavily onto the hillsides and gullies, she stares across the camp toward the handcart, unable to see if her father's sweatshirt is there, unable to recall if he's wearing it. Already can't picture him any way except his drawn face, as though growing longer, mouth slightly agape, the shovel with its pile of gritty loam held out like a serving platter, trembling in his weak hand.

Footsteps approaching. Not a slow shuffle with one foot slightly dragging, but a steady crunch on hard sand, two sets, and their voices muttering, cursing, no laughter. She stands. They're not coming from the downhill side, not climbing up from the bus stop where the men would come home from work—they're approaching from up the hill, from the neighborhood. Reflexes somehow dulled, she's staring at Adrian's sleeping shelter under the tarp-draped sumac, already hiding there in her mind—inside, or better yet behind the bush, since her handcart in front is too much an announcement of an inhabitant—but she's still rooted midway between the fire pit and the rock, so she's not even watching as they come into view.

"Ronnie! What a fucking relief!" Adrian—already upon her, has her by the shoulders, her neck like a rag doll tipped back. "We've been at the fire, we thought you didn't get out, there's nothing left, and there's this little crater—" his face a sooty mask, his eyes like weird pale moons looking out, "—and the whole gully has burned off, right up to the top, those houses up there—" his ponytail only holding half his hair, the rest loose and darkened with smoke, even his breath in her face is smoky, "—and it also spread further up the gully, miles back, toward Box Canyon where they can't get trucks in, I though you were—We didn't know if you got out." Suddenly, for a second, he pulls her against himself, her nose crashes against his collarbone, the sooty smell of him isn't sweet woodsmoke, it's rancid and bitter, then she's released and even pushed away nearly as abruptly. "They found your baby highchair, completely toasted—the firefighters thought they'd be finding a burned-up kid."

Ronnie stares at him.

"Hey, where's the old man—your dad?"

"He . . ."

"Ronnie, he's wasn't . . . he didn't . . . was he unable to get out?"

"No, I left him—"

He has her shoulders again. "You didn't. Where? Were you away when it started? On your way to work? Didn't you even *know* about the fire? It started right where you live . . . your father—" His hands like talons against the bones in her arms.

Either collapsing or retreating, she sinks out of his grasp, once again sits on the rock. As though out of breath. As though physically exhausted. As though she hadn't been planted immobile on this same rock for over an hour. "No . . . he's fine . . . I mean, we both got out of the fire . . . I mean, we were never in the fire . . . we left before. He's . . . Then I left him . . ."

"Oh, at a shelter? A hospital?"

"No." She swallows, her throat as dry as though she'd been battling the fire alongside Adrian. "At the lagoon. He's at the lagoon."

"Why? Did you move your camp down there?"

"No." Swallows again. "There's no camp. Our stuff is all here." With her chin gestures toward the handcart, and Adrian glances that way also. For the first time she notices Hernando, who'd come back to camp with Adrian. She can't remember if the voices she'd heard approaching camp had been speaking Spanish or English.

"Then why the hell would you take him out to the lagoon and leave him there?"

"I . . . The other lagoon. *He's* the one who wanted to go out there. Then he . . ."

"What?" Kneeling in front of her so their eyes are level. "Did he have a stroke or heart attack or something?"

"No, he's fine. He got what he wanted."

"He *asked* you to leave him alone out there after dark?"

"No, he wanted to go back there and find where he'd buried my brother. His whole . . . his body. Not ashes after all."

"*What?*"

"And I left him because . . ." Her fists, clenched on her lap, gather fistfuls of the bottom edge of the hunting vest. ". . . because he . . . they let me take the blame."

"Hey! Hey, wait." He grabs her ankles, one in each hand, as though afraid she'll swing a leg out and kick him in the face. "That's no excuse to leave your father— How did he die—your brother?"

"I always thought I . . . ," watching her grimy knuckles turn white, "but . . . I just found out . . . My mother shot him."

"My *god*." His eyes fall to the dirt in front of his knees, then rise again. "But how did you get blamed? Did they tell you that *you* shot him?"

"No. I never used the gun."

"Then how did you get blamed?"

"I thought it happened some other way. I *thought* I remembered something, but . . . I remembered two separate things that happened, but remembered them as just one time. There were *two* times we buried something, two different times that I made the same mistake and both times we had to bury . . . something."

"What mistake? Did they *tell* you it was your fault?"

"No."

"Well, did you tell them you thought *you* killed him?"

"Sort of. I think they knew. We didn't exactly talk about it. Why should we? I guess we all knew!"

"Ronnie, I don't get it, who knew *what*?" He stands, hands in his pockets then out again. "I mean it's a horrible tragedy, it *was*, but how long ago, twenty years? Thirty? What could make you angry enough *now* to leave an old man alone at night out in a field?"

Something bright and hot, like fear, flares in her stomach. Her body abruptly doubles over as though retching, her voice pouring out dark and guttural. "He knew I threw away my life—he *knew* I thought I killed my brother. They let me forfeit my life because I thought I robbed them of *his*." So many words had never come out of her mouth so fast before. And they keep coming. "He let me grow up thinking I could never do anything my whole life except continue to make up for . . . losing Chad. He knew that's why I was . . . the way I was. At least I thought he knew." It feels, even tastes, like vomiting. "I thought that's what he meant . . . today . . . that he *knew* I thought it was my fault. And that he'd decided not to say anything, to just let me go *on* assuming it was my fault . . . so I wouldn't hate my mother. But actually—he didn't realize what I really thought, and *I* never knew what they—"

"Because you never talked about it."

"Maybe he didn't think we had to. Because, in a way, he already *did* know. And he was right. *I* was the one who had it wrong. I had two different hunting-accident memories glued into one. I was presuming my brother died when he fell out of the tree. I felt guilty for the wrong thing. Because it turns out . . ."

"It wasn't your fault at all."

"No," she looks up, cold tears on her face, "it actually *was*. It *was* my fault." Rubbing her cheeks with her palms, feeling grit on her hands— dirt from the trench her father was digging—rasp her skin. "Because I ducked. It's what we were always supposed to do when game came in sight. He was playing and not watching and I wanted to show him, to scare him into . . . I wanted to teach him to pay attention. So I ducked when there was no game. To startle him and make him realize he should be watching. But she thought I saw game, so she just turned and shot."

After a moment, Adrian turns his back and walks away to where Hernando is sitting, his back also to Ronnie, on the other side of the fire pit. Does Adrian want her to leave—is he giving her a private moment to slip away and take her thirty-five-year-old distress with her, out of his prudently negotiated, precariously balanced life? Hernando must have made a fire. She can now hear the pop of flame and smell the smoke, fresh greasewood and straw. The two men exchange some conversation. Ronnie wipes her face on one sleeve, knowing she's only smearing dirt from one place to another. Hernando lifts dripping feet from where he'd been soaking them in a plastic bowl of warm water. Adrian tosses a towel into Hernando's lap then takes the bowl, flings the water into the grasses outside camp—an almost invisible sparkling arc pattering into the darkness.

With an empty soup can Adrian dips into a blackened bucket sitting in the fire pit, pours steaming water into the bowl, adds to it from one of the plastic jugs lined up under a small sumac, takes another towel from a branch, then returns to Ronnie. Squatting, he sets the plastic bowl on the ground near Ronnie's boots, wets one end of the towel, wrings it out, then hands it to her. With both hands, Ronnie presses the warm, wet towel to her face. It smells like the dusty leaves of the sumac.

"As soon as you catch your breath and start to see straight," he says quietly, "we'll go back out there and get your father. Tonight."

Her face still in the towel. "Okay." She draws a shaky breath, then lowers the towel. He takes it, re-wets it, wrings it again and hands it back to her.

"You didn't need me to tell you."

"I know."

Single file and silent, Adrian in front, they make their way down the trail in complete darkness. She can see streetlights on the boulevard at the bottom of the hill, the lit parking lot of the hardware store, traffic lights and neon commercial signs and Christmas light displays, but can't see ten feet off either side of the trail.

At the bus stop, neither sits at first. It might be around 6:30, possibly approaching 7:00. She knows it's a weekday but doesn't know which day nor the date. Christmas trees with their branches still tied up are leaning against the chain link fence that separates the sidewalk and bus stop from the hardware store parking lot. An area of parking lot has been cordoned off with twinkling colored lights. Under a picnic shade tarp, a man who sells the trees sits on a stool, smoking.

Squinting into the approaching headlights, Adrian says, "You know, Hernando, he sends more than half his pay back home to his parents, so he'll never have enough for his own place. His father's all broken down from . . . well, he doesn't work, his mother has seven or eight other kids—Nando's the oldest, he's twenty, the youngest around eight or nine. And look how Manuel went back to Mexico to make sure his mother and aunts had someone to take care of them, even though he could make a lot more up here." Holding onto the bus stop sign pole, Adrian looks down, using the edge of the curb to clean mud from the bottoms of his boots. "Manny—Manuel—he's older, around my age, thirty-one or two, an old man and stuck on this career path."

"You're only. . . ?"

"*Only*? Thanks. Anyway, and here *you* are traipsing around the county with your father who probably needs to be looked after full time—"

"He can manage his own basic care." Ronnie sits on the bench, staring with throbbing eyes at the blurs of passing traffic.

"Can he? But still, you've been with him all along, you *stayed*, you never went out on your own."

"I know. That's because—"

"Wait, hear me out. Specific circumstances don't really matter to what I'm getting at. I'm just noticing the common strain. Filial responsibility. They say it doesn't exist in the United States where the individual is revered. Don't we grow up expecting *not* to remain in a primary family with our parents once we're adults? It's interesting, how the predisposition is shared after all. That's all I'm saying."

"Are you always studying something?"

"That's exactly what my parents would ask." He turns but doesn't flash the expected grin. "And yes, I realize the irony of that statement, considering the topic of discussion. I was just about to throw myself into the case-study pool." Now the grin. "Or maybe out into traffic."

Either because it's rush hour or perhaps mere days from Christmas, nobody's out buying a tree. What will happen to all these trees, still bound and bundled? During their last years on the farmstead, in January they used to go to the county recycling yard and fill trashcans with free mulch from pulped Christmas trees. For a few weeks afterwards, the garden beds smelled vividly of pine.

"I think individual circumstances *do* matter," Ronnie blurts. "My whole filial duty was completely misguided."

"But do you regret what you've done?"

"I've been in a dungeon."

"Isn't that a little too dramatic?" Adrian raises a hand to the Christmas tree man, who nods. "Besides, your parents' grief may've given you the tools to build your dungeon, but you built it yourself." He sits beside her, not so close that he can't turn sideways to face her, drawing one foot onto the bench and wrapping his arms around his knee. "And that's just assuming it really *was* a dungeon. Everyone's in some sort of dungeon, from their own little limited point of view, but maybe it's an honorable, rich or meaningful road seen from another perspective."

"Like you? Your life living under a bush?"

His brief smile is wan. "I do like to think of it as honorable and meaningful. It's my parents who see it as the dungeon . . . and the dungeon I *chose* . . . for no reason they can fathom."

"Can you blame them for worrying?"

"Worrying's one thing . . . bribery's another."

Ronnie's exhaustion is settling over her like a blanket, so she doesn't ask for an explanation. When she tips her neck and lays her head on the back of the bus stop bench, her face to the starless sky—gray, not black, because city lights reflect off the dome of smoke—she can smell the Christmas trees on puffs of breeze, tinged also with exhaust and soot. And it's like her voice is another vapor, wistful and frail, "I feel sorry for these trees that won't get bought."

It's either Adrian's laugh or his hand on her knee, for just a second, that sends a flush from her gut to her neck. The white lines around his eyes remain creased, his crescent eyes sparkling. "I guess things aren't too bad if you can worry about feelings for dead trees." He stands, hands once again in his pockets. "It's not like they're from a real forest, like now there's a bare mountainside somewhere and the trees they took from it are just going to waste." He steps into the gutter again to scan the oncoming traffic.

"That's not what I mean."

"Oh?" Arms folded, one foot on the curb, still grinning. "Tell me, then."

"Well, they were going to be Christmas trees and make someone happy," she sits up, almost smiles but can't seem to find it. "I know that's awfully sappy. But they were going to mean something and now they'll just whither and get thrown in the chipper."

Although he doesn't laugh again, he seems so buoyant and full of energy, and she feels the opposite, leaden. "Hey," he bounces up from the gutter, comes back to the bench, sits on her other side, actually straddles the bench, facing her. "This won't make you feel better, but I don't think the trees make anyone that happy. Not anymore. I remember how going out to get our tree was such a big deal. But haven't you noticed that the big tree lots—the ones that aren't part of a hardware store or nursery—they put up one of those air-tents with a big balloon floor where kids jump around, or one of those tents full of plastic balls kids go plowing into, or some train ride, and those big goofy Santa balloons? That's because just going out to pick a tree isn't exciting enough for kids anymore—they have to have a carnival."

"That's true," she murmurs. "A few days before Christmas, my father used to cut a branch from this big long-needled pine on our property. He had to go up into the tree with a saw. My brother would be on his tiptoes down below until the branch came flying down."

"What would you be doing?"

"I don't remember."

They sit in silence. Tinny speakers in the tree lot play a tape loop of carols. In the glow of the street lights, she watches airborne particles swirl, then realizes they are particles of ash. "This week, putting up those fancy decorations," she says, "I remembered how my parents hung just one string of lights across the front of the house—on a dead end lane, no one else would even see them. When it got dark—*barely* dark the first night because he couldn't wait—they turned the lights on and my brother shrieked and danced on the front lawn."

"We sound like we're a million years old." With one finger, he traces a name carved in the bench. "Did your dad continue to cut a branch even after . . ."

"I guess so. Eventually he had to take the whole tree down because the roots were causing eruptions in the lawn and could've in time ruined one of his rock walls." She stands, her knees surprisingly not jelly. The bus is approaching, brakes hissing.

"He could take a whole, mature tree down by himself?"

"Yeah, why?"

The inside of the bus is lit up. Sometimes, just after dusk, walking home instead of taking the bus, she noticed how the buses were lit, showing all the people sitting together, the first seats facing each other, some people standing in the aisle. It was like watching a warm evening living room roll past down the street. But boarding the bus really isn't like going inside a house—with gusts of exhaust as they mount the steep steps, then the hard plastic seats and smeary windows and gritty vinyl floor. Before leaving camp, Adrian had used the warm water left in the pan to douse his face, had re-gathered his ponytail and exchanged his dirty, smoky sweatshirt for one that just smells a little musty. Except for wiping her face with the wet towel, Ronnie isn't any cleaner than several hours ago, but this time the bus is already thick with the smell of end-of-the-day bodies.

Adrian slides onto the middle of the first seat, the one that faces across the aisle. A sad-looking or sullen man is already on one end. There's just enough room for Ronnie on the other end. She holds the vertical pole to keep herself balanced. But at the next traffic light, the bus lurches and her forehead knocks against the cold metal pole and Adrian's arm is around her, steadying her, then pulling her against himself, and she feels her body settle slowly, as though giving up.

Above her head, far above it seems, his voice says, "So, are you not interested or just being polite?" He shifts, leans something against the top of her head, his cheek perhaps, or jaw. His voice a little closer, "I know compared to your protracted family drama, my little dilemma is a big nothing." Is he making fun of her? Her mind tries to tense up for a response, but nothing comes to the surface. He goes on, without waiting, "But it sure feels like a sell-out."

Ronnie closes her eyes. Did she sleep, for just a second?

"I deserved that," he says with a laugh.

"Deserved what?" Her voice muffled against his side.

"That big sigh. Here I am whining about my petty problems."

"No, I didn't . . . I wasn't . . . meaning anything. In fact," she tries to lift her face, but barely moves, "I'm sorry for not listening better."

"I haven't told this stuff to any of the guys, I don't know why I'm wanting to blather now. I'll have to tell the guys something, though, when I leave, and it's gonna sound bad, no matter how I put it."

"What is?" A week ago, this news might've caused a lump of dread in her stomach. But now, although she's sitting crushed up against his body, his arm around her, she knows she's no longer even part of what he's leaving. "Where are you going?"

"I'm moving back home and going back to school. My side of the bargain. If I do, then they'll set me up with a trust fund to start a non-profit organization to help migrant workers. But that's so far down the line, the guys'll only see I'm going back to suburbia."

"They're not like that."

"No?" He stirs, the warm weight is lifted from the top of Ronnie's head. "Just think of how life looks to them. This is what I was talking about with all the filial responsibility stuff." The bus stops. The grim man on Adrian's other side gets up, but doesn't get off. He moves further back on the bus. Simultaneously, Ronnie and Adrian sit up straighter, push slightly apart and turn to face each other. His arm still connecting them, a hand on her shoulder and a finger quietly stroking the back of her neck, he says, "*You're* like them, but I'm not. They send money home to their families—but it's been the other way around for me. And now I run completely back and let my parents support me . . . it's soft, is what it is. But . . . I . . . I'll tell you, I would've loved to be in your shoes, in your family."

"You want to not exist?"

"What—? Wait, don't go there again." A brief squeeze of her neck as the bus lurches forward. "I don't get your beef about no life, Ronnie. You had a life, *have* one. For every gallon of experience you've had, you've only told me three drops, yet I can tell it was deep and—"

"But I also meant how, to the world, my brother never existed. Literally."

"How's that?"

"He didn't even have a birth certificate. He was born at home and they never . . . did whatever it is people do to document that a new person is alive. So . . . when they—when we buried him, there was no mystery. No one wondered where he went, why he disappeared. Then we never even talked about him. Like he'd never been born. Except my mother . . ." Trying to ignore being blinded by tears, but can't any longer, she uses one shoulder to wipe half her face, turning slightly away from him.

"I think he did continue to exist one way or another all that time . . . 'cause I'm guessing *you* didn't forget anything he said or did." His hand slips up onto the back of her head, into the slightly matted dusty hair that's still not yet two inches long.

Despite the low ceiling of smoke reflecting the city's lights, the bottom-land is black dark. They stand on the edge of the lighted boulevard, on the road's sandy shoulder, traffic whizzing behind them, across the street a brightly lit parking lot and neon bus stop. In front of them the airy puffs of breeze through grasses, rustles of mice or rabbits, but so dark even the trail doesn't show.

Adrian locates a tiny flashlight on his key chain. "I must be some sort of idiot to come out here no better prepared than this."

With the whisper of a light beam sweeping in front of his feet, he begins to move forward, reaching back with one hand which Ronnie obediently takes.

When her eyes adjust as much as they're going to, she can see enough to discern the top half of the lone eucalyptus up ahead, slightly uphill and to the left—south-south east—but for now can't make out the stand of fennel on the level knoll across the trail from the tree. They won't hit the fennel until the trail—if they're still on a trail—turns to the east. Remapping the terrain in her mind, she tries to remember what landscape features she passed after she left her father and ran out of the bottomland toward the bus stop, the same topography they would've passed through together, much slower, on the way in. Maybe it was all the spreading wild mustard, which would be nearly as tall as the fennel, and in the dark neither would overtly distinguish itself, except by smell.

"The fire, or something, has obliterated the smells—isn't everything supposed to smell stronger at night?"

"What do you mean?"

"Or maybe it's closer to dawn, after the dew point, when you can just smell everything better, the swamp areas or mud, sandstone or tidal backwash, sage or fennel or eucalyptus or . . . whatever."

"Okay, Ol' Yeller, did you learn to track game too?"

"Huh?"

"You're like a virtual hound dog."

"In more ways than one." She keeps her eyes up, on the silhouette of the shaggy eucalyptus. "Maybe it's me that's covering all the scents. I think I smell pretty bad. So bad I can't even tell anymore."

"And neither can the rest of us dirty migrants, so don't worry." He tangles his fingers with hers, not the way she ever held Chad's hand. "It doesn't bother me, if that's what you think. Who says the smell is *bad*, anyway?"

Their footsteps begin to fall more quietly—a soft crunch with a thick padded feel underfoot. "We're off the trail."

"Yeah, I know." His penlight is more like a pale moth darting around above the ground. "This damn thing's useless."

"My eyes're getting adjusted."

They can't possibly get lost—with the pinprick beams of headlights moving like beads on a string on the freeway to the west, the hulking tree in front of them to the south—knowing that the trail will bend to the east and shift the tree to their right and the freeway behind them. But several more times they stray from the trail, discovering they've gone afield when one or the other stumbles over a rock or bone-white driftwood branch lying under tangled dead grasses, or when their progress is abruptly halted by a stiff buckwheat bush nearly wrapping their legs. Once Ronnie's boot hits against four or five bricks still mortared together. Each time they backtrack and relocate the trail.

"It's not that far. We were right in the middle. A high place. The other side of the fennel. Not that far."

"It's okay, we'll find it. Him. We'll find him."

The same time she realizes their progress, like a breeze, has subtly shifted and they're now facing east, they're also suddenly at the stand of fennel. It's unmistakable, impossible to miss, abruptly in front of them like a dark wall with a darker crevice where the trail briefly penetrates the hedge, and the licorice smell difficult to blot out, even with smoke. By day swarming, even vibrating with buzzing bees, wasps and dragonflies, but at night it's sewn in the lace of a million spider webs. Every two or three steps her face breaks through one, and she's not even in front on the trail. A tickle on her neck, and her fingers mash a bug there. The hollow stalks and stiff, tiny starburst blossoms rattle and whistle softly in gusts of wind, and it feels colder, as though they've left sunshine to duck into a deeply shaded thicket.

It seems they stay enveloped in the fennel forever, but finally Adrian ducks under a broken stalk, steps into the clearing and stops, with Ronnie, behind him, still in the thicket. She drops his hand, pushes past him, batting at a last sticky strand of silk across her eyes. "Yes, it's here. Right here. We were right up in here somewhere. *Dad!*"

But there's no sound. No shovel in sand, no rolling pebbles, no soft grunt, no panting effort . . . did she really think he would still be here digging, scraping . . . excavating, exhuming . . .

"Where *is* he? Dad? *Dad!*"

"Ronnie—"

"Where could he have *gone*? *Dad!*"

"We'll find him, let's just—"

"It's too dark. We can't see to follow footprints." Hands cupped to her mouth, "Dad! Can you hear me? *Dad!*" When Adrian puts a hand on her shoulder, she whirls in place to face him. "Is this even the right spot? Give me the light. Don't move."

"Why?"

"We might be stomping all over . . ."

The dim beam barely makes it to the ground. Ronnie squats to hold the penlight a foot off the surface, slowly zigzagging the faint yellow circle. She looks up at the fennel, the way it makes edges of a clearing. "It's got to be the place." The muted colors of evening make the dirt all look the same, whether freshly turned or undisturbed crust or matted with dead roots, and the light, as faint as it is, is still a ray, so every rock and pebble and blade of grass throws a small shifting shadow as she moves the beam. But finally, "There!" and she reaches out to touch the stiff blades of the iris. "He filled it in."

"What?"

"The hole, the trench . . . He filled it back in. This is all loose dirt, this patch," with one hand she pats the surface, "this . . . square area." She stands again. "*Dad!* Can you hear me?"

"Hey, my voice is louder," Adrian says, "but how should I call. . . ? Oh well," and his voice resounds across the bottomland, "*Dad!*"

"Dad! Can you hear us? Dad!"

"*Dad!*" His voice booms again. Then, "Shhhh." He takes Ronnie's arm, and she catches the breath that would've been her next shout. The freeway hums. A confused mockingbird pipes a call. "Wait," he whispers.

"Ho!"

"That's what I thought I heard."

The air rushes out of Ronnie. "It's him. Where is he?"

"Coming from that way," Adrian turns. "Sounds like over at that big tree. We might've tripped over him if we kept going when we were off the trail back there."

"Dad! We're coming."

"I'm at here," he answers, like a voice from across a valley.

Not bothering to look for a trail, Ronnie and Adrian plow through ankle-high grass and push through waist-high mustard and sage. There's little danger of stepping on a rattlesnake at night; but, night or day, rain or fire, if stepped on, wasps won't hesitate to swarm from nests built in rocks and covered by sedge. But they cross the distance without mischance. A few times she calls, "Dad?" And he responds "Yup," or "Here." Then, within the last twenty yards, she can see him, a dark form standing among the tree's drooping branches, holding one aside like a curtain, like a tent flap.

"He found shelter," Adrian murmurs.

"I should've known he would, he's not brain-damaged."

"Hey," Ronnie's father says, "I already. Know you. You're not—"

"Dad, it's Adrian, remember?"

"But . . . he called at me . . . dad."

"You're shivering." She peels Adrian's jacket from her arms and slings it like a cape over her father's shoulders. He's still wearing a flannel shirt but his undershirt is gone.

"I've. Been lating."

"Waiting."

"Yes. Didn't hear how. How dark. It did dark."

"You had plenty of daylight," she says, holding a sleeve out as her father's hand searches for the opening. "I thought you'd have time to build a rock wall, mix some topsoil and manure and start some boysenberry shoots."

Adrian laughs.

"This is ours. No person to help."

"Yes, we did need help, Dad. *I* did." Arms across her chest, she hugs her shoulders.

"Now everything done. We can get at home now."

"So . . ." Adrian's voice seems to come from darkness even though he's standing no further than two feet away. "Should we take him back or stay here tonight? It's not that far but he's probably pretty tired."

"What's with your boots, Dad?" Ronnie bends to get a closer look at the boots gaping open on his feet. There are no laces. "We have no camp to go back to," she says softly, still crouched at her father's feet.

"C'mon." Adrian holds hanging branches aside, touches Ronnie's back, and they move underneath the tree. The ground inside the tree's hanging branches is not clear but strewn with leaves and dead branches—branches still fully foliated with dry, brown leaves that rattle as Adrian begins to gather armloads. He's creating an open space with piles of the boughs and broken shoots on four sides. There are also dead and dying branches still in the tree, either caught in the living branches or partially attached and half-alive, with leaves that are going dry, a slowly fading dusty green, even though it's too dark to actually distinguish the color. Adrian pulls several down, ripping them from where they're connected by a strip of bark or a half-broken green bough. Ronnie's father has squatted down close to the tree, his hands on something on the ground, as though protecting it from being swept up with the debris Adrian is rearranging. The army shovel upright, blade in the ground, is leaning against the trunk.

The space surrounded by piled branches isn't bare dirt—it's overlaid with loose leaves. As Ronnie begins to recognize the nest Adrian is making, she uses her hands to rake piles of loose leaves and adds them to the bed.

"There," Adrian says. "Let's hunker down."

Ronnie goes to her father, behind him, and puts her hands near his armpits to help him stand. "Wait," he says.

"What do you have—?" She freezes, looking over his head at his hands on the ground holding a long bundle wrapped in his undershirt and tied—actually bound, from one end to the other—with the long laces from his boots. She stands without helping him up.

"Ronnie?" Adrian moves up behind her. With one hand holding her father's arm, he pulls him to his feet, his other hand again touching Ronnie's back, nudges her toward the closest edge of the nest. "Spread out your vest to lay on, if you want."

She does, then kneels beside the flattened hunting vest, in the center of the nest, doesn't look up as Adrian helps her father step over the pile of boughs, doesn't know if her father has brought the tied bundle to sleep with. Adrian guides her father to the vest, and her father quickly settles there, curled on one side, his back to Ronnie.

"Get close and keep him warm," Adrian says.

As she straightens her legs and nudges her body close to her father's back, Adrian drapes his jacket over Ronnie and her father, then he's rustling, stretching out behind her, moving up against her spine, his legs against her legs, making the same curled shape. She can feel his arm crimped between them, then he pulls it out, moves up tighter against her, drapes his arm over her.

Adrian releases a big sigh against the back of her neck. "Let me know if he starts to shiver," he says softly. "I thought his lips might've looked a little blue."

"He's okay. He's asleep."

"Not yet," her father says.

She can feel Adrian's silent chuckle. Then he says, "We should probably have him between us, but . . . I don't feel like moving. Do you?"

She waits, suddenly feels his other hand cupping the top of her head. Maybe he doesn't expect an answer, or no answer is an answer. But she says, "No."

The whispering, rustling quiet is missing the drone of aircraft. They must quit after dark.

He says, "We'd make a pretty good team."

A jolt in her quaking stomach. Now aware of the dull ache, remembers she hasn't eaten since the candy bar. Neither has her father. "What . . . do you mean?"

"Oh, you know, like primitive man and woman making shelter, furnishing their lodge. Nesting. Except it wasn't until there was *some* civilization that people took care of their old." His fingers on her head—gently lifting some of her hair, slipping it through his fingers. "Although . . . most prehistoric humans did already have burial rituals."

Ronnie blinks, staring at the grizzled back of her father's head. "Do you think the stuff you learned in college is useful?" Someone's gut growls, but does she hear it or feel it? High up above them, birds ruffle their feathers, a few mutter, a distinctive hollow murmur.

"Well . . ." his voice almost trails away, as though he's falling asleep. But he does continue, "To run my nonprofit organization, I'll need to know something about business, something about government . . . and . . . yes, broad cultural knowledge is going to be important." One finger taps on her head. "That's what I meant though, you could work with me in the nonprofit. That is, when I get it going."

"You mean . . . in a couple of years."

He demurs with the same "Well . . ." Then, "You could go to school too."

"I don't know . . ." She pulls her arm from her father, picks up a leaf that's scratching against her neck, holds it to her nose and breathes in the lavish but faint eucalyptus scent. "I mean . . . maybe I could've once, but . . ."

"You never said." Her father's voice rasps.

"What, Dad?"

"Never said. To let you to go." He coughs. "At school."

Something rustles, it seems close enough to be under the tree with them. Adrian says, "So, what are you planning to do?"

"To give them. At home," her father says. "Finish."

"What does he mean?"

"You know, his . . . *our* . . . the family thing we came out here to do." She breaks the leaf in her fingers and the fragrance intensifies. "Anyway, it's kind of obvious what I have to do next. Earn money, find us a place to live . . . Maybe someday . . ."

"What?"

"Work for myself. Landscaping."

"Oh yeah. I forgot about your landscaping company. What if my corporation helped other people—like Hernando—start *their* own landscaping company."

The birds stir again, voices humming, a little gurgle like a purr. "Dove," Ronnie whispers. "We didn't see any all day."

"More like pigeons. We may wake up covered in birdshit." He picks up a sleeve from his jacket and lays it over her face. "You cold? Are you shivering?"

"I don't think so."

An owl calls, high enough to be gliding somewhere over the tree. "This doesn't make you, like . . . um, scared, does it?"

"Being outside? No."

"No. Being like an old married couple in bed. That should scare anyone." He stirs, scratching one leg with the other foot. "Not that I know what that's like."

"Me either." She picks a tiny spider from her father's collar. "I slept in a tent with my . . ." The owl calls again.

"No wonder those pigeons are nervous."

"Either that or it's the smell of old bird blood on this vest." But she's still smelling the now fading bite of eucalyptus oil.

Adrian blows out another long sigh. "But I would've had to get married pretty young to be a worn-out old husband at thirty-two."

"Yeah, I did once think you were closer to my age . . ." her voice little more than a mumble. "Maybe just a few years younger."

"Does it matter?" Again the soft rhythmic tapping of one finger on the top of her head. "You know . . . for some of us, our parents stayed married for decades, and not just convenience—it really worked, the marriage, they relate so perfectly, understand each other intimately, and even like each other's company, care and worry about what the other needs, still flirt and . . . make love . . . I think it's somehow too hard to live up to that . . . you can't imagine succeeding, at the same level . . . having it as good—"

"Wait, excuse me." She tugs the jacket away from her father's face. "What, Dad?"

"You take. Promises." He hacks, rough and phlegmy. "Should take them. Even if never easy."

"Yeah, I know you promised, and you kept your promise."

"Too very late."

"What do you mean?"

"I tell him when it gets safe . . . I'd give our brother . . . back home. Our home. Not here." He wheezes softly for a moment. "But can never do it. Years. Just wished to . . . forget. Our sister— No, our mother— never forgot. Couldn't live it. It was because my not doing."

Ronnie abruptly sits up. Adrian's hand slides down her back. She's slightly dizzy.

Her father continues, "Only later after our mother— He was gone in ocean. So I give his ashes. Out at here. And give the iris to bloom flower. But that wasn't the thing . . . our mother wanted. *Now* I do the right one. My promise." Chest heaving, tries to clears his throat, wipes his mouth with one hand. "But very too late. Because me, our mother in ocean."

"Why didn't you ever tell me." Her hand on her father's shoulder, she rolls him to his back so she can see his face. His eyes dark, filmy and murky.

"I try."

"I don't mean a month ago."

"Tried. But I didn't. Talk good. Way ago."

Adrian, also on his back now, brushes her arm with one hand. "What's he saying?"

"It's . . ." Looking up into the dark, shaggy tree, her head whirls. "I'm so hungry I feel sick."

From the cupboard: bread, jars of jam, bags of dried beans, rice, macaroni, flour, sugar, rolled oats, our own canned tomato sauce. From the refrigerator and baskets in the cool laundry room: lettuce, cabbage, chard, eggplant, peppers, tomatoes, Brussels sprouts, potatoes, carrots, radishes, quince, tangerines, oranges, grapefruit—it wasn't peach or apricot season, no berries except frozen strawberries. From the basement, long, heavy banana squash, hard head-sized pumpkins, pomegranates he'd been collecting to run through the press for juice, and fava beans drying for next year's seeds. I told him he had to reach for each one with his weak hand—both hands for the larger things— hold it and say its name, and what dish it might be cooked into. Pie or bread for pumpkin, salad or sauce for tomato, slaw or stuffed for cabbage, pasta é fagoli for beans, sauce for quince. And so on. When he couldn't say it—couldn't find the word or remember how to make the sound—he looked at me, at my mouth, slowly reciting.

Next the dishes and utensils. Every gadget from drawers and cupboards. Plate, bowl, glass, spoon, fork, butter knife, paring knife, bread knife, butcher knife, vegetable peeler, slotted spoon, whisk, potato masher, potato ricer, spatula, pancake turner, tongs, butter brush, bottle opener, can opener, corkscrew, cheese grater, orange juicer, colander, steam basket, pressure cooker, cast iron fry pan, pasta kettle, cake pans and bread pans, various appliances. The name of each, show me how it works, what does it make or what is it used for?

"Open glass with wine. Scrape 'cumber. Make so cheese—so cheese—so cheese can . . . scatter. Saw the bread . . . back-and-forth. Potato . . . make squish . . . push down. Spaghetti stay, water go. Mix egg. Cook . . ."

What kind of cooking?

"In oil."

What's it called when you do that?

"Fly."

No, but close. Frrrr—

"Free."

Keep trying.

Clothes from his bureau, items from his desk—pencil, pen, paper, envelope, ink pad, stamps, stapler, paper clip—same with the bathroom counter, the medicine cabinet, the linen cupboard. The hall closet yielded only a raincoat, an umbrella and a suitcase. The bedroom closet stayed closed, the shotgun remained unnamed, unaimed, unexplained.

The first one wasn't a small stroke, but not massive either. He was weak, he slept, he woke to look out of his face with eyes that seemed too liquid to understand much, then he slept again, his slack face falling back into his head, his arm curled as though cradling a stuffed bear, fist clenched. He woke and stared at me. He didn't speak.

They said bring pictures from home, he needs to remember faces and names.

He doesn't need pictures, I'm standing right here.

Pictures of your mother, they said, other family members . . .

I pulled a chair up and sat down beside the bed.

They said he might regain some of his former self, some of his former abilities, a modicum of his life—with rehab, with speech therapy and physical therapy and something called occupational therapy, which didn't mean turning last year's pepper plants under the soil's surface to provide nitrogen for winter produce nor mortaring rocks into a retaining wall nor grafting a tree limb, but buttoning a shirt, holding a spoon, brushing his teeth, turning a doorknob.

They recommended a rehab facility, fixed the paperwork to be signed, and even before he could be transferred, a therapist came to his hospital room to begin sessions. The first three weeks are the most crucial, she said. She'd brought a painting of people strolling in nineteenth-century Paris, a map of the world, a stuffed German shepherd, a coffee pot, a toy piano, a felt cutout of a round face—with felt pieces making eyes and nose, red cheeks, eyebrows and half-circle smile. I checked my father out and brought him home.

The second stroke came about a month after the first . . . intensive care and a long hospitalization, this time the unavoidable decision to sell the property to pay for medical care. He came out of a brief coma physically no worse—in fact retaining most of the restoration we'd managed—but as though the second stroke hit only his constitution, and he was suddenly older.

It was between the two strokes, when there were almost three weeks at home on the farmstead with him . . . when every day, twice a day, he climbed and descended all ninety-six steps plus the concrete wheelbarrow ramps that meandered from terrace to terrace on various parts of the farmstead. With a worn straw broom in his good hand as a cane, a hammer in his weak hand encouraging the kinked arm to unfurl, with tin cans of pebbles tied with rope around his weak leg's ankle, and with me hovering behind, in his outline: he lifted his feet up to each of the concrete steps . . . steps that he had, over the years, poured then smoothed the concrete . . . then the next step, and the next. Across a fallow vegetable bed or past a row of trees—touched each trunk and named the fruit as he passed—then painstakingly descended another set of steps or the steep ramps. Two or three hours in the morning, two or three in late afternoon, sometimes stretching into twilight . . . zigzagging the hillside property, barely looking right or left and yet preserving the land's contours in muscle memory.

Middle of the day, lessons in name-and-explain, make your body do the motion, make your mouth say the words, everything has a name, a purpose, a product or accomplishment. After every room in the house, nearly every cupboard, drawer, closet and shelf, it was time to take on the basement. Too chilly to stay in there, and not enough room to maneuver, so by the armload, tools brought out and spread on the lawn, laid down side-by-side. Three kinds of rakes, the straight-bladed hoe and the triangle-blade, round-blade shovel, square-blade shovel, trench digger, cultivator, pick, sledge hammer, post-hole digger, fruit picker, push broom, ax, ladder, tree-pruner, two-man saw, hedge clipper, long-handled lopper.

He went down to one knee to grasp a tool with his good hand, transferred it into his weak hand, put good hand on the grass to shove himself backwards, onto his feet, then used whatever tool he held to push himself upright.

What's it called?

"Cake."

No. Like rrr-river. Like rrr-rope.

He watched my mouth and repeated, "Rrr-ake. Scrape leaves." *The handle slipped through his weak hand like a cue stick, his good hand doing all the thrusting and pulling.*

The fruit picker: "Reach . . . in tree."

The hoe: "Cut dirt."

He couldn't raise the sledge hammer, ax, nor pick off the ground, so he wielded invisible ones over his head. With the hedge clipper, he limped to the eugenia and used both hands to close the big scissors over a tendril, but the shoot just folded, uncut, between the blades. "Needs . . . stone. Rub on stone."

What's it called?

"Sharp."

No.

If I was feverish and incessant, if I went past guidance into obsession . . . It was self-centered, for myself, for none but selfish reasons, that I prodded him toward recovery, worked him to exhaustion and frustration—wanting him back, but for my sake, wanting to keep him, to keep him going, keep him from . . . deteriorating . . . okay, from dying. Because he was the last one. Because without him, what would I do, literally WHAT—and who would know if I did it? Yes, I made noise—silent noise behind my solid face—about wanting my own life, about sacrificing my life for compensation I wasn't completely sure was my debt. But I also knew all along—knew without knowing I knew, without ever realizing or admitting the shaky course of thought—that without him, with no one left to atone to, who would even know I was alive? I'd have no purpose, no real use. He was the last one, and if he was gone . . . there'd be no reason for me to do anything, any of the things I did every day, there'd be no reason to get anything accomplished—the things that always needed doing in the right order. No reason to prune the fruit trees in December and net them in January to protect the buds that would start to appear in March. No one would need me to scald the skins off a bushel of tomatoes and preserve them whole in jars so tomorrow's bushel wouldn't spoil unused. Who would notice if the figs over-ripened and split and fell and smashed on the ground luring beetles and bees and filling the air with a thick, sweet stink of ferment—that is, if I didn't daily strip the tree of ripe fruit, lining up most of it on drying racks, moving yesterday's rack up a space, and the rack from the day before up a space, and so on, and so on, finally removing the last rack of properly shriveled fruit to store in plastic bags in the freezer. It wouldn't matter if I didn't keep the weeds from choking out the lettuce seedlings or if I forgot to check the hard shell squash every day to cut the largest one from the vine and rotate the others so the side touching the ground didn't rot or become drilled by pill bugs, then, if dinner was already scheduled with eggplant and artichoke and greens, make sure I used the harvested squash in bread or cookies. The same things, year after year, season after season, everything I did advanced our world into the next day, the next week, the next month . . . It was how I knew I was alive. It was how I stayed alive— Somehow, it seemed . . . that once he was gone too, not only would I no longer exist, I would've NEVER existed.

Maybe that's how I missed it. When he tried to tell me. Preoccupied with my own . . . with dim and hazy uneasiness. Probably that's why.

The wheelbarrow brought out the smaller tools all at once, a heavy entangled load. Hammers, pliers, wrenches, wood saws, screwdrivers, paint brushes, hand gardening tools, hand-held trimmers and pruners, crow bars, cement trowels. He was leaning on the push broom like a crutch, the long head of bristles under both arms, the top of the pole dug into the grass. Getting toward mid-afternoon. Warm winter day, bright slanting sunlight. Had we skipped lunch? Did light-headed sunspots float across my vision? Did I shut my eyes against the glare, behind him, flaring off a spray of water from an automatic sprinkler over the strawberry patch in the side yard?

Hands shading my eyes: he'd already let the broom fall flat onto the grass and, from the jumble of tools in the wheelbarrow, he'd selected the folding army spade. Green paint almost chipped free of the handle, blade folded, tucked up. He seemed to bounce it slightly in his hands, as though testing its weight. The same motion as cleaning blood from the spine of a fish: with his thumb he pushed at dirt, dry and crusted and cemented into the groove on the back of the blade.

Not twenty minutes ago he'd said "shovel" for the others—the long-landed garden shovels: square-edged and trench-digger and standard round-blade.

"Trunk."

No, you know this.

"Car."

Are you getting tired?

"Time for come to—the place. Way ago I tell him. Time for do it." He was trying to pry the blade open. "Safe now. But so much late. Give her home."

What are you trying to say? Let's stick with what we're doing, unless you need something. Do you have to go to the bathroom? Do you want to rest before we start walking?

"He wanted. He . . . my sister . . . my mother wrote . . . writing, drawing . . . no, not that . . . like telling . . . a question."

ASKING.

"He ask. For me to. SAY. An important say. When you say and you then DO."

Calm down, getting upset will make it harder—

"Word means . . . when you SAY. And have to DO."

I didn't know a little shovel could do so much.

"*No. Look at the—thing. The thing I never come do. I say but never do. This needs in trunk. Get under in car. My sister . . . no, daughter . . . mother . . . he ask me please. You take to me. This thing—use this thing for. Dig. When we take to go. Go . . . up? No. Go . . . before. Go* BACK. *Back. Go back. Go back.*"

Let's go lie down for awhile.

That was the time, it was during those three weeks, when I found the army shovel up on the back patio, on the picnic table that had long ago become a way-station for items on their way from one place to another: from the garage and needing to go down to the basement, from the washroom and needing to go to the garage, from the car and waiting to go to the pantry, from the basement and needing to go into the house or garage or the car. I put the shovel back in the basement, into the wheelbarrow of hand tools that was never emptied, it just sat inside the basement door, until the estate sale, and we weren't there to see if one person bought everything or each tool went where it was especially needed.

Chapter Twelve

Tickling. Something tickling. Need to stop it, brush it away. But she's paralyzed, rendered forever loose and languid by an unremembered fall, back broken, everything fat and numbed, but not too numb to feel . . . the impression of each touch that remains where it alights, on her cheek, her neck, an unusual buzzing on her lips . . . and the warm, tight pressure leaning against her . . . from being cradled, lifted or covered, held or shielded . . . from being carried from place to place, with no guilt for her deadweight, her helplessness, no obligation to even look at her guardian. This being carried . . . it's not like flying. Flying takes effort, vigorous breathing muscles, red-raw lungs. But is attainable. Can do it. In a way. She can be completely airborne. In flight. Gliding. Yet no matter how hard she flaps her arms, she can barely do more than skim inches off the surface. If she tucks her legs and kicks off from the ground, she can, but temporarily, go higher—beating against the air as though submerged and paddling to break water's surface before a last breath expires—but decline begins as soon as the thrust's brief lift wears off. Passing under something, an awning, an arch, a swing set, a branch, something clips her back, that's what it was, that's the fall, the blow to her back, the backbreaking blow, that has curled her into this thick, impotent ball without regret because now the exertion, the labor to move, to act, is no longer hers.

"Ronnie . . ."

She finally raises a heavy, twice-as-thick arm . . . it flops monstrously and a fat sleeping hand splats against her face to crush the bug.

"Ronnie, we let you sleep late." Adrian is squatting beside her. Dangling from his fingers, fluttering over her face like a fly, a stalk of wild oats. "Didn't want to wake you too fast and have your wandering spirit not return in time."

"Huh?"

"You know, the Native Americans believed that when you sleep—"

"He wake?"

"Dad? Where is he?" Her voice low, words coming slowly.

"He's been off . . . taking care of business. We let you sleep in." Adrian stands, twirling the oats. "Don't get up too fast. I don't think you moved all night."

"How do you know?"

He just smiles, picks up the rumpled hunting vest and shakes leaves from it. Her waking arm throbs heavily and tingles like glitter. A flock of ravens is softly bickering, then falls quiet. Closer, crickets still chime. It is before dawn. Adrian is holding the vest out for her father to put his arms into the holes.

"No, it's too heavy," she says. "Let him wear the . . . your jacket." She's finally sitting, pulls her knees up under her chin. She's never had trouble getting up early, but she's still pushing through oil instead of a cool, lacy pre-dawn.

"I thought the sooner we get up and get him someplace warm where he can lie down—eat first then lie down—the better." He drapes the hunting vest over one of Ronnie's shoulders. "We'll go back to my place, I think I have some bread there. Then we can think about your immediate options."

She stumbles to her feet.

"We'll stay here so you can go . . . take care of yourself."

Her feet have swollen to fill her boots, feel like cut logs at the ends of her legs. She blinks hard to try to remove the film or membrane fuzzing her vision. Behind a clump of sage, she has to grasp handfuls of the bushes to keep from falling backwards when she squats. She can't get her feet very far apart when the spandex pants are pushed to her ankles. Despite it being over twelve hours since relieving herself last, she has hardly any urine.

Morning air is calm. Still too dark for flight, bush tits, sparrows, and thrush revel—a ringing jumble of simultaneous chatter, rustling in bushes all around. Soon, before hawks start soaring, doves will be leaving the trees up on hillsides and come in to drink from waterholes. Hunters should already have arrived, would already have laced up their boots and wet their throats with orange juice from one thermos or hot chocolate from another. Would have already loaded the guns, stocked vests with shells, and tugged long brimmed hats onto the backs of their heads—which they'll pull lower, shading their faces, when the sun begins to glint over the eastern hills.

When Ronnie shuffles back to the eucalyptus tree, her father is sitting, practically at Adrian's feet. "He's real tired," Adrian says, "I'm gonna help him, you take the shovel and . . . whatever it is he's got there."

"Chad," her father says, his throat so wet it could've been a cough.

"Huh?"

"Never mind." Ronnie moves between them, her back to Adrian—as though blocking him from seeing what she's doing—takes the half-filled-with-dirt mayonnaise jar from where it sits between her father's feet. Pushes it into a vest pocket, barely glancing at it. The thin bundle is still in his hands, but he releases it to her, looking into her face. She won't meet his eyes.

It's not a residential bus stop, at the college across the street—the parking lot lights still on, probably set on timers to go off at six. No students would be departing the campus until the scheduled stops at ten or eleven, but the bus stops anyway, the driver watches them board without a question on his face. The newspaper folded on his dashboard has the same headline as the one in the box at the bus stop. *Twenty-seven homes destroyed in La Costa Blaze.*

"Mind if I borrow this?" Adrian asks, taking the paper. Ronnie is already sitting, her father slumped beside her, maybe already asleep, the bus already moving. The bundle lies across her legs, but she doesn't look down. The shovel is upright between her knees.

Adrian sits in the seat that faces her, back-to-back with the driver. Ronnie stares at an ad on the back of the newspaper, for a Christmas sale for furs. It feels like her head is a too-large pumpkin balancing precariously atop a long stick, or as though she's wearing a stiff Elizabethan collar preventing her from looking down and seeing the rest of her body.

"A lotta these houses are right up the hill from your camp," he says, flipping the paper down. "Or were. Completely gone, just like that."

He seems to be waiting for her to speak. "That's what fire does." She means burning up the sides of hills is the natural direction. Burning *down*-hill hits water. Anyone knows that. So if fire has all the features of life—breathes in one gas and exhales another, takes in fuel and leaves waste, can move, grow, reproduce . . . and die—why not say it can learn or use logic, or at least can perceive what's dangerous and avoid it. How many characteristics of being alive is she managing this morning?

"Someone's gonna think your camp caused all this."

"The camp's burned up."

Ronnie's father snorts, snores, his head lolls sideways onto Ronnie's shoulder, then he jerks upright. His chin drops, head slumps forward, he snores again. Rising slightly from his seat, Adrian takes her father by both shoulders and gently leans him against the side of the bus, tucks the folded newspaper between his face and the glass while he says, "But they can find where it started, the flash-point. And there's usually less burned at the origin. Even I could see there had been a camp there."

She hadn't moved while Adrian settled her father. She feels the bundle lying on her inert palms the same way she sometimes feels the weight of something she was holding in a dream still shimmering in her hand after waking. "In that case," she says, "they'll find the . . . bomb. Whatever it was."

"There was a *bomb?*"

"I think so." She's talking toward the front of his shirt, not his face. "I swear, I thought, once they found the camp, it would be reported, then bulldozed by some authority, the county or immigration—I never thought they'd burn their own houses down in the process."

"How did you think they'd find it. Smoke?"

"Yes, but—" She meets his eyes. "You don't think *we* started that fire?"

"Not on purpose, but—"

"Shanes." Her father sits up. The newspaper falls to the floor. "Boys. Did that."

"What're you gonna do, huh?" Adrian smiles. "Boys are hellions, can't live with us, can't live—" He stops. Glances at Ronnie. "Sorry." He looks down and clears his throat. She still feels like a statue, dipped in mortar and solidified.

"I'm giving. My boy home." He reaches to put his hand on the bundle, but his fingers fall on Ronnie's wrist.

It's light, close to seven already, when they cross the street from the bus stop to the Home Builders store. Moving so slowly, they can't even get across the street before the light changes. Adrian holds one hand up toward the approaching cars, grasping Ronnie's father's upper arm with his other hand. As the cars start to whisk past behind them, a blurred shout is thrown from a window, impossible to interpret the words.

They enter the parking lot through the entrance closest to the building. If they keep going straight, along the front of building, they'll pass a row of black barbecue grills, each bigger than the last, each with a basketball-sized red bow on its hood. They'll pass three or four backyard chippers, yellow-and-green or red or shiny black, also adorned with massive bows. A pyramid-display of garden tools decorated like a Christmas tree, with blond-wood handles wrapped in ribbon like candy canes, and red or green-painted metal parts. And the outdoor hotdog stand, a kiosk outlined in white lights and sliver garlands, that starts selling hotdogs off the grill at 6 a.m., but also offers coffee and doughnuts and bear claws. One morning last week when they arrived early, before her father's pals were there to share their breakfast, she'd bought him coffee from the kiosk, and they'd stood silently, sipping coffee, looking at the glossy chippers, the generators, tractor lawn mowers, tool boxes for pickup trucks.

But immediately inside the parking lot entrance, instead of walking past the store, Adrian turns left to cut through the cordoned-off Christmas tree area, heading toward the back of the lot where he needs to leave a message with Hernando to pass on to their construction boss. "Hey," he turns and walks backwards, "got any money? Go get your dad something to eat. Meet me back there with the guys."

Near the kiosk, Ronnie has to hand the bundle to her father, steps up to the window to pay, then takes the Styrofoam cup and napkin-wrapped plain doughnut in each hand. Her father is standing beside a plastic table where the hotdog man keeps covered trays of relish and onions, squeeze-bottles of ketchup and mustard, sugar dispensers and powdered creamer. As though evading her eyes, he's looking out into the parking lot, not toward the back but the part nearest the front door where contractors and handymen who arrive earliest get the closest parking spots. She puts the coffee and doughnut down on the table, reaches to take back the bundle, and also turns her head to follow her father's gaze. Two boys on bicycles are making circles around the first row of cars. They're wearing jackets, like raincoats, one with a hood, the other more of a trench coat that flies behind him like a cape. A third boy joins the others, making slow laps around the first row of cars. One rides close to a trashcan that's chained to a light post, kicks out one leg and his foot booms against the metal can. Another rides close and kicks the can. The third, instead of kicking, drops something into the can. The bundle is back in her hands, so she motions with her chin toward the back of the lot, "Let's go, can you carry those?" The doughnut is almost half gone. Her stomach kinks.

As she steps off the front curb to cut through the parking lot toward the back, her father veers on an angle to follow where Adrian had cut through the Christmas trees. "Dad it's shorter if we just go straight—"

But he doesn't waiver, already halfway to the tree lot, so she hurries to join him, the jar in the vest pocket bouncing against her thigh. He's finished with the doughnut, the napkin wadded in his hand, when they get to the trees. At the front of the lot, trees are nailed to crossed pieces of wood so they'll stand upright—they're the most profuse trees, trimmed as they grow to force additional branches to sprout from the trunk, so they'll not only be thicker but also perfectly conical. Some are flocked, a snowcapped forest. A $75 price tag brushes Ronnie's arm as they pass. Behind the grove of garnished trees, a man with a tool apron is reading a newspaper, sitting on a stool under the canopy. On another stool beside him, a cup of coffee and a radio playing a morning traffic report. Additional standing trees, also nailed to crossed boards but allowed to remain green, are aligned around three edges of the roped-off tree area, under an outline of Christmas lights, just dull pinpricks in morning light. But the majority of the trees are still bundled. Ronnie's and her father's boots crunch on fallen needles in the aisle passing between piles of trees—on one side of them the taller trees, the eight to twelve footers leaning against the fence that separates the parking lot from the sidewalk, the street, the bus stop where she and Adrian waited last night. The smaller six-foot trees are tied in groups, the bundles lying parallel, heaped on top of each other, the ends of their trunks all facing the aisle. Ronnie counts eight fresh-sawed trunks in each bundle. A bus pulls up to the stop outside the fence. When the bus leaves, two or three women on the sidewalk, or maybe a woman and a man, speak softly in Spanish.

Through the row of standing trees, she sees a familiar truck—the landscape contractor who used to hire her—pulling into the back entrance of the parking lot, continuing to move slowly up to where men will be gathering to wait for work. She sees a few men sitting on the curb at the back of the lot, on the only part of the curb she can see. She can't see Adrian with them. Those men stand but don't start to wander into the lot to get closer to the truck, so it's not their ride to work, or not their turn, because there are many more men in the parking lot, blocked from Ronnie's view by cars and Christmas trees. The bus's last puff of exhaust finally filters through the trees. Several men call to each other and laugh. A thumping stereo draws closer, heavy and thick, a mob pulsation, as though everyone's hearts have begun beating together, a single engorged heart. The men on the curb look up, look toward the street. A car pulling into the back of the lot stops there, blocking the entrance. Stereo booming, rhythmic thunderclaps, a protest rally of synchronized hand-clapping and feet pounding, thudding, throbbing, surging . . .

Her father's body slams into her . . . her father's shoulder or his chest knocks her sideways . . . he's been shoved or hit . . . or he bulldozes into her all on his own . . . her father rams into her . . . knocking her over . . . throwing her into a pile of Christmas trees . . . she's tripping into a bundle of pines . . . lurching off her feet . . . crashing face-first into a forest of culled trees . . . the parcel in her hands cushioned between her body and the mattress of compressed branches . . . her father awkwardly on top of her . . .

"*Dad*, what—"

"—WITH WHITE JUSTICE—" A loud speaker? A recording? "—YOU BURN OUR HOMES—" a voice chanting to the cadence of the stereo's artillery, "—SO YOU BURN IN HELL—"

"Dive—" her father says. "No, *bend*—get—under. *Get below.*"

"Dad, what's going—" Popping in the parking lot, then a blast, and another. Screams coming from several directions. Car alarms shrieking. "That's . . . *gunshots*—" More popping, short and quick, not like the blast and ring of a shotgun. A sharp shatter of glass.

"Duck," her father says.

"Not *that* kind of shooting—"

"*Duck*. Head *down*."

"GO HOME . . . GO BACK TO THE MUD YOU CAME FROM. OR WE'LL SEND YOU HOME IN A . . ."

"They're *shooting*—"

"Stay."

"No, I've got to—"

"Stay at here. Stay under—*down*."

"No, get off, how many times am I gonna sit on the ground while someone I . . . love is shot to death—"

"That always was. *Different.*" Her father with a hand on her head pushing to put her face back into the mound of trees. Needles scrape her eyes, her face, smears of sap gummy on one cheek, thick musk of pine, broken sprigs and more needles up her nose. The jar like a fist digging into her groin, one knee twisted, ankle cocked insanely off to one side. Still holding the bundle with one hand against her breast-bone, Ronnie pushes into the trees with her other hand. Branches crack, her hand sinks, arm scratched by broken twigs and short needles—finally grasping a sticky trunk, thick as an ax handle, lifts her head enough to see through the blur and prickle of branches, digging to make a window in the tangle of evergreen. Can see the landscaper's truck, cab empty, windows shattered, lights flashing in back, sparkle of glass on the pavement, a bicycle flying past—maybe it's the fluttering cape cracking in the wind and not the crack of a pistol. Still pushing on the back of her head, her father's hand is strong—where's Adrian?—it's his weak hand—she can't see anyone, no one standing on the curb or surrounding the truck or approaching through the parked cars and trucks. Car horns honking repeatedly, alarms of all kinds, tooting, trilling, hee-hawing, a voice still screaming up at the front of the store, faraway and persistent, breathless, shrill, and the stereo's heavy heartbeat still pulsating as though coming from an aircraft hovering low directly overhead . . . but also . . . something has stopped—no more popping, no shots cracking. A whiff of metallic firecracker smoke puffs past, a man shouts—Adrian?—somewhere a trash can kicked over, rolling on pavement, footsteps running, another shout. Now she can see people moving, the upper halves of their bodies, several men sprinting, dodging between cars, zigzagging different paths, holding a stick, a brick, a two-by-four, a rock. The back of Adrian's head, his dirty blond ponytail?

"They're chasing them."

"Who?" Her father now clutching the back of the hunting vest, pulling himself up, dragging her down, the neck of her sweatshirt tight on her throat.

"Maybe Adrian. And the others. Chasing the boys. The Shanes."

The popping now replaced with curses "—*fucking wetbacks, stinking Mexican fuckers, go trash and burn down your OWN shithole country—*"

More men converging, three or four lean over the back of the landscaping truck and grab tools, the landscaper now sitting upright in the cab, a bike lying on the asphalt in front of his blinking truck, the car blocking the entrance jerks forward, then screech of tires on pavement, the stereo is suddenly snuffed, an engine roars, more squealing rubber, dissonant wail of at least two sirens. The thumping car is gone—replaced in an instant by the up close scream of one siren, the other warps as it passes and dwindles down the street. No more screaming, no inflamed yelling, no cursing, but one voice barks, giving orders, a loud speaker crackles—words are too jagged to understand, as though jumbled by the flashing, flickering convulsion of red light blue light red light blue—

Her father's hand lets up the pressure on the hunting vest. Ronnie rises, straddling a bundle of trees. She takes her father's flailing arm and gives support while he gets to his feet. "Dad, put this into the game pouch." She hands him the wrapped bundle and turns to let him slip it into the vest's back pocket. Then she swings her leg over, gets off the trees and stands beside him. The landscaper is getting out of his truck, a phone in his hand. A jumble of men in the far corner, possibly one or several are lying on the ground. More sirens approaching, pulling into the parking lot. The landscaper pointing and gesturing. Uniformed, helmeted police multiplying. Suddenly starting to outnumber everyone else. Speakers crackling from the flashing cars, giving orders, repeating commands. Ronnie and her father moving forward now, leaving the trees and out in the open parking lot. A knot of uniforms milling at the fence near the far corner. Barely visible between them, three sets of legs like inverted V's, bodies pressed against the fence, hands on heads. An ambulance pulls in, then more blinking police cars block the exits. Still more cars block traffic from going either way past the hardware store. A fire truck is parked at the bus stop. One by one, car alarms in the parking lot stop blaring, honking, squealing. Talking to two police up by the front of his truck, the landscaper saying, ". . . no . . . those are my employees . . . some kind of bombs in the trash cans . . . my men surrounded them after the shooting stopped . . . they emptied the gun . . . only one gun, I think . . ." One of the policemen has the tools that were taken from the truck. A crowd of people from the hardware store beginning to gather—customers in jeans and boots, mostly men this time of the morning, and clerks, both men and women, in red aprons—the small throng held back by several police cars, blocking each parking aisle. Firemen in heavy yellow coats are near the front of the store, examining the blackened trashcans that had held bombs, probably the same kind that had ignited the fire at their camp . . . just yesterday. As she passes beside the landscaper's truck, crunching glass beneath her boots, she finally finds Adrian, spots him returning from the corner with two cops. Ronnie and her father approach the group standing with the landscaper within a circle of flashing lights near the truck's front fender, the same time that Adrian arrives from the other side. As though no one else is there, he looks past the uniformed men and through the frantic lights, looks at her and says, "Are you okay?"

Most of the police turn and glance at her. One says, "Ma'am, you'll need to return—"

"Are they the same kids who threatened you, Ronnie?" Adrian interrupts.

"You know these kids, ma'am?"

"I . . . don't know." She's trying to see past the half circle of uniformed men. "Where is everyone?"

"They're out there," Adrian murmurs, "where they're safe." His eyes dart toward the brushy hill slope outside the parking lot fence.

"Safe?"

"Survival," he ducks his head and mutters so low she's not sure she hears him.

"Ma'am," a policeman touches her arm. "You say you've seen these kids before?"

"Shane," her father says.

"First or last name? Which one?"

"No," he says. Clears his throat. "Something else."

Another cop is asking Adrian for identification. He reaches into his pocket for his wallet. The three boys are being handcuffed. One kid is speaking loudly, almost shouting, "*They're* the criminals—" A policeman over there says, "shut up."

"They started the fire, tried to burn down our—"

"Shut *up*."

Each boy held by one arm and guided toward three different cars. Feet shuffling, one boy's pants fall around his knees, shackling him as he walks. Someone laughs.

"Ronnie?" Adrian gets her attention, then says, "She doesn't have any, they stole her wallet."

"When, today?"

"No, it was—Ronnie . . . you want to tell them?"

"They've been bothering my men for a while," the landscaper says, "the guys who work for me. Just kid stuff. I told them to ignore it, don't start anything. I never realized—"

From a radio speaker on the closest car, in monotone and surrounded by static, a woman's voice speaks in numbers, street names and code words. One of the police answers, more numbers, into a microphone on his shoulder.

"Is this your current address, sir?"

"No," Adrian says. "Well, yeah, I guess so, my mailing address."

"Is it or isn't it?"

"Yes, it's current."

"The investigating detectives are going to need to talk to you. Is there a phone number?"

Adrian recites some numbers.

"Sir," the cop hands the license back to Adrian without looking at him, "was anyone else firing a weapon?"

"No," the landscaper says, "these are my employees."

"Who, sir?"

The landscaper turns toward the back of the lot, the curb where the men usually wait, sweeping an arm behind himself, the hand holding the cell phone, but freezes, arm extended. Then drops his arm. None of the men who'd been there waiting for work this morning when the shooting started—the men she'd seen with Adrian chasing the kids into a corner—not one remains in the parking lot. Adrian is grinning, looking down, easing his license back into his wallet. Again he mutters, "survival."

With a cop's hands guarding the tops of their heads, the kids are being loaded into the backs of the cars. The kid with the falling pants is trying to hold his trousers up with handcuffed hands. The third one, brought to a car just in front of the landscaper's truck, turns and grimaces, or smirks . . . or smiles. His front teeth are broken.

"Wait!"

It's startling, her own voice blurting out. The cop holding the kid looks over, the other police also turn toward her, Adrian looks up. The strobing red, blue and white lights on the cars make any movement look jerky, or like her head is vibrating, her eyes unable to remain steady. "That one . . ."

"Know this boy, ma'am?"

The radio pops, the robotic female voice says a number. One yelp of the fire truck siren, its fog horn blows, then the truck pulls away. The kid spits, "dyke bitch." Clears his throat and tries to shoot a glob of saliva, but most dribbles down his chin. "Fuck you, bitch." He's trying to wipe his chin on his shoulder and the cop is shaking him, saying "shut up," the boy's head snapping back and forth as though on a spring.

"I just never before recognized one a second time . . . I thought he would . . . I thought he wouldn't . . . Never mind."

The cop finishes stuffing the kid into the car, slams the door. The kid slumps sideways, his head in darkness in the car's far corner.

The car blocking the entrance turns off its flashing lights and leaves the parking lot. The ambulance follows. Clenching her jaw and her fists, she hadn't realized she was quaking until Adrian's arm is around her. He moves her around the truck's fender, opens the door with the broken window. The glass rasping underfoot sends shivers up her neck. Adrian sweeps nuggets of glass from the seat, then she steps up into the cab.

"He's going to bring us to a shelter to clean up," Adrian mutters. "You can eat and get some clean clothes, and we'll figure out what to do." She's scooting over on the seat and her father is climbing in beside her, boosted by Adrian from behind. The door slams.

"Was anyone hurt?" Her voice nearly a whisper. She clears her throat, softly, as though in hiding.

"Who knows?" Adrian, still at the truck window, looks away but continues calmly speaking, "Maybe someone was winged. They aren't going to stick around when cops show up, even if they're bleeding. They can just disappear into the landscape when they have to. No one *I* saw was hit, but I'll find out." He looks back at her once, then leaves.

Between herself and the seat, Ronnie feels the long t-shirt-wrapped bundle in the game pocket, diagonal across her spine. She slowly tips forward, hands on the dashboard, voice whispering, "Take it."

Rustle of her father moving, but his hand doesn't dig into the vest. "Her," he says.

"What?"

"Not *it*. Her."

"It's her gun, isn't it?"

"Her. Our brother."

"*Him*, Dad. Him." Her forehead down on her knuckles. More soft rustling, then the drag on the vest as his hand goes in. The bundle noiselessly sliding out.

"Okay now." His hand on her shoulder, he tugs, to get her to lean back again. His pull is feeble, or gentle. She lifts her head then rises and eases backwards. A plain car pulls into the lot, followed by a van with an emblem on the front doors.

She whispers, "This is so . . . unbelievable."

"If them—the people—pol—"

"Police."

"If police do metal search— Search with machine—"

"Metal detector."

"If looked in all—every person. Would give this."

"Good thing we left the shotgun at Adrian's camp."

"That one. Too. But *this* one would. Worse." He taps the bundle with a fingertip.

"It's just a rusted old gun barrel, no one would—"

"And bone. Probably from this," he pats his thigh. "L—leg."

"*Dad,* a—a leg bone? A whole. . . ?"

"Almost all."

A few policemen are cordoning off the entire parking lot with yellow ribbon, others are returning to their cars and leaving. Some leave their flashing lights on, others don't. The three cars with the three boys—dark forms slumped low in the caged back seats—form a caravan and move slowly toward the exit.

"Could we put him over. This trouble age?"

"He would've been this age over twenty years ago, and you wouldn't have been . . . sick."

"Old. Just hear old."

"Okay. You'd have been younger. Did you ever worry about getting me past . . . a certain age?"

"Our sister—no, mother—he tried. And tried. And. Tried to. Give another one. For you. You needed. Baby."

"What I *needed*—"

"Our mother thought it's the—thing— To take you to forgive him. But when the change. Started. Men— Meno— When no more period. He—*she* had nothing. Nothing left to do . . ."

"She still had *me*."

"And you always after have we—*us*. Your people all together—family. Our life."

She turns, but he's not looking at her.

The last uniformed men speak for several moments with two men in suits and a woman in high heels holding a trench coat around her body with both arms, her hair in a tight knot on her neck. Shoulder-to-shoulder, Adrian and the landscaper continue to stand in the parking lot, no longer accompanied by policemen, ignored by a photographer and some other men and a woman with tool kits and medical bags who are bent over and searching the ground around the bicycle.

"I'll take the . . . that." She reaches for the long bundle on his lap.

"My promise."

"Let me hold it for now." She lifts the bundle. His hands hover. She only holds it tight enough to feel the padding of the shirt wrapped around it, something hard but fragile inside. Lowers her hands, rests the bundle between them, on her right thigh and her father's left. One man wraps the bike in a plastic sheet and carries it to the truck.

Ronnie says, "I wish we could go home."

"We will come. That's where we. Get next."

"No, I mean I wish we could go . . . back to our life, the way we were. I want to go *home*."

It isn't until every police car is gone that Adrian and the landscaper begin to drift slowly toward the curb at the back of the lot, strolling past the front of the truck, still side-by-side, talking quietly, Adrian's arms folded, the landscaper with hands in pockets, their eyes trained slightly downward, as though watching the ground for obstacles, heads turned slightly toward each other. Occasionally one will glance up at the other. By the time Adrian and the landscaper reach the curb, most of the men who'd been in the parking lot that morning are returning, some still holding sticks or rocks, tramping quietly through the brush outside the fence.

The landscaper stops in front of a defunct department store, in the old section of one of the North County coastal cities. Adrian hops out of the back of the truck and comes to the door to help Ronnie's father step over the gutter to the sidewalk. Ronnie follows them through the double glass doors, painted-over opaque brown with *St. Paul's Shelter of North County* in faded white. Inside, a linoleum-floored room, half taken up with a double row of long tables end-to-end, the other half mostly empty except a few spindly tables and two old sofas with flattened cushions, and an assortment of chairs: old desk chairs, ripped vinyl chairs, stained upholstered arm chairs, and one lumpy recliner where a young dark-haired girl is nursing a baby, half covered with an olive-green blanket. A bald man with a beard is snoring softly on one of the sofas. A woman who could be thirty or fifty—hair hidden in a baseball cap, a scar on her upper lip—sits beside another man on the other sofa, playing cards, both smoking, each holding a deck, alternately one shuffling while the other looks at cards spread face up on a coffee table. The woman has a gray cockatiel on her shoulder, pulling strands of her hair one at a time out from under the cap. A tint of disinfectant and bleach mingles with the cigarette smoke, a rank urine smell, a faint whiff of coffee.

Adrian leads them, winding through the tables, to the back of the room. Hanging above a wide stairway, a sign with a down-pointing arrow says *sleeping quarters*, and, near the corner in a small side room, a woman with silver hair is sorting through a bag of clothes. The thin cries of two or maybe three babies or small children echo up from the stairway.

The old department store's restroom had been remodeled to allow one of the toilet stalls to become a shower. While Ronnie stands there— hands holding the two shoulder-high partitions on either side of her, lukewarm water pelting her breastbone—someone takes her clothes from the hook, replacing them with clean, very worn brown corduroys, and a long-sleeved turtleneck. The socks waiting for her on the short bench are worn tube socks with slightly yellowed heels, but the underwear is new, still creased from a package. Her bra has not been replaced. Good thing she hadn't brought the hunting vest into the shower. It's hanging on the back of a chair beside her father and Adrian in the main room, where they are eating cheese sandwiches and drinking tomato soup from mugs. Before entering the shelter, her father had once again slipped the long padded bundle into the vest's game pocket in back.

Then her father and Adrian shower in the men's room while Ronnie sips soup. The waistband of her new pants, half a foot too big around for her, is puckered under a cracked leather belt. The knit turtleneck clings to her loose breasts. When she'd finally opened her eyes in the shower and soaped a cloth to wash herself, she hadn't seen a trace of ink on her chest and stomach. Her period still hasn't started and she hasn't felt a cramp in days.

The woman with silver hair brings a sandwich and asks Ronnie if she wants to donate her old clothes—the shelter throws out anything too soiled or torn, and washes and recycles the rest, or they can wait and get their old clothes back clean from the laundry, whatever's still wearable. Ronnie thinks about the spandex pants, but before she answers, the woman hands her a brown sack containing everything from their pockets: wadded dollar bills and some change, a fish hook with the point dug into a smooth piece of wood and fishing line wound neatly like a spool, a pocketknife, her father's glasses, three small pebbles—lucky stones with rings that go all the way around. After removing the two crumpled dollars, Ronnie stuffs the bag in one of the vest's side pockets, balancing the mayonnaise jar on the other side, and tells the woman she can do whatever she wants with the old clothes, but leave the vest and the jacket. She means Adrian's jacket, slung over the chair where her father had been sitting.

"No one's taking your coat," the woman says, already leaving.

Her father comes out in old suit pants and a college sweatshirt. He's holding up the pants with one hand. Adrian, his hair wet but wearing his same clothes, says, "wait a sec," goes looking for the woman and comes back with green canvas trousers with pockets up and down the legs. "She didn't have any more men's but had some boys'." His hair is combed back, behind his ears, but is loose, not clasped in a rubber band. Beneath their feet, at least two babies continue crying downstairs.

"Smoke?"

Ronnie gasps, jerks around. The sleeping bald man has quietly come up behind her.

"No," Adrian says, "take off."

"Need help, Dad?" She crosses her arms over her breasts, over her startled heartbeat.

"No." He heads back to the restroom, still holding up the suit pants, the green trousers over his arm. The bald man retreats back to the sofa as quietly as he'd approached.

"While you were showering, I called a friend," Adrian says, his finger touching a shaving nick on his throat.

"Did you find out if anyone was hurt?"

"No, he wouldn't know that. But they probably still don't know. They'll probably never find out. The guys'll take care of each other. There are a few doctors they can go to who won't report knife or gunshot wounds. If they need anything else, I'll hear. This friend's just bringing a car over for me to borrow. Maybe we can find you a motel or something."

The girl in the recliner sings softly, the baby now over her shoulder.

"Okay." Ronnie's grip tightens around her ribs. "But . . . no. We have something else we have to do."

"Oh . . ." His calm eyes on her don't falter. "Are you cold?"

"No." She looks at the vest then takes it off the back of the chair. Adrian holds the collar while she threads her arms through. She turns, clutching the vest closed over the clinging turtleneck. "Do you have time? Can you . . . Want to come with us?"

"Be glad to." He smiles.

Ronnie nods, her face getting warm.

The bald man is already snoring again. A stringy-haired woman comes up the stairs with one of the wailing children, passes through the room toward the front door. The girl in the recliner swears in Spanish and her baby starts to cry too. The man playing cards shouts, "Shut up, no one can think!" The scarred woman beside him slaps the table with her baseball cap, scattering cards, and says, "Bitch." The cockatiel screams, flapping its wings. There might be an adult weeping softly as well. Adrian puts his hand against the side of Ronnie's hot face, a gesture that would brush back hair, if she had any. He folds one of her ears down and lets it spring back.

When her father comes out of the restroom, Ronnie uncrumples the two dollar bills in her fist and says, "Should we pay something for the food?"

Laughing, Adrian closes her hand back around the money with both of his.

The whole thirty or forty miles down the coastal freeway to the city's downtown, her father sleeps in the back seat, head thrown back, mouth open, hands palms-up loosely cupping the wrapped bundle on his lap. He doesn't wake when Ronnie slips her arms out of the hunting vest, takes the jar out of the pocket then spreads the vest over him. She puts on Adrian's jacket, zips it up. It isn't clean but doesn't smell smoky and covers the absurdly puckered corduroy pants and clinging turtleneck. This dull, tired-eyed sluggishness feels like she's been crying, even when she's sure she hasn't. Her father stays sleeping as they drive around and round the coiled ramps of a parking building and even when Adrian jerks to a stop in the dark, chilly echo chamber. So Ronnie goes into the bank alone where, with the key that was pinned inside the hunting vest, she gets her social security card out of the vault drawer then reports the loss of her wallet. Using Adrian's post office box number as her address, she fills out paperwork for a checkbook and replacement bank card, and discovers her account hasn't been cleaned out. Now, in fact, the account is a little bigger, since her father's last social security check was electronically deposited on the first of December. Leaving the bank, she realizes the entryway is a metal detector.

Yesterday's fire cloud in North County couldn't have been seen, forty miles south and twenty miles east, in Dictionary Valley. Here it's not unusual for a December day to be bright and clear, even warm. Their camp in the gully, just two miles from ocean surf, had frequently stayed socked-in with coastal fog until late morning, sometimes noon. But Dictionary Valley—where the winter grasses that appeared after the first rains are already turning yellow—has plainly not been denied the sun these past weeks. Even rare nights when fog does roll in twenty miles from the coast, the farmstead on Hannigan Hill always woke in sunshine and looked over a sea of mist flooding the valley. Only when Pacific winter storms blow ashore, and only when they aren't pulled north by the jetstream, are skies above Hannigan Hill steel-gray with clouds, and the air pumped with eager energy of imminent rain. But not today. The eucalyptus are darkly green, standing in their hundred-year-old rows along sandy sidewalks, draping branches over the streets. The wild oats already heavy with fat maturing kernels, gray-green and drying as they ripen in the sun. The foxtails have already gone to brown and dropped their grain, waiting for a future day of rain to germinate and turn the roadsides, ditches and empty lots green again.

Ronnie guides Adrian through the turns—Olive Grove to Skyland to Santa Rosa to Central. Then the winding county road that changes its name as it climbs, Hardy Dell then Hannigan then Valley View, and finally Lakeview, the part that dips and curves below the farmstead property. She's squinting but Adrian wears sunglasses. Her father is awake now, occasionally says "Here," before Ronnie directs the way, even though the populated road lined with landscaped yards looks so different. Houses have even been built on the steep part of Lakeview, some with tiny front yards well below street level, old enough now that thick hedges with gates protect privacy as though Lakeview is a four-lane boulevard with a busy sidewalk. Lakeview has no sidewalk, barely even a shoulder. Outside the hedges or border bushes, tumbleweeds and wild grasses still cling to the last sandy dirt before asphalt starts.

"Here," her father says.

"It's right up there," Ronnie reiterates, gesturing out her open window. Here, after Lakeview's steep slope has leveled, the hillside to the right rises directly from the edge of the road's surface. Twenty or thirty yards up the natural strip of hill, the huge nopale block any view of the property. Down on Lakeview, they're too low to see the house.

"There's nowhere to park."

"There's a—"

"Oh!" Adrian spies the graded dirt leeway that runs over the aqueduct, veers off the road, jolting over bumps and rocks. Ronnie holds the top of her head as though she's about to lose a hat in the wind. Her teeth snap together.

"No!" her father blurts. "No cars at here!"

"Stop here," Ronnie says, more quietly. "You won't be blocking traffic. No one drives here."

Adrian sets the brake and her father's door is already open. They've gone far enough up the leeway that the top of the house is now visible, a small satellite dish mounted on the roof where the corroded-green brass rooster weather vane used to be. Her father's boots grind pebbles outside on the leeway. The seat creaks when Adrian turns toward her. "Ready?" Then her father comes around to her window, bends and peers in.

"I'm coming," she mutters. Reaches into the back seat for the hunting vest and puts it on after stepping from the car.

Side by side, they walk several more yards up the leeway path. To the side of the dirt road, buried in matted dry grass from several seasons, vestiges of the piles of rocks, dynamited from the hillside farmstead, lugged by her father with hundreds of others and piled just off the property line, side-by-side heaps or elongated mounds, waiting to be retrieved when he constructed his walls. Became home to tarantulas and stinkbugs, black widows, wasps and lizards.

Adrian grabs Ronnie's arm the same moment she gasps, "Wow." Up ahead on the leeway, a large iridescent bird struts, dragging a long tail, pauses to turn and regard them, barely warily. It hops up onto a circular concrete platform that's an access to the county waterline.

"Roadrun," her father says.

"No, Dad, a peacock."

"People keep them like guard-dogs," Adrian says. "They can make a lot of noise." With a quiet rustle, the bird opens its tail, a huge shimmering fan, turns slowly on the cement platform. "Or maybe I'm thinking of geese."

"Roadrun Road," her father says.

"Oh," Ronnie murmurs, "that's what you meant. Roadrunn*er* Road."

"Right one. Roadrunner Road."

"That's pretty good," Adrian says, "is that the name of this?"

"Kind of. We named it. But there aren't any more roadrunners. They were gone even before we were. Too many people."

"And Dove Pot," her father says. "Rocky Flat. Polly—frog Sinking—?" His head turns quickly, his eyes on Ronnie's mouth.

"Okay," she mutters. "Sink*hole*. Poll*ywog* Sinkhole."

"Sinkhole. Pollywog Sinkhole. And Wasps Crate."

"No, it's Wasp Crat*er*."

Adrian chuckles, "Huh?"

"Names of places," Ronnie says dully. Takes a deep breath, closes her eyes. At the end of a long quiet sigh she finds a small, silent laugh. Opens her eyes, smiling. "My brother's names for places around here." Looks at her father—his glasses glint, his eyes distorted behind smudged lenses, but she can tell he's smiling too. "I didn't know my father knew."

"Why Dove Pot?"

"I don't know why Chad thought of that. Dove sat on the ground in a flat place, up there, the other side of the house."

"Sinkhole? There's no groundwater around here to make sinkholes."

The peacock's feathers rattle softly as the bird vibrates and flourishes its tail. And Ronnie laughs out loud. "We got that from a book my mother read to us. It was just a place in the creek where we played."

"Jeez, you were like pioneer homesteaders," Adrian says, one hand on her father's shoulder, the other for a second cupping the top of Ronnie's head, "not only eking out a living from the land, but identifying and naming your landmarks and landscape, making unknown territory known, and your own history preserved in the origin of the names."

"Okay . . . so we have one more pioneer thing to do."

Her father is standing beside a barely perceptible short trail through the grass that leads from the leeway—Roadrunner Road—to the edge of the nopale property barrier. "See this trail?" Ronnie says, her back to Adrian, following her father toward the nopale, "how it looks like one of those Indian highways that get blazed through brush or forest?"

"Sometimes they were actually traveling on deer paths, but . . . some of those ancient highways can be seen from the air, etched in straight lines across deserts."

"Yeah, well . . . this one, it's where my brother and I went out and back, over and over, hundreds of times, lugging clippings to dump over the side of the hill, or on our way to cross through Wasp Crater to play in Pollywog Sinkhole at the bottom of the hill." She turns toward Adrian, shading her eyes and grinning, almost giggling, "And no amount of years or different civilizations can erase our trail."

Adrian chuckles. Ronnie's father says "Shhhh. Quiet now. Hear if. Those . . . people. If those—people—from before. Are down there."

"We were chased off by kids," Ronnie says to Adrian, then, "Dad, how can they possibly scare us now?"

Her father kneels, the same place they crouched on the ground their first day out of the hospital. He reaches under the nopale, pulls out the shrunken, blackened banana peel. "Where's the. The . . . tool. To dig? The . . ."

"Oh, the shovel. Don't you have it?" But she knows he doesn't. He hasn't carried anything except the bundle. Quick glance at Adrian. "Damn, I must've . . . how could I lose it? Oh!—I must've left it on the bus . . . or dropped it when we jumped into the Christmas trees." She digs into the vest pocket, then unrolls the top of the brown sack and fishes inside. "Here." She hands the pocketknife down to her father. He fumbles with it, so, crushing the bag under her arm, she kneels beside him, reaches into his hands and opens the knife without taking it back from him.

While her father brushes away the layer of rotting nopale lobes and starts to dig, Adrian stays standing behind them. She hears him take several slow quiet steps backwards, but when she peeks over her shoulder, he's not very far away. Her father hacks at the ground, gripping the knife in his good hand, using his bad hand to scrape away the dirt as he scoops out a deep but narrow trench. It's not as easy as digging directly in front of himself, he has to reach under the nopale, avoiding spines on the lowest lobes. The sound of the knife digging dirt seems loud in the midday calm—no radio blaring or dog barking or voices laughing and cursing, no splashing in the pool. Far up on the satellite dish, a mocking bird twitters every song he's ever heard. Her father measures the trench— about eight inches deep—and he keeps digging. No person is ever likely to disturb the earth under the nopale, but possums or gray fox—if the fox can still persist in a populated region—will dig in moist mulch, looking for grubs and worms. They used to raid the earthworm beds, could even gnash their way through a barrier of chicken wire. A nopale spine scrapes a red line on her father's forearm, but he doesn't seem to notice it and Ronnie doesn't stop him to attend to the scratch. She picks up the bundle from where he'd set it beside his leg. His breath begins to grunt low in his chest. He measures again—ten inches, maybe close to a foot. He starts to widen the trench, chopping at the dirt with the knife point then running the blade back and forth against the rim of the hole as though honing the cutting edge against a stone sharpener, but this blade will be worthless after this.

"Rocks," her father pants. "Two." When she doesn't move right away, he turns and takes the bundle from her.

Ronnie doesn't get up, just swivels around, stretches out on hands and knees then feels through the grass for the rocks that hadn't ever been used in her father's retaining walls. There won't be any flat ones—those were always set aside in separate piles to be used for the tops of the walls— but she finds one oblong rock the size of a big shoe and another not quite the same the size. Cupping the rocks to her chest, she scoots on her knees back to her father's side. He hasn't put the bundle into the trench yet. Meets her eyes, his glasses now flecked with dirt, then tucks the bundle into the bottom of the trench. It fits without hitting the sides. Then he holds out two hands for the first stone, crams it in tight over the bundle. Takes the second stone, packs it into the trench beside the first. With both hands starts pulling and sweeping the loose dirt back into the trench, over and beside the two rocks. His fingers press the dirt in tight around the rocks. He adds more dirt, continues pressing, mashing the dirt with fists, then with thumbs, until all the dirt he'd dug out of the trench is jammed back in around the two rocks. The top of the filled-in trench is slightly mounded. He slaps it hard with flat palms, then rakes the mulch back over the top.

The ground under the nopale looks undisturbed. Dirty hands on knees, her father sits staring at the place. "Done," he says. Ronnie brushes soil from the red scratch on her father's arm. He lifts his arm and peers at the line, rubs it himself. "It was a . . . good life. All of us." Then he looks at Ronnie. A fly or bee buzzes nearby and she waves a hand at it, but slowly. Then she nods.

Her father nods too. "So. Forever did the thing—"

"*Finally* did."

"Finally . . . gave the thing . . . what our mother—"

"*My* mother."

"My . . . *your* mother. What your mother. Asked. Wished about." He brushes his hands together but his soiled palms aren't going to be cleaned without water. "Now get me— Think to me— What would she .. *he* . . . our brother. What can . . . Chad wish?"

"*My* brother," Ronnie whispers. She knocks a ladybug from a blade of grass into her cupped hand, then says, "None of this was ever about what Chad wanted. Chad was a little boy . . . all he wanted was . . . new games, something different and fun to try every day." Reaches under the nopale and drops the ladybug in the shady mulch. "Adventure. The things that boys—" She stands so suddenly, spots flash across her eyes and her head spins. "He was a *boy*." She turns toward Adrian. "*You* were a boy . . . what do boys *want*?"

"Um . . . Okay, let's see . . . to try whatever you're told not to do?" He steps forward, hands in pockets, grinning.

"To slide down a hillside of dry grass on a cardboard sled. To pee into electric heaters. To jump on your bed 'till your hands hit the ceiling."

"To squirt water. In the hose," her father says. "Straight to sky. Not onto dirt—for roots."

"Yes, and bring the sprinkler indoors when you want to play rain forest!"

Adrian laughs. "Okay, yeah. To throw things and watch them splat against something else. To drop things off the roof. To squish worms in rain puddles."

"To find trapdoor spiders just to dig them up. To keep spiders as pets. To keep a preying mantis and crawdads and pollywogs and lizards and frogs and salamanders and . . . *sand crabs* as pets."

He'd found a plastic pail with a broken handle, filled it with sea water and smuggled it home in the back of the station wagon, kept it upright with wadded towels, and he rode back there with it, kneeling behind the back seat, looking out the back window at the dark, unrolling coast road, pretending we were in a car race, and all the cars behind us were losing. His head and upright tufts of hair on his crown would've blocked the rearview mirror, but our father didn't say anything. Everyone was tired after an August day in the sun, in the ceaseless roar of waves, fighting the riptides with air mattresses in cold water, or, for our father, fighting the pull of undertow as he stood in the surf keeping the heavy fishing pole taut. I slept, stretched out on the back seat.

At night, at home, Chad poured his seawater into a plastic jug pilfered from the washroom, one that was waiting to be refilled with distilled water for our mother's iron. Hid it under his bed, almost touched by our mother's toes when she came in to kiss him goodnight.

He wasn't supposed to go into the tree. He wore an elastic brace that went around each arm and stretched tight between his shoulder blades, to keep his cracked collarbone still. Still, he could climb to the tree house—a funny, upright, stiff-bodied monkey. From the basement he'd already taken one of our father's gallon-size glass jars, used to cure olives—brought it up the tree, set it up beside our freshwater aquarium. With our metal bucket and rope, he pulled the seawater into the tree and sloshed it into the big jar. Three kidnapped sand crabs, females full of eggs, plopped out with the wet sand at the bottom of the jug.

We hadn't gone to the beach for a week, since his fall from the tree. For a while his lip had been puffy, like a beak. He could only take the brace off in the bathtub. He hadn't been allowed to go into the surf with our mother on an air mattress. So while she and I were out riding breakers, he was starting a saltwater aquarium project to enter in the next year's fair.

When the sand crabs died he turned each one over in his hand, peeled back the flap and poked the orange eggs out with his finger. The three hard bodies he set along the edge of the tree house to dry and add to his shell collection, but the eggs, like the eggs we gathered from the quail coop, might hatch with a substitute mother. He dropped the globs of eggs into the freshwater aquarium so our crawdad could brood them.

The orange color started to wash out and fade, the globs got looser, as though melting underwater, the water itself was even murkier. And yellow jackets came to the tree to swarm over the stinking bodies of the crabs. We stayed out of the tree for several days, until the crabs' bodies were thin, empty shells. Then we lay on the platform, faces to the glass aquarium, to search for little sand crabs that would be filling the water like brine shrimp, like the baby guppies that came from pregnant mosquito fish. The crawdad was in the mouth of his rock cave, his eye-feelers waving, his claws pushing thin gluey sand crab eggs into his moving mouth parts.

"Hey!" Chad bolted upright and plunged his arm up to his elbow into the water, poked a finger at the sand crab. With a cloud of muck, the crawdad backed into his cave, but also snapped a claw on Chad's finger. Chad pulled his arm out, the crawdad hanging from his dripping finger, tail curled. "You bad boy!" Chad scolded the crawdad who then dropped off Chad's finger, plopping back into the water, and Chad turned to me, the stitches inside his mouth made it hurt to smile, so he kept his lip stiff and straight as he looked at me, giggling. His dark eyes fiery with silly joy.

"It's all coming back to me," Adrian laughs again. "To spit. To kick things. To make footprints in wet cement."

"To chase tumbleweeds rolling down the street and thwack them with sticks." She pulls the mayonnaise jar of dirt from the vest pocket. "To take a driftwood gun and go hunting the fierce bad rabbit. To have rock fights with bumblebee nests."

"To splash and roll and wrestle and dig and—"

"To make mud in the back yard even when it hasn't rained for three months. To play flying-trapeze out of your tree house."

"Yeah—to make clubhouses and forts. To hide treasure. To crush things . . . to build things only to destroy them."

"To stomp on stink bugs and make stink bombs. To get stuck inside the old dishwasher behind the garage because it was a perfect place to hide."

"To make things break and crack and burst and crash . . ."

"Of course . . . yes!" Her knees flex, her body braces, arm cocks . . . *fires*—

With a fluid overhead, straight-armed swing, she heaves the jar over the nopale and catches a glimpse of her father's face—thin lips cracked open, nearly a smile, sunken eyes gleaming as he follows the flight of the jar. It sails in a high arc, glinting in the sun, flipping end-over-end, before it disappears . . .

Then shatters, then bursts, then smashes, then explodes with a tinkle of splintering glass . . . when it hits the side of a rock wall constructed by hand . . .

When it hits the side of our father's handmade rock wall, the dirt will fall, sift down and cling to the face of the granite—but our mother's ash, together with the dust of bones and baby teeth, will glitter into the air.

Biographical Note

CRIS MAZZA'S first novel, *How to Leave a Country*, while still in manuscript won the PEN / Nelson Algren Award for book-length fiction. The judges included Studs Terkel and Grace Paley. Some of her other notable earlier titles include *Your Name Here: ___*, *Dog People* and *Is It Sexual Harassment Yet?* She was also co-editor of *Chick-Lit: Postfeminist Fiction* (1995), and *Chick-Lit 2 (No Chick Vics)* (1996), anthologies of women's fiction. Mazza's fiction has been reviewed numerous times in *The New York Times Book Review, The Wall Street Journal, MS Magazine, Chicago Tribune Books, The Los Angeles Times Book Review, The Voice Literary Supplement, The San Francisco Review of Books*, and many other book review publications. In spring 1996, Mazza was the cover feature in *Poets & Writers Magazine*.

A native of Southern California, Cris Mazza grew up in San Diego County. Her BA and MA were completed at San Diego State University, then she crossed the country to finish an MFA in writing at Brooklyn College before returning to San Diego where she lived several years training and showing her dogs, completing her first four books, and teaching at various local colleges and universities. Mazza has taught fiction writing at UC San Diego, and was Writer in Residence at Austin Peay State University in Clarksville, TN, then at Allegheny College in Meadville, PA. Since 1993 Mazza has lived outside Chicago. She is a professor in the Program for Writers at the University of Illinois at Chicago. In spring 2000 Mazza was the Chairholder in Creative Writing in the MFA program at the University of Alabama, and was an NEA grant recipient in 2000-2001.

In the past several years, Cris Mazza's work as a novelist has expanded as she has continued to consider psychological and emotional complexities of life in the last decade of the twentieth century (and the beginning of the 21st century), but has begun to do so with the contributing complication of place: how regions or localities that still have their own unique characteristics of landscape, society, and culture impact the human experiences (sexuality, family, authority, gender) that Mazza continues to explore in fiction.